# "The C
# ana
# "The Third Shadow"

## TWO CLASSIC ADVENTURES OF

™

## by Walter B. Gibson
## writing as Maxwell Grant

### Foreword by Dick Ayers

### with New Historical Essays by
### Will Murray and Anthony Tollin

Published by Sanctum Productions for
# NOSTALGIA VENTURES, INC.
P.O. Box 231183; Encinitas, CA 92023-1183

International Standard Book Numbers:
1-932806-60-1    13 digit 978-1-932806-60-1

First printing: May 2007

Series editor: Anthony Tollin
P.O. Box 761474
San Antonio, TX 78245-1474
sanctumotr@earthlink.net

Consulting editor: Will Murray

Copy editor: Joseph Wrzos

Cover restoration: Michael Piper

The editor gratefully acknowledges the assistance of Kirk Kimball.

Nostalgia Ventures, Inc.
P.O. Box 231183; Encinitas, CA 92023-1183

Visit The Shadow at www.nostalgiatown.com

## Volume 7

## CONTENTS

Two Complete Novels From The Shadow's Private Annals As told to Maxwell Grant

### Thrilling Tales and Features

Foreword: THE SHADOW OF THE GHOST RIDER
by Dick Ayers ............................................................. 4

THE COBRA by Walter B. Gibson
(writing as "Maxwell Grant") ..................................... 6

RIVALS OF THE SHADOW by Will Murray ................. 60

THE THIRD SHADOW by Walter B. Gibson
(writing as "Maxwell Grant") ..................................... 63

THE SHADOW'S SHADOWS by Anthony Tollin ........ 127

**Cover art by George Rozen**
**Interior illustrations by Tom Lovell**

The Shadow knows—what lurks in the imagination of the artist!

I was only six years old when I first heard The Shadow's sibilant tones and mocking laughter emerging from my family's Philco Radio in 1930. At that point my toy soldiers were the actors in the stories I imagined. Radio drama was a perfect inspiration and simulant for the development of the imagination of a young artist. The *Shadow* programs kept me wide-eyed in front of the radio.

My father coached me into drawing what I thought the characters in the programs looked like—which evolved into making up stories with them—comic stories like I saw in the daily and Sunday papers. *The Shadow* radio stories became even more exciting than a horror movie in the '30s as my radio-prompted imagination went uncensored. Only having heard The Shadow on the radio, I drew what I imagined he looked like. As the years progressed I continued to enjoy the comic strip form of telling stories and my art teacher at school began coaching me.

When I was 13 years old, my family moved to upstate New York. It was very rural in 1937, and radio reception was primitive. My radio listening was limited. I had no *Shadow.* I was also isolated from reading *Shadow* magazines due to distance and lack of money, but The Shadow still lurked in my imagination. His voice was embedded in my brain. After serving in the U.S. Army Air Corps through World War Two, I began illustrating comic book stories. Even in my twenties, the radio dramas were my background inspirations when I worked at my drawing table. As I worked in Joe Shuster's studio, Martin Stein, Ernie Bache and I would imitate the radio actors' voices and scenes as we drew Jerry Siegel's and Joe Shuster's *Funnyman.*

Working with other artists, it became fun to imitate voices of actors or celebrities. I remember doing "The Shadow Knows," never knowing who the actor was. One day as I was doing my Shadow voice, another artist shouted out *"Orson Welles!"* Now I finally knew who did the radio Shadow voice. No wonder the voice of the Shadow remained such a strong memorable phrase in my imagination. Welles was my favorite movie star.

One of my first solo series was The Calico Kid, about a federal marshal who posed as a salesman selling merchandise from a covered wagon. As I picked up my third script, publisher Vin Sullivan told me The Calico Kid was becoming The Ghost Rider. Some renegades were to overpower The Calico Kid and his assistant and kill them. They would meet the spirits of successful famous lawmen in Purgatory who would teach The Calico Kid their superior skills. The publisher had the first script written and The Ghost Rider debuted in 1949 as a backup feature in *Tim Holt.* By 1950, Ghost Rider had his own magazine and it sold so well that he was also featured in *Best of the West* and *Bobby Benson's B-Bar-B Riders.*

In developing the character of Ghost Rider, Vin Sullivan told me to think about *The Headless Horseman* by Washington Irving, and also asked me to draw The Ghost Rider thin and lanky so he would appear "ghostly." We thought of having his clothes and horse have glowing phosphorescent paint on them and the cape with a black underside so that when he wrapped his body or head in it against the night sky he would look headless or bodiless. Of course, The Ghost Rider also utilized this black lining to completely disappear into the darkness just like The Shadow.

As my good fortune continued, I visited a fellow art student from the art school atop the Flatiron Building on 23rd and Broadway in Manhattan. That afternoon I also met Carl Memling, a young author who wrote children's books and westerns for pulp magazines. Though he wasn't interested in writing for comic books, I asked him to let me show a sample story to Ray

Krank, my editor at Magazine Enterprises. He gave me a one-page story he had published and I took that story to show Ray. Vin Sullivan and Krank immediately assigned Carl Memling to write the scripts for The Ghost Rider. I familiarized Carl with the format of comic book script writing and described The Ghost Rider characters to him.

I had the image of The Shadow in my mind when I drew Ghost Rider, and I visualized him talking and sounding like The Shadow when he frightened villains. I asked Carl to think of The Shadow when he wrote his dialogue balloons. It was at this stage that I thought of how I could give The Ghost Rider the sound of The Shadow in his speech balloons. I decided to letter his speech balloons with a different outline than the others.

I asked Carl, when writing the dialogue, to have Ghost Rider speak in a Shakespearean style as he scared villains. I also suggested that Ghost Rider use ventriloquism—another Shadow specialty—to project his voice to where the "magic lantern" used by his assistant cast his image about the darkness. The Ghost Rider became even more fun to draw as Carl wrote every story I illustrated. Ray and Vin assigned me the *Bobby Benson* comic with Carl writing that also. Our telephones kept us working closely together.

Carl Memling kept the Shadow flavor in the stories. He had become a very prolific writer and together we did stories for other publishers. It's a sad note that through that time period writers didn't get credit for the stories that they wrote.

From 1952 to 1955, I had an artist assist me with the inking of the stories. I would pencil and then outline my drawings with pen or brush and ink. Ernie Bache would finish the art, adding weight to my lines and the blacks and halftones that gave the feature a shadowy look. We worked together in my studio, bringing out the best in each other's talent.

I had not recalled The Shadow's influence until recently as I reread the Ghost Rider stories. I now see there was a blending of my enthusiasm into my interpretation of Ghost Rider's speech, but it was just my imagination at work after being an avid radio fan hearing "The Shadow knows!"

Unfortunately, I didn't see many issues of *The Shadow Magazine*

**Dick Ayers at his drawing board in 1949, illustrating The Ghost Rider.**

during my Ghost Rider production years. However, the memory of the radio show remained, and thankfully still remains.

As I reread my original 1950s Ghost Rider stories, I realize that my hours of listening to *The Shadow* unconsciously seeped into my story interpretations. One story in particular, "Magico versus The Ghost Rider," features an exaggerated master villain in the tradition of The Shadow's Cobra, with a heavy dose of the stage magic beloved by The Shadow's raconteur, Walter Gibson (who also pounded out scripts for Magazine Enterprise's *Straight Arrow).*

Magazine Enterprises lost the Ghost Rider trademark to Marvel in 1965, when Stan Lee assigned me to do a new Ghost Rider series. The character was changed but I drew him in the same costume. I no longer had any story influence, and the revamped Ghost Rider lacked the dialogue similarity to the Shadow. Marvel's *Ghost Rider* series only lasted seven issues and the hero was later given a different interpretation. However, this revival of the western Ghost Rider is featured in the new *Ghost Rider* movie, with Sam Elliott costarring as the haunted horseman opposite Nicholas Cage.

Of all the features I illustrated for Magazine Enterprises, Ghost Rider is the one I penciled, lettered, and inked—and is still being published.

In recent years, AC Comic's publisher Bill Black obtained the rights to publish the Ghost Rider art I had done for Magazine Enterprises, and reprints The Ghost Rider, calling him The Haunter or the Haunted Horseman, in a revival of *Best of the West.* No matter what he is called, he is recognized as *my* Ghost Rider—and he still sounds just like The Shadow in the theater of *my* imagination.

The Shadow knows what lurks in the imagination of this artist. I definitely would have the voice of Orson Welles surging through my mind as I worked.

Alas, radio drama has disappeared and I note that when I tried working while listening to music, it didn't work as a substitute. These days I still work at my 56-year-old drawing table, sometimes breaking out into a "Yowsah, yowsah!" I long to hear *The Shadow* again while I draw a good horror detective story!

*The famed might of The Shadow seemed to be on the wane, giving way to a new and more destructive warrior—*

# THE COBRA

From the private annals of The Shadow, as told to

# Maxwell Grant

Book-length novel complete in this issue.

## CHAPTER I
## THE CRIME TRAIL

FOGGY darkness swirled beneath the superstructure of the East Side elevated. Dim lights, glowing through the murk, showed the dingy fronts of dilapidated buildings. Shifty, skulking figures shambled along the street. A bluecoat, twirling his club, watched them idly from the corner; then resumed his beat.

This was a bad spot on the fringe of the underworld. The officers who patrolled this section of Manhattan were chosen members of the force. Always on the lookout for the paths of crooks, they kept a wary check of sullen faces and sly, stoop-shouldered prowlers.

Less than one minute after the patrolman had continued on his beat, a man stepped forward from the cover of the elevated steps. Well-dressed, but inconspicuous in his dark suit, he was of better appearance than the usual denizens of this district. Like the bluecoat, he watched with wary eye.

A taxicab rolled slowly by. The man by the steps noted it with a sidelong glance. He saw a gray-haired man of middle age peering keenly from the window, as though engaged in study of the district. The cab rolled on. The man by the steps lighted a cigarette.

The flicker of the match revealed his face. It was a hardened countenance, with curling, ugly lips. A long scar showed from chin to cheek. That scar was buried by the hand that held the match.

As he flicked the match away, the man by the elevated steps used his other hand to draw the collar of his coat across the telltale scar. His action showed further effort to hide the mark.

With head hunched slightly to the side, the man squinted up and down the street, then moved along by the curb with an easy, swinging gait.

There was method in his wariness. This man was known in the underworld. "Deek" Hundell, leader of the toughest holdup crew in Manhattan, was a person whom any lurker in the badlands could have spotted instantly by his familiar scar.

THE strolling patrolman had missed an opportunity tonight. Standing openly at the corner, he had been spotted by Deek Hundell. The holdup expert had waited for the policeman to depart; and there had been method in his waiting. Deek Hundell was wanted for murder.

A disdainful smile showed on Deek's ugly lips as the crook passed the front of a lighted shop. Deek had dodged flatfeet before. Cops did not worry him. His caution now was for the benefit of chance passers.

Among the slouchers on this gloomy street, Deek knew that he might encounter enemies who would betray him. These were the stool pigeons, the spies of the police.

Deek Hundell turned to peer at a display of cheap suitcases in a pawn shop window. His hand, rising to pluck the cigarette from his lips, remained there, adding its hiding palm to cover the scar.

A ragged, stoop-shouldered prowler was shambling from the fog. Moving close to the window, Deek caught the reflection of a pasty face. The passing man was going straight ahead. Deek waited.

More footsteps. Two foreigners, jabbering in their own tongue, moved past the standing crook. Then came an old woman, carrying a basket on her arm. Footsteps died along the sidewalk. Deek turned and resumed his course.

Twenty paces brought the gang leader to the entrance of an alleyway. Here, with head still hunched, Deek gazed in both directions and flicked his cigarette to the gutter. Satisfied that no one was watching, he moved into the darkness. A muttered laugh came from his lips.

Deek Hundell had passed the crossroads of the underworld. From now on, his course would be untraceable. On this visit to the badlands, the notorious crook had taken no chances. His laugh was one of surety.

Silence dominated the street by the elevated.

The swirling, chilly fog seemed to creep about the iron pillars like a living monster. A thickened spot of darkish mist spread slowly away from the shelter of a pillar directly opposite the alleyway that Deek Hundell had taken.

BLACKNESS remained, but in the blackness glowed two spots that shone like coals of fire. Metamorphosing from the mist, they showed as living eyes, poised in an inky background.

Then blackness moved; a tall, uncanny shape stepped forward from the elevated post. The owner of those glistening eyes had manifested himself.

A spectral being clad entirely in black—a form shrouded by the folds of a sable-hued cloak; above the eyes, the brim of a dark slouch hat.

The strange figure paused momentarily, while the piercing eyes studied the course that Deek Hundell had taken. Then, with a quick swish of the cloak, this watcher crossed the sidewalk and merged with the darkness of the alleyway.

Deek Hundell had congratulated himself too soon. Convinced that he had reached the alleyway unnoticed, the crook was continuing his course with no fear of pursuit. He did not know that his trail had been taken by the most vigilant tracker who had ever entered the badlands—The Shadow!

A creature of the darkness, a phantom being whose guise of black rendered him invisible to the sharpest eyes, The Shadow was on the trail of impending crime. He had picked up the course of Deek Hundell and he was following it to a certain objective.

There could be but one reason for Deek's appearance in the underworld. Wanted for murder, the gang leader had chosen other spots until tonight. His arrival here was a sure indication of a rendezvous between Deek Hundell and his gangster henchmen.

Motion in darkness: such was the only indication of The Shadow's presence. The swish of the black cloak sounded faintly as the master trailer moved through the alleyway and took a turn into a passage between two houses. He could not see his quarry up ahead, for Deek was moving cautiously through the gloom; yet The Shadow followed the slight sounds of the gang leader's footsteps.

When the mobster trailer reached the end of the passage between the houses, his keen eyes peered across a narrow, gloomy street. They spied Deek Hundell entering the battered doorway of an old brick house, where only darkened windows showed.

A weird specter, The Shadow crossed the narrow street and reached the darkened doorway. The opening of the barrier seemed imperceptible. The black figure entered. The Shadow stood in a narrow, gloomy hallway which terminated in a flight of rickety stairs. A gas jet, its flame turned low, furnished the only illumination.

Slowly, The Shadow advanced. His gliding progress ended at a door on the right of the hall. A creeping hand, gloved in black came from the folds of The Shadow's cloak. It turned the knob of the door. Keen eyes peered through the narrow crevice.

BEYOND was a small flight of stairs; then a stone-walled room where a few dozen men were seated about at tables; bottles and glasses were set before them.

The Shadow knew this place; it was a sordid dive of the underworld where lesser mobsters were wont to meet. The entrance was opposite the door through which The Shadow peered. It opened on a side alley that led from the front street.

Deek Hundell was not in the underground den. The door closed silently. A soft, whispered laugh sounded in the gloomy hall. Its echoes clung there as The Shadow turned to the stairs and ascended. The steps terminated in the center of a second-story hall.

Like the one below, this hall was lighted by a flickering gas jet. At the rear was another flight of stairs that led down to the back of the building. The front of the hall terminated in a door.

The Shadow turned in that direction. He passed two doors on the right; just beyond the second one, he paused to listen. A muffled, growling voice was sounding from the room beyond the barrier.

Swiftly, The Shadow continued to the end of the hallway. His hand turned the knob of the door at the end. The door was locked. Muffled clicks sounded as The Shadow applied an instrument of steel. The lock gave. The door opened and The Shadow entered the front room.

Dark, deserted and illy furnished, this room extended to the right—a fact which The Shadow had anticipated by his study of the building itself. To the right was a connecting doorway that led to the room where the voice had sounded.

The Shadow reached the intervening barrier and applied the pick. This time, there was not the slightest sound of the yielding lock. The knob turned noiselessly; the door opened inch by inch until a narrow slit was formed. Silent and motionless, his hand still on the knob, The Shadow gazed into the room beyond.

Five men were seated about a broken-down table. Their evil, sordid faces marked them as desperadoes of the badlands. Their eyes were turned upon an individual who sat facing the doorway to the hall. In the illumination of the gaslit room, that man's features were plain.

Deek Hundell.

Glinting eyes and snarling lips; a scar that ran an ugly, jagged line from chin to cheek—this was the quarry that The Shadow sought. Deek Hundell, murderer, had reached his destination in the underworld. Joined by his squad of killers, he was building new schemes for crime.

The eyes of minions were on the gang leader. Attentive ears were drinking in Deek's growled words. Gloating faces showed eagerness for evil deeds that lay ahead. Little did these crooks realize that another listener was present; that eyes keener than their own were watching the sordid countenance of Deek Hundell.

The Shadow, master fighter against crime, was listening in on Deek Hundell's plans. With those schemes learned, The Shadow would be prepared to strike from darkness. Criminals, confident in their security, were doomed to failure before their plans were formed.

## CHAPTER II
### THE NEW AVENGER

"WE'RE pulling the job tomorrow night." Deek Hundell's growl had an emphasis that held his henchmen. "Out on the Boston Post Road is a swell place where there'll be lots of palookas with dough. I've picked the spot—I'll lead you to it when we go."

"O.K., Deek," came a response from one mobster. The others joined with nods.

"Maybe," resumed Deek, leering, "some of you guys are wondering why I'm taking places outside of the city. I'll tell you why. It's because these spots are outside. Don't get the idea that these New York bulls have me worried."

Laughs from the mobsters indicated that they, as well as Deek, were contemptuous of the Manhattan police.

"I've been living here in New York," continued Deek, "in an uptown hotel and there ain't a bull that's had an eye on me. Wanted for murder— that's rich—and that dumb dick, Joe Cardona, thinks he's going to grab me.

"Him? For two bits, I'd poke a gat in Cardona's ribs and take his badge from him. That's what I think of Joe Cardona!

"Why are they hollering about me? Because I bumped off a flatfoot two weeks ago. That's not the only bird I've plugged, but they're hollering because a dumb cop got his. Let 'em holler! When I feel like it, I'll go downtown shooting for the whole force!"

A pause. Gloating smiles showed that Deek's confidence was impressing his followers. The very fact that Deek was here in the badlands showed his disregard for the police who sought his trail.

Eying his companions in crime, the gang leader saw that he had gained his point. It was now possible for him to proceed with cautious remarks without damaging the authority that he held over his band.

"The trouble here in New York," declared Deek, "is too many cops. They pile up on you before the job is pulled. They'll never get me—but I'm thinking about you guys.

"That ain't all. There's too many stools here in town. They know me—and they can spot this scratch I've got on my jaw. It's O.K. for you fellows to lay around here until I want you—but it's best for me to be out of the district."

Nods. One of the mobsters tapped the table with his knuckles; then ventured a chance remark.

"You got the right idea, Deek," he declared. "Between the cops and the stools, a guy's got to keep his mug shut. Then there's The Shadow—"

"The Shadow!" Deek snarled the name with contempt. "Listen to that, you fellows! Bulker, here, is talking about The Shadow! Say—we ain't had no trouble with The Shadow, have we?"

HEADS shook as Deek looked about the circle. The gang leader grunted new contempt. Before he could make another statement, there was a rap at the door. A new mobster entered as Deek growled.

"Hello, Gringo," greeted Deek. "Sit down here—and listen to the pipe that Bulker just made. He's talking about The Shadow!

"Say—who is The Shadow? I'll tell you—a guy that goes around in a black shirt and mooches in on jobs. He ain't never given us no trouble and he never will. Say—have any of you bimbos ever seen The Shadow?"

"The guys that have seen him," protested "Bulker" weakly, "ain't around to tell it."

"Yeah?" Deek laughed. "Well, if The Shadow ever tries to cross me, he'll get his! What say, Gringo?"

The newcomer raised his hands for silence. There was something in his manner that betokened tenseness.

All sat silently—Deek included—as "Gringo" approached the table and leaned forward. A hard-faced rowdy, the toughest of Deek's henchmen, Gringo's manner of unfeigned alarm commanded interest.

"Listen, Deek." Gringo was serious. "You've been out of sight for a while. You don't know what's been going on—and neither does the rest of the mob—because they ain't in the know. What I'm going to give you now is something to think about."

"Are you figuring that The Shadow is in it?"

Gringo shook his head emphatically. "The Shadow is out—he's a has-been compared to the guy that's in the picture now. Say—you know how The Shadow works. Lays back and watches—then hits some big shot or cleans up his mob.

"The Shadow's tough all right, but while he's on one trail, the others are running wild. That's because The Shadow waits until he's got a fellow with the goods. Savvy?"

"I know that," growled Deek. "He'll never get me—"

"I'm not talking about The Shadow," interrupted Gringo. "Listen, Deek—what would you say to a guy that began knocking off big birds while they were laying quiet? Picking them before they had a chance to move?"

"Who's doing that?"

"A fellow that calls himself The Cobra." Gringo's tone was an awed whisper. "He spots his man when the guy has a crowd about him. He walks in and bags the guy he wants. You know what happened to Hunky Fitzler, don't you!"

"The guy with the apartment-house racket? Sure—somebody gave him the works up in that swell joint of his—"

"That's right. And I'll tell you who put Hunky on the spot. It was The Cobra. What's more, he bumped Cass Rogan, the guy that had the gambling racket sewed up. There were fellows that saw him do it!"

"They ain't shouting about it."

"You're right they ain't! I'll tell you why. When you see a big shot get his—and know that that guy who did it could have plugged you just as easy, you're going to keep mum, ain't you?"

Deek considered. At last he nodded; his face was sober. Gringo added a pointed remark.

"I'm telling you this, Deek," he warned, "because you're big enough to have The Cobra on your trail. I'm telling you—The Cobra is lopping them off. They say The Shadow listens in—well, The Cobra walks in—"

DEEK HUNDELL thumped his powerful fist on the table. His snarling growl broke off Gringo's discourse. The wide flame of the gas jet wavered beside the door. Deek's sullen face gleamed viciously in the light.

"Forget this hokum!" he rasped. "We ain't got time for pipe dreams. The Shadow ain't never tackled this mob of mine. The Cobra ain't going to take a chance on me alone.

"I'm going to give you fellows the dope on tomorrow night. I'm only waiting for Corky Gurk

**THE COBRA!** Who, or what, is this new avenger on the horizon of the underworld? What purpose is behind this new threat which lops off the heads of gangdom with more daring, more success than even The Shadow?

Small-fry gangsters quaked at mention of The Shadow, but the Big Shots felt that they could outsmart the man in black. But The Cobra? The leaders of gangdom left the city in tremendous hurry. Those who stayed met their end. The small fry, wonder-

ing, felt themselves secure.

Even The Shadow, himself, was outsmarted! Where The Shadow came to thwart crime, he met The Cobra, who had already served Justice!

Here, at last, was some one who would supersede The Shadow. And he, too, fought on the side of the law. He served those who sought to bring an end to crime.

There was room for but one avenger. The Cobra or The Shadow? Which would it be?

---

to show up, so he'll be in on it. Then I'm sliding out that hall to the street—and you birds can ease into the joint down in the cellar. One-by-one—get me? There's nobody ever wised up this meeting place yet—and there ain't nobody going to—"

Deek stopped as a rap sounded at the door. Mobsters started. Deek laughed; then scowled as he saw them shift uneasily.

"That's Corky," he scoffed. "Time he was here. Who did you think it was? The Cobra?"

The mobsters joined in the laugh as Deek, half rising from his chair had his hands upon the edge of the table as he rasped the order:

"Come in, Corky."

The door opened. It seemed to swing inward of its own accord. Each mobster, showing indifference, was glancing toward the barrier.

Suddenly wild gasps came from bloated lips. Deek Hundell alone gave no outcry. His scarred face was frozen.

IN the doorway was a grotesque figure that looked like nothing human, although it had the stature of a man. Clad from head to foot in a close-fitting, dark brown jersey, this individual was entirely masked.

The single garment formed thick wrinkles on the limbs and body. Above the narrow jersey, it terminated in a broad hood, which was topped by a small, tapering knob.

There was something snakelike in the costume; but the feature that gave it weird realism was the hood which hid the entrant's face.

It was the hood of a cobra!

Two white spots appeared like eyes, about them, broad white circles that terminated in downward pointing lines. The effect was that of a terrifying face which seemed to survey the startled mob with expressionless gaze.

There was no mummery about The Cobra's painted visage. The gangsters who saw it cringed as though it had been a living countenance. It was a sign; an identity that brought instant recognition. Men of crime were face-to-face with the new avenger!

To each gazer, the eyes of The Cobra's hood seemed fixed in his direction. Then came The Cobra's warning—a hiss that sizzled from lips beneath the hood—the perfect mimicry of a snake about to strike!

Like a flash, a hand swung from the central fold of the pleated brown jersey. A revolver glistened beneath the gaslight. Deek Hundell, an answering snarl coming from his own lips, yanked a gun from a pocket to meet The Cobra's aim.

The new avenger had hissed his warning. His swift revolver was the coming stroke. Deek Hundell, murderous gang leader, was forced to a fight for life!

Gangster eyes were bulging. Hands were trembling. The witnesses of the duel were powerless. Beyond the door to the front room, other eyes were on the scene. Another hand was acting. The Shadow, sensing grim events, was drawing an automatic from beneath the cloak.

Stern avenger who roamed the underworld, The Shadow had become the witness to the power of a new figure of mystery who was there to deal death to a startled murderer!

### CHAPTER III
### THE COBRA WINS

THE sound of The Cobra's venomous hiss ended with the bark of the revolver. Deek Hundell, rising, stopped short. The gun which he had whipped from his pocket dropped from loosening fingers. The gang leader clapped his hand to his stomach; his snarling lips twisted in agony as Deek collapsed face forward on the table.

Deek's henchmen were stunned. Then came another hiss. Wild eyes stared at the smoking gun barrel in The Cobra's hand. They saw a brown arm sweep upward to the gas jet; a twist—the room was plunged in darkness, save for a slight flicker of illumination from the hall.

The Cobra's form was blurred, except for its hood. There, against a darkened background, glowed the painted eyes and their surrounding lines. Weirdly luminous, The Cobra's false face was peering toward the gangsters whose chief had died.

Then came a sweeping barrier—the closing door. A fierce hiss dwindled as The Cobra swung the portal behind him.

An oath came from Gringo's lips. A flashlight glimmered in the mobster's hand. It was followed by others, as Deek Hundell's cohorts suddenly sprang to avenge the death of their murderous chief.

Gringo was the first to reach the gloomy hall. The action required a leap across the room; then the opening of the door. The hall was empty. Gringo stared in both directions.

"I'll take the backstairs," he rasped. "You're with me, Bulker. The rest of you pile into that front room—maybe he ducked that way."

There was a call from below. Gangsters in the underground dive had heard the muffled sound of The Cobra's shot. They were coming to find out what had happened. Gringo shouted down as he headed towards the back.

The body of Deek Hundell lay sprawled upon the table where it had collapsed. The mobsters had piled from the room; now the door that adjoined from the front was open. The Shadow, standing in the dim gloom, was surveying the victim The Cobra had slain.

SWIFT had been The Cobra's work. The killing—the departure—both had been timed with precision. The Shadow had come here to forestall Deek Hundell's plans for crime. The Cobra had gone The Shadow one better. He had slain Deek in cold blood.

The Shadow held no grief for Deek Hundell. The man was a self-admitted murderer. He had deserved to die. The ringleader of a dangerous mob, his death meant the end of that gang's crimes; for Deek Hundell had held the whip hand over the crew.

For once, The Shadow had been forced to stand by as a mere watcher while another hand of vengeance had delivered doom.

The Cobra!

Gringo, the gangster, had spoken well when he had described this new avenger as a rising menace to the underworld. The Cobra had struck in the presence of a crowd of witnesses. His deed was one that would reverberate through all gangdom.

A whispered laugh came from The Shadow's lips. It was a tense, foreboding laugh—one that told of impending trouble.

The Cobra had made a perfect getaway. Maddened gangsters, augmented by those below, were turning this hovel into a hornet's nest. The Shadow, silent witness of The Cobra's might, was left in the thick of it!

Mobsters were coming now—back into the room where Deek's body lay. They were lighting the gas while others were trying to open the door to the front room, from the hall.

The Shadow had locked that door behind him. Swiftly, he was regaining the front room through the connecting door. He closed the barrier as the gas came on. He turned the lock and stood silently in darkness.

Mobsters were working at the connecting door. They had hopes that The Cobra might be here.

The Shadow was faced by a dilemma. His choice lay between a quick departure or a futile struggle.

The Shadow was a fighter who did not deal in flight, save when it formed a portion of his strategy. Tonight, he was faced by a situation which was unique even in his long experience.

He could gain nothing by remaining. Mobsters would fight The Shadow as quickly as they would The Cobra; and the hordes of gangland would know that The Shadow had stood idly by while his new rival had delivered death!

Picks had failed on the door from the hall. Mobsters were battering the barrier as The Shadow swept to the front window of the upstairs room. Up came the sash. The Shadow's tall form swung over the sill, just as the door from the hall was flattened by a surge of mobsters.

Two gangsters tumbled as the door gave. Behind them was a third, holding a bull's-eye lantern; beside him, two gorillas with ready guns.

As chance had it, the rays of the lantern shone straight upon the open window. A cry came from the mobster as he saw the blackened form swinging from the sill.

REVOLVERS barked wild shots as the gunmen responded to their companion's shout. Had The Shadow continued his swing from the window, the next shots would have beaded him. Instead, The Shadow delivered his response.

Clinging to the sill, he swung his right hand inward and pressed the trigger of a mammoth automatic. His target was the bull's-eye lantern. Darkness, crashing glass, and the howl of the wounded lantern-holder was proof of The Shadow's perfect aim.

Again, the automatic spurted flame. Tongues of fire; driving bullets that smashed hot against the walls of the hallway sent mobsters ducking for cover. Amid the echoes of the gunshots came the strident tones of The Shadow's laugh.

Time was precious. More than twenty mobsters were close by; should The Shadow remain, this room would become the focal spot for hastening fighters from all parts of the underworld.

With a sweep through the window, The Shadow poised with one hand clutching the sill; then dropped catlike, a dozen feet to the sidewalk below.

The plunge was timely. Mobsters had reached the street. They had heard the bark of guns from above. With The Shadow's poise, flashlights glimmered upon the window—just in time to reveal the huddled shape in black as it dropped to the street.

Down came the glimmers. Focused lights played on The Shadow's shape as it showed, half-sprawled upon the sidewalk. Cries of recognition; shouts of triumph! These came as the men with the flashlights aimed revolvers toward what appeared to be their helpless prey.

They had reckoned wrong. The Shadow, as he took the plunge, knew that split seconds would be precious. The fall had neither stunned nor crippled him. He had chosen to use his guns instead of rising.

Automatics blazed. They were held by hands that were less than two feet above the sidewalk. Crouching with back against the brick wall of the old house, The Shadow delivered an enfilading fire along the street.

Gangsters staggered or dived for cover. The Shadow, rising as he pressed the triggers, sent shots that ricocheted from walls and paving. The street was cleared except for a trio of crippled mobsters who had failed in their dive for safety.

The Shadow's laugh came in ringing challenge. His emptied automatics dropped beneath the folds of his cloak. Another pair of .45s—fully loaded—appeared instead of the exhausted weapons.

LEAPING from the wall, like a black projectile, The Shadow gained the center of the street in two quick bounds; there, still moving toward the opposite side, he whirled and brought his automatics into play.

The Shadow did not choose men as his targets. Instead, he picked the spots where men must be. The doorway through which he had trailed Deek Hundell; the entrance of an alleyway, thirty feet along the street; the front windows of the old house—one on the ground floor; the other on the second—the very window through which The Shadow had escaped.

These were the points upon which The Shadow rained his leaden hail. As The Shadow fired, shots came from those strategic spots. The Shadow, in his lone game, held a strange advantage.

His retreating figure, weaving toward the gloom of the opposite side of the street, was a hopeless target even for skilled marksmen.

Bullets sizzed past that phantom shape in black. Metal messengers flattened against old walls beyond the further sidewalk. A single shot that seared The Shadow's shoulder with a trivial flesh wound was the closest of the mobster bullets.

Doorways and windows—these were the targets which The Shadow had chosen. It was purely through superiority of numbers that the mobsters had gained their chance to open fire. The Shadow's shots, blazing back, stilled those nests from which frenzied sharpshooters were sniping.

Quick shots sent mobsters scurrying back along the alleyway. Timely bullets picked two gangsters at the door; one crumpled within the doorway, the other staggered back. Shots to the downstairs window dropped a sniper there. Then came the upturned blaze of an automatic.

A gangster, leaning from the second-story window, was aiming for the last spot where he had seen an automatic spurt. He never found his target. The Shadow's bullet clipped the mobster's shoulder. His revolver dropped from his hand and clattered to the sidewalk. Then, with a wild scream, the mobster lost his hold and hurtled forward to the street below.

As this final enemy landed headfirst upon the paving, The Shadow's laugh came as a mocking peal.

The mobster's rolling form lay still. It was the last motion in the street. The Shadow had gained the passage between the buildings opposite. Stanch warrior of the night, he had returned to darkness.

POLICE whistles were sounding in the distance. Cries rose from afar. Excitement was arising in this section of the badlands. Ringing gunfire had been heard for blocks around.

The Shadow no longer remained in the vicinity where confusion reigned. His was a fleeting figure, traveling unfrequented byways. The swish of a cloak; the soft whisper of a laugh; these alone marked The Shadow's escaping course.

The Shadow had fought well tonight, yet he had been forced to a struggle which he had not sought. Battling for his own protection, he had borne the brunt of a conflict which another had precipitated.

Hollow victory had been The Shadow's gain. It was The Cobra who had won tonight. The new avenger who had risen to strike down fiends of crime had not only gained the end which he had sought; he had left The Shadow—his rival—in a desperate predicament.

What Gringo had told Deek was true. The famed might of The Shadow was on the wane. One whom the underworld had feared was giving way to a new and more destructive warrior—The Cobra.

Terror—swiftness—action—these were the weapons with which The Shadow had kept the hordes of gangdom at bay. Another had adopted those very methods; The Cobra was using them with repeated strength that eclipsed The Shadow's tactics.

What was the meaning of this rivalry? Only The Shadow knew; and his whispered, fleeting laugh was the only token of what the future might hide.

Tonight, The Shadow's power had been no more than an anticlimax.

It was The Cobra who had won. He had delivered vengeance while The Shadow tarried!

## CHAPTER IV
## THE COMMISSIONER HEARS

DEATH in the underworld!

The headlines of Manhattan dailies screamed this legend. The killing of Deek Hundell, added to the deaths of other notorious crooks, had made The Cobra's work sensational.

Yet rumors—not facts were all upon which the reporters could draw. Men of gangdom, though they might mutter among themselves, were loath to talk freely of the new scourge that had arrived within their midst: The Cobra.

Of all the readers of crime news, none could have displayed more interest than a dignified, gray-haired man who was seated at the table in a large, well-furnished study. This individual wore a quiet smile as he read the wild accounts in the newspapers that were spread out before him. He seemed to be amused by the manner in which rumors had been padded into column stories.

A telephone rang. Still reading a newspaper, the gray-haired man reached for the instrument and spoke quietly into the receiver:

"This is Caleb Myland speaking... Yes... Hello, Townsend... No, I don't expect to be in town on Thursday... Sorry, old man... Tonight? No, I'm staying here on Long Island. An important appointment..."

Caleb Myland hung up the receiver and continued his perusal of the newspapers. He looked up as the door opened. A long-faced servant was standing there.

"What is it, Babson?" questioned Myland.

"Commissioner Weston is here, sir," replied the servant.

"Ah!" exclaimed Myland, warmly. "Usher him in at once, Babson."

The servant left. A minute later the visitor entered. Caleb Myland arose to shake hands with Ralph Weston, police commissioner of New York City.

RALPH WESTON was a heavily built man of military bearing. His face was a firm one; a pointed mustache added to its commanding appearance. A man of middle age, Weston had the vigor of youth and a dynamic personality that befitted his official position.

At the same time, his expression was a troubled one, and his eyebrows narrowed as he noted the newspaper spread on Caleb Myland's table. Weston's first action, after seating himself, was to indicate the journals with his hand.

"You've been reading that stuff, Myland?" he questioned.

"Yes," returned the gray-haired host. "From what you told me over the telephone, Weston, I assumed that the news reports would have some bearing on your visit here. I was looking for information, I found very little."

Weston helped himself to a cigar from a box which Myland placed beside him. The gray-haired man had taken his chair beyond the table. There was something in his manner that gave him the appearance of a counselor. Weston noted it. The commissioner's troubled look faded to some degree.

"Myland," said Weston, seriously, "you have given me excellent advice on occasions in the past. I need your help at present."

"Regarding this?" Myland indicated the newspapers.

"Yes," admitted Weston. "Something is going on in the underworld—something more baffling than any phase of crime we have ever known. You, Myland, are a criminologist of international repute. Your books on crime have formed a foundation for the study of the criminal mind. I want your opinions—and your advice."

"You shall receive it."

"Good. I want to ask you a question to begin with. Did you ever hear of a person called The Shadow?"

Caleb Myland stared solemnly. He made no reply for a moment; then nodded slowly.

"Who is he?" demanded Weston.

"I do not know," declared Myland. "In a sense, The Shadow is a myth. He is supposed to be a master who battles crime, yet no one has ever traced him—"

"Exactly!" interposed Weston. "That is why, Myland, I officially labeled The Shadow as a non-existent factor. His name—or title—was to be kept out of all police reports."

"Until you could establish the identity of someone who passed as The Shadow!"

"Yes, I had a lot of trouble with my best detective—Joe Cardona. He insisted upon working The Shadow into his reports. He finally dropped that policy until now. Cardona is working on these mysterious deaths that have occurred in the underworld. Yesterday, he came to me with the astounding statement that he could not proceed unless allowed to consider an unknown person as a definite entity."

"You mean The Shadow?"

"Yes—and more. I put that very question to Cardona and he came back with a most astounding answer. He wants it to be conceded that The Shadow is a figure who enters the affairs of the underworld; more than that, he wants me to accept the fact that there is another crime fighter of equal mystery—a new fighter who calls himself The Cobra."

"The Cobra?" questioned Myland. "I have heard talk of The Shadow—but never of The Cobra. This is indeed amazing."

"Either amazing or insane," corrected Weston. "Cardona had his nerve to bring up the matter of

CRAWLER GORGAN, Cardona's under-cover man who serves as contact man between the police and the underworld in this strange hunt for The Cobra, whose aid to the police proves so great that the prestige and power of The Shadow, most amazing of all crime avengers, wanes in comparison. The fear of The Shadow has left the underworld, to be replaced by awe of The Cobra. And all the strange, unusual mutterings of the underworld are revealed, in this amazing chronicle of The Shadow's epic battle, by Crawler Gorgan, most extraordinary of all the under-cover agents of the police.

The Shadow. When he added to that by introducing The Cobra, his boldness passed all belief."

"What did you tell him?"

"I asked for his resignation."

"And he gave it?"

"No. He requested a chance to convince me. He said that all the underworld is talking of The Cobra; that Deek Hundell was killed by The Cobra in the presence of half a dozen mobsmen. He added that The Shadow was seen in the same vicinity; that the sanguinary fray which followed Hundell's death was a fight between the mobsters and The Shadow."

"And he has proof—"

"He is bringing a man to testify in his behalf. For several years, Myland, we have used the services of undercover investigators who represent a higher group than stool pigeons. One of these is a man called Crawler Gorgan."

"Gorgan." Myland was thoughtful. "Ah, yes— he used to run a small pawn shop. He sold out his business after he became a dope addict. He deals in petty crime, spends all his money on dope, and is regarded with pity even by those in the underworld."

"How do you know all this?" quizzed Weston.

"From my files," returned the criminologist, with a smile. "In studying crooks, I have gained sketches of many characters in the underworld. Crawler Gorgan is one; I happened to remember his story as it looked like an unusual case. It is news to me, however, to learn that Gorgan has served as a police agent. I suppose that his reputation as a dope addict is a false one."

"It is," assured Weston. "Gorgan has played an excellent part. Always undercover, he forms contact only with certain men from headquarters. Joe Cardona is one. Gorgan has given us some excellent reports, which I've commended.

"Hence when Cardona told me that Gorgan could substantiate his statements concerning The Shadow and The Cobra, I told him to bring Gorgan to me in person. That is why I arranged for them to come here tonight."

"Here?" Caleb Myland raised his brushy gray eyebrows in anticipation.

"Here," repeated Weston. "Myland"—the commissioner leaned forward and brought his heavy fist emphatically to the table—"I want to settle this matter. No detective—not even Joe Cardona— has the real insight into gangland. They all go by what stool pigeons tell them; by what they force out of small-fry crooks. If Gorgan can amplify Cardona's statements, I can count on them. If not—well—Cardona can turn in his resignation."

"A valuable man, Cardona," observed Caleb Myland. "I have heard much about his work. But why, Weston"—Myland was smiling dryly—"did you arrange to have the interview here? You told me merely that you wished to call and to discuss crime activities."

"I'm not sure of anything, Myland," returned Weston, soberly. "I've fought against these rumors concerning The Shadow, but I must admit that things have happened which made me believe that such a personage might exist.

"So long as the efforts of this being—mythical or otherwise—were a retarding influence to crime, I felt that the matter could pass. Imagine it, Myland! A weird creature crook-hunting in the underworld, terrifying wolves of crime! It passed belief; that was why I tried to reject it.

"Now there are two! The Shadow and The Cobra! Crooks have been put on the spot. The underworld is in a furor. Can I, as the highest police official in New York, stand by and view this turmoil as a mystery?"

"No," returned Myland, quietly. "You cannot afford to do so, Weston. You are wise to have arranged this meeting here. I take it that you want my opinions on what Cardona and Gorgan have to say?"

"Precisely."

"Very well. I shall aid you. I can promise you that my analysis will prove of value. If—"

Myland paused to look toward the door. Babson was standing there. At Myland's wave, the servant entered, and handed his master an envelope.

"For Commissioner Weston, sir," said Babson. "Two gentlemen are here to see him."

Weston opened the envelope and read words scrawled on a card within. He nodded as he turned to Myland.

"They are here," he remarked.

"Babson," ordered Myland, "usher the gentlemen in at once."

As Babson left, Commissioner Weston settled back in his chair. Caleb Myland copied the motion. Their faces showed intense interest as they waited the entry of Joe Cardona and "Crawler" Gorgan.

## CHAPTER V
## MYLAND ADVISES

THE two men who next entered Caleb Myland's study presented a marked contrast. To a criminologist such as Caleb Myland, they represented definite types.

One was a swarthy, dark-haired fellow of short, stocky build. His face, firm-jawed and stern, showed his bulldog characteristics. Myland needed no introduction to learn the man's name. This was Detective Joe Cardona.

With the sleuth was a tall, stoop-shouldered individual, whose pasty face and nervous twitch were suggestive of the dope addict. The man's eyes were blinking in the light. In his scrawny hands, he held an old felt hat that fitted with his ragged attire. This was Crawler Gorgan.

Cardona made the introduction in gruff manner. He pointed to his companion as he spoke to the commissioner.

"This is Gorgan, Commissioner," he said.

Rising, Weston proffered his hand. Gorgan accepted it awkwardly. He showed a trace of firmness in his grasp. Weston, turning, introduced both men to Caleb Myland. The criminologist merely bowed and pointed to chairs. Cardona seated himself and Crawler Gorgan followed.

"Cardona," announced Weston, "I have told Mr. Myland substantially what you told me. I said that you were bringing Gorgan here to add his statements to your own. Mr. Myland is a criminologist of high repute. I want him to hear Gorgan's testimony. After that, Cardona, you will be free to add further remarks of your own."

Cardona nodded as the commissioner ceased speaking. Weston and Myland sat silent. Cardona took this as his cue. Turning to Gorgan, he said:

"Tell them about it."

Gorgan licked his puffy lips. His blinking ceased momentarily as he turned his eyes back and forth from Weston to Myland. The man seemed to be steadying himself to talk. When his voice came, it delivered direct words.

"I look like a hophead," declared Crawler Gorgan. "I ain't one, though. Joe here told you that, Commissioner. I used to run a hockshop; and when I saw I was likely to get listed as a fence, I made a deal with the police. That was seven years ago, Commissioner.

"I knowed the joints and I knowed the crooks. I wasn't one of them, but it didn't take much to make them think I was. They all knowed Crawler Gorgan—yeah, they thought they did, the scum!

"I wouldn't play no stoolie—why should I? I'd never done nothing against the law. But when I got the chance to work undercover, I took it. Down in the Tenderloin, they figured poor Crawler Gorgan had gone blooie."

Crawler paused to grin. He raised his right hand and rubbed it along his nose in the manner of a cocaine sniffer. The gesture was a perfect pantomime.

"That's what they think I am," resumed Crawler. "A dope. The hockshop sold out; I hang around the joints; and they figure I pull some small jobs every now and then. All the time I'm listening—and what I get goes to Joe Cardona."

"I AM aware of that, Gorgan," stated Weston. "You have an inside knowledge of affairs in the underworld. Therefore, I want you to answer this question. Have you ever seen a mysterious personage called The Shadow?"

"The Shadow!" Crawler blinked as he uttered the name. "Say, Commissioner, it didn't use to be healthy to see The Shadow. The guys that lamped him didn't stay around to talk about it.

"But there's some that have seen The Shadow—and I've heard what they've had to say. They were birds who didn't get too close—like them that was battling with The Shadow the other night, after Deek Hundell got bumped."

"Did The Shadow kill Deek Hundell?"

"No. I'll tell you who got Deek. It was another guy that's beating The Shadow at his own game. Listen, Commissioner. The Shadow don't pick the open. He stays in the dark and when he comes out of it, he's ready for business. That's why he's a mystery. All in black—with eyes that glitter like fire. That's The Shadow! When he opens up with those big automatics of his, there's no stopping him. When he's through, he slides back into the dark."

"So I have heard," interposed Weston. "But what about The Cobra?"

"He's different." Crawler's tone was emphatic. "The Cobra is out for the big shots, Commissioner. He picks the guy he wants; then walks in and gets him. He don't wait, like The Shadow does, until there's some crime being done. He lops off the big boys right when they don't expect it—and he likes to have witnesses on deck."

"You have seen The Cobra?"

"Me? Not yet. But I've met a dozen guys that have seen him. When he bumped Deek Hundell, there was a whole crew there. The Cobra comes in on them"—Crawler paused to make his description graphic—"right through a doorway. He was dressed in a sort of sweater—all brown—with a hood over his head. Painted eyes—like one of those cobra snakes—and he hissed, like a warning.

"They say Deek Hundell didn't have a chance. The Cobra plugs him and douses the light. Bang goes the door and there's a bunch of scared guys sitting around with Deek laying dead. That's the way The Cobra worked."

"Cardona tells me," observed Weston, "that The Shadow figured on that occasion."

"Yeah," asserted Crawler Gorgan. "That was the part that came after. The Cobra made his getaway; and the crew didn't have no chance to stop him. They were looking for The Cobra and they found The Shadow."

"How did he happen to be there?"

"Nobody knows. Some guys have figured it out that he was checking up on Deek Hundell. Maybe

**"… I hang around the joints … listening—and what I get goes to Joe Cardona …"**

he was out to get Deek, too. Anyway, the Cobra got in ahead of him and left The Shadow holding the bag. The Shadow had to fight his way out of it."

COMMISSIONER WESTON pondered. Crawler Gorgan's story was convincing. Despite the fact that the undercover man had seen neither The Shadow nor The Cobra, it was evident that he was telling accepted facts.

"Cardona," Weston addressed the detective, "I find myself forced to accept your theories. I have doubted the existence of The Shadow. I doubt it no longer. As for The Cobra—well, I can supply a statement of my own."

Weston paused to puff reflectively upon his cigar. When he spoke again, he addressed Crawler Gorgan.

"You have told me something, Gorgan," he said, "that Cardona did not mention. You have spoken of The Cobra's hiss. That was the one point that I required. I have heard that hiss."

The listeners stared at the commissioner in surprise. Weston nodded seriously.

"Two nights ago," resumed Weston, "I received a mysterious phone call. I heard a hiss over the wire—for all the world like the hiss of a snake—and then a voice. It said: 'I am The Cobra. Tonight, I shall strike.' That was all.

"I took it for a hoax. I hung up the receiver. That night, Deek Hundell was killed. The next day, Cardona came in with his story about The Cobra."

"You didn't tell me about the phone call, Commissioner," observed Detective Cardona.

"There was no use," returned Weston. "I wanted to know more before I mentioned the fact. I am convinced now that The Cobra is a figure in the affairs of the underworld; and I have every reason to expect that I shall hear from him again. I made a mistake to hang up without engaging in conversation with this mysterious caller."

Weston threw his cigar in an ash stand. His reflective tone turned to one of challenge. He pounded the table with his fist and issued a demand.

"What is the game?" he questioned. "Who is The Shadow? Why has he been mixing in the underworld? Who is The Cobra? Why has he entered? Who can answer it?"

"I can tell you plenty about The Shadow," declared Joe Cardona. "I've seen him—even if Crawler here hasn't. He's pulled me out of jams—and you, too, Commissioner. You didn't know it, but I did; and if I'd tried to put you wise, you wouldn't have believed me.

"Crooks are scared of The Shadow. He nails them when they're working. Some of the biggest crimes have been solved and ended by The Shadow."

"And The Cobra?" questioned Weston.

"I'll tell you about him." It was Crawler Gorgan who volunteered. "He's muscled in on The Shadow's game; and he's pulling stuff The Shadow never did. He's knocking off the big shots, Commissioner. They haven't got a chance to stop him!"

WESTON wheeled toward Caleb Myland. The criminologist had been a close listener to all that had been said. It was evident that Weston was seeking his opinion as that of a judge.

"What do you think of all this, Myland?" was Weston's question. "What is the game behind it? The Shadow and The Cobra—what are they after?"

"The Shadow," observed Myland, "has long made it his business to offset crime. His work has been notable in that direction. He has played a crafty game, from all that I have heard.

"It is apparent that The Cobra has chosen a similar purpose. He is outdoing The Shadow. From Gorgan's statements, it seems obvious that The Shadow's fame will wane while that of The Cobra rises."

"Granted," agreed Weston, "but what should I do about it? So long as The Shadow seemed a myth, I took it for granted that if he did exist, his purposes were to be commended. Now matters are different. Can I afford to keep hands off while two unknown individuals take the law into their own grasp?"

"So long as men such as Deek Hundell are the victims," declared Myland, "it is to your advantage to let The Shadow and The Cobra alone."

"To accumulate power," added Weston. "Then, if they wish, to turn crooked. I want evidence, Myland—evidence that these fellows are on the level. Why should they fight crime to no gain? Answer that!"

Caleb Myland laughed. He leaned forward on the table and began to speak in the tone of a lecturer.

"There," he said, pointing to Joe Cardona, "is a man who could head the detective force of a good-sized city, with twice the pay that he receives in New York. He prefers to retain his present job. Why? Because he likes to fight crime—the biggest that he can find.

"There is another." Myland indicated Crawler Gorgan. "He has chosen to live in the underworld, posing as a dope addict, risking his life should his true status as undercover man be discovered. Why does he keep up that work? Because he, too, has felt the lure of fighting crime.

"You, Weston, are a man of high social standing. You could head a huge corporation. Instead, you retain the office of police commissioner. Why? Because you have felt the challenge that crime offers.

"Let me speak for myself. I have wealth. Look at this home. Behind that paneled wall, I keep thousands of dollars in my safe. I have fifteen bank accounts; and a private yacht that could take me anywhere.

"Instead, I stay here in New York, or visit other large cities; I go to prisons and view their conditions; I stroll through districts where crime is fostered; and I complete the chain by writing books on criminology. Why? Because I like to battle crime. Not for money—not for glory—but for the fascination that such work offers."

WESTON was nodding. He was getting the point to which Myland was working.

"Four of us," testified the criminologist, "are here in this room. We are all inspired by the same motive. We like to meet crime and defeat it. We can say the same for The Shadow; and for The Cobra. They are crime fighters. We must accept them as such—for the present."

"You mean—"

"I mean that too close contact with crime may cause an individual to embrace it. There is always the chance of a crime fighter turning crook. For that reason, Weston, I always considered The Shadow as a danger. I feel now that the danger has been removed."

"Why?"

"Because of The Cobra. There are two in the field. Should one of them turn crook, the other will combat him."

"Ah!" Weston exclaimed in satisfied fashion. "You have struck it, Myland! Your statement is an excellent one. But how can we tell about their motives?"

"Easily. Two nights ago, The Cobra struck against crime. We know, therefore, that his motive was a good one. The Shadow was also present. We are in doubt concerning his motive."

"That's right."

"We must, therefore, analyze each episode in which either or both of these strange characters figure. Should conflict arise between them, we can then tell which one has turned to crime. The law can side with the one who is in the right."

"Excellent, Myland!" exclaimed Weston, rising. "Such shall be our course. There is your duty, Cardona; and yours, Gorgan. Learn all that you can regarding The Shadow and The Cobra. We must be ready for the climax"

"All right, Commissioner," said Cardona, grimly. "You can count on me. I'll let Gorgan duck back where he belongs; and he'll keep me posted right along."

"You will bring him here again," ordered Weston. "We are going to follow Mr. Myland's advice throughout this new campaign. However, you must avoid all risk in bringing Gorgan."

"That's all right, Commissioner," interposed Crawler Gorgan. "I've got my own hideout; and when I duck out of sight, nobody knows where I'm at. They didn't hand me my moniker for nothing. When I want to see Joe Cardona, I call him; and nobody sees him meet me. I'll keep him posted, Commissioner."

The detective and the undercover man made their departure. Ralph Weston remained a short while, to talk with Caleb Myland. Then the commissioner left also.

Caleb Myland, criminologist, remained alone behind his big table. A smile showed on his keen face. Myland chuckled in anticipation.

Brilliant student of crime, Caleb Myland scented the approach of a strange combat which would develop from the rivalry between the two unknowns: The Shadow and The Cobra!

## CHAPTER VI
## THE SHADOW MOVES

A CLICK sounded in a darkened room. A bluish light appeared in a corner; its downward shaded rays were focused upon the surface of a polished table.

Into that sphere of light came two long-fingered hands. Upon the left gleamed a sparkling gem that showed ever-changing hues. The Shadow was in his sanctum.

This was the hidden room which The Shadow had long used as his headquarters. Once men of crime had penetrated here; they had not lived to tell the location of The Shadow's sanctum.

Somewhere in Manhattan—there lay the sanctum. The bluish light told the place; the sparkling gem, a matchless girasol, proclaimed the identity of its wearer—The Shadow.

Long fingers opened envelopes. Clippings dropped upon the polished table. These were the accounts which Caleb Myland had been reading in his study; they were amplified by later items. A day had passed since Myland had received Commissioner Weston at his home.

The Shadow studied news reports. They spoke of confusion in the underworld. Events were impending in the badlands. Big shots were in fear of their lives. The clippings failed to give the reason, but The Shadow knew the answer.

The Cobra!

Into the realm of gangdom had come a fantastic figure whose quick strokes had raised him to the summit. For years, The Shadow had been the unseen factor who had held the balance between justice and evil. His stern hand had always been ready to swing the scales to the side of right.

The Shadow's course had been a wise one. Well did he know the value of keeping crime at bay. The Shadow's strokes were body thrusts to the undying monster called crime. A being of retribution, The Shadow used tactics that had proven their worth over a prolonged period.

The Cobra, apparently, was attempting the impossible. He was out to lop off heads. Hydralike, new ones would form where the old had been. To The Shadow, The Cobra's course seemed futile.

That was not all. The Cobra, through his sudden rise as a terrorist, had become a problem to The Shadow. The menace of The Cobra had eclipsed that of The Shadow. The episode that had marked the death of Deek Hundell had been the turning point.

IN all his battles against men of evil, The Shadow had taken advantage of the one phobia that lurks in every human brain—fear. Crooks noted for their steady trigger fingers had faltered when they faced The Shadow.

The scene had changed. The Cobra was the new terror of the underworld. He had struck down Deek Hundell amid a squad of protecting henchmen. Those men who had sat stupefied had later risen to do battle with The Shadow.

True, The Shadow had won a fight against great odds; but he had waged a futile conflict. He had been forced to retreat under fire. Skulking mobsters who had feared the very name of The Shadow were now boasting of what they would do should they meet him. The prestige of The Shadow was at stake.

Another envelope came between The Shadow's hands. It held a message, written in code. The Shadow perused the blue-inked lines; then the writing faded, word by word.

A report from Cliff Marsland, The Shadow's agent in the underworld. A low, weird laugh whispered from the darkness on the near side of the shaded lamp.

In his report, Cliff had emphasized the very pointers that The Shadow had realized. The underworld was speaking in awed tones of The Cobra; and boastful threats against The Shadow were being uttered in the same breath.

A pen appeared in The Shadow's hand. The fingers wrote brief comments that showed the trend of The Shadow's thoughts. The master sleuth was analyzing the situation which confronted him.

How had The Cobra learned Deek Hundell's meeting place? The Shadow had picked up Deek's trail through Harry Vincent, who had long been one of The Shadow's trusted agents. Harry had watched Deek at the uptown hotel where the gang leader had been staying.

But The Cobra had used no watcher. Somehow, the new crime fighter had learned of the meeting spot without tracing Deek at all.

What was the answer? The Shadow's whispered laugh showed that his keen brain had found an inkling.

A tiny bulb glimmered on the wall beyond the table. A hand moved forward and plucked a pair of earphones from the wall. The Shadow spoke in whispered tones. A quiet voice came over the wire:

"Burbank speaking."

"Report."

The Shadow's whispered order seemed to cling with weird echoes. Burbank's statement came:

"Report from Marsland. At the Black Ship. Members of Heater Darkin's mob waiting for orders from their leader."

"Instructions to Marsland," responded The Shadow. "Remain on duty. Side door code message."

"Instructions received."

The earphones went back to the wall.

The Shadow's laugh sounded as a sinister whisper. Through Burbank, his hidden contact man, The Shadow had received this special word from Cliff Marsland. It was the very type of information for which The Shadow had hoped.

CLIFF MARSLAND, when stationed in the underworld, had frequent opportunities to gain advance notice of impending crimes. Accepted as a gunman of importance, Cliff had the run of various hangouts, including the Black Ship.

During the past few days, Cliff had been roaming the badlands at The Shadow's order. His present information, concerning "Heater" Darkin, a notorious gang leader, was exactly what The Shadow wanted.

Here was opportunity. The Shadow specialized in swift strokes dealt while crime was taking place. Heater Darkin was recognized as a big shot who dealt in merciless tactics. It was time that his evil career should be broken.

Gangdom was talking of The Cobra. It was time that such talk should end. The trend of gangland's fears must return to the master whose prestige The Cobra had usurped. The Shadow! His fame would benefit through a meeting with Heater Darkin, while the big shot was engaged in crime.

A sibilant laugh crept through the confines of the sanctum. Black gloves appeared upon the table. Thin, smooth fitting cloth, they slipped over the long-fingered hands. Clippings and envelopes were pushed aside. A black hand rose; the light disappeared with a click.

The swish of The Shadow's cloak sounded in the pitch-black gloom. Then came a repetition of The Shadow's laugh; the whispered mockery took tone as it rose to an eerie crescendo.

The gibing mirth came to a sudden ending. In its place were echoes that reverberated from jet-black walls, as though uttered by a myriad of ghoulish tongues. The creepy echoes died. Complete silence followed.

The sanctum was empty. The Shadow had departed. Faring forth on a new mission, the master fighter was out to combat crime. Two purposes lay before The Shadow on this night.

One was the cause of right: The Shadow's unceasing desire to bring disaster to crooks whom the law could not forestall. The other was a vital point that concerned The Shadow's future dealing with affairs of the underworld.

Upon his success in frustrating Heater Darkin's culminating crime, The Shadow was staking his reputation as the greatest of all menaces to evil.

This would be The Shadow's counter challenge to the rising fame of The Cobra!

## CHAPTER VII
## THE COBRA'S LAIR

SOMEWHERE in Manhattan. Such was the location of The Shadow's sanctum. The same phrase alone could be used to mark the position of another strange abode—the lair of The Cobra!

A stone-walled room, its musty, cobwebbed crevices gaping where plaster had fallen; a low ceiling from which glowed a single frosted incandescent—this was the spot which The Cobra had chosen for his headquarters.

The furnishings of this room consisted of a table, a cot and two chairs. A rounded wicker basket of Oriental design rested in one corner. At one side was a battered door, raised above a single stone step. Opposite, another door that evidently led to an adjoining compartment.

One chair faced the wall. Directly in front of it was a projecting box that looked like a radio cabinet. This was fitted with numbered holes, from one to thirty-six. Hanging in front were wired plugs. Wires ran from the big plug box to the wall behind.

Muffled footsteps clicked outside the room. The door opened above the step. The Cobra, clad in wrinkled garb of brown, stepped into his lair. Behind him showed a dim stone stairway which he had used to reach this underground den.

The Cobra closed the door behind him. He moved toward the basket in the corner. He raised the lid and uttered his strange hiss. An answer came from the basket; the hood of a snake rose into view.

The reptile was a cobra; its brown skin made it appear like a miniature of its master. A forked tongue darted from the head above the hood. Again, The Cobra uttered his fierce hiss as he leaned toward the basket.

The venomous snake lowered its hood. The Cobra clapped the cover on the basket. His hiss had cowed the serpent.

THE COBRA seemed to enjoy this bit of by-play. His hiss became a chuckle as he approached the chair in front of the plug box.

Seating himself, The Cobra waited. His weird hood with its painted front gave him a fierce appearance in the dull light of the underground lair. A low buzz sounded from the box. The Cobra inserted a plug in an unnumbered hole below the thirty-six.

"Ss-s-s-s-s-s!"

The Cobra's hiss was the signal that connection had been formed. A voice came from the box on the wall; its distant tone increased as The Cobra turned a dial.

"Fang Eleven," announced the voice. "The time is set at ten o'clock."

"You will guard the passage?"

"Yes."

"Ss-s-s-s-s-s-s!"

As he concluded the conversation with the hiss, The Cobra pulled the plug from the hole. He then moved the plug along the line above and pressed it into a hole numbered eight. There was a short pause; then a voice:

"Fang Eight."

"Ss-s-s-s-s-s! You are ready?"

"Yes."

"Wait fifteen minutes. Proceed if I do not call again. Ss-s-s-s-s!"

The Cobra moved the plug to another hole. This time a voice reported as Fang Four. The speaker received the same instructions as Fang Eight. Again, The Cobra plugged and gave the identical word to Fang Eighteen; his final action was a telephone call to Fang Nine.

Fangs of The Cobra! These were agents reached in some mysterious fashion through the telephone connection of The Cobra's plug box. In touch with workers in the underworld, The Cobra was utilizing a system which neither The Shadow nor the police had recognized.

Tonight, The Cobra was on the move. From his lair, this new power in the underworld was planning another stroke. His men had been posted; the statement from Fang Eleven had caused The Cobra to order action by the others who were waiting.

The Cobra remained in his chair. He opened the bottom of the plug box and drew forth an instrument. It was the dial of a telephone, connected by wires to the plug box.

A brown-coated finger turned the dial. The sound of a busy signal came from the plug box. The Cobra pressed a switch. The clicking ended.

This dial represented a portion of regular telephone equipment. By using it, The Cobra was connecting his own apparatus with the regular telephone line. The person whom The Cobra had sought to call was evidently busy on the wire.

AFTER a short wait, The Cobra again dialed the number. This time the connection formed. The sound of ringing came from the plug box. Then a click; a brisk voice came from the cabinet.

"Police Commissioner Weston speaking."

"Ss-s-s-s-s-s-s-s-s-s!"

The Cobra's prolonged hiss brought a startled gasp over the wire. There was a pause. Then, in a low voice, The Cobra spoke:

"I am The Cobra. Tonight I shall strike!"

Another pause; then came the commissioner's voice in an easy questioning tone:

"Good. Where is your objective?"

"Follow instructions," hissed The Cobra, "and

you shall be there. One false step—your chance shall end. Do you understand?"

"Yes." Weston's voice sounded agreeable. "Tell me what you want me to do."

"Forty-seventh Street west of Seventh Avenue," hissed The Cobra. "Nine-thirty o'clock. Enter the gray sedan that you will find waiting there. Bring one companion. That is all. Ss-s-s-s-s!"

The Cobra pressed the switch. The call was ended. The brown-clad figure arose. The snake-like hiss sounded in gloating fashion as The Cobra stalked across his den.

He opened the door on the opposite side of the room. A large closet was revealed; hanging from hooks were various garments, among them two other costumes that were identical with the one which The Cobra wore.

Pushing these aside, The Cobra reached to a shelf and obtained two articles: one a large revolver, the other a small flashlight, which The Cobra tested to make sure it was in working order.

The Cobra left the closet and closed the door. He went back to the switchboard and inserted a plug. A voice was prompt in its response:

"Fang Two."

"Ready!" warned The Cobra. "I shall want the coupé in fifteen minutes. At spot three."

"I am ready."

"Ss-s-s-s-s-s-s!"

The Cobra removed the plug. He strode to the door at the steps. The door closed behind him as he ascended from the lair. Clicking footsteps came muffled from the stone stairs. The light in the lair went out.

LIKE The Shadow, The Cobra was moving to strike crime. Bold in the past, he had evidenced a new disregard of hazard. The Cobra had extended an invitation to the police commissioner to witness the stroke that would be dealt tonight!

With the aid of those workers whom he had termed his fangs, The Cobra had prepared for this event. More than before, his power was to be known in the underworld.

This night was destined to produce a new and startling chapter in the strange rivalry that had arisen between two fighters of crime in New York: The Cobra and The Shadow.

## CHAPTER VIII
## THE TRAIL

"AT nine-thirty, Cardona."

Detective Joe Cardona nodded as heard the police commissioner's statement. Cardona was seated in the little office of Weston's apartment. He had just heard the commissioner's account of the call from The Cobra.

"It was eight-thirty when the call came in," continued Weston. "Just after I had hung up from my talk with you. I knew that you were on the way here, so I didn't call back to headquarters. Instead, I telephoned to Caleb Myland."

"What did he have to say, Commissioner?" questioned Cardona.

"He was not at home," declared Weston. "Out of town, his servant said. I wanted to get Myland's advice. However, I feel sure that he would recommend the course that I intend to follow."

"To keep this appointment with The Cobra?"

"Exactly. Taking one man along with me. You, Cardona, are the man that I have chosen."

"You're running a risk, Commissioner," declared Cardona, gravely. "This looks like a phony game to me. Let me take a squad out on this job."

"And ruin it?" The commissioner laughed. "No, Cardona, that would be futile. I have made arrangements for our protection. I called Inspector Klein at headquarters, just before you arrived. He is sending men to act as our reserve."

"You mean they'll follow us?"

"Yes. I am in charge tonight, Cardona. I have made my plans. Come. We are going to Forty-seventh Street and Seventh Avenue."

As the two men rode in the commissioner's car, Weston recalled a question which he had intended to ask Cardona. He put it eagerly, realizing that it might have a bearing on tonight's expedition.

"You have seen Gorgan?"

"Yes, Commissioner. About an hour before I called you. He hasn't learned anything new as yet. They're still talking of The Cobra—but it's all been rumor."

"This is no rumor, Cardona." Weston spoke with assurance. "That voice over the wire tonight was the same one that spoke to me the evening that Deek Hundell was slain by The Cobra. Ah—here we are. Come on; we'll look for the gray sedan."

WESTON and Cardona alighted near the spot appointed by The Cobra. There was no sign of the gray sedan. Cardona noted two men standing a short distance from the curb. One was Detective Sergeant Markham; the other, Detective Logan, both from headquarters. They had evidently been dispatched here by Inspector Klein.

It was exactly half past nine, by the big clock on the Paramount Building. Cardona turned to the commissioner.

"We'll learn quick enough," began the detective. "If this is a stall—"

Weston stopped Cardona with a wave of his hand. Joe turned in the direction of the commissioner's gaze. A gray sedan had pulled up by the curb. Weston stepped forward and accosted the driver; at the same time, he made a beckoning motion which brought Markham and Logan from their spot of obscurity.

"You're waiting for me?" questioned Weston.

"Came here to get two passengers," returned the driver. "I guess you're the ones who are waiting."

"Who sent you?"

"New Era Garage, over on Tenth Avenue. Fellow came in there tonight and hired this car."

"Do you work for the garage?"

"Yes, sir."

"Where have you been instructed to take us?"

"Down Sixth Avenue. The fellow that hired this car said a cab would pass us on the avenue. I'm to follow the cab that blows its horn."

Weston turned toward Markham. The detective sergeant nodded. He and Logan hurried away. Weston motioned Cardona into the sedan. The car started.

"Clever," mused Weston. "This driver knows nothing. Paid to take us down Sixth Avenue. Hmm. Wait until the cab appears. We may find out something then."

The sedan had reached Sixth. It was rolling beneath the superstructure of the elevated. Past Thirty-fourth Street, a cab swung by on the left. The taxi driver blew his horn; then slowed speed. Weston leaned to the rear window of the sedan and drew a flashlight from his pocket. He flicked the light twice.

A black sedan swept past the gray. Cardona grinned. In the black car were Markham, Logan and other detectives. Weston and Cardona watched the police sedan overtake the cab and order it to the curb.

"Pull up in back of the taxi," ordered Weston. The driver of the gray car complied.

Markham was quizzing the cab driver when Weston alighted on the sidewalk. The detective sergeant shrugged his shoulders.

"He don't know anything, Commissioner," said Markham.

The cab driver looked startled. The word "Commissioner" had given him the identity of this big man with the pointed mustache. Fearing arrest, the taxi driver became voluble.

"I haven't been doin' nothin', Commissioner," he said. "A bloke give me a ten spot an' told me to stick here on Sixth Avenue until I seen a gray sedan. I was to go by an' blow my horn."

"Where were you to lead us?" demanded Weston.

"Down Fourth Avenue, Commissioner," responded the cab driver. "Another cab is supposed to be waitin' down there. When he blows his horn, that means for me to quit."

WESTON turned to Markham. He motioned to the detective sergeant and drew him aside. He called Cardona into the conference.

"A clever game," asserted the commissioner. "There may be one cab after another. These chaps know nothing about The Cobra. Here is our plan.

"Follow us, Markham, until we reach our destination. Keep in the offing. Form a cordon and be ready for a whistle. If it looks safe, Cardona and I shall go ahead alone. Do not approach unless you see my light; if we get out of sight, wait for the whistle."

"Yes, sir," affirmed Markham.

"Go ahead," said Weston, as he approached the cab driver. "We are following."

The cab headed for Fourth Avenue. The gray sedan, with Weston and Cardona as occupants, took up the trail.

On Fourth Avenue, near Fourteenth Street, another cab rolled by and honked. The first cab pulled to the curb. The driver of the gray sedan took up the trail of the second cab.

This vehicle headed eastward. The driver seemed to be following a charted course as he turned from street to avenue. Suddenly another cab passed. Its horn blew. The second cab pulled to the curb; the third took up the lead.

The course led to a dingy district. They had reached the fringe of the badlands when the cab came to a stop. The sedan rolled up behind it. Weston bounded to the curb and spoke to the taxi driver.

"Is this where you were supposed to lead us?" he questioned. "How did you know where to stop?"

"I didn't know until just now," returned the cab driver. "I was told to come along this street until I saw a cab parked the wrong way, with only one light on. There it is."

"Quiz the other driver," ordered Weston, to Cardona.

Joe hurried ahead. He flashed his badge as he reached the cab. The driver growled.

"I figured it," he said. "Parked the wrong way, I knew somebody would land on me. I thought it would be a copper though. I didn't know the dicks were on traffic duty."

"Forget it," rejoined Cardona. "What I want to know is how you came to be here."

"Don't think I'm cuckoo," said the driver. "A guy gave me ten bucks to pull up here and park with only one light. He said if anybody asked me any questions, to tell them to go in that house over there."

The driver pointed to a dilapidated building on the other side of the street. Its windows were unlighted.

"What then?" questioned the sleuth.

"I'm through," returned the cabman. "That's all I'm supposed to do."

Cardona went back to where Weston was standing. He told the commissioner what he had learned. Weston shrugged his shoulders.

"These men know nothing," he again affirmed. "Check on their cab cards and order them to report to headquarters in the morning."

While Cardona was doing this, Weston returned to the gray sedan and told the driver that he could go back to the Tenth Avenue garage. The driver protested:

"I was hired to wait here, sir," he said. "I guess they figured you would be going back. I'm to take you wherever you want to go."

"Wait here, then."

THE cabs were pulling away. Weston beckoned to Cardona. The commissioner and the detective crossed the street. They ascended the steps of the dilapidated building.

"Ring the bell," ordered the commissioner. "We're going in here. We can summon Markham and his men if we need them. There's a second police car with them; they'll surround the place after we enter."

The bell button failed to push. Cardona struck a match and examined it. He whistled softly.

"Say, Commissioner!" he exclaimed. "I ought to have known this place. That bell's out of order, but there's a name card over it. Eliaphas Growdy."

"Eliaphas Growdy?"

"Yes, Old Growdy. This is where he lives. Worth a million dollars, they say. Owns a lot of real estate down in this district. Has his office in his home—lives here like a recluse."

"Try the door."

Cardona obeyed. The door was locked. Cardona produced a flashlight and examined the fastenings. He turned to the commissioner.

"I can open this," declared Cardona. "It's an old lock—I always carry a bunch of keys."

"Do it."

Cardona turned locksmith. He drew a ring of keys from his pocket and worked on the lock. He was successful. The door opened inward on rusty hinges, to show a darkened hallway.

"Leave the door open," ordered the commissioner. "Come inside, Cardona. We'll wait here for five minutes, to let the cordon form. Then we'll investigate the place."

The commissioner drew back his cuff to show the dial of his wristwatch. It showed the time as exactly ten o'clock.

"Five minutes," repeated Weston.

Standing in the darkened hallway, the police commissioner and the star detective tarried before keeping the appointment that The Cobra had arranged.

## CHAPTER IX
## THE SHADOW ENTERS

WHILE Commissioner Ralph Weston and Detective Joe Cardona were following The Cobra's lead to the dilapidated abode of Old Growdy, Cliff Marsland was on the job at the Black Ship.

The Shadow's agent had picked up a hot tip. When Heater Darkin and his crew forged forth on crime, the underworld invariably found much to talk about. Buzzing rumors usually preceded Heater's expeditions; and it was one of these that had caused Cliff to report to The Shadow.

Heater Darkin, himself, avoided the Back Ship, but the notorious dive was a rendezvous for his henchmen. Cliff Marsland, seated near the side door, had spotted four gangsters whom he knew were with Heater Darkin. Nevertheless, as ten o'clock approached, the men remained idle.

This perplexed Cliff. It began to worry him. This quartet of mobsters represented less than half of Heater Darkin's contingent. None of the others had appeared. Cliff wondered where they could be; and he decided to find out.

There was something in Cliff Marsland's bearing that marked him apart from the crowd seen in the Black Ship. Cliff was as firm-jawed as any gangster; but there was an intelligence in his expression that placed him out of the gorilla class.

This had its effect upon the mobsmen whom Cliff Marsland met. They recognized him as a superior.

Hence when Cliff arose from the table where he was sitting and sauntered across the room, the men whom he approached looked up in greeting. Puffing at a cigarette, Cliff did not appear to notice any of them until a tough-faced rowdy gripped his arm and leered a welcome.

"H'ar'ya, Cliff."

Cliff had anticipated this. Nevertheless, he turned with feigned surprise. The man who had caught his arm was "Bullet" Conray, one of Heater Darkin's lieutenants. He was the very man whose attention Cliff had sought to attract.

"Hello, Bullet." Cliff spoke in a matter-of-fact tone. "Didn't notice you sitting here. How's everything?"

"O.K.," growled Bullet. "Sit down, Cliff. Have a drink. Wotcha been doin'?"

"Taking it easy," returned Cliff, seating himself at Bullet's table. "Looks like you're doing the same."

Bullet laughed. The man showed the effect of liquor that he had been drinking. Cliff's reminder caused him to push glass and bottle aside.

"I've had enough," he grunted. "So've the other boys sittin' around here. I may get the word any minute now—an' it ain't good judgment to show up crocked when you're workin' for Heater Darkin."

CLIFF made no comment. He was lighting a fresh cigarette from the butt of the old one. His silence seemed critical. Bullet Conray became apologetic.

"I lay off the grog," he said, "when I go out on a job. But tonight's kinda different. Me an' these other guys—we're just waitin' here until we get a call from Heater. He ain't usin' a full crew tonight."

Cliff nodded as though he understood. Bullet reached for glass and bottle; then pushed the articles aside.

"Had enough," he insisted. "I don't want Heater to be sore. Maybe he's goin' to call me—maybe he ain't. It all depends on how much swag he gets. These gorillas here are waitin' for word from me. They don't know where Heater's gone; but I do."

"Raiding a warehouse, eh?" prompted Cliff. "Say—when you've got to call in a fellow to lug away the swag, it's a big job."

"Warehouse?" Bullet snorted. "Say, Cliff"—the tone was becoming confidential—"you ought to know that Heater Darkin don't go in for rackets like that. He's got somethin' big on tap. I'm tellin' you."

Bullet was reaching for the bottle. Cliff, in matter-of-fact fashion, plucked it away to pour himself a drink. Bullet grinned. Cliff had saved him the trouble of denying himself another drink. Impressed by Cliff's nonchalance, Bullet resumed his confidential tone:

"You know who Old Growdy is, don't you?"

Cliff nodded in reply.

"Well, he's the guy that Heater's takin' tonight." Bullet's grin widened as the gangster spoke. "Nobody ever thought of tappin' Old Growdy, did they?"

"Why should they?" Cliff seemed unimpressed. "The old geezer's got nothing."

"Yeah?" Bullet laughed. "Well, that's where you've been fooled, Cliff. Fooled like the rest of 'em. It took Heater to get wise. Old Growdy's got a gold mine in that shack of his. Heater's goin' to get it."

A pause; then Bullet added:

"Gold hoardings, Cliff. A lot of silverware, that's real stuff. Heater's wise to plenty. Old Growdy's got a regular mint in his cellar. When Heater finds the storeroom, he's goin' to call here—over Old Growdy's own phone. I'll bring the gang to help haul the swag."

Licking his lips, Bullet reached for bottle and glass. This time he poured himself a drink. It steadied him for the moment. Bullet stared suspiciously at Cliff.

"You're stickin' around here, ain't you?" he questioned.

"Sure thing," rejoined Cliff. "Why?"

"Well"—Bullet was speculative—"maybe it ain't wise to talk the way I just done. That's all. I wouldn't have talked, maybe, to nobody but you, Cliff."

"Listen, Bullet." Cliff's tone was firm but low. "I didn't ask you to talk. What you told me doesn't mean anything to me. I work on my own—and I don't go after tinware. Get me?"

Bullet nodded.

"I'm here for the night," resumed Cliff. "If Heater's job goes blooie, it won't be on my account. But I'm giving you some advice. If you're going out to haul swag, you'd better be sobered up. Take a walk—you and the rest of your crew."

WITH this statement, Cliff arose. He clapped Bullet on the shoulder and laughed. Apparently, he and Bullet had been exchanging jests.

From the corner of his eye, Cliff noted the others who were members of Heater Darkin's corps. Like Bullet, they were showing the effects of liquor.

Strolling across the room, Cliff neared the side door and sat down to chat with a flat-nosed mobster whom he recognized. This fellow was not one of Heater Darkin's men. While he talked, Cliff watched Bullet Conray.

The gang lieutenant had remembered Cliff's advice. He was on his feet. Staggering slightly, he was approaching the men who formed his crew. The group talked.

Bullet and two others arose and made for the side door. Cliff knew that Bullet must have instructed the fourth member of the crowd to be on hand for the phone call. Bullet and the other pair were going out for air.

Cliff's right hand was in his side pocket. His fingers gripped a short, two-inch pencil and pressed its point against a tiny pad. Secretly, Cliff was writing a brief, coded report. He released the pencil. He pulled the top sheet from the pad and crumpled it into a pellet. Holding the tiny ball between his fingers, he arose from the table.

Bullet and his companions had gone outside. The last man was staring stolidly across the room. He was not noticing Cliff Marsland. Lighting a cigarette, Cliff strolled to the side door and opened it. He stepped into the darkness of an alleyway.

Bullet and his companions were forty feet away. Cliff could hear their voices down the alley; by peering from the edge of the doorway, he could glimpse the glowing ends of their cigarettes. To the right of the doorway was the blackened niche of a boarded window. Glancing in that direction, Cliff saw nothing but darkness.

Yet he sensed that a personage was waiting in that gloom. Cliff raised his cigarette to his lips with his left hand and gave short, quick puffs as a signal. In his right hand, he held the burnt match; with it the little paper ball. Reaching into darkness, he released both objects.

Beneath his hand, Cliff felt a slight swish of air. It was the only token of an unseen presence. Cliff knew that his coded message and the match had dropped into the hand of an invisible watcher. In accord with Burbank's order, Cliff had passed the word to The Shadow.

Cliff swung back into the Black Ship. He dropped at the lone table which he had first occupied. He poured out half a glass from his bottle and held the little tumbler in his hand. Slowly, his shoulders began to slouch.

A few minutes later, Bullet Conray entered. The sojourn in the fresh air had steadied the gang lieutenant and his two gorillas. Glancing warily about the room, Bullet spied Cliff.

The Shadow's agent was hunched in his chair. His left arm was stretched across the table. On it lay Cliff's head, twisted sidewise. With outspread fingers, Cliff's right was clutching its half-emptied glass.

Bullet Conray laughed.

"Look at that guy," he snorted. "He told me a walk would do me good. He needs one himself— but he don't look like he'd be able to take it."

Ceasing his banter, Bullet drew his men to the table where the fourth member of the crew was sitting.

"Outside, Curley," he ordered. "Time you sobered up, too. Lay off the booze, you guys. I'm waitin' for a call—an' we're goin' to move when I get it."

Another glance at Cliff. Bullet leered contemptuously. To all appearances, Cliff was out. Bullet's suspicions were completely ended. He believed that Cliff had probably forgotten all that he had heard; of a certainty, Cliff was in no condition to repeat or make use of anything that Bullet had told him.

If Heater Darkin should encounter trouble tonight, it could not possibly be of Cliff Marsland's making. So Bullet Conray reasoned, totally oblivious to the fact that Cliff had already passed the word!

ONE block from the Black Ship, a fleeting patch of blackness passed beneath a blinking street lamp. A cloak swished as a living form sought the shelter of a doorway. A tiny flashlight gleamed upon a crumpled scrap of paper that lay in a black-gloved hand.

The keen eyes of The Shadow were reading Cliff Marsland's coded message. The flashlight went out. A whispered laugh sounded while gloved fingers tore the slip into tiny bits.

Each lamp along that street showed a passing splotch of black. The Shadow, informed of the spot where crime was due, was on his way to Old Growdy's.

It was a dozen minutes after ten o'clock when keen eyes peered toward a block of old and dingy buildings. Between these dilapidated structures was a passage of cracked cement. As The Shadow watched, he saw a square-set man pause at the entrance to the alley, then pass on toward the other side of the block.

The Shadow knew the identity of this watcher. A detective from headquarters. Some tip must have been received there that Old Growdy was in danger. The Shadow was unperturbed. The forming of a police cordon did not hamper his plans for the present.

Swiftly, the tall form glided across the street. It reached the cement passage. The Shadow moved noiselessly through the dark. He reached the back of a house which he knew to be Old Growdy's.

A squidgy sound came from the wall. The Shadow, equipped with suction cups attached to hands and feet, was rising to the second floor. Crawling upward, The Shadow reached his goal. His form showed like that of a mammoth bat, clinging to the surface in the gloom.

Window fastenings yielded noiselessly. The Shadow's form moved over the sill. From the second floor of Old Growdy's obscure home, The Shadow was ready to begin his exploration in search of crime.

Somewhere in this house, Heater Darkin was at work. The Shadow was out to find the spot. He was planning a new and daring counterstroke against fiends of crime.

Yet even The Shadow did not know the surprising events that were already in the making!

## CHAPTER X
### AGAIN THE COBRA

THE SHADOW had chosen to enter Old Growdy's by the second floor because of the presence of the loose police cordon. From Cliff Marsland's brief report, The Shadow knew that any hiding place of wealth would doubtless be below ground. Hence his cautious course—rendered so because police were in the offing—was headed in that direction.

The cordon which caused The Shadow to exert caution had a directly opposite effect upon two others who were already in the house.

Commissioner Ralph Weston and Detective Joe Cardona had begun a rapid investigation.

While The Shadow was coming in the second-story window, Weston and Cardona were descending a flight of steps that they found leading to the basement. They had spent several minutes on the ground floor before discovering these stairs; Weston was eager to proceed downward.

The commissioner's flashlight was blazing its path to the darkened cellar. Cardona, close behind, was whispering a protest against Weston's speed: one that the commissioner did not choose to heed.

"Come along, Cardona," ordered Weston, briskly. "I'll handle the light; you be ready with the whistle. We can take care of ourselves if there's trouble below."

Weston was handling a revolver as he spoke. Cardona also had a gun in readiness. There was no arguing with the commissioner. Cardona kept pace with him as they reached the cellar.

A passage stretched off to the right. It showed a door, opened inward. Weston moved forward and reached the door. He turned off his flashlight and gripped Cardona's arm.

A light showed dimly as the two peered past the doorway. It came from the right. This doorway was the entrance to a second passage that led in that direction. Beyond was an illuminated room. Weston and Cardona could hear voices, but no one was in sight.

"Move up to the door," whispered Weston. "We'll cover them in there."

Cardona nodded.

Near the door, the commissioner paused. Then, with Cardona, he began to edge forward. He whispered instructions; Cardona began to nod in reply. Suddenly both men stopped short as a footstep clicked behind them. Nudging muzzles of revolvers pressed into their ribs.

"I got 'em!" snarled a rough voice. "Drop them gats, youse mugs, before I plug you!"

INSTINCTIVELY, Weston and Cardona let their revolvers fall. Their hands came up in response to the menace from back. At the same time, a grinning, hard-faced man popped into view beyond the door.

Joe Cardona knew him. It was Heater Darkin.

The big shot held a revolver with which he covered Weston and Cardona from in front. His grin turned to a fanglike laugh as he ordered the prisoners to move into the room.

The scene that greeted commissioner and detective was a strange one. This room, buried below the level of the street, was fitted like an office. Quivering in a chair behind a battered, flat-topped desk, was an old man with white whiskers, whose eyes showed fear.

It was Old Growdy.

Cornered by one wall was a trembling young man whose hands were upward. He was covered by a gangster, who was also watching Old Growdy. This prisoner was evidently Old Growdy's secretary.

As Cardona and Weston backed against the wall at Heater Darkin's order, they saw the man who had covered them from the passage. He was a two-gun mobster who flourished his gats in businesslike fashion.

"Cover them, Luke," ordered Darkin.

The two-gun gorilla obeyed. Heater Darkin chuckled. Pocketing his own revolver, he strolled across the room and seated himself on the desk. He laughed in contemptuous fashion.

"Visitors, eh?" he scoffed. "Joe Cardona—the smart dick—and say! Well, if it ain't the police commissioner!"

Heater's eyes hardened.

"Come here to make trouble, eh?" he snarled. "Well, you'll see it—but you won't make it. You know who I am. They call me Heater Darkin. I'm the boy that gives the heat. I'll let you watch me hand it.

"Dumb clucks! Coming down those steps with a flashlight. Luke here saw the flash. That's why I stuck him behind the door in the passage—just to trap you guys. If there's any more of you, it'll be bad for them. I've got another guy laying out there for any more smart mugs."

Heater laughed raucously. Then, continuing to relish this situation that had brought the police commissioner and the ace detective into this predicament, he again became loquacious.

"I guess Old Growdy suspected trouble," he scoffed. "Sent word out and you came down here to see what was the matter. Well—there's one thing Old Whiskers kept to himself. That was his own private entrance to this place.

"That door you just came through has a steel front. It was locked and Old Growdy and this bird Tomkins, his secretary, were here in this room. Going over accounts. Safe behind a steel door—and very safe because of that other way out—over there."

Heater Darkin pointed to a panel at the side of the room. Weston and Cardona could see that it might be the entrance to a secret passage.

"You guessed it," jeered Darkin. "An underground passage that leads a block away. If you've got any smart cops waiting outside, it won't do them any good.

"I learned about that passage. I brought my crew in from the other end. I got a guy waiting back where we came in.

"Do you know what's coming off here? I'll tell

you. I'm going take Old Growdy's swag out through that passage.

"What's more, nobody's going to stay around to squawk. Old Growdy gets the works—and so does Tomkins. Maybe you two get it, too. Maybe you'll go along with me. But there's no shooting coming until Old Whiskers coughs up the mazuma."

WHEELING, Heater turned to Eliaphas Growdy. The old man trembled as he saw the viciousness of the crook's gaze.

"What about it?" demanded Heater. "Where do you keep the dough?"

"I have nothing," protested Growdy. "Nothing of value—"

"Listen." Heater's tone was hard. "Just because two mugs blew in here, don't think you've got a chance. You saw what happened to them. That's why I opened the steel door; just to nab any smart eggs who might come around. If any more show up, I'll get them too. Come on! Squawk!"

"I shall tell you nothing," quavered Old Growdy. "If you intend to kill me, why should I speak?"

"So that's it?" Heater laughed in ugly fashion. "No use to talk? We'll see."

Striding past the desk, Heater reached to the floor. With one hand he seized both of Growdy's legs. He gave a twist that sent the old man revolving in his swivel chair. The turn ended as Heater plopped Growdy's feet squarely on the desk.

"Look at those old shoes!" scoffed Heater. "Saving every penny, you old miser. Well, Whisker Face, here go the boots."

Roughly, the crook tore the shoes from Growdy's feet. The old man's toes showed through holes in the ends of his socks. Again, Heater laughed.

"That makes it simple," he asserted. "All set. Here's where I give the heat. Ever have your toes singed, Old Whiskers?"

Bringing his left arm down on Growdy's ankles, Heater produced a matchbox. He held it in his left hand. He extracted a match with his right. He lighted the match. He brought the flame close to the old man's toes and held it there.

Old Growdy began to writhe as the match went out.

"Want more?" snarled Heater, as he struck another match. "Want more? Or are you going to squawk?"

Old Growdy tried to squirm away. He was helpless. He shrieked as the second match approached his toes. He was clasping his hands in agony, swaying back and forth in the swivel chair, while Heater watched him gloatingly.

WESTON and Cardona stood helpless. The commissioner was wild with repressed fury at sight of this preliminary torture. Cardona was grim. Yet neither could make a move, in the face of the two revolvers that covered them.

Biting his lips, Commissioner Weston turned his head away as the second match went out. He knew that this first torture was but a taste of what was to come. Heater had not commenced to work. He was bringing out a third match, ready to strike it.

Futilely, Weston stared toward the panel on the opposite side of the room, as though expecting aid from that quarter. The commissioner, alone, was gazing toward the secret exit. Hence he was the only person to witness the surprising occurrence that took place there.

With a slight click, the panel slid open. Framed before a dim background stood the most fantastically garbed man that Weston had ever seen. Clad from head to foot in a wrinkled brown jersey, this tall arrival was masked by a hood that covered his head.

Part of the brown garment, the hood was painted in fantastic fashion. Circles of dull white; tapering lines below them—these gave the head the exact appearance of a cobra's hood, with a topping bulge above it.

A gasp came from the lips of Commissioner Ralph Weston. Into this scene of terror had come the man whose promise had brought Weston and Cardona to this place.

The man at the panel was The Cobra!

## CHAPTER XI
## QUICK STROKES

EVEN as Commissioner Weston gasped, The Cobra took action. He had walked into a setup. All that he needed was promptitude and nerve. His revolver spurted as he whipped it from his jersey.

The Cobra had picked Luke. His bullet found its mark in the gorilla's body as Luke turned to learn the cause of the panel click.

The gangster who was guarding Tomkins swung also. He did not have a chance. Before he could aim, The Cobra had swung the revolver in his direction. Again the brown finger pressed the trigger. The second gangster fell.

Leaping up from the table where he was holding Old Growdy by the ankles. Heater Darkin turned to face this foe. His plight was worse than that of his henchmen. The Cobra had caught them unaware. He now had Heater Darkin unarmed. The big shot fumbled in his pocket, seeking his revolver.

"Ss-s-s-s-s-s-s-s!"

The Cobra had reserved his warning hiss for

**The detective delivered an upward swing that sent Luke's shot toward the ceiling.**

the one man whom he had come to get. He had shot the others only because they were armed.

The hiss ended while Heater was still striving to yank out his gun. Deliberately, The Cobra fired. Heater Darkin slumped to the floor.

For one long moment, The Cobra stood watching the body of his victim. Then, with a backward step, he went into the passage. The panel clicked shut.

The Cobra was gone.

"Look out, Commissioner!"

Weston turned as he heard the cry from Joe Cardona. Luke, the big two-gun gorilla, was swinging a revolver. The Cobra's shot had wounded his left arm; his right was still ready with its gat.

Cardona was leaping for Luke as he cried his warning. The detective delivered an upward swing that sent Luke's shot toward the ceiling.

With a snarl, the big gunman dived for the passage. Cardona snatched up the gun that had dropped from Luke's left hand. Weston seized the revolver that had been held by the gangster who had covered Tomkins. The secretary had rushed to aid Old Growdy, who was now slumped helplessly in his swivel chair.

Cardona fired down the passage. His aim was wide. Bullets ricocheted past Luke, who was fleeing to the other end. Cardona hurried after; Weston followed. They reached the door where the passage turned.

Cardona was first. The detective stopped short. As he clicked a flashlight toward the cellar stairs, he realized that he was trapped. Luke had turned; with the big man was a second mobster. For the first time, Cardona remembered what Heater Darkin had said about another gorilla stationed in the cellar.

SEEKING safety, Cardona dropped to the floor, firing wildly. He slipped as he tried to dive back along the passage. He heard snarls; and caught the gleam of turning revolvers.

Then came a roar from the cellar stairs. It was repeated with quick precision. Cardona's flashlight, turning upward, showed the mobsters toppling. For a brief instant, it revealed a form in black; but Cardona did not catch that glimpse.

Weston was standing above Cardona. The commissioner was following Cardona's wild shots with bullets of his own. His own flashlight gleamed as Cardona's dropped. Weston ceased firing as he saw the two bodies of the dropped gangsters.

"Good work, Cardona," he commended. "You bagged them."

The commissioner's words reached the darkened stairs. They brought a faint, whispered murmur of a laugh from a being who stood shrouded there. It was The Shadow.

The master fighter had reached the cellar stairs just as The Cobra was making his departure from the room below. Before The Shadow had gained the bottom of the steps, Luke had come dashing forth from the passage.

Waiting, The Shadow had seen the arrival of Joe Cardona. With timely precision, he had saved the life of the detective; and probably that of Commissioner Weston, for the latter had come blundering after Cardona.

As The Shadow lingered to make sure that all was well, the door swung open at the top of the cellar steps. The Shadow pressed against the wall. A flashlight glimmered past him. The voice of a detective came down the stairs.

"Hey! Cardona!"

It was Commissioner Weston who shouted in reply. His words were an order to the man above.

"Search the house!" he cried. "There may be more of these crooks. Let no one out! Close the cordon!"

The detective shouted the order to those on the ground floor. Then he began to descend the stairs. He twisted his flashlight as he came downward. Its rays flickered squarely on The Shadow. The detective let out a shout as he faced a pair of burning eyes. He raised his revolver.

The sleuth failed to fire the shot that he intended. Like a flash, The Shadow sprang forward and upward. His powerful hands caught the detective's wrists. Flashlight and gun went bouncing down the steps as the startled sleuth sprawled in The Shadow's grasp.

A twisting hold sent the detective sidewise. The man gripped the rail of the cellar steps to save himself. Dazed by the swift attack, he clung there, as The Shadow sprang upward to the door above.

Detectives were in the hallway as The Shadow appeared. They whipped out revolvers, in accordance with Weston's instructions to let no one escape. The Shadow was quicker; an automatic showed in his right hand. He delivered two shots above the heads of the detectives.

The men jumped for shelter.

The Shadow made the stairs to the second floor. As he swept rapidly upward, the balked detectives fired. Their shots were too late. They took up the pursuit.

The Shadow reached the rear window on the second floor. As he raised the sash, a flashlight gleamed from the alleyway beneath. The shout of a detective came from behind the light. The Shadow hurried back to the hall.

THE inside detectives were at the top of the stairs. One shouted as he spied The Shadow. He fired—again too late. The Shadow was on his way, still moving upward; this time to the third floor of Old Growdy's home.

The Shadow reached the top of those steps as the detectives neared the bottom. His flashlight glimmered. It showed an opening in the ceiling; a trapdoor that led to the roof.

Out went the flashlight. Turning deliberately to the steps, The Shadow fired two quick shots, aimed high. They served their purpose. The detectives dived away from the bottom of the stairs. They shouted below for reinforcements. Their quarry was trapped. They wanted aid to take him.

A whispered laugh came from the dark. The Shadow's cloak swished as its wearer swung himself upward upon the newel post at the top of the steps. Firm hands pressed against the trapdoor in the ceiling.

The barrier was locked. A rusted bolt shrieked as The Shadow forced it open. Pressing with amazing strength, The Shadow forced the trapdoor free from its catches. A puff of fresh air entered as the trap toppled on the roof.

Cries from below. Other detectives had arrived. The voice of Detective Sergeant Markham issued a command:

"Rush the steps! We'll get him!"

Detectives surged upward. Their course was unwise. They would have been easy targets in the darkness.

But there were no shots to receive them. The Shadow had no quarrel with the law. As the detectives rushed, The Shadow's strong arms gripped the edges of the opening in the ceiling. His body swung upward. An instant later he had gained the roof.

A flashlight from a detective's hand picked out the opening just as The Shadow drove the trapdoor shut. The detective opened fire.

The Shadow was already on his way. By the time the detectives had raised the trap and had reached the roof, he had reached the rear roof of a house four doors away from Old Growdy's home.

The passage between Old Growdy's row and the string of houses in back was more than a dozen feet in width. The Shadow, however, did not need to bridge that chasm. His swiftly moving form leaped forward as it reached the rear of the roof. With a perfect broad jump over a space thirty feet deep, The Shadow reached the roof of another house. His course continued.

More than a block away from Old Growdy's, The Shadow picked a wall that was to his liking. Its side, descending to a narrow street, was dark and obscure. A short wait; then came the squidge of rubber suction cups. With smooth precision, The Shadow descended the wall.

A police whistle sounded. The cordon was tightening. An officer, throwing his light along the street, caught a momentary glimpse of a shadowy form that was heading for a passage opposite. The policeman fired—too late to stop the progress of the moving figure.

THE SHADOW had passed the cordon. Like The Cobra, he had departed from Old Growdy's. But where The Cobra had gone in triumph, recognized as one who had saved helpless victims of crime, The Shadow, trapped in a situation that could not be explained, had been forced to flee in order to avoid a battle with the law.

The Cobra—that night when he had slain Deek Hundell—had left The Shadow to bear the brunt of surging mobsters. Tonight, he had again left The Shadow in an embarrassing position.

Instead of regaining his lost prestige, The Shadow, tonight, had discredited himself with the police. First with the underworld; now with the law. For the second time, The Shadow had been belittled by the craft of The Cobra!

## CHAPTER XII
## WESTON ORDERS

"WHAT have you learned, Gorgan?"

The speaker was Ralph Weston. The police commissioner was seated in Caleb Myland's study. Before him were Joe Cardona and Crawler Gorgan. Behind the desk sat Caleb Myland. The criminologist was listening intently to the commissioner's quiz of the undercover man.

"Not much, Commissioner," replied Crawler Gorgan. "I've been listening down in the badlands. News travels fast down there. They're all talking about The Cobra. But there ain't none that have spotted him."

"What about the affair at Old Growdy's?"

"They got the details of that, all right, Commissioner. Say—everybody knows that you and Joe were there. The Cobra plugged Heater Darkin—the toughest crook in the business! That's what they're saying.

"And they're talking about The Shadow. How the cops went after him. I'm telling you something, Commissioner—if The Shadow shows up again, he's liable to get his. There's plenty of tough birds that are ready to take a shot at him."

"The Shadow," decided the commissioner, "is a doubtful character. Cardona still persists that he is fighting on the side of the law. I insist that his behavior at Growdy's points to the contrary."

"Don't condemn The Shadow, Commissioner," protested Joe Cardona. "He has stepped in plenty of times to make trouble for the crooks. I think he was at Growdy's in order to stop Heater Darkin. The only reason that he didn't was because The Cobra got there first."

"Ridiculous!" exclaimed Weston. "The Shadow waged battle with our cordon."

"No one was shot by him—"

"Because they drove him away. He was in flight. The Shadow's bullets were wide."

"Not down in the cellar, Commissioner—"

Weston pounded the table in angered interruption. He glared at the detective, then turned to Caleb Myland.

"Cardona has propounded a preposterous theory," explained Weston. "Down in the cellar of Old Growdy's home, Cardona and I trapped two thugs. We riddled them with bullets. Cardona, however, thinks that The Shadow, standing on the cellar steps, fired shots to aid us.

CALEB MYLAND, criminologist of repute, whose aid in this case is summoned by Police Commissioner Weston. It is Myland who first suggests that possibly close contact with crime has made The Shadow change his allegiance from Justice to Gangdom!

"I saw no such shots. I believe that Cardona's imagination was at work. I have told you all that occurred the night that The Cobra so valiantly came to our rescue. What is your opinion, Myland?"

"I REGRET," declared the criminologist, "that I was not at home that night. I should have liked very much to have been with you, Commissioner. Unfortunately, I was delivering a lecture in Baltimore.

"It appears to me, however, that your analysis is correct and Cardona's is wrong. I shall tell you why. We have two occasions on which both The Cobra and The Shadow appeared.

"On one, The Cobra slew Deek Hundell. On the other, he disposed of Heater Darkin. Both were murderous characters. Hundell was a self-admitted killer. Darkin had stated that he intended to deal death. Therefore, we know that The Cobra is opposed to crime."

Weston nodded in response to Myland's reasoning.

"On each occasion," resumed Myland, "The Shadow was also present. Why? To deal with criminals also? Perhaps. But we may also consider the possibility that The Shadow was there to offset The Cobra. He apparently had opportunity to deal with the crooks, but failed to do so.

"Therefore, I am inclined to revert to my original opinion. Crime battlers sometimes turn crook. The Cobra has not turned crook. The Shadow, in all probability, has."

"But you can't prove that, Mr. Myland—"

The interjection came from Joe Cardona. Commissioner Weston stopped it with a wave of his hand.

"You cannot prove otherwise, Cardona," he declared. "Therefore, you should not interrupt Myland's theory. Go ahead, Myland. Excuse Cardona's interruption."

"Watch events in the underworld," advised Myland. "Do not molest The Cobra in his excellent work. But at the same time, be on the lookout for The Shadow. Should you gain proof that he has gone crooked, you can use every effort to thwart him."

"Good advice," nodded Weston. "You are to follow it, Cardona. In the meantime, Gorgan, do your best to get information on both The Cobra and The Shadow. I am disappointed because you have learned so little."

"I've heard a lot, Commissioner," protested Crawler. "The only trouble is—what's phony and what isn't. I'll tell you what's been said about The Cobra. They figure he's working a game that'll put crime on the fritz."

"You mean by eliminating criminals?"

"The big ones—yes. But not the little ones. The Cobra's got them scared. He's making some of them work for him like stool pigeons—and they're afraid to blab. That's what's been said."

"More power to him!" exclaimed Weston. "The Cobra is showing masterful tactics. Undermining the structure of gang organization. Wonderful! Who are these henchmen whom he has drafted?"

"That's what I can't get," replied Gorgan. "You ain't going to find any guy admitting he's with The Cobra. That would be suicide, Commissioner. You can take it from me—The Cobra is wise enough to tell nobody much. He's got 'em all scared."

"What about The Shadow?"

"Everybody thinks he's laying low. I told you that, Commissioner. The Cobra has made him look cheap. But I've got an idea—if you want it. It's just an idea, Commissioner—"

"Let's have it."

"I think The Shadow will try to stage a comeback. I heard what Mr. Myland just said about The Shadow going crooked. I ain't ready to agree with that, Commissioner. Not just yet, anyway. The Cobra's got him licked though—beating him at his own game. If The Shadow ain't on the job pretty soon, they'll all be laughing at him. And any guy that gorillas get a laugh out of don't amount to much—you can see that, I guess."

"Good theories, Gorgan," commended the commissioner, briskly. "However, I should like

"KING" ZOBELL, biggest of the Big Shots, leader of all in New York's underworld. He alone believes himself invulnerable, and refuses to be stampeded by the great fear of The Cobra. Why?

facts. Return to your hideout and learn all that you can concerning both The Cobra and The Shadow.

"I promise you that you shall be rewarded for any tangible information that you can produce. At the same time, you are too valuable a man to run serious risks. Gain your information in your own manner."

This was the final comment. Cardona and Gorgan were dismissed. The commissioner sat alone with the criminologist, Caleb Myland.

"CARDONA is efficient," commented Weston, "and Gorgan is useful. But, after all, their abilities are limited. They cannot be pushed beyond their capacities."

"Quite so," agreed Myland. "Nevertheless, Weston, I believe that these problems in the underworld will solve themselves."

"How?"

"Through the actions of The Cobra. He has shown the fairness of his purpose. His willingness to have you observe him combat crime is evidence of his sincerity."

"But The Shadow?"

"There is the doubtful quality, Weston. I foresee a struggle between these two factors who have made it their business to ravage the underworld."

"But who will cause it?"

"The Shadow. His prestige is at stake. He may reveal new traits—criminal ones, perhaps—in his efforts to combat The Cobra's rising power."

"And the outcome?"

"We shall see. The time will come when you will find it necessary to side with either The Shadow or The Cobra."

Caleb Myland said no more. Commissioner Weston, however, remembered the criminologist's words when he was riding back to Manhattan in his official car.

A combat was impending. The Shadow and The Cobra—both could not follow the parallel course indefinitely. As Myland had said, sooner or later, one would be outlawed.

Myland had not specified which, but Weston had caught the criminologist's innuendo—and the police commissioner agreed with it. With one of these fighters beyond the pale, the other would deserve the protection of the law.

Which?

Commissioner Weston had his answer. It was induced by his own experience; it was backed by the opinion which Caleb Myland had cautiously expressed.

Commissioner Weston was convinced that when the showdown came; when the duel between The Shadow and The Cobra was actually in view, the one with whom the law would find it best to side would be The Cobra.

## CHAPTER XIII
## THE SHADOW HEARS

DAYS had passed since The Cobra had ended the nefarious career of Heater Darkin. Since then, The Cobra had struck again. His victim had been "Smokey" Bragland, head of a big gambling racket. Smokey had been shot down in one of his palatial gaming rooms, with a dozen witnesses present.

Although the public did not know it, Police Commissioner Weston had received advance notice of The Cobra's deed. On this occasion, the hisser who spoke over the wire had not invited Weston to be present.

But The Cobra's action had satisfied the commissioner. Smokey Bragland was an unconvicted murderer. His warranted death had brought new consternation to the underworld.

The Shadow had not appeared on this occasion. That had caused new comment in the badlands. It produced the general opinion that The Shadow had admitted his own inability to keep up with The Cobra's prowess.

Night had come to Manhattan, and among the hordes of scumland, The Cobra was again the topic of awed conversations. At the Blue Crow— a hangout where the most disreputable of rowdies met—uncouth mobsters were speculating on The Cobra's next victim. While they were talking, a mobster entered. It was "Duff" Berker, a member of Heater Darkin's disbanded crew.

"Hi, Duff!" called a sweatered gangster. "We was just wonderin' who The Cobra was goin' to get next."

"Don't talk about that guy," growled Duff. "He's going to get the works himself, someday."

"Yeah?" the first speaker was sarcastic. "Who from? Say—he knowed more about what Heater Darkin was doin' than you did, I bet. Where was you that night?"

"Outside," retorted Duff.

"I'll bet you was," grinned the gangster. "You oughta have been coverin' up for Heater. Yeah— that's where you oughta have been. Then The Cobra mighta handed you the bump, too."

Duff Berker made no reply. He shuffled from the joint. Buzzing comments followed.

"He's the guy could handle Heater's old gang, Duff is."

"You bet he could, but he's wise enough to lay low. He ain't goin' to get what Heater got."

OUTSIDE, Duff Berker was shuffling along the street. He come to an old house and entered. He went through a hall to a little back room. He entered, turned on a light and closed the door. A pay telephone was on the wall. It bore a placard: "Out of order."

Duff picked up the receiver. He turned the mouthpiece with his other hand. A hissing sound reached his ear through the receiver.

"Fang Eleven," reported Duff.

A hissing voice responded. Duff spoke in reply. His conversation ended, Duff twisted the mouthpiece and hung up the receiver. He shambled from the room and left the obscure house.

Duff Berker's action was a justification of Crawler Gorgan's theory that The Cobra had gained the services of mobsters in the underworld. More than that; it showed how The Cobra had been able to move more swiftly than The Shadow.

The Cobra's agents were minions of the big shots whom The Cobra had eliminated. Thus had The Cobra kept exact tabs on the movements of his prospective victims!

BACK at the Blue Crow, mobsters were still talking of The Cobra. An hour passed while gangsters sipped their grog and jested.

These lesser minions of crime felt themselves to be fish too small for The Cobra's net. At the same time, they were visibly impressed by The Cobra's power; more so than if he had been warring on such small fry as themselves.

A sweatered, dull-faced creature shambled into the dive. Questioning eyes turned in his direction. No one recognized the newcomer, but his appearance was sufficient to grant him entrance.

This arrival slouched into a chair by a table and threw a grimy dollar bill into view. A hard-faced waiter took the money, and plunked bottle and glass upon the table. With trembling hand and bulging eyes, the newcomer tried to help himself to a drink. The effort was too much. He sprawled out on the table.

"Booze or hop?" questioned a rowdy.

The waiter raised the man's head and stared at the grimy face with its closed eyes. He let the man's head drop on his arm, where it rocked like a pendulum and finally became motionless. The waiter picked up the bottle and set an empty one in its place.

"Hophead," he said. "When dose birds get looney, they start out for a drink. When dis guy wakes up, he'll t'ink he's finished de bottle. Leave him lay. I'll t'row him out when we close de joint."

Mobsters resumed their conversation. Another man appeared. This fellow was recognized. It was Crawler Gorgan. A cigarette clung to Crawler's pasty lips.

Slouching to a table, Crawler called for a bottle. He received it. Staring straight ahead, he poured one drink and finished it; then another.

Mobsters resumed their conversation. They paid no attention to Crawler until he had swallowed a third drink. Then, when he arose with fixed stare and moved dopily through the door, a gangster made comment:

"Looked like Crawler has been hittin' de pipe. He won't last long—dat guy."

"You bet he won't," affirmed another. "He'll be like that bimbo over there."

The speaker pointed to the sweatered man who still lay sprawled upon the table. Listeners laughed. The denizens of this hangout had little regard for hopheads.

A SHORT while later, a new arrival appeared. This was a frail little mobster, whose face showed a crafty look. His appearance brought greetings from seated mobsters. Glasses of liquor were offered to the newcomer. He licked his lips, sat down and took a drink.

"What's doin', Ears?" questioned a mobster.

"Yeah. Give us the lowdown," piped another.

"If anybody knows what's blowin'," declared a third, "it's Ears Findler. Come on, Ears. Let's hear your spiel."

"Been talkin' about The Cobra?" questioned "Ears," with a wise look.

"Yeah," came the reply. "Who's he goin' to get next?"

"Why're you askin' me?" quizzed Ears. "Think I'm his pal?"

Mobsters grinned.

"Come on, Ears," asserted one tough character. We know you ain't wid de Cobra. We was just figurin' maybe you had a hunch who he was after."

"I know who's dodgin' him," declared Ears, warily. "When a guy's dodging The Cobra, it looks like he was on The Cobra's list. That's the way I figure it."

"Who's de guy?"

"King Zobell."

Grunts of astonishment greeted this assertion. One mobster, a scar-faced individual, voiced his disbelief.

"Say," he growled. "King Zobell is the real big shot. How's The Cobra goin' to get at him?"

"Don't ask me," retorted Ears. "I'm only tellin' what I've heard—and I don't go around listenin' to nothin'. Here's the lowdown.

"The Cobra knocked off Hunky Fitzler an' Cass Rogan, didn't he? All right—who did he get next? Deek Hundell an' then Smokey Bragland. There's four big shots for you. Who's next?"

"There's a couple of birds—"

"Yeah, but King Zobell is the best bet. I ain't givin' you just my own idea—I'm talkin' what I've heard from guys that are in the know. I'm tellin' you somethin'—the big shots are duckin' out of town. There's only one guy willin' to stand the gaff. That's King Zobell."

"Say—he's got a half a dozen rackets, King has. He wouldn't duck. You're right, though, Ears. King's the bird The Cobra oughta be out to get."

"An' King knows it." Ears grinned as he gave this information. "I'll tell you why. This is the hot stuff. Somethin' I learned tonight. How many bodyguards has King Zobell got?"

"Two," said a mobster. "He had Duster Corbin an' he's just taken on Diamond Rigler—"

"Right," interrupted Ears, "an' he ain't satisfied yet. How does that hit you?"

"You mean he ain't got enough bodies?"

"He needs another. Duster Corbin is out to find one. An' you can bet that the guy Duster picks will be a tough egg."

"Whew!" One mobster drew his breath. "One grand a week—that's what King Zobell pays for a body. Say—he must be scared if he's hiring a new one. Who do you think he's going to get?"

"Whoever Duster Corbin picks," returned Ears. "An' I'm tellin' you this—Duster ain't goin' to pick any guy that don't look tough enough to give The Cobra a battle. Think that over!"

"Where's he lookin'?"

"When I seen him," informed Ears, "Duster was on his way down to the Nugget Club. You know that joint—over the old garage. Say—there ain't any guy gets in there that ain't known—an' he's got to have a roll on him, too.

"If Duster is lookin' for a bird that's in the money an' is worth one grand a week, he'll find him there. I don't know who he's goin' to pick; but I'll tell you this. King Zobell will have a new bodyguard by tomorrow night—an' the reason he's gettin' one is because he's scared of The Cobra."

WITH this final reiteration of his former statements, Ears Findler polished off another drink and slouched from the Blue Crow, leaving the mobsters talking among themselves. It was a few minutes before the conversation changed; then the result came as a chance interruption.

"Take a look at de hophead," laughed a gangster. "He's comin' to."

Eyes turned toward the neighboring table. The sprawled figure was moving. A shaky hand was reaching for the bottle. The sweatered man was staring with wild eyes, while his fingers slipped against the smooth glass.

The bottle eluded the man's clutch. It toppled and rolled from the table. As it broke on the stone floor, a hoarse, distorted scream came from the lips of the wild-eyed man. The waiter approached and grabbed the fellow by the neck.

"Outside, bummer," he ordered. "We don't want no hopheads here. Get goin'."

The mobsters caught a glimpse of a drawn face with sharp-pointed features. Dull eyes peering from each side of a beaked nose stared at the waiter. The man staggered through the door and slouched off into the night as the waiter slammed the barrier behind him.

Boisterous laughter followed.

Had any of those mobsters trailed the departing man, however, their mirth would have changed to awe. Half a block away from the Blue Crow, the shambling dope changed his gait. His figure straightened as he paused at the entrance of an alleyway.

Beneath the fringe of a street-lamp's glow, his distorted face changed. His hawklike visage took on a stern expression. His dull eyes seemed to brighten until they glowed with the intensity of fire.

As the visitor who had left the Blue Crow turned to merge with darkness, a sardonic laugh came from his firm, unyielding lips. That burst of repressed merriment was a sign of identity. The pretended hophead was The Shadow!

Into the underworld, The Shadow had come to listen for information that concerned The Cobra. He had chosen the Blue Crow as a listening post. There he had gained a clue.

Duff Berker, fang of The Cobra, had left too early to hear the utterances of Ears Findler. Crawler Gorgan, undercover man for the police, had also departed before the proper moment. But

The Shadow had remained. He had learned facts that only Ears Findler could have gained.

"King" Zobell feared The Cobra. That was sufficient. It gave The Shadow the inkling that he required. He could foresee The Cobra's next stroke.

The eerie laugh trailed in the distance as The Shadow, still guised as a chance prowler, moved rapidly through the dark.

## CHAPTER XIV
## CLIFF PLAYS HIS PART

ONE hour after The Shadow's departure from the Blue Crow, Cliff Marsland entered an obscure cigar store and found a telephone booth in a deserted corner. The night was yet young. Cliff, despite the fact that he had learned nothing in the underworld, was putting in a routine call.

Cliff dialed a number. He heard the ringing over the wire. Then came a click; after that, a quiet voice:

"Burbank speaking."

"Marsland," replied Cliff. "No report."

"Instructions." Burbank's tone was solemn. Cliff listened to the words that followed.

Orders from The Shadow!

As Cliff heard them come in Burbank's quiet tones, he stared in amazement. In all his career as an agent of The Shadow, he had never received instructions such as these.

As Burbank continued, Cliff's eyes brightened. He began to see the purpose behind it. His head was nodding instinctively. His jaw was set as Burbank concluded.

"Instructions received," affirmed Cliff.

Walking from the cigar store, Cliff thrust his hand in his trousers pocket and brought forth a roll of bills. He had a good supply of cash with him tonight—sufficient to command respect at the Nugget Club, where only those with bankrolls were received.

With his other hand, Cliff reached to his hip, where he had an automatic in readiness. Shoving the bankroll back in his pocket, he strolled along to a busy street on the fringe of the badlands. There he hailed a passing cab. The driver blinked as Cliff gave an address.

The cab pulled up beside an old garage. Cliff entered. A watcher eyed him. Cliff paid no attention to the fellow. He strolled to the rear of the garage and reached a door. He pressed a push button. A buzz sounded; the door opened to show a flight of stairs.

Cliff went up. He reached a door where a little peephole opened. An eye surveyed him. The door opened. Cliff entered to meet a stocky, sharp-eyed fellow in tuxedo.

"You're Cliff Marsland," stated this man. "Been here before."

"Right," declared Cliff.

"Go on in," ordered the watcher.

CLIFF grinned as he entered a swanky, well-carpeted room with luxurious furnishings and hanging curtains. Despite the precautions here, this place could be easily entered if one used craft.

The Shadow, for instance, would have no trouble eluding the watcher in the garage and picking the locks on the two inner doors. Cliff's smile denoted anticipation.

Voices were coming from an archway on the right. Cliff entered to find a dozen men assembled along a long mahogany bar. Some were attired in tuxedos; others in street clothes.

Two men who recognized Cliff waved a greeting. Cliff responded. He strolled to the far end of the bar and took his position there.

The Nugget Club was a gambling joint frequented only by mobsters of class. No ordinary gorilla could wander into these preserves. The passport was money. Cliff could see the barkeeper eying him. As Cliff pulled his bankroll from his pocket, the man turned away, satisfied.

Slot machines were in operation at the end of the room. Silver dollars were in play. Cliff smiled to himself at the thought of these wise crooks trying to beat a game as crooked as their own.

While he stood at the end of the bar, Cliff took in the layout of the room. There was a door at the further end; that door was seldom used. It could be reached from the big room, close by the spot where Cliff had entered the door with the peephole.

After a brief study of the door, Cliff turned his attention to three men who were standing near the center of the bar. One was "Duster" Corbin, bodyguard and right bower of King Zobell, the bigshot racketeer. Despite the low growls of the conversation, Cliff could make out what it was about.

The two men to whom Duster was talking were applicants for the job that Duster wanted filled. King Zobell needed a new bodyguard. Duster was demanding qualifications. He was getting boastful replies.

"Say"—one of the men raised his voice—"who do you think it was that put away Crazy Louie? I was the guy that did it."

"Crazy Louie?" The other applicant snorted. "Say—he was bugs. Listen, Duster. If you're looking for a guy that's worth a grand a week, you'd better talk to me. I'm worth twice that dough, easy—but because it's you, I'll listen."

"Ease up," ordered Duster. He was a stocky, heavy-browed fellow whose scowl was a warning. "I'm not figuring on what you've done. What I'm after is a guy that's not scared of anybody. Get me? That includes all."

"You mean The Shadow?" quizzed one of the applicants. "Say—that guy would be my ticket. Show him to me and I'll—"

"Phooey," interposed the other job seeker. "The Shadow is a has-been. Nobody worries about him anymore. You mean The Cobra, don't you, Duster?"

"I mean anybody," asserted Duster, with a growl. "I want a guy that's got nerve—like I've got. I passed a job to Diamond Rigler and I've got another job just like it—for the right guy—"

DUSTER'S voice broke off. With it came a lull throughout the room. To the ears of the dozen men assembled there came a chilling sound that broke with sinister foreboding.

It was a weird utterance long feared in the underworld; one that had been derided of late. But as that token of sardonic mirth manifested itself, Duster Corbin, along with the two behind him, dropped away from the bar in sudden terror.

The laugh of The Shadow!

Fierce mockery, delivered with a sneering whisper, it rose to a shuddering crescendo. All eyes turned toward the spot from which the laugh had come. That was the door at the end of the long barroom. With involuntary haste, these big fellows of the underworld raised their arms.

Guns lay ungripped in ready pockets. Not one man tried to draw. A dozen paling faces showed twitching lips while bulging eyes stared at the black-cloaked figure that had entered.

With burning eyes that peered from beneath the brim of his low-turned slouch hat, The Shadow was watching every man in the room. From his black-gloved hands projected huge automatics. The very sight of those guns brought fear.

The Shadow's laugh ended. Weird echoes seemed to linger. Then came a sneering voice, in a tone that resembled a magnified whisper.

"You speak of The Shadow." The words were mocking. "I am The Shadow! I am here to meet those who think they do not fear me."

With this statement, The Shadow moved slowly forward. Boastful mobsters cowered. Braggarts were silent. Every man could see those gun muzzles looming toward himself.

"Who dares to meet me?" The Shadow's tone was scornful. "Now is his opportunity. Let him speak for himself!"

As The Shadow paused, Cliff Marsland calmly edged one hand below the level of the bar. He drew his automatic from his pocket. He hunched his body backward as he rested the barrel on the woodwork. With steady, calculated aim, he pressed the trigger.

WITH the unexpected roar, The Shadow staggered. His gloved hands dropped as his tall figure broke toward the door. Rising to full height, Cliff Marsland flashed his gun and fired a second shot that burst with a long flame.

The Shadow leaped headlong through the door, swinging the barrier as he fled.

Cliff delivered two quick shots that splintered the woodwork of the door. Then, with a ferocious leap he cleared the bar, thrust the barkeeper aside and dashed in pursuit. He yanked open the door and emptied his gun down the passage which The Shadow had taken.

The room was in a clamor. Every petrified mobster was leaping to action. Revolvers were flashing. Men reached the spot where Cliff was on guard; others dashed through the archway that led to the head of the stairs. There they found the watcher groggy as he lay slouched against the wall.

Pursuit was too late. The Shadow, though obviously wounded by Cliff's first shots, had made his escape. Would-be pursuers were returning to the barroom. There they found Cliff Marsland reloading his automatic.

"The Shadow!" jeered a gang leader. "He was trying a comeback. Say—here's the guy that showed him where he stands. Give me your mitt, there, Marsland."

Others were offering their congratulations. Cliff received them in indifferent fashion. Among those to shake his hand was Duster Corbin. King Zobell's right bower turned his head toward the two men with whom he had been talking.

"Scram, you punks," he ordered sourly. "Afraid of nobody, eh? Why didn't one of you take a chance when The Shadow showed up?"

The rejected applicants sidled away. Duster gripped Cliff by the arm and drew him away from the congratulating throng.

"I've heard of you, Marsland," declared the heavy-browed gun handler. "Now I've seen what you can do. You had me beat. I was standing there like a dummy while you took a plug at The Shadow!"

"I didn't drill him," commented Cliff, in a disappointed tone.

"You nicked him," asserted Duster, "and you're the first bimbo that ever beat him to a shot. Put it there—and listen"—Duster's voice became a buzz—"how would a job with one grand a week suit you?"

"I could use it," affirmed Cliff.

"It's yours," rejoined Duster. "You're on—new body for King Zobell. You're going over to his place with me tonight."

He yanked open the door and emptied his gun down the passage which The Shadow had taken.

FIFTEEN minutes later, Duster Corbin and Cliff Marsland sauntered from the Nugget Club. Acclaim from the men remaining was still ringing in Cliff's ears.

The Shadow, jealous of The Cobra's rising power, had attempted a comeback. Cliff Marsland had achieved the hitherto impossible. He had put The Shadow to flight.

Cliff grinned grimly as he clambered into a cab with Duster Corbin. He had reason. At The Shadow's bidding, he had aided in the duping of a dozen witnesses. Cliff had played his part to perfection.

The carefully aimed shot that he had delivered was well calculated. Cliff had sent it a full foot wide of The Shadow's body. The Shadow's stagger had been a well-feigned pretense.

The second shot, delivered to the top of the

door through which The Shadow was passing was another token of Cliff's ability to miss the mark which others thought that he had hit. Again, The Shadow had made a deliberated plunge.

Tonight, The Shadow had deliberately arranged to injure the fame which he had gained. There had been method in his action. What The Shadow had lost, Cliff Marsland had gained. Through his sudden fame, he had gained the berth as King Zobell's new bodyguard.

King Zobell would be The Cobra's next prospective victim. Through some crafty plan, The Cobra would manage to meet King Zobell on his own ground, in the presence of his friends.

Two could play at that game. With Cliff Marsland working for King Zobell, The Shadow could match The Cobra by appearing when he chose. Cliff, as inside man, would pave the way.

What was The Shadow's purpose? Why did he desire a direct meeting with this strange character whose purposes were apparently as just as The Shadow's own?

Only The Shadow knew!

## CHAPTER XV
## AT KING ZOBELL'S

TWO nights had passed since Cliff Marsland had played his role. The Shadow's agent, new hero of the underworld, was working at his new job of bodyguard for King Zobell.

The big shot lived in an old-fashioned apartment house in a decadent neighborhood. There was reason for this choice of residence. King Zobell, controller of half a dozen rackets, had purchased the building outright. He had fitted it like a stronghold.

Zobell's apartment was on the fourth floor. It could be reached only by a private elevator which opened in a little anteroom near the rear of the apartment. Crossing the anteroom, one reached Zobell's living room, the spot where the big shot spent most of his time.

Barred windows—sheer walls four stories to the ground—these were the protections which King Zobell demanded. The fourth floor—the top story of the building—was above the level of the neighboring structures. Hence King Zobell dwelt in apparent security.

King Zobell, himself, was a portly, fat-faced fellow who looked like a cross between a politician and a corporation president. It was business ability, a well as nerve, that had enabled him to merge some of the most active rackets in New York.

Wary as well as enterprising, Zobell had learned to play his hand in crafty fashion. Lesser racketeers did duty for the big shot. They were on the firing line; King Zobell pulled the strings. It was seldom that the big shot left his apartment. Most of his business was conducted by telephone. When personal interviews were necessary, visitors were brought to his apartment.

Of late, however, King Zobell had not been at home to visitors. Duster Corbin, his chief lieutenant and ranking bodyguard, fared forth to treat with those who had business with the big shot.

This explained why King Zobell had chosen to have two lesser bodyguards. He wanted one on constant duty; and he wanted Duster Corbin free to leave at any time required.

CLIFF MARSLAND had quickly recognized the fact that King Zobell was a nervous, troubled man. The big shot could have surrounded himself with a whole corps of henchmen; instead, he preferred to trust to picked bodyguards. He was afraid of traitors. He knew that his secluded abode, guarded by capable gun wielders, would give him best security.

As for the cause of his fears, the big shot was prompt to make that known immediately after Cliff Marsland entered his employ. The facts came out during a conference between King Zobell and his bodyguards.

Duster Corbin—stocky, glaring and heavy-browed; "Diamond" Rigler, a rangy, long-legged fellow with sharp, ever roving eyes; Cliff Marsland, keen-faced and determined—these formed the trio that King Zobell took into his confidence.

"I'm sticking it out," informed the big shot. "Staying here in town, while others scram. The Cobra wants me for the spot—and I'm counting on you three to nail him if he comes to get me.

"Don't kid yourselves, boys. The Cobra is tough. Those mugs that he picked off were no softies. I thought that maybe it would be a while before he slated me. But when other guys that he's due to gun for began their fade-out, I figured I'd be next.

"Duster Corbin, here, is an ace. He picked you, Diamond, or you talked him into it—I don't know which. Anyway, you've got the goods. As for you, Marsland, you showed your stuff when you took pot shots at The Shadow.

"But we're not dealing with The Shadow now. The Cobra has The Shadow licked. The Cobra is after big shots. That's why I'm worried. The biggest boys in New York now are the ones that are working for me.

"That's why they're safe. The Cobra goes to the top, every time. I'm the one he'll pick—and I'm telling you, if he gets me, there won't be a big gun left. Not one—and there won't be anybody with nerve enough to try to be big.

"But The Cobra isn't going to get me—not so long as I count on three like you, and no more. This place of mine is as good as any castle. Keep your rods ready and The Cobra won't have the chance he wants."

Cliff, when off duty, had reported these statements to The Shadow. Nor was that all. At other times, King Zobell had chatted with Cliff alone; and the big shot had shown a keen insight into the affairs of the underworld of New York.

It was Zobell's firm belief that The Cobra worked through traitors. In his campaign against the big shots, he enlisted the services of small-fry lieutenants who were close to their superiors. It was probable that he dominated these men by fear; whatever his way, it was a fact that not one trail had been gained to The Cobra himself.

CLIFF could feel the tenseness of the atmosphere at King Zobell's. Here, on this second night that he had been stationed on duty, Cliff was beginning to sense the strain. He had reasoned one fact to his own satisfaction.

If—as King Zobell feared—The Cobra intended to get the big shot, there was only one place where the job could be accomplished. That was in this living room, where King Zobell dwelt in confident security.

How would The Cobra manage it? Cliff could see no way.

A startling thought, however, occurred to him. The Cobra must certainly know that he could reach King Zobell by cracking this stronghold. Was The Cobra trying to figure out a way to do it—or was he biding his time with a plan already formulated?

Cliff felt a strong inclination to the latter belief. Had he witnessed anything like a manifestation of The Cobra's interest in King Zobell's abode, he would not have gained his hunch. But the fact that The Cobra had made no move was significant to Cliff.

Cliff was seated in Zobell's living room when the idea struck him. Duster Corbin was also present. King Zobell was giving instructions to his chief lieutenant. Duster was to visit racketeers tonight.

"You can go off duty, Marsland," declared Zobell, suddenly. "I'll keep Duster here until Diamond Rigler shows up. Then Duster can go out. I'll count on Diamond for tonight."

Cliff nodded. This was a change from the regular routine. According to schedule, Cliff was to stay here until Diamond arrived. As bodyguards, Cliff and Diamond took separate shifts. Rising, Cliff started toward the door; then paused.

"Say, King," he said to the big shot. "It'll be O.K. if I stay here for the night, won't it?"

"Right," acknowledged King. "You can stay here anytime you want, Cliff. I've got no kick to having two men ready. At the same time, you're welcome to the night off. You don't have to stick while Diamond's on the job."

"I've got nowhere to go," declared Cliff. "Might as well be around here. I'll be back in a little while, King."

"Good idea," decided Duster Corbin, as Cliff headed for the elevator. "It won't do any harm, King, to keep Marsland sleeping here at nights. He's got the easy shift—the day one—and I'm here most all day. But at night—well, that's the time to worry—and you've only got Diamond Rigler to depend on. Diamond's good enough, though."

Cliff Marsland had reached the ground floor of the apartment house. He stepped from the elevator and closed the door behind him. This lift, traveling upward through a solidly walled shaft, was a specially designed device that added strong protection.

Once the elevator had descended, it could not rise again unless a special switch was pulled from above. Anyone could send the car down from upstairs, by use of that switch.

When King Zobell's bodyguards reported, they gave a special signal by ringing a bell beside the shaft. Each man had his own call. Thus a bodyguard on duty could either send down the car or turn the switch so that the man below could use the elevator.

CLIFF sauntered from the lobby of the old apartment house. He strolled around the corner and followed a narrow street at the rear. Looking up, he could see the lights of King Zobell's barred living room. The sheer wall ended above those lights; it was topped by a projecting cornice.

Cliff reached a drugstore a block from the apartment house. He entered a phone booth and called a number.

In brief, steady phrases, Cliff reported his opinions. He told Burbank of his apprehensions regarding The Cobra. Then, by way of a checkup, he described the working of the elevator that went up to Zobell's abode.

"It's the only way of getting there," explained Cliff. "It would be easy enough to get up to the roof of the apartment building through one of the regular apartments—but that wouldn't help to get into Zobell's.

"The living-room windows are barred. Top floor, back, under a cornice. Thick, heavy gratings. Zobell talked about putting in bulletproof glass, but it wasn't necessary. There's no building anywhere near that would give a line on his window."

Cliff concluded with the statement that he was going back to King Zobell's.

He strolled from the drugstore, reached the street in front of the apartment building and sauntered along. He noticed a man in front of him. The fellow turned into the apartment house. Cliff caught a glimpse of his face. It was Diamond Rigler, reporting for duty.

As Cliff reached the entrance, he spied Diamond at the far end of the lobby. Cliff stopped short. He saw Diamond throw a crafty glance back over his shoulder.

Cliff was outside; Diamond did not see him. Then, still watching, Cliff saw Diamond go past the elevator shaft toward stairs that led to a basement.

Quickly, Cliff bounded through the door. He had an immediate suspicion of Diamond's action. Why was the man going downstairs? The basement had once held a barbershop. That room was closed; its equipment was still there.

Cliff reached the stairs. He moved downward. He observed a light in the old barbershop. He stole close to the open door. There he saw Diamond Rigler lifting the receiver from the hook of a pay telephone.

That phone was out of order! It bore a placard to that effect.

Cliff stared as Diamond adjusted the mouthpiece. Then came a strange sound from the receiver—a faint hiss that even Cliff could detect.

"Fang Nine." Diamond Rigler was speaking in a low voice. "All set to report at Zobell's... Yes... When Marsland goes off duty... Yes... The arrangement works if Duster Corbin is still there..."

Cliff edged back toward the stairs. The truth hit him with bewildering force. There was merit in his hunch. The Cobra, indeed, was ready to strike. Diamond Rigler, one of King Zobell's bodyguards, was a henchman of The Cobra!

DIAMOND had paused in his conversation. Cliff reached the steps just as he heard the man's footsteps coming toward the door of the barbershop. Evidently Diamond suspected a listener. Cliff managed to get out of sight. He heard the door of the barbershop close.

There was no reason to wait here. Cliff knew that it would be unwise to rouse Diamond's suspicions. At the same time, he realized that prompt action was essential. The Cobra was planning a stroke—for tonight!

Moving up the stairs, Cliff quickly formulated a plan. He must get word to The Shadow. At the same time, he could not afford the time that would be required by a trip to the drugstore a block distant. Cliff wanted to be in Zobell's apartment when Diamond Rigler arrived.

Cliff saw the way. With a grim smile, he stopped at the door of the elevator shaft. He rang the bell twice; then once—his call. Cliff tried the door. It remained for a few moments, then yielded. Duster Corbin had pressed the switch above.

Entering the lift, Cliff closed the door and pushed the button that drove the car upward. He still retained his grim smile as he neared the top of the shaft.

Tonight, The Cobra would strike again. This time, The Shadow would know before The Cobra struck!

## CHAPTER XVI
## THE MEETING

CLIFF MARSLAND was no longer smiling when he entered King Zobell's living room. The Shadow's agent seemed quite unconcerned. He plucked a cigarette from a box on Zobell's table and lighted it with a match from the stand.

"Where am I parking, King?" he questioned. "Little room in the front?"

"Yeah," affirmed the big shot.

"All right," returned Cliff.

With no other explanation, Cliff strolled in nonchalant fashion through the door at the front of the living room. Neither King Zobell or Duster Corbin evidenced any suspicion of the action.

The front room to the left of Cliff's belonged to King Zobell. There was a telephone in the room—an extension of the one which Zobell had in the living room. Cliff felt sure that neither King Zobell nor Duster Corbin intended to make a call. He chanced it.

Entering Zobell's room, Cliff raised the receiver and dialed Burbank's number. The Shadow's contact man responded almost immediately:

"Burbank speaking."

"Marsland," declared Cliff, in a low tone. "Diamond Rigler is working for The Cobra. Called him from downstairs. Reported as Fang Nine.

"Diamond is coming up to relieve me. I'm staying. Duster going out. The Cobra is due to strike."

"Report received."

Cliff was about to give further details when a shaft of light appeared upon the floor of the room between this bedroom and the living room. Evidently King Zobell was coming in this direction.

Cliff hung up with promptitude. He made a quick dive through the door. As Zobell appeared from the door of the living room, Cliff was apparently coming out of the little room which the big shot had assigned to him.

"I'll give you those papers, Duster." Zobell, half turned toward the living room, was speaking to his lieutenant. "They're in my room. I'll be with you in a minute."

Cliff walked by King Zobell. He reached the living room, dropped in an easy chair and picked up the cigarette which he had placed on an ash stand. As he puffed in silence, Cliff began to analyze the situation.

HE was sure that he knew The Cobra's game. Cliff's reasoning was precise. Since Diamond Rigler was The Cobra's minion, why had not Diamond opened the way for The Cobra in the past—on some occasion when Diamond was here alone with King Zobell?

Cliff saw the answer. The Cobra did not want it to be known that Diamond was a traitor. Tonight's scheme would cover that fact.

First, Diamond would probably wait until Duster Corbin had departed. Then Diamond would come in to relieve Cliff. The Cobra would follow. The purpose would be to kill both King Zobell and Cliff.

Diamond would make his getaway with The Cobra. Duster Corbin, returning, would find the bodies. Perhaps Diamond would stay instead of leaving! At any rate, the scene would indicate that The Cobra had arrived before Diamond came to relieve Cliff!

A perfect scheme—one that would keep Diamond as valuable to The Cobra as before. Cliff settled back into his chair. All was well for the present—particularly as long as Duster Corbin remained in the apartment.

King Zobell was returning with a stack of papers. Duster received them and began to go through them. At that moment a buzzer sounded: once—then twice.

"It's Diamond," remarked King Zobell. "Let him in, Marsland."

Cliff went to the elevator shaft and pressed the switch. He could not withhold a grin. To his way of thinking, Diamond had made a bull. Sauntering back to the living room, Cliff took his seat and lighted a fresh cigarette. Diamond Rigler had evidently tired of waiting and had taken it for granted that Duster Corbin was already out.

A minute later, Diamond Rigler appeared from the anteroom. Cliff watched his face, looking for signs of surprise.

There were none. Diamond had a poker player's countenance. Nevertheless, Cliff figured that Diamond was probably annoyed at finding Duster Corbin here.

For if Duster went out leaving both Cliff and Diamond with King Zobell, each of the secondary bodyguards would share in blame should The Cobra appear and slay King Zobell. Cliff's feelings were those of mingled elation and disappointment. He was pleased because a block had apparently

stopped The Cobra's plans; he was annoyed because the showdown would probably be postponed.

Ten minutes passed. Duster Corbin completed his examination of the papers. He pocketed them. He arose to leave the apartment.

"I'll be back by midnight," he informed. "See you all later."

Cliff felt calm security as he puffed his cigarette. Duster passed the door of the anteroom. Diamond seemed dejected as he slouched in a chair. Then, with quick succession of events, came the unexpected.

CLIFF heard the sliding of the elevator door as Duster Corbin opened it. A sharp, startled exclamation; then a revolver shot. Staggering with long, convulsive bounds, Duster Corbin appeared from the anteroom. His hands were clasped to his body. His lips voiced two hoarse words:

"The Cobra!"

Cliff was on his feet as Duster Corbin sprawled upon the floor and rolled over dead. As Cliff reached for his gun, an order stopped him. Diamond Rigler had risen; he had drawn a revolver. He was covering Cliff. The Shadow's agent had acted too late.

"Up with 'em!"

Cliff's arms raised at Diamond's command. Cliff was staring toward the doorway through which Duster Corbin had staggered. There he saw the author of the shot that had felled King Zobell's chief lieutenant.

The Cobra!

Clad in wrinkled brown, his painted hood a monstrous sight, The Cobra stood with smoking revolver in his hand. His painted eyes; the muzzle of the gun which he held—both were directed toward King Zobell. The big shot sat petrified. He was gripping the arms of his chair.

Cliff Marsland saw his own mistake. He had not calculated on this. He remembered Diamond Rigler's words over the telephone:

"The arrangement works if Duster Corbin is still there..."

This was the arrangement! Diamond Rigler, upon leaving the elevator in the anteroom, had pressed the switch so that the car would be ready for The Cobra! The snakelike slayer had come up in the elevator. He had been waiting for Duster Corbin!

Cliff saw death. He could picture himself slain with Duster and King Zobell. The big shot and two dead bodyguards. That would be a perfect smoke screen for Diamond Rigler's treachery!

"Ss-s-s-s-s-s!"

King Zobell cowered as he heard The Cobra's hiss. Trapped, the big shot was a pitiful figure. His big, bluff face showed terror.

The Cobra showed no mercy. Upright at the door, he pressed the trigger. The revolver barked. King Zobell uttered a hoarse gasp that ended sharply.

The big shot crumpled in his chair. His hands slipped from the sides and dangled loosely. A red splotch began to form upon his white shirt front— the life blood drawn by The Cobra's bullet!

THERE was no hiss as The Cobra turned toward Cliff Marsland. But those painted eyes formed a merciless expression. Cliff was due to die. Fiercely, he took the only course that offered life.

With a wild leap, Cliff flung himself on Diamond Rigler. He caught the man off guard. He grabbed Diamond's right wrist with his left hand; with his right arm he seized his foeman's body. Grappling, Cliff drew Diamond back across the room, using the man's body as shield against The Cobra's fire.

Coldly, The Cobra watched the struggle. It could be no more than futile. Sooner or later, the pair would break. Cliff's unprotected body would be an easy target for The Cobra's aim. Cliff realized this as he fought. He made a bold clutch for Diamond's gun and failed to grab it.

Diamond, lunging his left hand free, delivered a blow to Cliff's jaw. Cliff staggered and sprawled against the door to the front of the apartment. Half stunned, he lay there.

The Cobra was watching from the door. His revolver was idle in his hand. Cliff saw why, as he turned to gaze at Diamond Rigler. With a vengeful snarl, Diamond was raising his own gun to end Cliff Marsland's life.

Calmly, Cliff closed his eyes. He could not stop the shot. Murder was in the making; Cliff was to be its victim. Surging thoughts swept through Cliff's brain. They ended with a surprise that opened Cliff's eyes.

A crash came from beyond the spot where Diamond Rigler stood aiming. Impelled by a terrific smash from without, the entire glass of the window frame had been smashed inward.

Beyond the shivered pane were a pair of blazing eyes, peering from blackness. A gloved hand gripped the bars beyond the window; from another fist projected the muzzle of a mighty automatic.

The Shadow had arrived! He had come by the roof of the apartment house—over the precarious cornice to the window below.

Though too late to witness the death of King Zobell, The Shadow had come in time to fight for Cliff Marsland's life. Out of the night had The Shadow come—for his meeting with The Cobra!

## CHAPTER XVII
## THE SHADOW'S SKILL

THE SHADOW'S turn had come. That looming automatic, thrust through a shattered glass, was a weapon that could mean The Cobra's woe. The Shadow had gained his opportunity to cover The Cobra and demand the strange rival to reveal his purposes.

But the desired meeting held one flaw. To deal with The Cobra, The Shadow would have had to disregard the safety of his agent, Cliff Marsland. Diamond Rigler, vicious and frenzied, had finger on revolver trigger. He was about to loose the shot that would mean Cliff Marsland's life.

The Shadow's automatic thundered in the confines of the room. The flash of flame was not directed toward The Cobra. Its spurt was made toward Diamond Rigler. There was not time to stop that pressing trigger; Shadow's bullet accomplished its appointed end.

Diamond Rigler's body twisted as his hand fired. Sprawled by The Shadow's shot, Diamond's aim went wide. A bullet splintered the door a foot above Cliff Marsland's head.

Deliberately, The Shadow had given opportunity to The Cobra. The black-clad arrival was risking his own life to save that of Cliff Marsland. As The Shadow dropped Diamond Rigler, The Cobra wheeled. His warning hiss came as he aimed point-blank and fired at The Shadow.

A fighter who worked in split seconds, The Shadow had foreseen this quick reply. Even while he fired at Diamond Rigler, The Shadow was working to thwart The Cobra's aim. His black form was dropping as the automatic spoke. Eyes and right hand fell from view while the left hand slid down the vertical bar which it gripped.

The Cobra's shot, aimed for The Shadow's eyes, whistled through the top of the slouch hat and zimmed on into space.

The Cobra aimed a second shot. This one was for the hand that clutched the bar. Again, The Cobra was a split second late. The Shadow had caught the window ledge with his right hand. His left dropped as The Cobra pressed the trigger. A bullet from The Cobra's revolver clanged the upright bar which The Shadow's hand had left.

The roaring gunplay had brought Cliff Marsland to his senses. Leaning against the wall, The Shadow's agent was pulling his automatic from his pocket. As The Cobra's gun delivered another futile bark, Cliff aimed for the grotesque figure in brown.

SOMEHOW, The Cobra sensed the menace. He wheeled. Cliff fired hastily; his shot went wide. The Cobra did not fire in response. He had no time for aim, as Cliff was steadying for a second shot. Still whirling, The Cobra gained the anteroom, just in time.

With the bark of Cliff's gun, The Shadow had reappeared beyond the window. His automatic, resting at the bottom of the bars, with his blazing eyes beside the muzzle, loosed new fire just as The Cobra leaped from view. Only the projecting edge of the doorway saved The Cobra in his flight.

Cliff, still a trifle dazed, missed a second shot; then clambered to his feet. With automatic in hand, he dashed across the anteroom. The Cobra had taken the elevator to the lobby below.

Cliff hurried back into the living room. The Shadow was gone from the window. Cliff stood looking at the bodies on the floor. Duster Corbin—Diamond Rigler—both were dead. The form of King Zobell lay slumped in its chair.

This was one of those emergencies in which The Shadow relied upon his agents to use their own ability. The Shadow had saved Cliff's life. He had balked The Cobra. The Shadow's rival was in flight.

The iron bars, set in the wall beyond the window, were a barrier that would have taken too long to break. Cliff realized that The Shadow, forced to depart by the precarious way up to the roof, would be delayed.

It was, furthermore, unwise for Cliff to remain. He saw how he could aid The Shadow! There was still time to bring up the elevator and descend to the street before The Shadow could arrive there. Cliff had a slender chance to trail The Cobra.

Dashing back to the elevator shaft, Cliff pressed the button to raise the car. He entered the lift and descended. He hurried through the lobby to the street. As he paused there, he fancied that he heard the distant sound of a police whistle, off in back of the apartment building.

A cab was standing by the curb. Cliff approached the driver. The man reached to open the door.

"See anyone come out of the apartment house?" queried Cliff.

"Yeah," returned the driver, gruffly. "A funny looking guy—"

"Which way did he go?"

"Grabbed a cab that was down the street. Pulled out toward the avenue and—"

"Get going. See if you can catch him."

Cliff bounded into the cab as he spoke. The driver slammed the door. As Cliff leaned through the front window, the cab jerked away from the curb. It shot toward the corner.

Something moved in the darkness of the cab. Cliff turned, startled, as he heard a hiss beside him. He was staring squarely into the muzzle of a revolver; behind it, luminous in the gloom, loomed the painted hood of The Cobra.

CLIFF rolled against the door as the cab whirled the corner. The form of The Cobra fell upon him. A cloth was pressed over Cliff's face. The pungent odor of chloroform was overpowering. Cliff slumped helpless.

The Cobra had tricked The Shadow's agent. The man at the wheel of this cab was one of his trusted fangs. Lurking in the taxi, The Cobra had been ready to trap Cliff should he arrive in pursuit.

Rescued by The Shadow, Cliff had thrown himself into the net. He was a prisoner of The Cobra!

As the cab passed around the corner, a figure appeared at the door of the apartment building. The Shadow had arrived. Up to the roof; across and down through an apartment window, he had come in pursuit. He was too late to see the fleeing cab. Yet his keen eyes seemed to sense what had occurred.

Another whistle—this time from the avenue. A reply—at the other end of the street. A whistle from the back of the apartment house. Police had heard the shots from high up in the building. They, too, had arrived.

The Shadow sprang from the doorway. His tall form swept forward like a phantom figure as he headed for a passage beside a garage across the street. Shots came from the corner. An officer raised a shout. Policemen dashed up to the scene. They were too late. The Shadow had disappeared.

With swift strokes from the darkness, The Shadow had broken The Cobra's power. Fighting from disadvantage, he had thwarted the killing of Cliff Marsland and had driven The Cobra into flight.

But The Cobra, realizing his own advantage, had used cunning when he fled. He had slain King Zobell as he had intended. He had left Duster Corbin dead. His own man—Diamond Rigler—had been blotted; but in return, The Cobra had captured the man whom he had sought to slay with the others: Cliff Marsland.

The underworld would never know of The Shadow's counterstroke. New credit would be The Cobra's. Defeated, The Cobra had turned events to his own advantage. The Shadow, as at Old Growdy's, had been left to face the arrival of the police.

Far from the apartment house where bluecoats now had charge, a grim laugh sounded in the darkness of a silent street. It was not a laugh of defeat; it was a laugh of determination. The laugh of The Shadow!

Whatever opinions might be formed, The Shadow knew the vital facts—and The Cobra knew them also. Let the underworld gasp in awe about The Cobra's prowess; let them deride The Shadow. Such did not alter the facts.

The Shadow's skill had prevailed. Only circumstances had aided The Cobra. The serpent-hooded fighter had been forced to flee The Shadow's might. War had broken between these two whom gangdom feared as grim avengers.

Once again, the advantage lay with The Cobra. The Shadow's task was heightened. Yet through his skill, The Shadow had forced the issue.

Whatever The Cobra's plans might be, The Shadow remained to block them. Until he could fully frustrate The Shadow, The Cobra would be forced to inactivity.

Tonight had brought the two in definite conflict. Their trails—supposedly parallel—were drawing closer. Another event such as this one would bring them face-to-face.

That was the reason for The Shadow's laugh. It betokened safety for Cliff Marsland. It presaged another meeting with The Cobra. It indicated secret knowledge of the hooded fighter's ways and purposes.

The Shadow had good reason to wage combat with The Cobra. The Shadow had divined the hidden goal which The Cobra was seeking through his warfare on gangland's big shots!

The time would come soon when The Cobra would again be forced to match his keen strategy against The Shadow's skill!

## CHAPTER XVIII
## THE DECISION

"LAST night, Myland"—Commissioner Ralph Weston was speaking—"I received another call from The Cobra. It was as before—the hiss—the statement that a stroke was to be delivered."

Myland nodded from behind his big table. "Here, then," he said, tapping a newspaper that lay beside him, "is the result."

"Exactly," declared the commissioner. "To The Cobra we owe our thanks for the elimination of King Zobell, the biggest of all Manhattan racketeers."

Caleb Myland pondered.

"One might call it crime," he stated, "when three men are slain—even though one is a racketeer and the others are his henchmen."

"They were armed," returned Weston. "That makes a difference, Myland."

"Yes," agreed the criminologist. Then, with a slight tinge of doubt: "But they were not engaged in crime, Weston."

"You mean—"

"That they could have been armed for self-defense."

"That's right, Myland," observed Weston. "Your opinions are important in this case. Personally, I have favored The Cobra's work. But if—"

"There is no cause to change your idea," interposed Myland. "Consider this point, Weston. The Cobra, obviously, was there alone. Zobell—his henchmen Corbin and Rigler—were three against one.

"You can safely give The Cobra the benefit of the doubt. He can be said to have fought in self-defense. That, Weston, would be my decision."

"And it is mine!" exclaimed the police commissioner, emphatically.

Caleb Myland smiled wanly. The criminologist seemed pleased. He tapped the table methodically; then propounded this question:

"What of The Shadow?"

"He was there again!" declared Weston. "The newspapers do not know it—but police reports show it. He was seen outside of the apartment house. Apparently, he was there to interfere with The Cobra."

Babson entered. The servant announced that two visitors had arrived. His manner indicated that they were Joe Cardona and Crawler Gorgan. This proved to be correct.

CRAWLER GORGAN appeared eager when he entered. He wanted to talk. Weston gave him an immediate opportunity.

"It was The Cobra, Commissioner!" asserted Crawler. "You can bet it was The Cobra that put King Zobell on the spot. He was the only guy that could have done it!"

"So I have decided," commented Weston, dryly. "I am glad to learn that the underworld shares my opinions. What else, Gorgan?"

"The Shadow was there, too," added the undercover man. "Everybody knows it. He had to duck the cops. Say—The Cobra has them worried in the Tenderloin. But The Shadow—well he—"

"Well, what?"

"Well, he's getting the razz. It don't look so good for him. I ain't convinced that he's gone crooked, Commissioner, like Mr. Myland here says; but if he hasn't, he's gone looney, for fair."

"What makes you believe that?"

"Listening around the joints. Here's the way they all figure it—and those birds are wise. The Cobra's knocking off the big shots, ain't he? Well what does The Shadow want to butt in for?"

"Professional jealousy, perhaps," suggested Weston, with a smile.

"Listen, Commissioner," protested Crawler. "You don't know The Shadow. He didn't used to waste his time. Why should he be fooling around where guys are going to get plugged anyway?

"He ain't helping The Cobra—that's a cinch. So it looks like he's trying to hinder him, don't it? That's why the smart guys figure the way they do."

"Mr. Myland and myself," declared Weston, "have come to a definite opinion. We feel that The Cobra's actions are justified. He is worthy of support. We can base all of our findings on the affair at Old Growdy's. There, The Cobra acted to save lives—including those of Cardona and myself.

"We find, therefore, that he acted in self-defense in the other cases, including this one of King Zobell. The Cobra is deserving of police protection. He shall receive it. Do you understand that, Cardona?"

The detective nodded.

"As for The Shadow," resumed Weston, "we can only presume that he, by obstructing The Cobra, is trying to confuse the law. The Shadow, Cardona, is wanted."

"For what?" questioned the detective. "There's nothing on The Shadow. He made a couple of getaways—but we don't know that he was doing anything crooked."

"Cardona is right," observed Myland, wisely. "You must use discretion, Commissioner."

"Why do you say that?" demanded Weston. "I thought your opinion, Myland, was that The Shadow had turned crook."

"Indications," returned Myland, "show The Cobra to be working in behalf of justice. They also show The Shadow in a very unpleasant light. We can say that we have established The Cobra's status, through your own experience at Old Growdy's. Conversely, you must establish The Shadow's status by a definite observation."

"I understand," nodded Weston. "Cardona, I am ordering a strict watch for The Shadow. Should he be traced in criminal activity—or anything that resembles it—we will not stop until we have captured The Shadow, dead or alive.

"At the same time, The Cobra is immune. He is doing splendid work. Perhaps, through his efforts, we may be able to disclose facts concerning The Shadow."

"You hit it, Commissioner!" The eager statement came from Crawler Gorgan. "You've said just what's going to happen."

"How is that, Gorgan?"

"HERE'S the lay, Commissioner. Understand—this ain't all my own idea. It's what I've been hearing—specially since last night. Do you know what King Zobell was?"

"A big shot racketeer."

"More than that, Commissioner." Crawler was nodding wisely. "He was the only real big shot left. The Cobra got some of them—the rest have taken it on the lam."

"Is that right, Cardona?" questioned Weston, in a surprised tone.

"It looks that way," agreed the detective. "All the other big shots have beat it. Some of the fellows who were running Zobell's rackets are sliding out, now that King has taken the bump."

"Revolution in the underworld!" exclaimed Weston.

"Say chaos, rather," interposed Myland, sagely. "Mobsters galore—but no leader."

"And none of the little guys want to be big," declared Crawler. "That's something, Commissioner."

"On account of The Cobra?"

Crawler Gorgan nodded.

"Good logic," decided Myland. "The Cobra has lopped off the heads. As new leaders rise, he will cut them down. But apparently, there will be no new leaders. There is opportunity, though." Myland shook his head in worried fashion. "If anyone should dare to organize those bands, in opposition to The Cobra—"

"There's only one guy big enough to do it!" blurted Crawler Gorgan.

"The Shadow!" exclaimed Weston.

Crawler nodded. Myland did the same. Joe Cardona looked glum. He had faith in The Shadow's integrity.

"Get me right, Commissioner," continued Crawler. "I don't want to give you a bum steer—and there ain't nothing to prove that The Shadow has gone crooked.

"I'm just telling you this: there's plenty of mugs down in the badlands who would follow any guy that they thought was tough enough to pull jobs in spite of The Cobra.

"They've razzed The Shadow, but he's still got 'em buffaloed. He's played a lone wolf game. There's no telling what he could do with a mob behind him. So I'm telling you what to watch for— that's all."

"Gorgan," decided Weston, "this is the best report you have produced. There is our task, Cardona. The Cobra, alone, is stronger than The Shadow. If mobs reorganize, there can be but one answer. The Shadow will have become their leader."

THE commissioner turned to Caleb Myland. The criminologist was sitting with his hands upon the table. His eyes were gleaming. He seemed to be looking into the future.

"I can predict it now!" he declared, with

emphasis. "Chaos always produces a leader. Contact with crime produces criminals. Weston, the stage is set!

"I can see but one course for The Shadow. He has lost credit. He has behaved in a suspicious manner. His power has waned; but it can be regained. He has seen a way to take advantage of The Cobra's deeds. That is why he has sought to block The Cobra.

"The Shadow has failed; but in failing he has won. The Cobra still remains as an avenger; but mobsters, far and wide are looking for a leader. Petty crime may exist for a short while; after that will come a master stroke.

"Backed by a supercrew of ruffians, The Shadow will deliver crime. The law will find it difficult to thwart him. We can only hope that The Cobra will aid."

"I believe you, Myland," declared Weston, soberly. "Nevertheless, we are handicapped for the present. We need proof!" The commissioner thumped the table. "Proof! Cardona has shown that. I believe that The Shadow will appear with dangerous men at his heels—but until he has done so, we cannot act with surety.

"Captured now, The Shadow could not be held. We must wait, Myland—wait in watchful readiness, to see if your prediction is fulfilled."

"You will see my statements justified," prophesied the criminologist.

"It looks like something is due to happen soon, Commissioner," asserted Crawler Gorgan. "Still, I ain't saying anything. I'll keep my eye out—that's the best that I can do."

Joe Cardona made no comment.

"On Wednesday night," said the commissioner, rising, "we shall meet here again. Is that all right with you, Myland?"

The criminologist nodded.

"You be here, Cardona," ordered the commissioner. "If Gorgan is available, bring him with you. If it is unsafe for him to come, get his report. Use your own judgment in that matter.

"Perhaps, by Wednesday night, we may have evidence of the sort that we are seeking. At any rate, I shall confer with you, Myland."

The criminologist nodded to close the conference. There was something in his knowing smile that made the observers feel that he was sure his convictions would be proven when that next meeting took place within this room.

## CHAPTER XIX
## THE SHADOW'S CLUE

THE police vigil had been raised from the apartment house where King Zobell and his two bodyguards had been slain. The smashed window in the big shot's apartment had been attributed to a wild bullet dispatched in that direction. Hence all investigation had been directed to the elevator shaft, which now was barred shut.

The lobby was deserted near the closed shaft. Hence, when a long streak of blackness appeared upon the cracked marble floor, there was no one present to view its strange, creeping motion.

Blackness that moved like a living thing—a streak of inkiness that terminated in a hawklike silhouette. There was a meaning to that splotch. It foretold the appearance of The Shadow!

Into the sphere of light glided a tall, cloaked form. A swish sounded softly as The Shadow's garment swung to reveal a flash of its crimson interior. The Shadow had returned to the spot where The Cobra had eluded him.

What was the purpose of The Shadow's visit?

The keen eyes beneath the hat brim were peering along the lobby. Their gaze was searching. They spied the stairway that led below. The Shadow descended.

A tiny flashlight glimmered. Its small circle of bright light focused upon the door of the deserted barbershop. The Shadow entered the unused room. His flashlight glimmered about the walls. It centered on the telephone which bore the placard:

Out of Order.

The light moved closer. A black-gloved hand rested upon the coin box. The Shadow's keen eyes studied the object before them. Long fingers, prying here and there, reached the mouthpiece and turned it a scarce quarter inch.

A laugh whispered gloomily through the room. The Shadow had found the clue he wanted. Working on the report received from Burbank—the contact man's account of the last call from Cliff Marsland—The Shadow had made a discovery.

Cliff, in his call had stated that Diamond Rigler had called The Cobra from downstairs. That was why The Shadow had come to investigate. To an ordinary sleuth, the card on this telephone would have cleared the instrument from suspicion. To The Shadow it denoted that this must be the telephone that Diamond Rigler had used for his call.

Further, The Shadow had quickly detected that the phone, to serve The Cobra, must actually be out of order so far as the public was concerned. Eying the instrument, The Shadow had noted finger marks upon the mouthpiece. They had given him the clue to the operation of the instrument.

THE SHADOW made no attempt to use the telephone. That would have warned The Cobra. The light went out; a laugh again sounded, this time in darkness. The Shadow had solved the riddle of The Cobra's fangs!

Throughout the decadent district which represented the badlands of Manhattan, there were other telephones like this one. When such instruments went out of order, they were seldom replaced. Every pay phone marked "out of order" was a potential report station for The Cobra's agents!

The Shadow glided from the apartment building. He reappeared, near the side door of an old garage, on the very fringe of the underworld. Entering the door, The Shadow found a telephone in an obscure corner. He put in a call for Burbank. His instructions came in whispered tones.

Sometime later, a young man appeared strolling along a side street of the Tenderloin. He walked into a cigar store and purchased a pack of cigarettes. As he strolled out, he spied a telephone in a corner and noted that it bore no "out of order" placard. The young man continued on his rounds.

This quietly dressed, clean-cut young chap was no stranger to the badlands. He had been here before at The Shadow's bidding. He knew the district well. The young man was Harry Vincent, a trusted agent of The Shadow.

In another quarter, another keen-eyed young man was making rounds of his own. Like Harry Vincent, he knew the underworld. Clyde Burke, police reporter of the New York *Classic,* was a frequent visitor to gangland's dives. He, too, was an agent of The Shadow.

With the aid of his two agents, The Shadow was checking up on the location of potential calling stations. Following his first clue, he was tracing The Cobra's operatives to learn the workings of those secret helpers whom The Cobra termed his fangs.

IN a gloomy room where only a single lamp was glowing, a man was seated facing a small switchboard. In response to a glimmering bulb, he pushed in a plug. This man had earphones and mouthpiece attached to his head. He spoke in a quiet tone:

"Burbank speaking."

A reply came through the earphones. Burbank spoke again:

"Report from Burke. Gangster identified as Gringo Volks made a call from Cobra booth one block west of the Blue Crow. He received no reply. Burke tracked him. Gringo is at the Blue Crow."

Fifteen minutes later, a black-garbed form moved silently along the street where the Blue Crow was located. Stealthily, The Shadow lowered himself into a small pit outside a grimy window. His keen eyes peered through the dirty pane to survey the scene within.

Gangsters were assembled, talking in low, confiding tones. The Shadow recognized faces that he had seen before. Among them was the one The Shadow sought. Gringo Volks, formerly chief henchman of Deek Hundell, was seated at a table with some others.

Gringo was the one who had spilled word of The Cobra on the night when Deek Hundell had died. This was a tribute to The Cobra's craft. It proved how The Cobra had learned of the meeting which Deek had called. Gringo, Deek's most trusted henchman, a minion of The Cobra. Thus had The Shadow learned from Clyde Burke's report.

Seated apart from other mobsters was a visitor who had been in the Blue Crow when The Shadow had come there in the guise of a sweatered dope addict.

This was Crawler Gorgan.

The Shadow knew the pale-faced undercover man for who he was—an agent of the police. He watched Crawler rise and slouch from the dive. This was sufficient proof that no conversation of importance was going on within.

Crawler reached the street and shambled along past the spot where The Shadow lurked. The undercover man had no suspicion of the black-garbed watcher's presence. The Shadow paid no attention to Crawler's departure. His keen eyes, still close to the smudgy window, were fast on the thug called Gringo Volks.

The hard-faced mobster seemed restless. He pushed back his chair and took the path to the door. Coming from the Blue Crow, he, too, went by the spot where The Shadow was in readiness. This time, The Shadow emerged from his hiding place.

Gringo had no idea that he was being followed. He did not glance behind him; had he done so, he would have failed to see the form that followed him. When The Shadow stalked prey through the underworld, his stealth was superhuman.

Not even a swish of the black cloak betrayed his presence. Like Gringo's own shadow, he followed silently until the gangster came to a disreputable dwelling which appeared to be unoccupied. Gringo opened a basement door and entered. He failed to close the door behind him.

THIS was the spot where Clyde Burke had watched—one block west of the Blue Crow. A pile of barrels, near the opened door, showed where Clyde must have stationed himself. The Shadow avoided this hiding place. Stealthily, he moved to the door and listened—less than a dozen feet from Gringo.

The gangster was fumbling with the mouthpiece of a telephone. A buzzing sound was audible. There was no further response. Gringo grunted

**A hissing sound from the receiver was plain to The Shadow's ears.**

impatiently and turned toward the door. The Shadow moved back into darkness. Once again, Gringo had called The Cobra with no reply.

This time, however, Gringo did not move back to the street. Instead, he lighted a cigarette and stood smoking it in the shelter of the basement. When he had reduced the cigarette to a tiny butt, he flicked the lighted end out into the street and went back to the telephone.

Again, the twisting of the mouthpiece. This time the reply came. A hissing sound from the receiver was plain to The Shadow's ears. Gringo spoke in low tone:

"Fang Two."

Clicking of the receiver. Then came Gringo's further conversation:

"I get you... Yeah... That's tomorrow night... Outside the Black Ship... You're putting me in charge... Nine o'clock... I'll take care of the mob..."

The call ended. Gringo stalked from the basement. He passed The Shadow in the darkness. His footsteps clicked on the sidewalk as he headed back toward his favorite hangout, the Blue Crow.

A whispered laugh sounded softly after Gringo's footsteps had faded. The tall figure of The Shadow glided mysteriously from a spot beside the door. Gringo Volks had finally reached The Cobra. From his chief he had gained definite information.

Tomorrow night. That was Wednesday night. The Cobra was planning some action with the aid of fangs whom he had used before. From a hidden lair, the unknown chief had issued an important order.

The laugh of The Shadow! Soft, but weird, it seemed to echo from the walls past which The Shadow moved with gliding pace. Whatever The Cobra's scheme might be, The Shadow would be concerned in its result.

Much was to be done before tomorrow night. Yet The Shadow's tone of mirth betokened confidence. For by watching through the window of the Blue Crow; by trailing Gringo Volks and observing the man's actions, The Shadow had gained another clue!

## CHAPTER XX
## CLIFF AWAKES

CLIFF MARSLAND opened his eyes. He was lying on a cot, in one of the strangest rooms that he had ever seen. Near him was a table and a chair; beyond that, a large cabinet projecting from the wall. Cliff blinked as a door swung open and a man stepped into the lighted room.

Cliff could not see the visitor's face. The man was dressed in dark clothes and his back was toward The Shadow's agent. He was stepping toward another door, which he opened to reveal a closet.

Cliff saw the man take down a garment. Stooping, he slipped trousers over his legs and drew a sort of cowl up over his back. Groggy, Cliff did not realize what this meant until the man turned and stepped from the closet. Then The Shadow's agent gasped.

He was facing The Cobra! This room was The Cobra's lair!

A hiss came from the painted, hooded face. It was the warning of The Cobra. Cliff stared as the brown-clad figure approached. He raised his arms and found them heavy.

"You have slept well," hissed The Cobra. "You will sleep again—for long intervals—while you remain my prisoner."

There was a forced tone to The Cobra's voice. It was that of a speaker who chose his words in an effort to disguise his natural way of speaking.

"There are not many," went on The Cobra, "who have become my prisoners. You are lucky. I am keeping you because I know your master— The Shadow.

"His time is up. Tonight, he will be outlawed. The police will be on his path. So will The Cobra. That is why I intend to let you live. You will aid me when I trap The Shadow."

Cliff's head was aching. The Shadow's agent sank back upon the cot. The Cobra laughed in snarling fashion. He turned to the chair before the switchboard and seated himself.

Cliff's eyes were closed, but he could hear The Cobra talking. Dully, Cliff heard the instructions which The Cobra gave.

Crackling through his brain was the thought that these words would be information for The Shadow; with it was the gloomy realization of total helplessness.

Cliff knew that he had been drugged. He had lain here probably for days and the effect of the dope had not worn off. Cliff's hands were trembling; at moments, they seemed to regain their normal strength, but when Cliff clenched his fists, all power seemed to leave him.

THE COBRA had finished speaking. He arose and again turned to look at the helpless form of Cliff Marsland. Again, his hissing tone delivered insidious words. Cliff's ears were pounding. He caught only momentary tones of The Cobra's voice.

"Tonight... The Shadow... a fugitive... the law will seek him... when I have done..."

Cliff closed his eyes in bewilderment. He was trying to connect these utterances. They were ringing in his brain—words that he half understood. The Cobra's voice ceased with a hiss. Cliff could hear his footsteps moving toward the closet.

Something was happening, but Cliff had only a hazy idea of what it was. He could hear The Cobra's hiss, coming as though faraway. Once Cliff opened his eyes; he stared in total amazement; then closed his lids and pressed his hands to his aching temples.

Wild visions gripped him. The Cobra's hiss—it seemed to bring The Shadow's laugh. Hope became despair. All was absurd and fantastic. Frenzied desire for The Shadow's aid was racking Cliff's brain.

Opening his eyes again, Cliff stared, glaring at the ceiling. It seemed to be whirling; as in a cloud, Cliff fancied leering faces.

The Cobra's hood—The Shadow's eyes—then

ugly faces of scowling mobsters. Steadiness came back only when Cliff closed his eyes and gripped the sides of the cot. He heard The Cobra's hiss. Then came the reply of a crackly voice, from the switchboard:

"Fang One."

"I am coming up," hissed The Cobra. "Is the way clear?"

"The way is clear."

"Turn out all lights. Above and below."

The lights went out as Cliff reopened his eyes. Complete darkness was the result. Cliff could hear The Cobra moving toward the door. He heard the barrier open; then close. A bolt shot. Muffled footsteps clicked from stone stairs beyond.

"The Cobra!" screamed Cliff. "The Cobra! The Shadow! Stop—stop—"

Cliff's voice ended in a gurgle. Weakly, the deluded man sank head back upon the cot. Darkness seemed to grip Cliff by the throat. He moaned piteously amid these moments of awakened fantasy. The clicking of The Cobra's footsteps seemed hours on those stairs, before they finally died.

YET The Cobra's ascent had required less than half a minute. At the top of the stone steps, The Cobra was opening a door. He moved into the darkness of the ground floor. In pitch blackness, The Cobra hissed.

An answering response came in a crackling whisper. It was Fang One—the guardian of The Cobra's lair.

"Which way, Master?"

"The side door," hissed The Cobra. "I shall be gone at least two hours. Wait here until I return."

"Yes, Master."

"Be careful with the lights. None until I have left."

"Yes, Master."

Footsteps thudded softly on a thin rug as The Cobra crossed the room. A door closed. Faint footsteps from a passage beyond. The Cobra had left.

Fang One chuckled in the darkness. He seemed to like its atmosphere. Then, a full three minutes after The Cobra's departure, a light came on as Fang One's hand pulled a cord. The illumination, shaded in a table lamp, revealed a plainly furnished room—also its occupant.

Fang One was an old, wizened man. His hair was thin and gray—on his crown he wore a little rounded cap of black. Many denizens of the underworld would have recognized that face, with its wrinkled, toothless smile.

The old man was "Crazy" Lartin, a recluse whom all regarded as almost penniless. Crazy had been a beggar in his time. Whatever hoardings he owned could not be large. This was the humble room of Crazy Lartin's abode. Below it was the lair of The Cobra!

A humble, crumbling old house in an ill-kept district. Such was the place that The Cobra had chosen as his headquarters. Crazy Lartin served as the guardian to the way below. He held the title of Fang One!

This was a room with many doors. One was the way by which The Cobra had come from his lair. There were four others. The old man was staring significantly across the room; his gaze indicated the direction which The Cobra had chosen for his departure.

Hands clasped and rubbing; lower lip protruding above the upper in a fiendish leer—Crazy Lartin seemed to enjoy the prospect of The Cobra's return. It was plain that he took pride in The Cobra's deeds. Fixed was Lartin's gaze—so fixed that the old man did not hear a sound behind him.

One of the other doors was opening. Upon the floor stretched a long, thin streak of blackness that crept forward in ominous fashion. Then came a figure from darkness; that of a being clad in black. The Shadow!

The old man turned—too late. He gurgled as he caught a flash of blazing eyes from beneath the brim of a slouch hat. Then The Shadow was upon him.

Fang One writhed with surprising strength. He was overpowered. The Shadow, stooping, trussed the old man with remarkable swiftness. He raised Lartin's body with one arm and dropped the old man on a couch in the corner.

Leaning forward, The Shadow held a gag above the old man's face. Before applying it, he put a stern, whispered question.

"Where is the prisoner?"

"Below," gasped Lartin. "Down the stone steps. The middle door—the light beside it—"

The gag wedged its way between the old man's gums. As he twisted the ends into a knot, The Shadow laughed. His whispered mirth boded no good for The Cobra!

## CHAPTER XXI
## THE SHADOW'S COURSE

CLIFF MARSLAND blinked. The light had come on again. The period of darkness had broken his dizziness. In the dim glow of The Cobra's lair, Cliff felt a returning strength. Surging through his mind were thoughts no longer scattered.

The Shadow must be reached! That was Cliff's one realization. Could The Shadow hear Cliff's story, he would know amazing facts! With that thought, Cliff Marsland flung himself sidewise from the cot and staggered to his feet.

The room spun. With crazy, whirling gait, Cliff plunged toward a wall as though his steps were taking him down a ramp. He slipped as his fingers failed to hold the cracks which they sought. Slumping, Cliff sprawled against the rounded wicker basket. It rolled over and the lid came off.

"Ss-s-s-s-s-s!"

Half rising, Cliff stared in the direction of the sound. A new creature of fantastic appearance was before him—a living snake—a cobra! Cliff uttered a gasp as he saw the venomous serpent lift its hood. This deadly creature—pet of The Cobra—was about to strike. It could deliver venom more potent than that of its master!

Cliff did not hear the click of the bolt behind him. He did not feel the swish of air that came from the opening door. The cobra's hood was poised to strike. Cliff was staring, powerless to move.

Suddenly the gleam of a flashlight was reflected in the wicked, beady eyes of the reptile. Blinded by the light, the snake paused in its stroke.

A terrific shot reechoed in Cliff's ear. It was the discharge of a heavy automatic; caught by the stone walls, the report was cannonlike. Hood and head were blown from the cobra's body. The writhing length of the snake wriggled on the floor.

Amid the repeated echoes of the pistol shot came the strident tones of a sardonic laugh. The fate of this real cobra was an omen. It was The Shadow's challenge to The Cobra. Slumped by the wall, Cliff Marsland gasped again as he stared into the eyes of The Shadow!

KEENLY, The Shadow discerned his agent's plight. With strong arm, he gripped Cliff's body and raised the half-drugged man from the wall. He carried Cliff to the cot and placed him there.

From beneath his cloak, The Shadow produced a small vial filled with a purplish liquid. He uncorked it and placed the little bottle to Cliff's lips. Cliff dropped back as a pungent odor filled his nostrils. Firmly, The Shadow pressed the vial. Gulping, Cliff took the draught.

The room whirled. Cliff collapsed upon the cot. Yet as he lay there, he could feel a potent fire that seemed to bring new life through his veins. The Shadow's keen eyes watched the blood creep to Cliff's forehead. Then The Shadow turned and stepped over to examine the switchboard.

Choosing plugs with care, The Shadow inserted them in the board. He spoke, in low, whispered tones. Cliff Marsland raised himself on one elbow and stared, despite his dizziness, as he heard a voice reply:

"Vincent speaking."

"Report," whispered The Shadow.

"Men assembled outside the Black Ship," came Harry's voice. "Cars waiting in an alleyway."

"Join Burke," ordered The Shadow.

The gloved hands were busy with the plugs. Again, the whisper. Another voice sounded from the plug box.

"Burke speaking."

"Report."

"Ready with the sedan."

"Await Vincent," ordered The Shadow. Then a pause: "Also wait fifteen minutes after his arrival. Marsland may join you."

"Instructions received," came Clyde's reply.

A soft laugh rippled from The Shadow's lips as the black hands pulled the plugs. Cliff stared steadily now; his head no longer swam; his eyes were filled with keen interest.

The Shadow had solved The Cobra's system. More than that; from The Cobra's lair he was using The Cobra's own equipment in order to instruct Harry Vincent and Clyde Burke on the work they were to do!

The Shadow arose. He approached the cot and stood above Cliff Marsland. The agent looked squarely into his chief's eyes. He felt the power of The Shadow's burning gaze.

"You heard The Cobra?" questioned The Shadow.

Cliff nodded.

"What did he say?"

"He gave orders," declared Cliff, as he strove to remember. "Orders—to men whom he called fangs."

Cliff paused; then, mechanically, he repeated disjointed phrases. There was not a full sentence among them. They were not in the order that The Cobra had uttered them. Yet The Shadow seemed to understand. More capably than Cliff, he was piecing together the broken statements.

"You saw The Cobra," whispered The Shadow.

"Yes," returned Cliff. "He—he came in here alone. I could not see his face. He went"—Cliff paused to point to the door of the closet—"over there. He—he came out as The Cobra. I was dizzy."

The Shadow moved toward the closet. He drew out garments—among them two long, wrinkled garbs of brown. He held them up to exhibit painted hoods. Cliff shuddered at the recollection; then steadied.

"He—he put on one of those," gasped Cliff. "It—it was after that he spoke. He—he said he would outlaw The Shadow. That—that tonight he—"

Cliff was weakening. He sank back on the cot.

He felt what he was sure could be no more than a last spell of dizziness. After that, he would have his strength. He was sure of it; but for the moment, he could not speak, so weak he was.

"And then?" came The Shadow's whisper.

"The Cobra!" blurted Cliff. "He—he went back to the closet. I—I saw him. I—I was dizzy. I—I thought that everything was going black—that I was falling—but that I would be safe for—"

A WHISPERED laugh came from The Shadow's hidden lips. Cliff Marsland had settled back upon the cot. His mind was secure; but he could no longer speak. It was unnecessary.

The Shadow's laugh was the sign that he had learned all that he needed to know. He had divined the full meaning of Cliff's disjointed statements. He had formed a complete report from wandering utterances.

Cliff lay quietly upon the cot. The Shadow moved about the room. Time was floating leisurely in Cliff's mind, although moments only were passing. With eyes still closed, Cliff felt himself raised up from the cot. He was moving to the stairs, gripped by The Shadow.

Cliff's footsteps clicked on stone. The dampness of the stairway revived him. Urged onward by The Shadow's arm, hearing The Shadow's whisper in his ear, Cliff reached the top.

In the furnished room, he saw the old man prone upon the couch. Cliff could see a fearful look in the bound prisoner's eyes. The man was staring at the figure of The Shadow. The glimpse ended as Cliff reached the door toward which The Shadow aided him. Then came the darkness of the passage; after that an outer door.

Through a blackened alleyway, Cliff Marsland still felt The Shadow close beside him. Across a street; another narrow way. Night air was reviving. It added the final touch to the potent liquid which Cliff had swallowed. They reached a street. On the other side, Cliff saw a parked car. He heard The Shadow's whisper.

"Are you ready?"

"Yes," replied Cliff, firmly.

"I have placed an automatic in your pocket," declared The Shadow. "Join Vincent and Burke in the car. They will tell you the rest."

Cliff nodded. With firm footsteps, he moved from the alleyway. He paused a moment to grip the wall and steady himself. He did not see The Shadow in the darkness. Turning, momentarily, he realized that his chief had withdrawn.

Cliff grinned. He was ready now. He headed across the street, steady and alert. As he advanced to join the other agents of The Shadow, he heard a weird whisper that rose behind him.

It was the laugh of The Shadow! From The Cobra's lair, the master fighter had rescued his agent and had dispatched him to join the others who were waiting.

The laugh faded, with echoing mockery. That was the token of The Shadow's departure. The Shadow, himself, had started on his way. He had appointed work for his men; for himself, a lone game.

This night would bring the climax. The meeting between The Shadow and The Cobra was due to come! Like The Cobra, The Shadow had decided on his course!

## CHAPTER XXII
### PASS THE COBRA

CALEB MYLAND'S Long Island home showed dimly in the night. Only a few windows were aglow. The quiet place seemed faraway from the teeming slums of Manhattan. Yet this secluded spot bore a close connection with affairs of the underworld.

This was where Caleb Myland, criminologist, was to hold another conference with Police Commissioner Ralph Weston. For this was Wednesday night—the evening set for the appointed meeting.

Myland's estate was skirted by a hedge. Beyond that clumpy barrier, three rakish automobiles slid into line. Lights out, men clambered to the road. They stood silent, listening to the low growl of one man who was undoubtedly their leader.

"Lay low, you fellows." The voice was that of Gringo Volks. "Ease in from the hedge—I'll lead you back to where there's a break in it. Spread out and move around the house.

"Keep the front clear. There's a big driveway there; we're not stopping people from driving in. There's bushes on the drive. Keep behind them—you guys that go to the front."

Low growls proved that the listeners understood Gringo's order.

"The Cobra's coming in tonight." Gringo's voice was still a low tone. "Maybe he's in already. Maybe he's coming later. We took our time getting here. It don't matter either way. Pass The Cobra—in or out. You get me? Pass The Cobra."

"We get you."

"When he comes out," resumed Gringo, "that's when the fireworks start. You won't see him at first. His signal will be a shot. That's when we cut loose. High and wide. To cover The Cobra in his getaway.

"Crowd close to the house. Raise a big row. Then back here to the cars, shooting all the way. Plaster the front, you fellows by the bushes. Plug the tires in cars. Then join the rest of us.

"We're working for The Cobra. But we're mum. This is the job that fixes things the way he wants it. From now on, we're in the money. And remember"—Gringo's tone was final—"pass The Cobra!"

Slouching gangsters grunted their understanding. A squad of more than a dozen, they filed toward the opening in the hedge. Spreading upon the darkened lawn, they edged away at Gringo's order.

THESE mobsters represented a picked crew. Never before had such a capable outfit ventured from the underworld. They were not ordinary gorillas. Each was a fang of The Cobra. Each could have told his own story of treachery in The Cobra's service.

Gringo's tale would have been typical. The former aid of Deek Hundell had been cornered by The Cobra. In return for life—with the added promise of remarkable gain—Gringo had worked from then on for The Cobra. He had betrayed Deek Hundell to his new master.

Among the others who were in Gringo's squad were the ones who had crossed other big shots. Only one was lacking: Diamond Rigler had been slated for a lieutenancy higher than the one which Gringo Volks was holding. But Diamond, alone of all the fangs, had died in The Cobra's service.

The nearer mobsters had reached the bushes on the close side of the drive. Others had circled the house and were reaching a similar position on the other side. Gringo had taken a vantage point close to the near side of the big house.

Fangs of The Cobra formed an armed circle! Steady hands with potent trigger fingers, these aides were ready for what might come.

A car came up the drive. Gringo eyed it from a distance. The night was still; he could hear the door slam; he could even hear footsteps crunching along the walk toward Myland's front door.

An interval; then came another car. Like the first, it remained in the driveway while an occupant alighted to enter the house. Gringo watched. Minutes passed.

In accordance with instructions from The Cobra, Gringo had brought his crew hither with no haste. Assembled at the Black Ship, he had waited until the appointed time to start. Then he had gone from car to car, instructing his drivers how to reach the road by Myland's hedge.

The Cobra was coming here tonight. It was probable that he had arrived before his crew. At the same time, there was a chance that The Cobra had chosen to wait until visitors had reached Myland's home.

The big house, as Gringo viewed it, would make a good lurking spot. Gringo, had he been in The Cobra's place, would have chosen to come ahead of the mob. Nevertheless, he saw merit in the other course, and appreciated The Cobra's wisdom in making provision for a later entry.

Somehow, Gringo began to lean to the belief that The Cobra had remained outside. Had he chosen this latter plan, he would be able to see how well the gang stationed itself under Gringo's order.

The night had been cloudy. The overcast sky was clearing. Gringo was glad that the fangs were stationed. Faint moonlight was now upon the lawn. Creeping men would have been visible. As it was, all were in their places. Not a sign could be seen of a single lurker.

THE lawn stretched out in back of Myland's house. A clear space showed a dull, silvery surface instead of blackened grass. Gringo turned. His ears had detected a faint sound that seemed familiar.

Was it a hiss?

Staring, Gringo saw a wrinkled shape, like a dark smudge on the silvered lawn. A bulky, stalking body, it was topped by a strange, outlandish hood. Upon that masklike headpiece glowed a luminous, painted face.

Circled eyes. Straight lines that tapered like chevrons to form a false face of venomous appearance.

The hiss was repeated.

The Cobra!

Gringo growled a low order. It was heard by a fang stationed closer to the house:

"Pass The Cobra!"

The next man whispered the word along:

"Pass The Cobra!"

Murmurs from the waiting fangs—murmurs no louder than a passing breeze. Awed eyes watched while lips were silent. Like a triumphant general passing beneath a bridge of swords, the figure of The Cobra stalked through the lines of his waiting, watching fangs!

The brown-garbed figure reached its goal. The Cobra had advanced to an obscure side door of the house. His snakelike form was swathed in darkness. The back of his hood was toward his men. The luminous face could no longer be observed.

"Pass The Cobra!"

The watchword had been obeyed. From now on, visitors could enter Caleb Myland's only by the driveway in the front; but none would be permitted to leave. The bars would not be lifted until the waiting fangs would hear the signal shot that would thrust them into action.

Then, amid the barrage of a besieging horde, The Cobra would depart, while his waiting fangs once more obeyed the order:

"Pass The Cobra!"

## CHAPTER XXIII
## MEN AT BAY

"WHERE is Mr. Myland?"

Commissioner Weston put the question. He was asking it of Babson, Caleb Myland's servant. Babson had ushered two visitors, Commissioner Weston and Joe Cardona, into Myland's study. They were awaiting the arrival of the criminologist.

"Mr. Myland should be here, sir," informed Babson. "He was out of town. I fancy that he missed his train and was forced to take a later one."

"Humph," grunted Weston, as Babson left. "This is maddening, Cardona. We need Myland's advice at once. I want him to hear the report that you received from Gorgan."

"It is still incomplete," reminded Joe. "Gorgan is going to call by telephone before—"

"That's just the trouble," interrupted the commissioner. "Myland should be here before Gorgan phones. Myland may have some important ideas on the matter."

The commissioner looked glum. He sat in meditative silence and Cardona did not disturb him. Then came the click of the opening door. Weston uttered an exclamation of satisfaction as Myland appeared.

"Sorry, gentlemen," remarked the gray-haired criminologist. "I was detained in Philadelphia. It meant only one hour's delay in reaching here, so I did not call by long distance. I came by taxi from the Pennsylvania Station."

"I didn't hear a cab drive up," observed Weston. "If I had, I would have come to the door to meet you."

"This study is secluded" was Myland's rejoinder. "One cannot hear automobiles when they arrive in the driveway at the front of the house."

"We have news for you, Myland," declared Weston, suddenly. "It is important news—from Gorgan. Tell the facts to Mr. Myland, Cardona."

"CRAWLER GORGAN phoned me," asserted Cardona. "He was near a dive known as The Black Ship. He observed mobsters gathering.

"Crawler could not recognize them in the dark. They were getting into parked cars; and to all appearances they were preparing for some raid.

"It was too late for me to reach Commissioner Weston by telephone, for I was at the place where I meet Crawler and I was ready to start here. I ordered Crawler to slide back to the Black Ship—to see what else he could learn—then to either call me here or to come with his report."

"I have used your telephone to call headquar-

ters," said Weston, to Myland. "Inspector Klein has sent two capable men down to the vicinity of the Black Ship. They have instructions to be cautious."

"A mob assembling," remarked Myland, thoughtfully. "A mob—despite the unsettled conditions in the underworld—"

The telephone bell rang. Myland picked up the receiver and handed the instrument to Weston. The police commissioner heard the voice of Inspector Timothy Klein. He held a short conversation; then hung up.

"The men have reported to Klein," informed Weston. "There are no cars near the Black Ship. All is quiet there. Yet we have not heard from Crawler Gorgan—"

"Crawler may be on his way here," interposed Cardona. "If he found out what the mob is doing, and had time to get here, he would come, rather than call."

"Of course," decided Weston.

"A mob assembling." Caleb Myland was repeating his interrupted statement. "That means leadership. Someone is reorganizing the forces of the underworld. Shattered hordes have been assembled by a mighty chief."

"The Shadow!" exclaimed Weston.

"I think so," nodded Myland.

"Listen, Commissioner!" Joe Cardona was on his feet. "This thing is coming to a showdown. I think you're all wrong about The Shadow. If he was going crook, he'd have done it long ago."

"He did not have the opportunity," reminded Weston, in an angry tone.

"I don't agree with you, Commissioner." Cardona was blunt. "He could have made the opportunity. I've got a theory of my own. Here it is.

"Who's been knocking off the big shots? I'll tell you. The Cobra! Why? Because by clearing them out, he's left the very opening you've talked about—but it's an opening for himself! The Cobra's the one that's ready to organize!"

"Preposterous!" exclaimed the indignant commissioner. "Cardona, such remarks at this critical time come almost as insubordination!"

"You'll hear me out!" insisted Cardona. "You accuse The Shadow of having tried to block The Cobra's work. All right—suppose he has. Maybe he knows that The Cobra is actually a smart crook—maybe he knows what's coming.

"Take it from me—that gang that Crawler's been watching don't belong to The Shadow. He doesn't deal with crooks. If some hidden hand is behind the outfit, The Cobra is the one!"

"No more!" Weston drove his fist against the table. "Cardona, you will answer for this absurd talk. The Cobra has proven his worth. The

Shadow has shown his questionable tendencies. Tonight, let us hope, we will gain positive facts. Perhaps this crook, The Shadow, will become too bold. Your theory, Cardona, is outrageous—"

"One moment, Commissioner," Caleb Myland was speaking with a placid smile. "We must not curb Cardona's statements. Any theory—given honestly—is worth consideration. Why not plan what should be done tonight? We need further word from Gorgan, but in the meantime, we can be discussing matters.

"I, like you, believe that The Shadow is a menace. But why mince words when the proof is probably in the making? Perhaps from Gorgan—perhaps from detectives—perhaps from crime itself, we shall know the answer before this night is ended.

"Let the crook reveal himself, as I believe he will—somewhere in New York. Speculation as to his identity will be useless until he has shown his hand."

Mollified by Myland's words, the commissioner subsided. He knew that the criminologist was right. Myland, like Weston, held the theory that The Shadow had yielded to the lure of crime; yet Myland was content to wait.

The door opened. It was Babson. The servant seemed nervous. He approached and spoke to Caleb Myland.

"Things aren't right outside, sir," he declared. "I was looking from a front window. I thought I saw a man behind a bush near the drive."

Weston looked up in surprise. Cardona became alert. Myland held up his hand to ease them.

"Babson is imaginative," he declared. "He knows that I have a large amount of cash in my vault—here in this room. He is always expecting trouble.

"There may be a man outside; perhaps someone from the underworld. I have feared this, but not on my own account. I have been worried about Crawler Gorgan. His job as undercover man is a precarious one. Perhaps he has been spotted making visits here.

"I shall take a look, gentlemen, at the place which Babson has mentioned. It is better that I should go alone. I can peer from the window without being observed. Come, Babson—show me the window—"

Myland was smiling serenely as he moved from behind the table. He was heading toward the door of the study, with Babson at his heels. Weston was watching the criminologist depart. So was Cardona. Both could see the door beyond.

Then came simultaneous gasps. Weston and Cardona leaped to their feet as Myland staggered back. Babson uttered a hoarse scream of terror.

All hands went up at the sight of the threatening form that stood within the doorway.

Armed with two automatics, a black-clad form was covering the four men. Tall, menacing in appearance, his features were completely hidden by the bundled collar of his black cloak. The broad brim of a slouch hat was turned down from his forehead.

An ugly laugh came from unseen lips. The automatics moved forward in the gloved hands that held them. Criminal in bearing, this intruder stepped toward the group of helpless men.

A cry of outraged recognition came from Commissioner Weston, as the official voiced the identity that was plain to all:

"The Shadow!"

## CHAPTER XXIV
## THE DUEL

COMMISSIONER RALPH WESTON scowled as he backed toward the wall in response to the gesture of the automatics. Myland showed a worried, bewildered countenance. Babson was terrified. Cardona's face was hard.

"You asked for crime." The words came in a harsh sneer from the lips that watchers could not see. "You shall have it. Open the vault in back of you, Caleb Myland."

Glumly, Joe Cardona stood with upraised hands while Caleb Myland turned to follow the bidding. Joe had staked all on the integrity of The Shadow. This turn of events was wholly unexpected to the detective.

Joe had seen The Shadow in the past. Always he had arrived as a grim avenger, to fight on the side of right. Now, his every action showing evil intent, The Shadow had come to rob.

Babson had reported a lurker outside. It must be one of a mob. The Shadow's mob! Joe could not have believed it, but for the presence of the black-clad intruder now engaged in deliberate crime.

A sneering laugh. It was like the laugh of The Shadow that Cardona had heard before; but it held a new tone—one that was ugly in its jeering. Joe Cardona glanced toward Ralph Weston. The commissioner's face was purple.

"You have looked for crime." The sneer of The Shadow seemed a snarl as it was addressed to Weston. "Watch it. Robbery—and murder. Turn out the law. I do not fear it."

Caleb Myland had opened the vault beyond the panel. Without awaiting bidding, the criminologist removed stacks of banknotes and placed them on the table. Thousands of dollars—all the wealth that the strong box contained.

"Close the vault!" hissed the unseen lips.

Caleb Myland obeyed.

"Death!" The word was ominous, as the black-gloved hands turned automatic muzzles toward Caleb Myland and his servant Babson.

Weston and Cardona stood helpless. They knew that they could not save the criminologist and the menial. One move would mean shots; then the guns would swing in their direction.

The money lay where the black-gloved hands could pluck it. Quick death to Myland and Babson—that, Weston took, was the intent of The Shadow. Then the money—unless Weston or Cardona should attempt to intervene. If they did, those automatics would bark new shots to end the lives of commissioner and detective.

WESTON could not watch. He heard the taunting laugh, delivered in spiteful hatred. He turned his eyes toward the door, to avoid a view of Myland's death. Cardona, glancing toward Weston's face, saw a sudden gleam appear in the commissioner's eyes.

At the same instant, Weston's lips blurted forth a cry of hope. The words swung Cardona's eyes in the direction of the commissioner's gaze.

"The Cobra!"

Framed in the doorway was the fantastic figure that had rescued Ralph Weston and Joe Cardona from a former plight like this. The folds of the dark brown garb seemed almost black against the gloom of the hall beyond. But the painted hood shone with luminous circles and pointed lines!

The moment that followed Weston's involuntary gasp seemed like a lifetime. Four men—those with upraised hands—stood motionless. They were but helpless witnesses to the amazing scene.

Weston's gasp had been an alarm. The black-cloaked figure of The Shadow whirled rapidly toward the door. Both automatics swung to cover the brown-garbed form of The Cobra. At the same instant, a long brown arm shot up from the folds of The Cobra's brown attire. A revolver flashed as the quick hand took aim!

A hiss came from the doorway. It was answered by a scoffing laugh. Then came the conflict.

Three shots resounded with a deafening roar. To the listeners, they came as a single, prolonged outburst. In this instantaneous duel between The Shadow and The Cobra, both mighty fighters had launched their lead with fierce defiance to the other's challenge.

But in that mighty burst of gunfire, one trigger was pulled a split second before the others. A quick, but perfect shot accomplished both vengeance and salvation. Brown finger, pressed to revolver trigger, had beaten the black with their automatics.

Turning, Joe Cardona saw the figure of The Shadow as it wavered. The arms had swayed in firing. A bullet to the body beneath the black cloak had caused the automatics to falter in their aim.

The black-cloaked form crumpled. It sprawled on the floor, a helpless, inert mass, while clattering automatics dropped beside it. The black hat, toppling forward, completely obscured the face beneath.

At the door stood the hooded figure of The Cobra. The painted face seemed to represent a gleeful smile. The muzzle of the revolver still was pointing; a wisp of smoke was curling from it.

Eyes behind the painted mask saw that the shot had gone home. The figure of The Cobra faded beyond the door.

"The Cobra!" exclaimed Ralph Weston. "He has saved us all. He has killed The Shadow!"

THE commissioner was pointing toward the motionless figure on the floor. Caleb Myland, leaning pale-faced on the table, nodded, as his hands pressed the stacks of rescued banknotes.

Joe Cardona was stunned. The Shadow—slain in the act of crime—by The Cobra! Mechanically, the detective moved forward from the wall. Stooping, he fumbled as he plucked up one of the automatics. A sudden stare came to Cardona's eyes. He grabbed for the other gun and stood, gaping, with one weapon in each hand.

These were not the famous .45s—those mammoth weapons with which The Shadow had mowed down many fiends of crime. They were .38s—powerful, but of lesser caliber than The Shadow's mighty guns.

As Weston stepped forward, Cardona stooped again. He dropped the automatics to the floor. With sudden inspiration, he seized the black hat and whipped it from the face that was beneath.

"Look!"

Ralph Weston and Caleb Myland obeyed Cardona's cry. Like the detective, they registered amazement. Cardona's expression turned to triumph.

The lifting of the hat had revealed an unexpected sight. The painted hood of The Cobra! An exact duplicate of the luminous, circled mask which had been worn by the fighter at the door!

Again, Cardona stooped. He seized the hood by the knot at the top. He yanked it clear of the head that wore it. This time, Joe Cardona, as well as the others, stood amazed and wordless.

The face of the dead man was that of Crawler Gorgan!

It was Caleb Myland who saw the light. Blurting, the criminologist gave the facts as he perceived them.

"Gorgan—The Cobra!" exclaimed Myland. "He turned to crime. He came here as The Shadow—to lay crime on The Shadow! The one at the door—we took him for The Cobra—was—The Shadow!"

As in corroboration of Caleb Myland's finding came a weird, chilling token from beyond the door. It was a whispered, creeping laugh, that broke with shuddering echoes—the laugh of the one who had slain The Cobra.

Saved men stood in silent awe as they heard the triumphant laugh of The Shadow!

## CHAPTER XXV
## VANQUISHED MINIONS

OUTSIDE of Myland's home, Gringo Volks was tense as he whispered orders to his men. The fangs had heard dull, muffled reports of gunshots within the house. They were waiting for another signal.

It came. From the side door which the fangs had seen The Cobra enter, a burst of flame appeared accompanied by the bark of a revolver. Fangs of The Cobra fired in return. High shots smashed against the walls of Myland's home.

Into a patch of moonlight appeared the figure of The Cobra, moving forward. A brown hand flung aside a glittering object—a revolver. The hand descended; two arms swung upward, holding blackened objects: huge automatics.

A peal of weird laughter. Strident, unrepressed, the battle cry of The Shadow struck the ears of the fangs as they paused in their fire. Wild exclamations followed. Before them stood The Cobra—but his weird call was the laugh of The Shadow.

Terror gripped the waiting fangs.

Then came bursts of flame from The Shadow's automatics, followed by screams about the lawn. Guiding his shots by the flashes of revolvers, The Shadow was aiming for The Cobra's henchmen.

"Let him have it!"

The order came from Gringo Volks as The Cobra's chief aide leaped from the bush where he was waiting. Flashing a revolver, Gringo sought to meet the challenge. Cobra or Shadow, this hooded figure was an enemy.

Gringo fired. His first quick shot was wide.

Gringo was aiming again. He was in full view of the house. An automatic barked. Gringo sprawled. His finger slipped from the trigger. His revolver bounded in the dirt beside a bush.

Staring fangs had seen the lieutenant's fall. With one accord they broke into frenzied flight. Cutting across the lawn, they fired hasty shots as they fled. They could no longer see the form at which they aimed. They could see only the bursts of flame from automatics.

Crouched behind a little wall that was beside stone steps, The Shadow was picking off the fleeing fangs. Responding bullets chipped off fragments from the wall; but the ricocheting shots missed the living target.

Fangs from the other side of the mansion were heading in a wide circle to escape The Shadow's fire. The automatics stilled. A weird laugh broke as five escaping crooks drove madly toward the opening in the hedge.

A searchlight's beam came flooding through the opening. The loud, eerie laugh had been a signal to men stationed in a car that had pulled up beyond the break in the hedge. Five fangs stopped blinded as they faced that glare. They raised revolvers.

Shots from beyond the hedge. They were delivered by The Shadow's trusted men, Clyde Burke and Harry Vincent—with Cliff Marsland revived to aid them—and broke the headlong retreat of the survivors who had obeyed The Cobra as their master.

Two fangs fell. A third remained firing, while his companions cut at an angle toward the house. The lone man aimed for the searchlight and missed his target. A burst of return shots dropped him.

RISING from his protected spot, The Shadow took long-range aim. One shot clipped the foremost fang; the next bullet sent the second sprawling. The last of the fangs had fallen. The Shadow's laugh rose triumphant; then faded as the master fighter—still garbed as The Cobra—turned to enter the house.

The Shadow's agents drove away from beyond the hedge as men appeared from Myland's. The fray outside had been furious, but fast. Not until its quick action had terminated did Joe Cardona appear, followed by the others from the study.

Moonlight showed sprawled and writhing forms upon the lawn. Cardona and Weston, carrying guns for protection, rushed forward to corral the dead and wounded mobsters. Aided by Myland and Babson, they carried in the bodies of those who were still alive.

Placing the crippled fangs in the front living room, Cardona and Weston hurried to the study to call for ambulances and reinforcements from headquarters. Joe Cardona was speaking as they moved along.

"These men will talk," said the detective. "The Cobra is dead. The Shadow spotted his game and picked off his whole crew. We'll find his hideout."

"How The Shadow did it is a mystery!" exclaimed Weston. "Commendable! Most commendable!"

Little did either realize the details of the work which The Shadow had accomplished as a sleuth in the underworld. They did not know how The Shadow had spied on Gringo Volks in the Blue Crow; how he had noted that while Crawler Gorgan was present, calls which henchmen sent could not reach The Cobra.

That was the clew which The Shadow had followed. He had trailed Crawler to his abode this very night. There, from Cliff Marsland's disjointed phrases, he had divined The Cobra's game. The Cobra had departed, attired as The Shadow! Cliff had taken it for a fantastic dream; The Shadow had understood all!

He had chosen the attire of The Cobra for himself. He had taken one of the additional garbs when he had left The Cobra's lair. Moving to the Black Ship, he had heard Gringo's final instructions to his men—corroborating facts which The Shadow had already fathomed.

It was The Shadow who had entered as The Cobra, passing through the lines of watching fangs; while The Cobra, wearing a cloak and hat to impersonate The Shadow, had been lurking within Caleb Myland's home!

CARDONA guessed this part as he spoke to Weston just outside the study door.

"The Cobra would have slain Myland and Babson," said the detective, solemnly. "Then, with the money, he was going to drop that cloak and hat to appear as The Cobra."

"So his men would pass him," asserted the commissioner.

"Yes," agreed Cardona. "They would have held us back. We would have blamed The Shadow for the crime—we would have thought the mob was his."

"We would have hounded The Shadow," admitted Weston. "Captured him—or driven him to hiding—leaving The Cobra free to sweep with crime."

"Those men of his," assured Cardona, "were lieutenants of the big shots that The Cobra killed. Each would have had his own mob—his own racket—his own crimes."

"With The Cobra master of them all!"

They had reached the study. Cardona uttered an exclamation as he pointed to the body of The Cobra, sprawled upon the floor. The black cloak and slouch hat were gone. Both Cardona and Weston knew the answer.

The Shadow had returned. He had taken away these garments in which The Cobra had masqueraded. Imitations of The Shadow's own guise, they belonged to The Shadow now—not to Crawler Gorgan, the traitor who had used his knowledge of the underworld to double-cross the law.

Commissioner Weston stood still as Detective Cardona raised his hand for silence. Faraway, barely audible in this rear room of Caleb Myland's home, came the echo of a parting laugh.

Ghoulish, chilling mockery, it faded from its strange crescendo. Yet the recollection of that bursting cry could not be forgotten. It was the note that sounded final victory over The Cobra and his evil minions.

The triumph laugh of The Shadow!

THE END

# RIVALS OF THE SHADOW by Will Murray

From his first appearance, The Shadow struck the popular consciousness like a thunderbolt. Overnight, "The Shadow Knows!" became a national catchphrase.

He so captivated the American public that just six months after the debut of *The Shadow Detective Magazine,* Street & Smith jumped it from a quarterly to monthly frequency. When in the autumn of 1932, they increased it to every other week, *Shadow* editor John L. Nanovic and writer Walter B. Gibson were the first to worry about imitators.

"We talked to [S&S business manager Henry W.] Ralston," Gibson recalled. "Nanovic and I said, Why not put out a magazine called *The Phantom?* He said, 'Oh, no. Concentrate on *The Shadow.*' But we said that somebody's going to put out one called *The Phantom,* because it's a natural. And sure enough, they did. We should have put it out ourselves."

The first issue of *The Phantom Detective* carried a February 1933 cover date. The new series chronicled the exploits of bored millionaire Richard Curtis Van Loan who was also the enigmatic master of disguise known as The Phantom. On the covers, he looked like Lamont Cranston in a top hat and domino mask. The novels were initially the work of Walter Gibson's friend and colleague, D'Arcy Lyndon Champion, who wrote

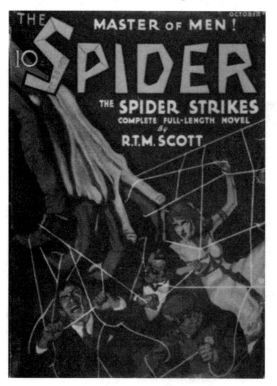

as D. L. Champion and Jack D'Arcy. For the Phantom stories, he was G. Wayman Jones and later Robert Wallace. In the 1920s, Champion had served as assistant editor under Gibson on *Tales of Magic and Mystery.*

That fall, Popular Publications produced a more brazen *Shadow* imitation. Owner Harry Steeger admitted frankly, "The reason we started the title *The Spider* was because of the success of Street & Smith's *The Shadow.* At this point in pulp history individual titles became very popular, so we decided to try out a few ourselves."

When the first issue of *The Spider* appeared, the cover image was modeled after all the Shadow covers showing the Dark Avenger's long-fingered hand, but with a signet ring emblazoned with a crimson spider symbol rather than the trademark fire opal ring. The originating author was R. T. M. Scott, but when he moved on, Popular replaced the byline with a house name commercially calculated to evoke Maxwell Grant—Grant Stockbridge.

In the beginning, the Spider was simply a masked alias of millionaire criminologist Richard Wentworth, but as the character was developed by replacement writer Norvell W. Page, he took up a black cloak and floppy hat in emulation of The Shadow. The Spider also practiced his own version of a creepy radio laugh designed to terrify crooks.

Just a few months later, Periodical House released another *Shadow* clone called *Secret Agent "X."* A mystery man and master of disguise, "X" was written by former Street & Smith editor Paul Chadwick under the house name of Brant House. Secret Agent "X" was actually a combination of The Shadow and Doc Savage. He whistled rather than laughed and maintained a host of alternate identities like The Shadow's.

Even Street & Smith borrowed from the Master of Darkness in conceiving Doc Savage. Like The Shadow, Doc possessed a striking signature sound. As Lester Dent once admitted to Gibson, from the beginning Street & Smith insisted on "... a 'trilling sound' he was to make, a patent steal from The Shadow to which I objected at the time..."

Nor did Street & Smith stop there. In 1936, they hired Laurence Donovan to pen the Whisperer series, about a gray ghost of a crime-fighter who spoke in a chilling whisper and blasted crooks with his supersilenced automatics. It ran only a year, but the series continued in the back pages of *The Shadow.* Clifford Goodrich was the nominal author.

About this time, Jerry Siegel and artist Joe Shuster were trying to interest publishers in a colorful new hero. Although Superman bore no

**The Black Bat debuted in 1939.**

obvious Shadow hallmarks, Siegel cited it as one of his formative influences:

"I read quantities of eerie hero-oriented pulp magazines like *The Shadow,*" he once revealed.

The year 1939 was a big one for Shadow clones. Batman debuted in the May issue of *Detective Comics.* Although he was what Walter Gibson later derided as a "clowned-up" takeoff of The Shadow, Batman caught the public imagination too.

Batman artist Bob Kane acknowledged the influence of The Shadow, among others.

"I have always been an ardent mystery and adventure fan. Some of my earliest heroes were The Shadow, on radio and in the movie serials.... I suppose both The Shadow's cloaked costume and double-identity role, as well as the extraordinary acrobatics of Douglas Fairbanks, Sr., did more to my subconscious to create the character and personality of Batman than any other factors."

Writer Bill Finger, who co-created Batman with Kane, concurred. "My first script was a take-off on a Shadow story.... I patterned my style of writing after *The Shadow.* Also after Warner Bros. movies, the gangster movies with Jimmy Cagney, George Raft, Bogart. I always liked that kind of dramatic point of view. It was completely pulp style. Sometimes I overdid it, writing phrases like 'Night mantles the city.' But, somehow, it all seemed to work."

Two months later, Leo Margulies' Better Publications launched a nearly-identical new pulp hero in *Black Book Detective.* Blinded District Attorney Anthony Quinn dons an ebony batwing cloak and hood to become the night nemesis known as The Black Bat. Like so many of his ilk, he brandished two .45 automatics and used them to punishing effect.

"Many years ago Leo Margulies asked me to come up with a series to be in competition with *The Shadow,*" explained originating author

Norman A. Daniels. "I concocted a set-up which, without change, became The Black Bat.... I was paid exactly what Gibson was paid and raised when he was raised." G. Wayman Jones was the byline that masked Daniels' true name.

The simultaneous bat-heroes created consternation in both editorial offices. It fell to DC editor Whitney Ellsworth to straighten it all out.

"It was a weird coincidence," Finger noted. "Apparently this character had been written and on the drawing board. Whit Ellsworth used to be a pulp writer for Better Publications. So through Ellsworth's intervention a lawsuit was averted."

Street & Smith introduced *The Avenger* that fall. Written by Paul Ernst under the house name of Kenneth Robeson, The Avenger was a naked attempt to capture the loyalty of both *Doc Savage* and *Shadow* readers, according to Walter Gibson.

"Both Les [Dent] and I were called in to talk with Paul Ernst," he recalled. "But what they really did, they decided to make a composite of The Shadow and Doc Savage. So they took agents like I had and they used a Doc Savage type of story... Les told him more about how to handle characters; I told him more about how to handle situations, make changes of pace."

The Avenger was another master of disguise. Unlike The Shadow, Richard Henry Benson never wore a cloak, dressed in black, or taunted criminals with his knowing laugh. He ran a crime-busting crew he called Justice, Inc. and lasted only four years while the Black Bat ran over a dozen.

Later that year another pulp house tried a variation of The Shadow. Kendall F. Crossen, the editor for Munsey's *Detective Fiction Weekly,* recalled that early in 1939, "I was asked by the head of the magazine department to try to work out a character to compete in the pulp market with The Shadow. A book had just been published about an American who had gone to Tibet and studied and had become a lama, the only white person who ever had at that time. The result was the Green Lama, which the company liked."

Originally, he was going to be called the Gray Lama, but that hue was judged too drab for cover-art purposes.

Returning to the United States, millionaire Jethro Dumont ("It was as close as I dared get to Lamont Cranston," Crossen admitted) donned the hooded emerald robes of the Green Lama to fight injustice in the pages of *Double Detective,* and later went on to become a popular comic book superhero.

"It never quite surpassed *The Shadow* but the Munsey Company were pleased with the sales," Crossen noted, indicating that even imitation Shadows were in high demand.

The Green Lama followed The Shadow to radio, but lasted only one summer.

Of course, they had been copying The Shadow on radio all along. In the fall of 1934, just as Frank Readick was returning to the airwaves as The Shadow, the originator of the role, James La Curto, debuted as The Menace and also was heard as a sinister-voiced master villain on *The Eel and The Serpent.*

By World War II, The Shadow's radio program was the medium's highest-rated daytime show. This led to a dark wave of imitators, who curiously copied the format of the original version of The Shadow, that of a mysterious narrator.

The Whistler substituted an eerie and haunting whistled melody for a knowing laugh—although he initially would laugh mysteriously at the close of each episode, too, adding, "I know" in direct imitation of the more famous tagline, "The Shadow Knows." *The Whistler* debuted in 1942, and ran for thirteen years. Gale Gordon played the title role in the audition show, and was succeeded by Joseph Kearns, Bill Forman, Marvin Miller, Everett Clarke and former-Shadow Bill Johnstone. The Whistler opened every episode with the grim line, "I know many things, for I walk by night."

This was followed by *The Mysterious Traveler,* in which the narrator told his strange stories as if to a fellow passenger on a night-traveling ghost train. Maurice Tarplin voiced the Mysterious Traveler throughout the 1943-52 series, and also starred in the similar *Strange Dr. Weird.*

Even Walter Gibson got into the act with The Avenger, a character who took the name of the pulp hero, but was otherwise a Shadow clone. Biochemist Jim Brandon used a black light device to accomplish his own brand of scientific invisibility rather than occult mind powers in the 1945 syndicated radio series. "We tried to make *The Avenger* radio series as much like *The Shadow* as possible, even hiring Walter Gibson to plot it," producer Charles Michelson explained. "But it worked against us. Stations resisted the show because it was too much like The Shadow!"

Even as *The Shadow Magazine* was winding down in 1949, Shadow imitators continued to pop up.

Inspired by the 1949 hit song, "Ghost Riders in the Sky," artist Dick Ayers conceptualized the comic book hero, The Ghost Rider. A phantom lawman of the Old West, frontier Marshal Rex Fury donned luminous white robes and blank-eyed mask as the feared Ghost Rider. The lining of his cape was jet black, and when he reversed it, the Phantom Rider of the Plains seemed to vanish. A favorite trick was to wrap the inner cloak around his skull mask so that he appeared headless!

Ayers, who drew the character from Carl Memling's scripts, credited the tricky concept to Walter Gibson's inspiration.

"I had the image of The Shadow in my mind when I drew Ghost Rider and asked Carl to think of The Shadow when he wrote his dialogue balloons," Ayers confirmed.

In the summer of 1951, there came the obscure Whisperer on radio, who had nothing to do with the earlier Street & Smith hero. After young lawyer Philip Glass' vocal cords are crushed in an accident, he infiltrates the crime syndicate as the hoarse-voiced Whisperer—the last Shadow clone network radio ever produced. Carleton Young voiced the title role in the NBC series.

All of these mysterious characters, as well as The Shadow himself, had disappeared from the airwaves by 1955. An era was over.

But The Shadow was never forgotten. His influence continued to be felt even into recent times.

Before he took on Spider-Man, director Sam Raimi executed a 1990 film about a disfigured crimefighter he called Darkman, which spawned two direct-to-video sequels. Raimi created the character of scientist Peyton Westlake AKA Darkman after he was unable to secure movie rights to Batman and The Shadow. Raimi is a self-admitted fan of The Shadow. But who isn't? The Dark Avenger cast an indelible shadow across the cultural landscape as few had before him, or would ever again...

This Nostalgia Ventures volume celebrates Shadowy doppelgangers. It's a requirement of pulp fiction that the hero must meet his evil mirror image eventually. *The Cobra* was Gibson's reaction to the flood of rival pulp heroes such as the Spider. And leave it to The Shadow's raconteur to turn the editorial suggestion that the Dark Avenger battle an impostor into a fresh twist on the oldest of pulp cliches.

Walter Gibson was asked many times about the many cloaked copies who followed in The Shadow's nebulous train: "People started asking me, What do you think of the other things, The Phantom and The Spider, and so on and so forth? Of course I didn't have time to read any of them. I didn't want to read them. They were just imitations. Without being egotistical, Babe Ruth—they asked him one time which pitchers bothered him the most. He said, 'They all look alike to me.' So all the imitations of The Shadow look alike to me. They were interchangeable. I never paid any attention to them.

"Now there is a difference between The Shadow and the others," Gibson once joked. "The Shadow was *taller,* wasn't he?"

# The Third Shadow

*Murder — bold robberies of gambling clubs — and the being behind the death-dealing gun was a creature in black cloak and slouch hat! Has The Shadow turned his wits to make himself the perfect criminal?*

**A Complete Booklength Novel from the Private Annals of The Shadow, as told to**

# MAXWELL GRANT

## CHAPTER I
## THE MAN IN THE CAB

TRAFFIC was jammed about Times Square. The rush hour was on; a heavy drizzle added its impeding influence. Umbrella-laden pedestrians were blundering across crowded sidewalks; while taxicabs and other vehicles were skidding to sudden stops along the slippery paving.

A sallow, long-faced taxi driver was peering from the wheel of his parked cab. He was stationed on an eastbound street, fifty yards east of Broadway. Though his spot was a gloomy one, the cabby had high hopes of a passenger. On nights like this, wise persons who were seeking cabs invariably picked those that were parked away from heavy traffic.

Looking backward along the street, the cab

driver was watching pedestrians on the other side. He was ready to hail any prospective customer who might be walking eastward. The cabby was counting upon a lucky break. He gained one unexpectedly. A man stepped up suddenly from the sidewalk on the right side of the cab, opened the door and clambered aboard.

The taxi driver heard the door slam. He swung about and looked through the partition to see a muffled man, whose overcoat collar was high above his chin. The driver spied the outline of a whitish face beneath a derby. He inquired:

"What address, sir?"

Huskily, the passenger gave an address near Park Avenue, on a side street. His voice choked as he completed the statement; and he followed with a spasm of heavy coughing. The driver started the taxi forward. The coughing ended; the passenger leaned forward and put a wheezy question:

"What time is it?"

The taxi driver pulled a cheap watch from his pocket and consulted it as he guided the cab toward Sixth Avenue. The light from a small hotel front enabled him to note the time.

"Quarter of six," said the driver. "I'll get you there in ten minutes, sir."

Swinging left on Sixth Avenue, the driver encountered trouble beneath the pillars of the elevated. Traffic was badly jammed; the cause was visible after the cab had managed to proceed one block. Smoke was pouring from the front of a little Chinese laundry; three fire trucks were on hand, dealing with the blaze.

A hoarse ejaculation of impatience came from the passenger in the cab. The driver responded. Without waiting for traffic to unsplice, he swung across to the left of the avenue; bucked oncoming cars, then thrust the cab between the "el" pillars toward his right. Skidding across the path of a southbound trolley car, he gained the slippery northbound tracks.

Safe from disaster, the driver regained control and spun for a right turn at the next eastbound street. An arm-waving traffic cop certified the driver's action. Away from the jam, the cab sped eastward.

THE cabby was still grinning over his smartness when he pulled up at the destination. He had made the trip in the ten minutes that he had estimated. A grunt of approval came from the muffled passenger. Then an inquiry:

"Do you have change for a large bill?"

The driver fished in his pocket.

"For five bucks," he stated. "Wait—maybe I've got enough change for a tenner—"

"A twenty is my smallest," interposed the passenger, huskily. "Here. Take this to the drugstore." He thrust a twenty-dollar bill from a gloved hand.

"Tell them it's change for Mr. Yorne. Bring the change to my house. The name is on the doorplate: 'Lucian Yorne.'"

The passenger stooped his head. The driver knew that he was reading the registration card, whereon the driver's own name—Luke Ronig—appeared with his photograph. A natural precaution, since the passenger was risking twenty dollars on Ronig's honesty. The driver saw his fare alight; he watched the muffled man ascend the brownstone steps of an old house.

Stepping from the cab, Ronig went to the drug store, which was at the corner, forty paces distant. The clerks were busy; it was a few minutes before one of them received Ronig's request to change a twenty. The clerk looked dubious, until he heard that the change was for Mr. Lucian Yorne. Then he changed the bill immediately.

"Talking to Mr. Yorne, were you?" he inquired. Ronig nodded.

"How was his cold?"

"Sounded pretty bad. His voice was husky; he coughed like he was goin' to crack apart."

"Too bad. He's been that way for a week. Only yesterday, I told him he ought to stay indoors. Said he was too busy—didn't even have time to see a physician."

Carrying the change in his fist, Ronig left the drugstore and went back to Yorne's house. He noted the nameplate as he rang the bell. A minute passed; then the door was opened by a tall, weary-faced servant whom Ronig took for an Englishman.

"Change for Mr. Yorne," he informed. "He told me to bring it to him."

"You may deliver the money to me," informed the servant, dryly. "I am Parlington, Mr. Yorne's butler. Kindly wait here a few moments, please."

The change amounted to nineteen dollars and forty cents. Parlington was counting it as Ronig watched him cross a gloomy hall and enter the distant door of a lighted room, which, from its location, might have been a study.

Ronig waited; the hall was silent except for the ticking of an old-fashioned grandfather's clock that registered a few minutes past six. The taxi driver compared the time with his watch. While he was doing this, he heard the sound of Yorne's hacking cough, coming from the open door of the distant study.

Half a minute later, Parlington returned. Eyeing the taxi driver rather dourly, the butler inquired:

"Your name is Luke Ronig?"

Ronig nodded.

"Mr. Yorne wanted to be sure," informed Parlington. "He does not trust cab drivers, as a rule. He saw your name on the card; so he told me to make positive that you were the right man."

"What's that got to do with it?" demanded Ronig. "I showed up with the dough, didn't I? Say—"

"Here is your tip," interrupted Parlington, frigidly. He handed Ronig forty cents. "Good evening."

RONIG pocketed the change. Parlington opened the door; the cabby went out and boarded his taxi. He headed for an avenue, swung southward and kept on until he reached a westbound street. Turning into that thoroughfare, Ronig looked over the pedestrians whom he passed. He pulled up to the curb and hailed a shabbily dressed man who was shambling through the drizzle.

"Hey, fellow!" greeted Ronig. "You walkin' over to Broadway?"

The shabby man nodded.

"Hop aboard," invited the cab driver. "I'll give you a lift; and a dime besides, for a cup of Java."

The shambler grinned as be climbed into the back of the cab.

"I get the idea," he chuckled. "Them coppers on Sixth Avenue won't let you jam into Broadway with an empty cab."

"You hit it, buddy," returned Ronig. "Half the cabs in town are over around Times Square, grabbing fares. The traffic cops keep us out until the lines get short. But they can't stop me if I've got a passenger."

Ronig was right. He crossed Sixth Avenue past the inspecting eye of a watchful traffic officer. When he neared the Times Square area, he spotted an opening and pulled up to the curb. The shabby man alighted and the taxi driver handed his fake passenger a dime.

"Here's your change," he said with a grin.

"And here's something for you, hackie," returned the shabby man. He held up an expensive umbrella with a gold handle. "Just found it on the floor when I was getting out. Guess your last passenger must have left it."

Ronig looked at the umbrella. Its handle bore the initials "L. Y." The cabby grunted and handed the shabby finder a quarter.

"I'll get a tip for takin' this where it belongs," said Ronig, "so the two bits is yours, buddy. L. Y.—those initials mean Lucian Yorne. That was the name of the guy I just dropped."

"Better charge him for the full distance on the meter."

"Naw! That won't matter. I'm not takin' it back there now. Too much business around here; and there'll be plenty clear through until after the show-break. Plenty of fares from the theater crowds on a night like this.

"Yorne will have to wait until midnight for his umbrella. If he's asleep when I stop by there, I'll keep ringin' until I wake up his funny-faced flunky. Well—so long, buddy."

RONIG stood the gold-handled umbrella beside the driver's seat. The shabby man strolled away; a minute later, the cabby opened the door for two passengers who had spied his waiting taxi. Soon, Ronig was on his way again, wangling through traffic, making the most of the rainy weather that every alert taxi driver welcomes as a boon.

The umbrella was jogging by the cabby's elbow, its gold head catching the colored glimmer of passing neon lights. It would serve as a reminder of Ronig's later mission. As he drove along, the taxi man was repeating the names of Yorne and Parlington. He was wondering, too, how much of a reward he might expect when he returned the expensive umbrella to its owner.

Had Ronig been able to foresee the future, he would not have looked forward to it with pleasure. For that umbrella was due to cost him much in time and trouble. By the time Luke Ronig returned it, the law would be investigating the affairs of Lucian Yorne. For crime was abroad upon this drizzly night.

## CHAPTER II
### DEATH AFTER DUSK

A DOZEN minutes after Luke Ronig had driven from Lucian Yorne's, two other cabs pulled up in front of the old house near Park Avenue. Two couples alighted from each taxi. Prompt greetings were exchanged in the rain; then the four—two men and two women—ascended the steps of the house. Parlington admitted them.

Gravely, the butler greeted the arrivals by name. One was a middle-aged man, whom Parlington addressed as Mr. Elward; the lady with him was Mrs. Elward. The other man was younger. Parlington spoke to him as Mr. Renwood. The lady with Renwood was Miss Arthur.

Parlington ushered the guests into Yorne's study. Elward spoke in surprise when he saw that the room was empty.

"Where is Mr. Yorne?" he inquired. "Ah—I see that he is somewhere about. His coat and hat are hanging here."

"Mr. Yorne has gone out, sir," put in Parlington.

"But his coat and hat!" repeated Elward. "They are here, Parlington—"

"Only because I insisted that he don fresh garments, sir. His cold is quite severe; it would have been a great mistake for him to venture forth in a soaked overcoat."

"Yorne is making a mistake to go out at all," interposed Renwood. "You should take better care of him, Parlington."

"What can I do, sir?" pleaded the butler. "It was six o'clock when Mr. Yorne arrived home. I had been awaiting his arrival since five. I thought surely that he would stay; instead, he spent only a few minutes here. He went out, despite my protests."

"Quarter past six," remarked Elward, as the big clock chimed from the hallway. "Mr. Yorne told us that dinner would be at half past."

"He told me to postpone dinner, sir," stated Parlington. "It will not be served until seven o'clock."

"Then Mr. Yorne will be back by that time?"

"I hope so, sir; but I am not positive. Mr. Yorne said that his guests should begin dinner even if he had not arrived."

WITH that Parlington left the study and crossed the hall to a kitchen. While the guests chatted among themselves, the butler brought drinks. After that, they could hear him busied in the kitchen. Parlington was a capable servant. Despite the fact that he was cook as well as butler, he kept paying frequent visits to the study to make sure that the guests were constantly supplied with preliminary refreshments.

Conversation was flowing well between the guests. Elward and Renwood were friends of some standing, although their talk showed that they had not met recently.

"It's good to see you again, Jerry," remarked Elward to Renwood. "I hope business has been picking up with you."

"Not much, Kent," returned Renwood, with a shake of his head. "Some brokerage offices have been doing fairly well; but ours has been practically at a standstill. How is the advertising game?"

Kent Elward considered the question, as he puffed at his cigar. He nodded slowly.

"Quite good," he stated, "so far as certain types of accounts are concerned. Jerry, if there happened to be a way of promoting advertising with certain untouched industries, there would be a fortune in it!"

**CLARK LOFTUS— from Detroit, in New York on a Diamond deal.**

"You mean that certain businesses do not advertise in proportion to their earnings?"

"Yes. That is when compared with businesses that do advertise. Take Lucian Yorne's business, for example. He sells jewelry. Does he advertise it?"

"I don't think he does."

"I know that he doesn't. He is connected with the Allied Jewelry Company. Not a line of advertising comes from their offices. Those offices, by the way, are important enough to occupy a full floor of the Tower Building, on Thirty-fourth Street."

"But they are wholesalers—"

"Granted. Yet wholesalers advertise in other lines of business. But let us take a more specific case. Lucian Yorne handles retail accounts. He does not advertise."

"Yorne handles retail? Does he have a store?"

"No. He has a little office on West Forty-third Street. He meets special customers there. That is the only way he does business. I have known him to carry jewels valued at more than a hundred thousand dollars, just to display them to special customers."

"Where does he keep all those gems?"

"In the vaults of the Allied Jewelry Company. Of course, I can see why Lucian should preserve secrecy regarding his present transactions. I find no fault with that procedure. But what I cannot understand is why he does not open a store of his own and keep his jewels there."

"You are right. His special customers could come to the store. He would gain other trade besides."

"Particularly if he advertised. We are back to the original premise, Jerry. If Lucian Yorne—"

Kent Elward paused as Parlington entered. The butler had come to announce that dinner was ready. The company went to the dining room and began their repast. They dined from seven until eight. Lucian Yorne did not return.

AFTER dinner, the four guests went back to the study. Jerry Renwood remarked that Lucian Yorne must have met some special customers. Kent Elward looked worried.

"I doubt that Lucian would have forgotten us,"

he stated. "He should have called by telephone, to tell us that he would be delayed. Unless he forgot the time."

Renwood pointed to the desk, where a large gold watch was lying. He turned to Parlington, who had entered with a tray of cordials.

"Is that Mr. Yorne's watch?" inquired Renwood.

"Yes, sir," answered the butler. "Mr. Yorne forgot the watch two times today. When he went out at noon; and when he went out just after six."

"That is why Yorne has forgotten the time," said Renwood to Elward. "Don't worry about him, Kent."

An hour passed. It was after nine when the doorbell rang. Parlington answered; the guests expected to see Lucian Yorne. Renwood remarked, chuckling, that their host must have forgotten his key as well as his watch. But it was not Yorne who entered the study. The man who came with Parlington was a tall, bald-headed individual, whose face was serious.

"My name is Loftus," he announced. "Clark Loftus, from Detroit. Two friends and myself had an appointment with Mr. Yorne, at his Forty-third Street office. We were to meet him there at half past eight. He did not arrive. His office is locked."

"Mr. Yorne left here a few minutes after six," declared Elward. "We arrived about six-fifteen. We came to have dinner with him—"

"So the servant tells me," interposed Loftus. "Frankly, gentlemen, it worries me. Mr. Yorne has jewels of mine, along with others that I had not yet purchased. That is why I came here personally, to talk to him. My friends are still outside his office."

No one had a suggestion. Loftus went to the telephone.

"Does anyone object to my calling the police?"

There were no objections. Loftus made the call. He turned to the solemn-faced guests.

"Detectives are to meet me outside the office," he stated. "Do any of you wish to come along?"

Elward hesitated; then shook his head.

"No," he decided. "It would be best for us to remain here, in case Lucian arrives. We shall have him call his office as soon as he comes in."

Clark Loftus bowed, and donned his drizzle-soaked hat. Elward and Renwood followed him to the door. They saw the stranger enter a waiting taxicab.

IT was fifteen minutes later when Clark Loftus arrived at a small office building on West Forty-third Street. A police car was already there; a man in plainclothes stopped the arrival. Loftus identified himself. The dick nodded.

"Thought it was you," he stated. "Come on up. We've broken into Yorne's office. Inspector Cardona wants to see you."

Yorne's office was on the second floor. Arriving there, Loftus saw his two friends standing by the door, a detective beside them. One started to speak; the dick ordered quiet. Loftus stepped into the office. His path was blocked by a swarthy, stocky man, whom Loftus guessed to be Acting Inspector Cardona.

"What about Yorne?" queried Loftus, anxiously. "Have you found him?"

In reply, Cardona stepped aside. Loftus stared aghast at the sight across the room. There, sprawled in a swivel chair, lay a man whose outstretched arms hung limply toward the floor. Loftus saw a bloodstained shirtfront; above it, a face that was rigid in death. He recognized the countenance.

"Lucian Yorne!" gasped Loftus. "He—he is dead—"

"Murdered!" added Cardona. "Shot through the heart."

Loftus choked; his words were inarticulate. At last, he managed to gasp:

"But—but we have been here—since half past eight. I heard no shots. Did—did my friends—"

Cardona spoke to a police surgeon who was standing beside the desk. The physician responded.

"This man was slain before half past eight," he stated. "He has been dead at least three hours."

"It is nine-thirty, right now," added Cardona. "That puts the murder at six-thirty or earlier."

"Six-thirty!" exclaimed Loftus. "That is just about the time when Yorne should have arrived here. He left his residence shortly after six. It's only a dozen minutes or so, by cab."

"A good point," decided Cardona. "We'll go up to the house. I've already ordered two men to be there. But before we start, there are some questions I'd like you to answer, Mr. Loftus."

IT was nearly eleven when Cardona and Loftus arrived at Yorne's residence. An hour and a half had cemented their relationship.

Joe Cardona had long been recognized as the ace detective on the New York police force. In the capacity of acting inspector, he had enlarged his fame. There were times when Cardona was quick to recognize persons who were free from blame in crime. Tonight was one of them; for Joe's initial suspicion of Loftus had ended by the time they reached Yorne's.

At the old mansion, Cardona found four very impatient people awaiting him. They were the guests, all detained by the police.

Cardona listened to Kent Elward and Jerry Renwood. He believed their statement that they had arrived at six-fifteen. More than that, Elward and his wife both established the fact that they had come directly from their home; while Renwood proved that he and Miss Arthur had been with friends at a tea dance in the Hotel Goliath.

"None of you could have been at Yorne's office," stated Cardona, "but that's not the point we're after. What I want to know is, when and where Lucian Yorne was last seen alive."

"According to Parlington," declared Elward, "he was here between six and six-ten. Long enough to put on another coat and hat."

"So I've been told." Cardona studied the hat and coat that were hanging in the study. "An old coat and an old derby just about like the ones that Yorne was wearing when we found his body. What about these?" Joe turned to Parlington. "Did Yorne generally wear them?"

"No, sir," replied the butler. "He wore them this afternoon because the weather was inclement. I insisted that he change to his new hat and overcoat, despite the drizzle. He was almost drenched, sir, when he arrived at six o'clock."

"You're sure it was at six o'clock?"

"Positive, sir! He sent the taxi driver to the drugstore to change a twenty-dollar bill. I received the cab man when he came to the front door."

"A twenty-dollar bill, eh?" queried Cardona. "How many of them did he have?"

"I don't know, sir. Mr. Yorne usually carried at least a hundred dollars."

"No money in his pockets when we found him. Whoever took the jewels must have lifted his cash, too. Suppose we find out who changed that money down at the drugstore."

CARDONA eyed Parlington as if he doubted the servant's story. Parlington noted it and looked troubled. He began to protest, swearing that his account was a true one. Cardona silenced him.

"Yorne was murdered before six-thirty," emphasized Joe. "He could have left here at six-ten and gone directly to his office. But we only have one man's statement—yours, Parlington—that Yorne was here. We need more than that—"

An interruption. An officer had arrived from the front door, bringing a man with him. The fellow was a taxi driver; he was carrying a gold-headed umbrella. Parlington uttered an ejaculation of happy relief.

"This is the man!" exclaimed the butler. "He brought Mr. Yorne home at six o'clock! He is the taxi driver who changed the twenty-dollar bill! His name is Ronig—"

"How do you know that?" snapped Cardona.

"His boss told him," put in Ronig. "He took a squint at my license card. Wanted to lamp my mug and my moniker, in case I didn't show up with the change for his twenty. Then he was dumb enough to leave his umbrella in my hack. I didn't have a chance to bring it back here until after the show-break."

Another policeman was arriving with the clerk from the corner drugstore. This fellow recognized Ronig and nodded to the taxi driver. Cardona began to quiz the hackie.

Ronig's account was concise. He gave every detail from the moment when his muffled passenger had entered the cab near Times Square. He gave an imitation of Yorne's husky voice. It was corroborated by the drug clerk; also by Elward and Renwood.

Parlington identified the umbrella. The initials on the handle supported the butler's testimony. Cardona took final notes; then announced that his quiz was finished. He departed with Clark Loftus. On the way to the Detroiter's hotel Cardona delivered an opinion.

"We've established the time of the murder," decided the acting inspector. "According to the facts at hand, it was between six-twenty and six-thirty. We knew that Yorne was killed before six-thirty; now we've found out just how long before. What's more, that time element has eliminated three persons who were pretty close to Yorne.

"Elward—Renwood—Parlington. Those three have a clean bill. The job is to find out who else could have known Yorne well enough to guess that he had jewels on him. I've got a hunch that the murderer won't be far away. It won't be long before I pick him out."

Though often blind ones, Cardona's hunches were usually correct. Such was the case with this one. Joe Cardona might have picked out the murderer tonight, had he used deduction with his hunch. That task, however, happened to be beyond Cardona's limit.

The murder of Lucian Yorne had been a clever crime; more than the direct killing which Joe Cardona supposed it to be. The ace detective had failed to guess the flaws. So far as Cardona was concerned, the crime would remain an unsolved one. Until some keener brain intervened, the murderer of Lucian Yorne would remain unpunished.

SUCH a brain would soon enter the case. For in New York was a master sleuth, whose specialty lay in solving crimes like this one. That being was The Shadow, mysterious avenger who dealt with men of evil. Perhaps Joe Cardona's confidence was due to the fact that the ace knew of The Shadow's presence.

It was The Shadow, not Joe Cardona, who would pick out the murderer of Lucian Yorne. Yet oddly, his detection of that crime when it came, would start a chain of other, unexpected circumstances. The Shadow, from the moment when he concentrated on this case, would be upon the threshold of crisscrossed adventures that would rival any that even he had previously experienced.

## CHAPTER III
## THE SHADOW DEDUCES

TWO days had passed since the death of Lucian Yorne. Joe Cardona was seated at his desk in police headquarters, fuming over a stack of typewritten reports. Across from him was a stolid-faced companion: Detective Sergeant Markham. He was listening to Cardona's comments.

"It's a one-man job!" Cardona thwacked his fist upon the desk. "And there are no thugs in it! They wouldn't have let Yorne get into his office. They'd have decoyed him—or snatched him—"

Cardona paused and shook his head. He glowered at a pile of newspapers—journals that blazoned the news of murder. The very sight of those stacked sheets was irritating to Joe.

"I talked with Barstow Leland," stated the ace, referring to a report. "He's the president of the Allied Jewelry Company. The only man there who knew that Yorne had gone out with a hundred thousand dollars worth of sparklers. Yorne left that office before five-thirty. At quarter of six, he entered Ronig's cab at Times Square."

A long, streaky shadow spread across the desk. Cardona looked up to see a lanky, stoop-shouldered man entering the office. Joe grinned at the sight of the wan-faced arrival who was carrying mop and bucket. The newcomer was attired in overalls.

"Hello, Fritz!" greeted the acting inspector. "Early again, eh? Five-thirty isn't soon enough for you. Every now and then you show up at five."

"Yah!"

Fritz uttered the reply in a guttural tone. He started to work with mop and bucket. Unmindful of the janitor's presence, Cardona resumed his talk with Markham.

"Yorne could have taken the subway to Times Square," declared the ace, "then hopped a taxi to avoid the jammed shuttle line over to the Lexington Avenue sub. Or he may have hopped a taxi right outside of the Tower Building, there at Thirty-fourth Street. If his cab got in that Times Square jam, he'd have been wise to ditch it and take another."

"He could have gone to his office," suggested Markham. "It was right there on Forty-third Street."

"I've thought of that," nodded Cardona. "But I can't see why he would have gone there once, then home and back again. If he'd gone to his little office and stayed there a half hour, that would have made sense. He could have had some work to do—some phone calls to make—"

"Maybe he stowed the jewels there, then got worried about them on the way home."

"Not a chance! There's no safe in the office. Yorne was no sap. He knew how to take care of gems when he carried them."

Glumly, Cardona began to finger the report sheets. One by one, he discussed the names mentioned there.

"CLARK LOFTUS was the only customer who knew that Yorne would be at his office at eight-thirty," declared Joe. "Half of the gems belonged to Loftus. The friends that he brought with him were reliable; they didn't know their destination until they arrived. I've double-checked on Loftus. He stands the strain.

"Kent Elward apparently knew a lot about Yorne's business. Elward is an advertising man of good standing; what's more, he has an alibi right up to the time when he arrived at Yorne's house. So the fact that he knew a lot doesn't hold against him.

"Jerry Renwood works in a stockbroker's office; he's sort of a man-about-town, so he doesn't rate as high as Elward. But Renwood didn't know much about Yorne's business. What little he learned was mentioned to him up there at the house, while they were waiting for Yorne to show up. That puts Renwood out.

"As for Parlington, the butler, he could have known a lot about Yorne. But Parlington was there at the house when Yorne came in at six. When Ronig, the cabby, showed up with that umbrella, it clinched Parlington's story. So there you have it!

"Beyond that, there's nothing. No customers of Yorne's; no friends who knew his business; no other servants who ever worked for him. I've tried to figure a team-up that might account for the crime; but that flops."

Rising from his desk, Cardona arranged report sheets in pairs and indicated them with his forefinger.

"Elward plus Renwood," he suggested. Then, with a shake of his head: "No. Their alibis are separate until they reached the house. The two women and Parlington substantiated the time that they arrived there.

"Another combination that don't click is Ronig and Parlington. You can't figure a cab driver and a flunky as pals; even if they were, what of it? Ronig could have laid outside the house and picked up Yorne for the trip back to the office; but how did he happen to get Yorne in the first place, except as a chance passenger?"

"Ronig is pals with the hackies who were in that line down by Times Square. Talking with some of them right up until the time he got his fare. I thought I was smart for a while, figuring Ronig as the one man in the game, but the more I quizzed him, the more I saw that he was out. And to try to tie him up with Parlington only made it worse."

Cardona picked up his report sheets. He donned hat and overcoat. Standing by the desk, he delivered final comment.

"It's a one-man proposition," he affirmed. "All five that I've mentioned are out of it, though. That's what I've got to tell the commissioner, when I see him at seven o'clock."

"Where?" inquired Markham. "At his office?"

"No," replied Cardona. "At the Cobalt Club. He's having dinner there. I'm going to grab chow before I drop in on him."

CARDONA stalked from the office; Markham followed. Fritz remained alone, conscientiously working with mop and bucket. Five minutes passed; then a change came over the stoop-shouldered janitor. A keen light awoke in his dull eyes. His frame straightened.

Even Fritz's blackened shadow seemed to gain life. Its profile formed a hawklike silhouette, as the janitor gathered implements and made for the door to the hallway. Spying no one in sight, Fritz showed briskness as he headed for an obscure locker.

There he put away the mop and bucket. From the locker, he drew forth folds of black cloth. A cloak settled over shoulders; a slouch hat fitted upon his head. Long hands drew on thin black gloves; a whispered laugh sounded from invisible lips.

This was not Fritz, the janitor. The masquerader had transformed himself into a weird, cloaked being, whose gliding course was an elusive path. A shape that belonged with night, the intruder edged out into the early evening darkness. Gloom swallowed his departing form.

He was The Shadow!

Made up as Fritz, The Shadow had listened in on Joe Cardona's findings. Thereby, he had gained his final check on circumstances involving the murder of Lucian Yorne. He had learned of Cardona's appointment with Police Commissioner Ralph Weston at seven o'clock. The Shadow had work to do before that hour.

HIS next appearance occurred within a black-walled room. A blue light clicked; focused rays spread downward upon the surface of a polished table. White hands came into the light. They fingered clippings; they made notations in ink of vivid blue, that faded away after it had dried. The Shadow was summarizing the case of Lucian Yorne.

His written comments concerned a most essential point: namely, Yorne's movements from the time that he had left the Tower Building at Thirty-fourth Street. The Shadow was banking on the testimony of Barstow Leland, president of the Allied Jewelry Company. He knew that others must have seen Yorne leave the offices of the jewelry company, even though they did not know that he was carrying gems with him.

Next: Times Square—after a gap of fully fifteen minutes. The testimony of Luke Ronig, the taxi driver. Circumstances alone had introduced Ronig to Yorne. Ordinarily, a cabby would have no guess as to the identity of a passenger, particularly on a drizzly night. That trip from Times Square to the house near Park Avenue was but a hazy episode in itself.

What gave it strength was the subsequent event: Parlington's testimony of Yorne's arrival and immediate departure. Ronig had talked with Yorne outside; he had given money to Parlington inside. The Shadow came to a definite conclusion that Joe Cardona had not actually considered.

Though Lucian Yorne's progress seemed distinctly traceable from the Tower Building to his home, it actually was not a trail. Only two men who knew Yorne had testified that they had seen him and talked with him in the light. One was Leland, president of the jewelry company; the other was Parlington, the butler.

Before five-thirty; after six o'clock. Therein lay a period that interested The Shadow more than the time space between six-twenty and six-thirty, the ten minutes upon which Joe Cardona had concentrated. Evidence—chiefly testimony—had caused the ace to establish the time of the murder; and therefore to minimize other factors.

Written words became concise deductions, as The Shadow inscribed them. He was putting down other facts that Cardona had mentioned. So far as his quizzes were concerned, Joe had done well. In a sense, he had done too well. He had swept himself away along a blind trail.

The Shadow's light clicked out. A whispered laugh resounded in this room he called his sanctum.

Then came silence. The Shadow had chosen a new destination. He needed time for preparation before he approached it.

SEVEN o'clock. Police Commissioner Weston was dining in the grillroom of the Cobalt Club, when someone approached his table. The commissioner looked up, expecting to see Joe Cardona. Instead, he recognized his friend Lamont Cranston.

An interesting chap, Cranston. He formed a contrast to the police commissioner. Weston was a man of military bearing, with brisk manner and pointed mustache. Cranston was of leisurely manner; his well-molded face was masklike and impassive. A globe-trotting millionaire, Lamont Cranston had gained his share of adventure. Yet when he was present in New York, he seemed indolent and bored with life.

Weston invited Cranston to sit down for a chat. Hardly had the millionaire taken his place across the table when Joe Cardona arrived. The ace nodded to Cranston; they had met before. Weston motioned Cardona to a chair. He asked for the reports. Joe gave them.

"Very unsatisfactory, Cardona" was the commissioner's verdict. "You are getting nowhere with this case!"

"But I have eliminated five men," protested Cardona. "That is something of a start, Commissioner—"

"A start that you had two nights ago." Weston snapped his fingers. "Those men were out of the case like that. Their very testimonies cleared them."

"You said to check up on them—"

"Certainly! Partly as a matter of procedure; partly to see if they could name persons concerned with Lucian Yorne. Since they know nothing, you should make inquiry elsewhere."

"I intend to do so, Commissioner. But in the meantime, I must know what to do about these witnesses. Some of them may want to leave New York City."

"Then let them."

"Very well, Commissioner."

Cardona arose and gathered his report sheets.

"They will all be up at Yorne's house, tonight," he stated. "I told them to be there. That's where I'm going right now, Commissioner."

"Wait here a few minutes," insisted Weston. "I shall accompany you, Cardona. Well, Cranston, would you like to come with us?"

"Sorry, Commissioner." Cranston had risen. "I have another appointment. One of my own, with a man whom I must meet privately. Good evening."

A SLIGHT smile showed upon the fixed lips of Lamont Cranston, as he strolled from the grillroom. Reaching the lobby, the millionaire walked to the street; a doorman signaled to the chauffeur of a parked limousine. The big car rolled up to the door. Lamont Cranston entered.

"Drive northward," he said, through the speaking tube. "Along Park Avenue, Stanley. I shall tell you when to stop."

The chauffeur nodded. The big car pulled away. Lamont Cranston opened a small bag that lay upon the floor; from it, he extracted garments of black. A cloak slipped over his shoulders; a hat

settled on his head. A soft laugh filled the closed rear of the limousine.

Like Fritz, Lamont Cranston was The Shadow. One guise served for visits to Cardona's office; another for meetings with the police commissioner. But when he traveled upon lone excursions, The Shadow preferred his chosen garb of black.

The Shadow was right when he had stated that he had an appointment with a man whom he must meet privately. But both Weston and Cardona would have been astounded had they known the name of the man and the place where the appointment was to be.

The man whom The Shadow expected to meet was the murderer of Lucian Yorne. The place that he had chosen for the meeting was the very spot to which Weston and Cardona would soon be on their way. The Shadow's meeting would take place at the home of the late Lucian Yorne!

## CHAPTER IV
## ONE MAN SEES

IT was nearly eight o'clock when Commissioner Weston and Joe Cardona arrived at Yorne's house. Cardona had deputed an officer to precede him. It was the bluecoat who answered the door and conducted the arrivals to a front reception room. Larger than Yorne's study, this room was a better place for such assemblage.

Elward and Renwood were present. They were seated, while Parlington was standing by the wall. Ronig was also at the meeting; the taxi driver looked ill at ease in these surroundings. While Cardona was introducing Weston to the group, the doorbell rang. The arrival was Loftus.

Commissioner Weston summarized the case. He made references to Cardona's report sheets; he repeated questions that Joe had asked before. They brought uniform responses from the witnesses. Weston was satisfied with the checkup.

"Apparently, none of you can offer further aid," decided the commissioner. "We appreciate the testimony that you have already given. We are sorry that any of you should have been inconvenienced. However, since developments are still pending, I should like to know regarding your individual plans."

"I should like to go back to Detroit," asserted Loftus, promptly. "Naturally, I shall be available at any time. Should you gain any trace of the stolen jewels, I can come to New York immediately."

Weston nodded his approval.

"I had planned a trip abroad," stated Elward, a trifle nervously. "My wife and I arranged passage one week ago. Of course, if—well, Commissioner, if you have an objection—"

"I have none."

Elward smiled in pleased fashion. He mopped his forehead with a silk handkerchief. Parlington spoke up.

"I am a British subject, sir," stated the butler. "I came to Canada a few years ago, with Sir Arthur Grendenning. I was anxious to visit the States, so Sir Arthur arranged to have me take service with Mr. Yorne. They were friends, sir.

"I can return to service with Sir Arthur. He is still in Montreal, and would be glad to have me in his household. That is where I should like to go, sir, at whatever time would be convenient. Should I be required here, I shall return at once."

"All right, Parlington."

Weston nodded as he spoke. He had referred to Cardona's report on Parlington. It contained full details of the butler's past service with Sir Arthur Grendenning.

"I shall be right here in New York," remarked Renwood. He was lighting a cigarette as he spoke; his manner lacked nervousness. "Any time you want to see me, Commissioner, just put in a call to my brokerage office."

Weston nodded and looked toward Ronig. The taxi driver grinned.

"My cab's outside, waiting," he said. "I'll be in it any time I'm wanted. If you don't mind doing me a favor, Commissioner, give me a pass so I can bust past them wise traffic cops on Sixth Avenue. I'd like to go right through 'em and make the show-break."

The commissioner smiled indulgently. He drew a card from his wallet and wrote a brief order of approval. He handed it to Ronig. The taxi driver started toward the door, to find Loftus waiting for him.

"I'll use your cab," remarked the man from Detroit. "I want to reach my hotel in a hurry. You can drive me there, Ronig."

THE two left. Weston looked about and noted that Elward and Parlington had also gone. He glanced inquiringly at Cardona.

"Elward's in the study," explained Joe. "He's calling Mrs. Elward, to tell her that they can take their trip to Europe. Parlington went upstairs to get his luggage. He's going to take the late train to Montreal."

Renwood was a listener to this statement. Puffing at his cigarette, the young man watched Weston and Cardona begin a review of the report sheets. Casually, Renwood strolled from the room and entered the front hall. The front door was closed; apparently the policeman had gone outside. Renwood turned about; then stopped.

Footsteps were coming down the stairs, which lay past the door to the study, at the end of the

long side hall. Renwood was standing where he could not be seen; but he chanced to notice a wall mirror that gave him a view directly to the stairway. There was a light at the foot of the stairs; hence Renwood's view was clear.

The man who had descended was Parlington. The servant was carrying two large suitcases. He turned right; Renwood knew that he had stepped into the pantry. It was then that Renwood saw the sight that held him spellbound.

Blackness moved. It came from the end of the hall just past the stairway. Shrouded, that mass looked vague, yet living. As it advanced, Renwood thought that it would take human form; then his view was clouded, for the shape had come in front of the stairway light.

Renwood blinked as vision cleared. The shrouded figure had faded into nothingness.

Where had it gone?

Renwood had two solutions. One was the pantry, where Parlington was; the other possibility was the study, where Elward was telephoning. The mirror gave no view of either door. Renwood had merely guessed that Parlington had taken to the pantry, for he had seen the direction of the servant's turn. But that shape in blackness had faded too mysteriously for anyone to guess its choice.

On tiptoe, Renwood moved from his place of obscurity. He went back through the hall. He stopped between two doors that stood ajar. On the right was the study; Renwood could hear Elward talking on the telephone. On the left was the pantry; a strange stillness reigned there.

On a hunch, Renwood edged to the left and peered through the crack of the door.

THE room was dimly lighted by a globe set in a wall niche. Within its walls, two figures formed a striking tableau. One was Parlington; the servant was standing beside the china closet in the corner. He had opened the door of the closet; from it, he had removed a stack of small black boxes. Turning, with these prizes in his grasp, he had stopped at sight of the being who had followed him.

This second figure was that of a black-cloaked intruder. Renwood could see the stranger clearly. The weird visitor was standing by the open door to the kitchen, turned half away from Renwood. Hence Renwood, though he saw the shape, was unable to spy the burning eyes that glared in Parlington's direction.

He could guess the power of those eyes only from his observation of Parlington's features. The butler's face had whitened; his whole frame was trembling. Then Renwood saw another threat: the muzzle of an automatic projecting from a black-gloved fist. He heard a whispered tone of sup-

The Shadow had stepped closer to his quarry .... one gloved hand
thrust a pen and paper toward Parlington.

pressed challenge. He caught the words that Parlington uttered:

"The Shadow!"

Parlington's recognition revealed the servant's caliber. It told that he was a man of crime; one who knew the identity of the avenger who trapped him.

Renwood heard a hissed command. He saw Parlington's hands lower. The servant laid the boxes on a shelf beneath the china closet. Trembling, he opened them. The glitter of gems sparkled in the light.

The Shadow had stepped closer to his quarry. Renwood saw one gloved hand thrust a pen and paper toward Parlington. Still quaking, the servant took them. Then Renwood listened to a sibilant statement, as The Shadow dictated words to Parlington.

"THIS confession," hissed The Shadow, "is made by—"

A pause. Parlington, himself, blurted out the name:

"Henry Durwell!"

"Henry Durwell," repeated The Shadow, "alias Parlington, the murderer of Lucian Yorne."

With twitching lips, Parlington was writing the words. New statements came, in The Shadow's voice. He was speaking for Parlington; the man was writing, despite his tremors.

"I knew that Yorne would be coming to his office." The Shadow paused to watch Parlington write. "I waited for him there. I shot him when he arrived. I took the jewels and his money. Yorne had worn his new hat and coat; I was wearing his old ones.

"I took a cab that happened to be Ronig's." Coldly, The Shadow was still speaking for Parlington. "I talked in a hoarse voice to imitate Yorne. I sent Ronig to change the twenty-dollar bill. I received Ronig when he arrived with the change. I pretended that Yorne was in his study.

"That was just after six o'clock. When Elward and Renwood arrived at six-fifteen, they established my alibi from that time onward. I had carried Yorne's umbrella. I purposely left it in the cab. I made Ronig think that Yorne had told him my name, so that, later, if necessary, I could have the police find him.

"I, alone, was responsible for the crime. I was glad to leave England"—The Shadow's tone was significant—"because of robberies that I had committed there. Crimes which had remained undiscovered."

Renwood stared. He wondered how The Shadow had guessed the past of Henry Durwell, alias Parlington. Then, suddenly, the answer struck

him. Parlington's recognition of The Shadow had been the clue. It proved the servant to be a man of former crime; one who feared this avenger, whose name was dreaded by all crooks.

"With this note"—The Shadow added final statements—"I leave the stolen jewels. The gun that you will find is the one with which I killed Lucian Yorne."

A pause, while Parlington completed the writing. The Shadow added:

"Your signature—and alias."

Fearfully, Parlington scrawled both names by which he had been known. Then came another order from The Shadow:

"The revolver!"

AMAZED, Renwood watched Parlington reach into his coat pocket and produce a .32. Trembling, the servant held the weapon, but dared not use it. The sight of the looming automatic made his gun seem puny.

Then The Shadow faded; his tall form blended with the darkness of the kitchen beyond the pantry. Parlington was alone, holding his revolver.

Yet the crook still felt The Shadow's presence. That mysterious visitor had completely sized Parlington's caliber. The Shadow knew what the crook would do, once his crime had been discovered.

Renwood watched Parlington raise the muzzle of the revolver to his temple. The murderer was bent on suicide. The shot that would produce his own death would bring Cardona on the run, to find the butler's confession lying with the reclaimed jewels.

As Renwood stared, a heavy hand clamped on his shoulder. The young man swung about, to be promptly thrust aside. The arrival was Joe Cardona. Stepping from the reception room, the inspector had seen Renwood peering at the pantry door. As he pushed the eavesdropper aside, Cardona gave a demanding growl; with his other hand, he shoved the pantry door inward.

Cardona saw Parlington, with gun still to his head. The ace sleuth spied the glittering jewels. With a roar, Joe drove inward, yanking a Police Positive from his pocket. His gun, like Parlington's glimmered in the light.

The effect was instantaneous. The Shadow's spell was broken. New murder—not suicide—became Parlington's desire.

As Cardona drew, Parlington jumped back and aimed his own gun for the ace. Renwood, back at the doorway, saw the snarling butler gain the bulge. He knew that Parlington would beat Cardona to the shot. But before Parlington could fire, a burst of flame spat from the kitchen; with it a reëchoing roar that came as sequel to The Shadow's judgment.

A sizzling bullet speeded from the kitchen, to find its lodgment in Parlington's gun-wrist. A howl came from the servant's lips as his finger refused its task of pulling the trigger. Then, before the crook could recover, Cardona's own gun barked amid the echoes.

Firing instinctively, Joe drove a stream of bullets into the murderer's body. Parlington succumbed.

Renwood's gaze turned toward the kitchen door. For the first time, the eavesdropper saw the burning eyes of The Shadow. Glowing orbs from darkness, they made the startled observer drop back into the hall. As he retreated, Renwood heard the whispered sibilance of a triumphant laugh.

It was The Shadow's knell for the deserved fate that had come to a man of evil. Parlington, slayer of his master, was dead. Not by his own hand, but from the bullet justly dealt by Joe Cardona. The ace had taken quick advantage of the respite that The Shadow had given him.

WESTON and Elward were dashing into the hall to find Renwood gasping like a man who had experienced an apoplectic stroke. Renwood could barely point to the door of the pantry.

Weston and Elward kept on; Renwood managed enough nerve to follow. They found Cardona holding the signed confession and the jewels, with Parlington's body on the floor beside him.

Renwood glanced nervously toward the kitchen door. He saw no sign of The Shadow. The master sleuth had completed his appointed task. He had vanished out into the night.

In the talk that followed, Joe Cardona listened sympathetically to Renwood. The young man stated that he had seen Parlington go into the pantry; that he had wondered why the servant did not come out. He had gone to the door—so he said—just in time to see Parlington raise the revolver to his head. The sight, Renwood claimed, had unnerved him.

Joe Cardona believed the story. He wanted to believe it, because he was glad that no mention had been made of the shot from the kitchen. Joe knew that he had been saved by The Shadow; he could guess whose influence had impelled Parlington to turn yellow at the moment when his getaway was clear. But Joe knew also that The Shadow would prefer his part to be forgotten.

When he left the house, Jerry Renwood gave way to nervousness that he had managed to repress until he walked alone. Striding along Park Avenue, he felt the fearful sensation that eyes were watching him; that somewhere, an unseen figure was stalking his path.

Until tonight, Renwood had been calm, although he had been a possible suspect in the murder of Lucian Yorne. Parlington's confession and death had cleared Renwood of all implication. It was odd, somehow, that he should feel terror now that the case of Lucian Yorne was solved.

There was an answer. Jerry Renwood had seen The Shadow. He had learned how that weird master dealt with evildoers. Jerry Renwood feared The Shadow; the reason, logically, was because Renwood held a secret of his own. Though blameless so far as Yorne's death was concerned, Renwood knew that he could be implicated otherwise.

Contempt for the law had been his motto. But he had quailed at the sight of The Shadow, who had stepped in where the law had faltered. Jerry Renwood had seen The Shadow; and deep within, he felt the sinking fear that The Shadow had seen him.

## CHAPTER V
### THE SECOND SHADOW

AT two o'clock the next afternoon, Jerry Renwood came from the doorway of a restaurant on Broadway. He spied a waiting taxicab; one look at the driver worried him. He was sure that he had seen the same man earlier that day, near the downtown brokerage office.

It was partly on account of that cab that Renwood had come uptown for lunch. He had wanted to test his hunch that he was being watched.

Renwood turned about and walked up Broadway. Looking over his shoulder, he made sure that the taxi did not turn about to keep him in sight. The cab remained stationary; but Renwood was lucky enough to spot another man who might be a follower. This stranger was a young chap who happened to stroll from the restaurant where Renwood had lunched.

Increasing his gait, Renwood thought of a hasty plan to shake off the man who was trailing him. He was on the west side of Broadway; he quickened his pace to reach the next street. There he darted into a subway entrance; pulling a nickel from his pocket, he pounded down the stairs in hope that he might gain a break.

It happened as Renwood wanted. Just as he neared the turnstile, a southbound local rattled into the station. Renwood dropped his nickel in the slot; he pushed through the turnstile and ran for the rear car. As he passed a newsstand, he suddenly changed course. Backing against the wall, he used the newsstand for cover.

Another man came through the turnstiles. It was the same fellow whom Renwood had seen coming from the restaurant. The arrival managed to squeeze aboard the local just before it started. The doors closed; the train rumbled southward. Renwood grinned as he stepped from his hiding place. This was a local stop only; the pursuer—if he was such—had taken it for granted that Renwood had boarded the train.

Still thinking of the taxi driver, Renwood dashed back through the turnstile and up the steps to the street. He ran into a frail, hunched man at the top, and nearly bowled the fellow from his feet. Mumbling an apology, Renwood resumed his dash and reached the street. There he dived into a doorway.

He was none too soon. As he peered from the obscure spot, Renwood saw the taxi that he had observed before. It was coming eastward along this one-way street. The driver had evidently made a quick trip around the block, hoping to spot Renwood somewhere.

Grinning to himself, Renwood watched the cab roll by and turn south on Broadway.

Sneaking from the doorway, Renwood remembered the man whom he had bumped on the subway steps. He threw a suspicious glance toward the subway entrance, but saw no sign of the man. Satisfied that he was no longer watched, Renwood threaded a circuitous course along various thoroughfares until he reached an old-fashioned building east of Sixth Avenue.

The door bore a sign that read: "Marimba Cafe."

RENWOOD entered. He ascended a flight of steps and came to a room that had only a few tables.

A man was seated alone; he looked up as Renwood entered. Dark-eyed, sallow-faced, the fellow delivered a suspicious glare.

"What was keeping you?" he demanded. "When I called you up, you said you would come uptown as soon as you had lunch. What's the matter with you, Jerry?"

"Nothing much, George," returned Renwood. "I—I thought I'd better get lunch uptown. That was all—"

"You could have called here. All you have to do is ask for Mr. Corbal. They'll look for me up here."

"I know. But—but—"

Corbal arose and shut the door. His eyes narrowed; his face hardened as he studied Renwood's worried countenance. Ordinarily, Renwood had an air of nonchalance that fitted with his light, well-featured face. Today, his ease was gone.

"Out with it," purred Corbal, his tone not unfriendly. "Come on, Jerry—something has taken your nerve. It can't be this Yorne business.

That was settled last night. You're in the clear, so far as that is concerned."

"I know it," acknowledged Renwood. "Just the same, I feel jittery—"

"But you didn't yesterday. So why today?"

Renwood fumbled for a cigarette. Corbal passed him one; then clapped him on the shoulder.

"Let's hear it."

"All right." Renwood nodded with an effort. "It's about Parlington. You've read the newspapers, George. Don't you think it was odd, the butler giving up just when he had the swag?"

"Yes," admitted Corbal, sourly. "And the worst part of it was that we didn't guess he had it. There you were, making friends with Yorne, so we could build up to a swindle. Along came Parlington and finished him. Kept the jewels and the gun right there in the house.

"We could have shaken Parlington for a divvy, if we'd known it. Bad business, maybe, dealing with a murderer; but he was a smooth one. Yes, it does look funny that the fellow turned things on himself. Why was he fool enough to write out that confession? Could you guess it, Jerry?"

"I saw him write it," stated Renwood, slowly. "I was watching, all the while."

"Did he look nervous?"

"Yes. He had reason to be nervous. That confession was dictated to him, George."

"Dictated? By whom?"

"By someone who was in the room with him—someone in black. Parlington called him 'The Shadow'—"

AN exclamation from Corbal. Renwood was surprised at its sharpness. It reminded him of Parlington's ejaculation.

"The Shadow," repeated Renwood. "He had the goods on Parlington. The fellow wilted. I would have, too, if I'd been him. Black cloak—slouch hat—an automatic that looked like a cannon. That describes him, George. When he spoke, his voice was a whisper—a fearful whisper that—"

"I've heard of The Shadow," interposed Corbal, as Renwood faltered. "I never met anyone, though, who had seen him. He must have a lot on the ball, to scare the daylights out of a cool card like Parlington. The fellow folded, you say?"

"Absolutely! He took it while The Shadow told him every detail of his crime. It left me woozy, George!"

"I'd like to have seen it."

"You wouldn't have forgotten it. Listen, George: After I left Yorne's, I'd have sworn that I was being tagged. Today, everywhere I've been, I've felt that eyes were watching me. A taxi driver—a man in the subway—"

"That's why you went to a different place for lunch?"

"Yes. Until I was sure I'd shaken off trailers, I was afraid to come here."

Corbal strolled about the room, eyeing his informant. At last he put a question:

"Getting cold feet, Jerry?"

Renwood nodded, though reluctantly.

"Don't want to go through with the next job?" queried Corbal. "Not anxious to help in the Garraway frame?"

"It's bad business, George," returned Renwood. "We don't deal in murder, either of us. Nor burglary, nor any regular crime. But we've staged blackmail—"

"Only when we've dealt with people who can't afford to squawk. There's no comeback from the law."

"I know that. But I've seen one different than the law. I've seen The Shadow."

"And if you saw him again, would you fold like Parlington did?"

"I don't know. I might. Anyone would."

Corbal laughed harshly. A slow hard smile appeared upon his features. At last he spoke.

"Suppose we call the Garraway job the last one," he suggested. "Make it the payoff; then travel our own ways. How would you feel about it, Jerry?"

"I'd rather quit right now."

"Suppose I can fix it so there's no comeback."

"There's still The Shadow—"

"That's what I mean—no comeback from The Shadow."

"If you're sure you can spring it, George—"

Corbal again clapped Renwood's shoulder.

"Eight o'clock tonight," he said. "You know where to meet me. At the new apartment. If you arrive ahead of me, open up the cashbox and count over the swag. That will make you feel good. Then we can talk over the Garraway deal."

"You've figured a way to pull it, George?"

"Just about. We'll talk it over when we get together. I'm going out from here by the back away. You stick around, have dinner here, then go out by the back and head for the apartment. You know you haven't been trailed here, so it's a good place to stay until after dark."

WITH that, Corbal departed. He left Jerry Renwood in a strengthened frame of mind; for his words had been persuasive.

Alone, Renwood pulled a large envelope from his pocket and took out a stack of investment literature. These papers would be useful in tonight's game. Renwood had worked his racket often, always with Corbal.

Renwood, because of his brokerage connections, served as the "blind"; actual blackmail was always staged by Corbal. That had lulled Renwood in the past, for it placed the burden on his pal. As Corbal had remarked, there had never been any "comeback." But Renwood had felt some worriment, for he had frequently supplied information to Corbal.

Through various connections, Renwood gained inklings of doubtful deals that had been worked by persons of good standing. Whenever such cases showed new developments, a trimming was in order. No one knew that Renwood was acquainted with Corbal; hence they set the stage so that Renwood would be a witness to Corbal's blackmail. Always, Renwood would soothe the victim afterward, advising him to say nothing; also promising to stand by him.

Experience had shown them that a blackmailed party would come across for the first time; but from then on, would constantly devise ways to prevent a second attempt. Hence they never played the same sucker twice.

They had gone through a fat list; the next man in line was Machias Garraway, the banker. Renwood had looked forward to this trimming. But last night, his enthusiasm had faded. Today, encouraged by Corbal's confidence, Renwood's interest was returning.

Afternoon waned. Renwood's plans were complete. The young man was nonchalant when he strolled downstairs to the cafe and ordered dinner. He sat by a front window that was heavily curtained. Peering through, he eyed the street.

A taxicab was dim beyond a street lamp. Renwood hoped that it was not the one that he had seen on Broadway.

There were few diners in the restaurant, a fact that Renwood noted with satisfaction. He saw no one who looked suspicious; nevertheless, when he left, he took the door that few persons knew about—the exit to the rear street. He walked several blocks; then became cautious as he neared a secluded apartment building.

IT was nearly eight o'clock. Darkness had brought worriment. More and more, Renwood had felt the strange fear that had gripped him the night before. The Shadow might be anywhere, Renwood decided. Perhaps he had learned of the Marimba Cafe; possibly he had discovered the rear exit and had lurked there.

Entering the apartment house, Renwood felt new terror as he ascended to the third floor. He had a key to the apartment; it was at the rear of the house. Its side windows overlooked the low roof of a garage that wedged almost to the apartment wall.

Renwood was nervous when he opened the

window and peered out into the darkness. The roof—the narrow space between the buildings—either might have held an unseen watcher.

Steadying himself, Renwood went to a corner of the living room. Stooping, he pressed a section of the baseboard. It clicked open, to reveal a cavity that contained a large metal box.

Renwood opened this container; from it, he removed stacks of currency, bundles of securities—all labeled with the names of former owners. As he counted this swag, Renwood kept darting new glances toward the window. Strained, he could think only of that menace; he gave no heed to the locked door behind him.

It was not until he heard the slight thud of a closing door that Renwood remembered the entrance. Hands filled with spoils, the crook came to his feet and spun about. Horror seized him; his face froze rigid. Renwood, indeed, became an exact copy of Parlington, as the crooked butler had been the night before.

The reason for Renwood's startlement was the same as Parlington's. Within the door stood a figure garbed in black—one whose cloak collar was high about his chin; whose hat brim, turned downward, obscured his visage. A gloved fist extended from the intruder's cloak; a steady hand gripped a leveled automatic.

In one brief instant, Jerry Renwood broke. Stolen wealth dropped from his hands; his quivering shoulders sagged. He had seen The Shadow once before; this time, he was faced by that formidable foe. Terror-stricken, the cornered crook awaited The Shadow's judgment.

## CHAPTER VI
### SPOILS TO THE VICTOR

STAMMERED words came to the lips of Jerry Renwood. Pleading, incoherent, he was begging mercy of The Shadow. Upon the floor lay proofs of crime; the spoils that he and George Corbal had gained from blackmailed victims. Renwood was ready to part with all such wealth, could he avoid the fate that had overtaken Parlington.

Renwood was not waiting for dictated terms. He was blurting all he knew; blabbing the name of Corbal; blaming all he could upon his partner in crookery. The vengeful form in black came closer. Renwood tried to back away. Quaking pitifully, he slumped to the floor, his hands raised piteously.

A harsh laugh sounded. Venomous, rather than sinister; yet the gibe had effect. To Renwood, the mere sight of The Shadow's shrouded shape had been sufficient. He expected instant flame from the looming gun muzzle. He buried his face in his hands. The laugh changed. It was raucous. Surprise made Renwood raise his head. He realized suddenly that no burning eyes were peering from beneath the hat brim. He wondered.

The slouch hat whisked backward as a gloved hand impelled it. The same hand threw aside the collar of the cloak. As the automatic lowered, Renwood saw a face he recognized. The man in black was not a strange unknown; he was Renwood's partner, George Corbal.

"YOU—you were at Yorne's last night?" Renwood sputtered the question, almost unbelieving. "You were—you were The Shadow?"

"No." Laughing, Corbal was laying aside his garments. "It was The Shadow who was there last night. The real McCoy. You gave me an idea when you spitted your story, Jerry. I rigged up this trick outfit, after I left you at the cafe. I wanted to see how it would work on you."

Renwood was losing his sheepishness. Fists clenched, he had risen from the floor. He was angered, now that his terror had passed. Corbal purred quieting words.

"Don't act sore, Jerry," he argued. "I had to spring this gag on you. I wanted to see how it would work. So you would be set for what's to come."

"You made a sap of me," interjected Renwood. "Because I was on the level; because I let you know that I was nervous—"

"Easy, Jerry. I could be peeved, too. You squawked a lot while I had you covered. Mentioned my name, as I remember. I'm willing to forget that part of it."

Renwood subsided.

"This rig is a swell idea," resumed Corbal, placing his discarded garb upon a chair. "It worked even better than I thought it would. I don't think that it would shake you, though, if you knew that I was inside it. That's why we're going to use it again tonight."

"Use it tonight?"

"Sure! After you've dropped in to see Machias Garraway!"

Renwood looked bewildered. Corbal chuckled.

"All this swag of ours," said Corbal, indicating the securities and the cash, "was plucked from people who had duped others. Garraway is just another in the crowd. You know why he wants to talk to you, Jerry. Garraway had juggled the trust funds of several estates. He switched bum stocks for good ones. He wants to unload the worthwhile paper.

"Garraway figures you're too dumb to know it. He wants to use you for a fence. Your job is to keep on playing dumb. Mine is to walk in when

**MICHIAS GARRAWAY—
banker.**

he's showing you the stuff; to tell him what it is and to make him come across. The trouble was just how to work it. I've found the answer."

"You—you're going there as The Shadow?"

"That's it! Remember that I'm the man behind this batch of crêpe and watch Garraway for your cues. Act just about half as scared as he does. Come along, Jerry—pull yourself together."

Corbal was stooping on the floor, picking up bundles of currency that Renwood had scattered. He saw his companion steady. Corbal motioned to the door.

"Slide on up to the Hotel Dothan," ordered Corbal. "You know Garraway's suite—No. 1200—and he's told you that he'd like to see you. Breeze in on him. I'll come later."

"But what about the cloak—"

"I'll put it on after I get to the twelfth floor. I'll carry one of the suitcases that we have here in the closet. It will do to lug the swag, as well."

Renwood donned hat and coat. His shaken confidence had been regained. He strolled to the door and nodded wisely as he gave a parting wave.

"I'll be there in ten minutes, George," he assured. "Waiting for you to show up. Pull the stunt as strong as you did; but make the laugh a little smoother. That's the one touch it needs."

RENWOOD made the trip in the time that he had estimated. Arrived at the Hotel Dothan, he went up to Garraway's suite. He rapped at the door. A slouchy, bald-headed man admitted him. This was Garraway, himself.

"Well, well!" greeted the banker. "So you have come to see me, Mr. Renwood! I had not expected you tonight, or I would have kept my servant here. He knows how to prepare refreshments better than I do."

"I have come on business, Mr. Garraway," returned Renwood, briskly. "About investments. I have prepared some lists that may interest you."

As they walked into the suite, Renwood pulled an envelope from his pocket. He noted that Garraway did not latch the door; that fact pleased Renwood at the outset. By the time they had reached a room that served as an office, Renwood had extracted papers from the envelope. He spread these upon the banker's desk.

"My assumption," stated Renwood, "is that you intend to purchase some substantial securities. Of course, I may be wrong. Sometimes I meet clients who wish to sell some of their own. In fact"—he paused wisely—"certain of my offerings are the property of customers whose names I never mention."

Garraway was looking over Renwood's data. Hearing the visitor's last remark, the banker raised his head.

"Do I understand," he inquired, "that you make a custom of handling such transactions? That you ask no questions; and answer none?"

"That has proven to be a good way of doing business, Mr. Garraway."

"And if you could acquire securities as sound as those that you have listed?"

"I should be glad to purchase them at a few points below the current market price."

GARRAWAY arose from his desk. He went to a safe in the corner. He handled the combination; then opened the door and brought out a narrow box. From its depths, he produced a bundle of securities.

"These should satisfy you," assured Garraway. "They happen to be some stocks that a friend of mine must sacrifice. An old friend—let us say a friend who is in difficult circumstances, one who would not care to have his name mentioned."

"I understand."

"Look them over. Confidentially, of course. Perhaps you may wish to buy some of them. Of course, if it requires too much cash, we can arrange some other method of transaction."

Garraway was rubbing his hands. He was just about to make reference to the mythical friend whom he had previously mentioned. Then, suddenly, words froze upon his lips. Renwood saw the banker stare toward the door of the little office. Catching the cue, Renwood swung about.

For the third time, he was viewing a figure cloaked in black. Knowing of the part that Corbal had planned to play, Renwood had imagined that he would need to fake startlement for Garraway's later benefit. Such pretense, however, proved unnecessary. Despite himself, Renwood felt a chill of fear.

Last night's episode with Parlington; the bluff that Corbal had staged tonight at the apartment— these had left Renwood in a jittery frame of mind. Past recollections made this spectral figure seem a living threat. The tension remained until the intruder laughed. A harshness in his mirth reminded Renwood of Corbal.

Slowly, steadily, the masquerader approached the desk. Garraway cowered before the gun muzzle. Renwood, feigning fear without great effort, heard another tone of whispered mockery. This taunt was an improvement; Corbal, apparently, had profited by Renwood's criticism. Then the intruder spoke.

"Stolen goods," he sneered, his tone smoothening as he proceeded. "Wealth that you have rifled from those who trusted you. I am The Shadow! I have come here to right a wrong! Tell me the names of those whom you betrayed." Lips quivering, Garraway confessed. He blurted names of persons; amounts of cash; the specific securities that had been transferred. All the while, he stared as though entranced, looking straight toward the black-clad inquisitor.

Renwood, standing at one side, remained motionless. "These holdings will be delivered to their owners," ordained the cloaked visitor. "I shall see that the right ones receive their property. You will do wisely, Garraway, to notify them to expect specific securities. Wise, also, if you remove the worthless paper with which you salted the trust funds.

"As for you, Renwood"—the cloaked figure wheeled—"I regard you as an accomplice of Garraway's. You are to leave this city. You are to maintain silence. If you fail to do so, you will suffer. Go, before I regret my merciful decision!"

MECHANICALLY, Renwood walked from the room, skirting wide past the figure in black. He reached the outer door; there he paused to dart a quick look over his shoulder. He could see the open doorway of the office. The figure in black was backing outward; beyond, Renwood could see Garraway.

The banker had crumpled; he was slumped upon his desk. Terror had overpowered him.

Closing the door of the suite, Renwood crossed the hall and rang for an elevator. He was still tingling when he left the lobby of the Dothan. Corbal's impersonation had been a marvel of realism. When he reached the apartment where the swag was hidden, the young man unlocked the door. Muttering to himself, he was planning the opening remarks that he intended to give when Corbal arrived.

"Great work, George!" mumbled Renwood, grinning. "You bowled out Garraway. You forced me clear of the picture. We're set to take it on the lam—before Garraway has sense enough to get wise—"

Renwood stopped short. He had opened the door; he was on the threshold of the apartment, staring into the lighted living room. On the floor lay the metal box, opened and empty. Beyond it was a sterner sight—a figure, bound and gagged, sprawled in a large chair. A man in a crumpled cloak of black, a slouch hat wedged hard upon his head.

With a cry, Renwood bounded forward. He yanked the hat from the bound man's forehead. He stared at the face beneath. Sullen eyes met Jerry Renwood's startled gaze. The helpless man in the chair was George Corbal!

IN that instant, Renwood knew the truth. His qualms about the opened window had been real ones. A watcher had lurked outside the window; one who had followed the trail from the Marimba Cafe. The Shadow had been here, a silent, invisible observer, when Corbal had first entered in his guise of black.

The Shadow had struck as soon as Renwood had gone. He had overpowered Corbal. He had taken the spoils from the metal box. It was The Shadow, not Corbal, who had followed to Garraway's. Gone, vanished, The Shadow had added Garraway's ill-gotten proceeds to the swag that Renwood and Corbal had accumulated.

Wealth would be returned to proper owners— by The Shadow. And here was the sequel to his successful exploit, a grim jest wherein one crook discovered his companion, that both might discuss the futility of crime. To murderers, The Shadow dealt death: to such schemers as Corbal and Renwood, he dealt ridicule.

Thus had The Shadow ended the masquerade of George Corbal, the man who had posed as a second Shadow. Upon it, he had allowed Jerry Renwood to return. Two crooks, deprived of spoils, had learned that their crimes did not pay.

## CHAPTER VII
## ONE MAN RETURNS

THE next morning, Jerry Renwood awoke in his old apartment; but it took him a full minute to recognize his surroundings. A deluge of scattered thoughts dominated his brain. Yorne's—the Marimba Cafe—Garraway's—the apartment where he and Corbal had kept their swag—all these formed a confused recollection. At last, he remembered releasing George Corbal; coming back here afterward.

Clear was his memory of The Shadow. A specter in black, who persisted even in daylight. Then to Renwood's ears came a repetition of the sound that had awakened him. Someone was pounding at the door of the apartment. Nervously, he donned slippers and dressing gown. He answered the summons.

A messenger was outside the door. The fellow handed Renwood an envelope and a pad to sign. Mechanically, Renwood wrote his name; then, as soon as the messenger had gone, he opened the envelope. From it, he unfolded a note that was inscribed in ink of vivid blue.

He read as follows:

> Environment aided you in crime. Therefore, my order for departure must be obeyed. Your companion in past activity will accompany you. He was the sponsor of evil deeds; it will be your part to show the way to honesty.
>
> Urge him to follow your lead. When called upon to report, do so. Good faith will be your only hope of safety. Follow instructions as you receive them. Your countersign is one word: *Black.*

There was no signature. The message did not need one. Renwood knew that it had come from The Shadow. As if in final proof, the note itself performed a mysterious deed—one that matched The Shadow's own performances. While Renwood stared, the written lines erased themselves, word by word, until blankness alone remained.

There were other papers in the envelope. Examining them, Renwood found that they were one-way tickets to San Francisco—two in number. He shoved them in the pocket of his dressing gown, then crumpled the blank paper and tossed it in the wastebasket.

The Shadow's purpose was plain. He was giving the partners in crime another chance. He was depending upon Renwood to see that Corbal went straight. Somehow, The Shadow must have looked into the affairs of the pair; for those tickets to San Francisco meant more than a mere trip.

Not long ago, Renwood had received an attractive offer of employment from a Pacific Coast bro-

kerage house. He had been asked to come West and bring along any capable man whom he might recommend. Renwood had passed up the offer at Corbal's urging; but he knew that the jobs were still open. The Shadow, too, had learned that fact.

THE telephone rang. Renwood answered it, to hear Corbal on the wire. Corbal had stayed at the apartment where they had kept the swag. This morning, he had received a mysterious telephone message, telling him to communicate with Renwood. Having given that information, Corbal said that he would arrive in fifteen minutes.

Jerry Renwood engaged in sober thought while he waited. He had formed a plan of discourse by the time George Corbal arrived. As soon as the two ex-blackmailers were together, Renwood produced the railroad tickets.

"From The Shadow," he stated. "It looks like a friendly gesture, George."

"Meaning that we're to grab those jobs in Frisco?" inquired Corbal.

"That's it," nodded Renwood. "I can fix it when we get there."

Corbal scowled.

"We'd better grab the chance," urged Renwood. "We've crossed The Shadow once. We're lucky we didn't get what Parlington did. How much money have you in the bank?"

"Five hundred bucks."

"I have about six hundred. That's eleven hundred—actually our own. Suppose we draw out the money, George. We can make a fresh start in Frisco."

"Who do you know there?"

"Only the head of the brokerage concern."

"Then we don't go to Frisco."

Renwood stared, puzzled. Corbal laughed, disdainfully.

"Maybe we did cross The Shadow," he asserted. "But what of it? Just because he piled in from the window and smeared us once is no reason that he can pull that gag again! We've lost a pile of gravy, Jerry. It's up to us to get it back."

"How? Where?"

"How? The way we did before. Where? Right here in New York."

Renwood shook his head.

"We'd be licked from the start, George," he insisted. "The Shadow has us ticketed. We've got to get out of town."

"But how can you stage the racket in Frisco? It will take you months to get acquainted well enough to build a new sucker list. If I'm in the office with you, we can't work together—"

"Not as crooks, no. But we can both make an *honest* living."

"Bah! So you've gone goody-goody, eh? Well, you've got your carfare. Beat it for Frisco if you want. But take someone else along with you."

"You mean that you'll stay here?"

"Yes. What's more, I'll play a lone hand. One that will drive The Shadow woozy! Listen, Jerry—I know a lot I haven't told you. While you've been getting the lowdown on respectable people, I've been looking into plenty of tough joints. That's how I happened to know about The Shadow."

"And now you've seen him, George. You know what he can do."

"What he can do, *I* can do!"

CORBAL eyed Renwood while making this final statement. Shrewdly, he noted the strained expression that showed upon Renwood's face. Corbal started to ask a question; then paused. Renwood spoke.

"I'm through with the racket, George," said Renwood. "I want you to drop it, too. For your own good. You showed the way when we worked crooked. Give me a chance to lead when we go straight."

Corbal nodded. His whole face had sobered. Renwood was surprised at the sudden change. He did not realize what was going on in his companion's mind.

"You're right, Jerry," declared Corbal. "Yes, you've picked the one way out of it. Let me see those tickets."

Renwood handed them over.

"Not a bad guy, The Shadow," purred Corbal. "He's staked us to the tickets. It's up to us to make the reservations. Suppose I attend to that, Jerry."

"All right."

"I'll go down to Grand Central. I'll arrange for a compartment to Chicago; another from there to San Francisco. We might as well travel comfortably. We can afford it."

Pocketing the tickets, Corbal strolled to the door. He paused.

"There's a good train out at nine o'clock tonight," he said. "I'll meet you on it, Jerry. Ask at the gate for the compartment number, if you don't see me waiting there. I may go in ahead of you."

TO Jerry Renwood, that day became a strange one. After Corbal's departure, Renwood dressed and went down to the office. He announced that he had taken the San Francisco offer; and gave up his New York job therewith. Later, he went to the bank and drew out his six hundred dollars. After that, he wired the concern in San Francisco, stating that he and another were coming to take the jobs.

Renwood had dinner at his favorite Times Square restaurant. With that farewell to Manhattan finished, he headed for Grand Central Terminal. He arrived at the train gate at quarter before nine. He asked the gate attendant if Mr. Corbal had gone aboard.

"What's your name?" came the query.

Renwood gave it. The attendant nodded. He nudged his thumb toward the gate.

"Mr. Corbal is on board," he said. "Compartment B, Car J 3. He has your ticket with him."

Renwood beckoned to the porter who was carrying his bags. As he did so, a man beside the train gate brushed against him. Renwood did not see the fellow's face. All that he heard was the word that the man whispered:

"Black!"

Renwood nodded without turning. A folded piece of paper was thrust into his hand. Ordering the porter through the gate, Renwood followed. Walking along the platform, he opened the wadded note.

He read the message:

Signal from car door. Up and down if Corbal is aboard. Across if not. If Corbal is still with you, wire if he keeps on from Chicago or decides to stop there. Address: Lenning Service, Sharon Building, New York. Expect new contact in San Francisco.

The writing faded as Renwood neared Car J 3. Renwood understood. This man who had slipped him the note must be an agent of The Shadow. One who had been on yesterday's trail. The man had been watching for Renwood, not for Corbal. He must have written the note while Renwood was talking with the man at the train gate.

Instructions from The Shadow; and Renwood was ready to follow them. Instructions without a clue, for the Lenning Service mentioned in the note was evidently a place that received telegrams and held them until the proper person called on the telephone to make inquiry. Renwood realized that he was working with The Shadow. He was pleased; for he knew that it would be to Corbal's eventual benefit.

Entering his car, Renwood reached the door of Compartment B. He started to open it; pressure blocked him. A query came in strained whisper:

"That you, Jerry?"

"Yes," replied Renwood. "What's up, George?"

"Nothing. I'll tell you later. Bring in the bags yourself. Keep the porter out."

"All right."

Renwood walked back to the platform, where the station porter was standing with the bags. He tipped the man; then waited while the porter walked away. Stepping to one side, Renwood saw a clear path to the train gate. He signaled with an up and down motion of his arm.

Corbal was aboard. That was all that Renwood had to flash. Yet he was puzzled when he walked back into the car. He could not understand Corbal's desire for secrecy. Nevertheless, Renwood stopped the car porter, just as the fellow was about to open the door of the compartment.

"I'll take the bags in."

With that remark, Renwood sent the porter on his way. Opening the door, Renwood pushed the bags into blackness. Again he heard the cautious whisper:

"Close the door before you turn on the light."

Renwood complied. When he clicked the light switch, he turned about, questioning words on his lips. He stopped short as he saw the man who was seated by the windows, backed by lowered blinds.

It was not Corbal. In his friend's stead sat a rough-faced rowdy who was holding a leveled revolver.

"Sit down!" growled the man with the gun. "Don't forget that I've got this gat. We're goin' to be friends, pal, after I've done a little talkin'; so there's no use gettin' funny!"

Renwood drew over the chair that was by the door.

"My name's Spike Gonley," grinned the thug. "George Corbal sent me in here. I've got your ticket, too, an' his, too. I'm ridin' through with you to Frisco. He ever tell you about me?"

Renwood shook his head.

"We was all set," resumed Gonley. "Goin' to knock off the joints together; with me slippin' the info to George. We figured he'd need a mob, though. While we was still waitin', George rigged up another racket. The one you worked with.

"A good pal of yours, George is. He ain't sore just because you got cold feet. He was just wise enough to know that you couldn't stand the gaff. When he talked with you this mornin', he knowed that you was ready to pull a fast one on him, because you thought it was for his good. So he switched it. Savvy?"

Renwood nodded automatically. "Spike" Gonley was looking for such a gesture. The thug grinned.

"Hit it right, didn't I?" he jeered. "Well, I'm just tellin' you what Corbal guessed. He's a smart guy, George is. What did you do—shoot a tipoff when I seen you go back to the platform?"

Renwood realized that Spike must have peered from the door of the compartment. Looking through the passage window, the thug had seen the signal. Renwood decided that partial admission would be wise.

"Yes," he stated. "I passed the word that Corbal was aboard. I thought he was."

"An' what's the gag in Chi?" demanded Gonley. "You're to send a telegram from there, huh?"

"Yes," admitted Renwood. "To the office of the Lenning Service, in the Sharon Building. Just to say that Corbal is still with me."

"He figured something like that," clucked Gonley. "An' after that—when we get to Frisco—what's the gag then? Another telegram?"

Renwood had his opening. He nodded. A jolt told that the train was starting. Spike Gonley pocketed his gun.

"We'll split, after you send that telegram from Frisco," he stated. "Until we get there, though, I'm watchin' you. Corbal says you ain't a bad guy; so we might as well be friends. Only if you try any wise stuff, it'll be curtains for you. That's why Corbal fixed it so we'd be by ourselves while we're travelin'; he knowed I could figure a getaway, if I had to plug you."

RENWOOD forced a smile. The train was gliding northward. It was too late to get word to The Shadow. Nor would there be a chance in Chicago.

Spike Gonley evidently intended to stick close, all the way. Renwood decided that the best he could do was grin. He felt a sudden, complete contempt for George Corbal.

His former pal was a criminal at heart, and Renwood knew it. Corbal had gained a fair chance to go straight. He had preferred to stay with crime. He had made his opportunity. By the time Renwood gained contact in San Francisco, Corbal would have the start he needed. That was Renwood's only regret.

For he could guess the part that Corbal intended. The same game that he had tried to play last night. Only this time, he would thrust himself into the affairs of the underworld, seeking to strike terror in the hearts of crooks upon whom he could prey.

Already, Renwood was picturing San Francisco, where he could shake loose from Spike Gonley, after sending a fake telegram. He could imagine himself speaking to some new agent of The Shadow, passing word that would be of value in the hunt for all evildoers.

Renwood was through with Corbal. He would be glad to tell the news that he had learned. He would state the truth as he was sure it must exist. For Jerry Renwood knew that George Corbal had remained in New York to continue the role that he had chosen.

Perhaps upon this very night, George Corbal was faring forth to crime, garbed as the second Shadow!

## CHAPTER VIII
## THE SHADOW LEARNS

FIVE days had passed since Jerry Renwood's departure from New York. Three nights had been quiet ones; the fourth had produced a startling event. On the streets, near the end of the fifth day, newsboys were proclaiming the sensation.

"Uxtry! Uxtry! Read more about De Shadow!"

Joe Cardona heard the shouts as he entered a building. He had finished a busy day; as a sequel, he was on his way to Commissioner Weston's office. Joe knew what the subject of discussion would surely be. This matter of The Shadow.

Cardona found Weston at his desk. The commissioner looked up when Joe was ushered in. Briskly, he told the ace to be seated. Finishing with letters that he was signing, Weston planked both hands upon the glass top of the desk and put a single word as query:

"Well?"

"About The Shadow?" asked Cardona.

"That's it," returned Weston. "He's a friend of yours, isn't he?"

"I suppose so, Commissioner. I know of others, though, who have counted on him in a pinch."

Weston nodded.

"Myself, for one," he admitted. "Yes, Cardona, we both owe The Shadow a great deal. And yet— this news today—"

"According to the newspapers," interposed Cardona, carefully, "The Shadow raided the Hilo Club and took what was on the tables. A pretty good haul, I guess. The Hilo Club was one of those places that we hadn't yet clamped down on."

"And after that?" queried Weston.

"The Shadow made a getaway," added Cardona, reluctantly. "Patrolman Jennings heard the shouts and tried to intercept him. The Shadow let him have it. Jennings is in the hospital. He may not live."

"That's just it!" Weston brought his fist down on the desk. "Cardona, we have allowed The Shadow leeway, because we believed that he opposed crime. Today, we know that he no longer deserves our loyalty. He has acted as a criminal! My order is: Bring in The Shadow!"

"It's tough about Jennings," agreed Cardona. "Yet we can't be sure that it was The Shadow who clipped him. Witnesses say they saw The Shadow fire when he reached the street—"

"If that's the case, Cardona, I'll change my present order. I want you to bring in the man who raided the Hilo Club. Bring him in dead, if you can't get him alive!"

"But that means The Shadow—"

"Does it?"

The question floored Cardona. A light came into the acting inspector's eyes. Weston had guessed an issue which, at first, had not occurred to Joe.

"I get it, Commissioner!" exclaimed the ace. "You mean that maybe it wasn't The Shadow at all! Instead, the fellow who raided the Hilo Club could have been a crook rigged up like The Shadow. Some fellow smart enough to go through with dirty work—to put The Shadow in a jam with us!"

"That is my thought, Cardona."

"If you're right, Commissioner," said Joe, "it explains a lot. For a guy named Zutz was outside man for the Hilo Club and it looks like he was bribed by the man in black. But we know The Shadow never deals with crooks.

"It is my suggestion we lay off this case temporarily, and let the other gambling places run wide open. Then we can wait for the being in black to attempt another holdup."

The commissioner pondered. Then he stated:

"Of all criminals, this unknown impostor has ventured far beyond bounds! His deed has been a deliberate challenge to The Shadow! Cardona, our policy is to keep hands off. The Shadow can take care of his own troubles. Come; let us discuss further details."

IT was an hour later when Commissioner Weston strolled into the grillroom of the Cobalt Club. Walking toward his accustomed table, he saw Lamont Cranston seated there. The millionaire smiled slightly as the commissioner joined him.

"Well, Weston," came the quiet remark, "I have suddenly dropped my aversion toward crime news. I have been reading of this latest development. Who is this person that they call 'The Shadow'?"

"He is a doubtful quantity, Cranston," replied the commissioner. "Once we thought that he sided with the law. Apparently, he has turned to crime."

"An odd circumstance. Well, at least he has shown his particular specialty. He raided the Hilo Club and came out a winner. From what I have heard, there are other places in town that should interest him."

"There are quite a few. We have been busy breaking the numbers racket. On that account, we have been slow in clamping down upon the gambling houses."

"This changes circumstances, however?"

"Not at all. On the contrary, we shall allow the gambling places to continue unmolested. Inspector Cardona made that suggestion this afternoon. He reasoned that since The Shadow has turned to crime, we might as well allow him to prove serviceable to us."

Later, when Lamont Cranston had entered his limousine, his thin lips delivered a soft laugh of whispered understanding. The Shadow had learned much through his conversation with Ralph Weston. He had divined the thoughts that were actually in the police commissioner's mind.

Two men, alone, had guessed the truth that even the underworld had not suspected. Those two were Weston and Cardona. They had reasoned that the raider at the Hilo Club had been an impersonator of The Shadow. Having conjectured that fact from Weston's guarded statements, The Shadow had also visualized the course that the law would follow.

Gambling houses would remain unclamped, in hope that the false, cloaked raider would continue his career of crime. The reason for such decision was another hope; namely, that The Shadow, himself, would take to the elusive trail and deal with the impostor.

The Shadow had learned news that he could use tonight.

ARRIVED at his sanctum, The Shadow turned on the blue light. He opened envelopes that he had picked up at an obscure office on the way. One contained a telegram signed "Crofton." It was from San Francisco and it had been sent to a New York investment broker named Rutledge Mann. The telegram discussed securities; but The Shadow interpreted its meaning.

Miles Crofton, The Shadow's contact agent in San Francisco, had contacted Jerry Renwood, to learn that George Corbal had not left New York. This, however, was news that The Shadow had already guessed. Since last night, he had been working on the assumption that Corbal was still the second Shadow.

A tiny bulb glittered from the wall as The Shadow drew earphones across the table. The Shadow was putting in an automatic telephone call. A voice responded:

"Burbank speaking."

"Report!"

"Report from Marsland. Watching the Club Torreo. Hawkeye had trailed Jake Lassop, lookout due on duty at eight o'clock. Jake made two phone calls."

"Report received. Further reports."

"Report from Vincent. Will be inside Club Torreo at eight o'clock."

"Report received. Instructions will follow."

A weird laugh chilled the sanctum. The Shadow had already gained results. Through Cliff Marsland, an agent who knew the underworld, he had checked on the disappearance of Zutz, the lookout who had been at the Hilo Club. The Shadow, like Joe Cardona, had figured how his imitator had worked.

Hawkeye was a spotter who worked with Cliff. In fact, Hawkeye was the little hunched-up man who had bumped Jerry Renwood at the top of the subway stairs the day he thought he was being followed. Hawkeye was a useful trailer; he had scored another hit. The Shadow had picked the Club Torreo as the next spot that a raiding masquerader would choose. Hawkeye had already gained suspicions concerning Jake Lassop, one of the Club Torreo's lookouts.

A GAMBLING house deluxe, the Club Torreo was difficult to enter. Yet Harry Vincent, an agent of The Shadow, had managed to fix it for himself. He had done this through Clyde Burke, a reporter who also served The Shadow. Thus Harry would be inside; Cliff and Hawkeye outside.

The Shadow knew George Corbal to be a man who had more nerve than cunning. Somewhere in Manhattan, the fellow had a hideout. From it, he would fare forth to further crime, impelled by his success at the Hilo Club. Crooks would not stop him; they were worried, for the present. Thinking that The Shadow himself had turned to crime, they had not guessed that a repeat performance would be next in order.

Corbal, perhaps, had figured out that much. But The Shadow knew that the rogue would be in the dark regarding moves intended by the law. He analyzed Corbal as a man who would be lulled by ignorance.

The Shadow, however, had wanted to know the plans of the police. If the law was ready to down the impostor, the law could have Corbal. If not, he would be The Shadow's quarry.

Through casual conversation with Commissioner Weston, The Shadow had learned the law's intention. Weston did not know that The Shadow passed as Lamont Cranston; nor had he guessed that through talking with his fellow club-member, he had passed the word to The Shadow.

Yet Weston had done exactly that. He had indicated fully that the law was counting on The Shadow.

Tonight, George Corbal would move to new attack. In turn, The Shadow would be present. Corbal had one aide: Jake Lassop. The Shadow would have three: Vincent, Marsland and Hawkeye. What Corbal thought would be a setup could well be turned into a trap.

The light clicked out within the sanctum. Silence thickened with The Shadow's departure. Tonight was a time for action; a potential murderer must be thwarted in new crime. Such was The

Shadow's purpose. The way was clear to end the menace of the second Shadow.

Yet no one—not even The Shadow—could foresee the episode that this night would bring. New freaks of chance were in the making. Crime was to take a new, more startling twist. All through the sudden loss of nerve by a man whose part was small.

Jake Lassop, traitorous lookout at the Club Torreo, was the minor factor whose action was to bring about strange consequences.

## CHAPTER IX
## THE MAN FROM HAVANA

IT was close to eight o'clock. Business was brisk at the Club Torreo. A gambling joint was clicking merrily on the floor above a pretentious nightclub. Visitors were subjected to close scrutiny. No trouble was expected.

Within a secluded office, two men were engaged in conference. One was "Duke" Hydon, the bearded proprietor of the Club Torreo. The other was a tall, sharp-featured man whose presence Hydon regarded as an honor. Small wonder, for the visitor held a reputation in the world of gambling. He was "Sparkler" Meldin, lately of Havana.

Sparkler deserved his nickname. The man had a flare for jewelry. Brilliant gems glittered from his finger rings; in his necktie, he wore an old-fashioned stickpin with a diamond that reflected like a spotlight. Only his teeth lacked gems; they shone with plain golden glimmer whenever Sparkler grinned.

"So you'll sell the joint?" Sparkler was quizzing. "Well, I ought to be glad to hear you say that, Duke. But I'm not."

"Why not?" queried Hydon in feigned surprise. "You just told me you wanted to buy."

"So I did. Revolutions have shot the racket in Cuba. But this place of yours is paying plenty, Duke. There's only one reason why you'd feel like selling it. The police."

Duke shook his head.

"You've got the wrong idea, Sparkler," he declared. "The racket is still good; and will be. But the grind is tough. It takes somebody who is known—like yourself."

"Nobody knows me in New York."

"They know who you are. That's enough. The best customers are scared for fear that joints are phony. There's been squawks about fixed roulette wheels, paying too big a percentage to the houses. What they want is a chance that they think is as good as Monte Carlo. If you take over the Club Torreo, the news will spread around that it's on the level. I'm putting you straight, Sparkler—"

DUKE broke off as someone knocked at the door. He nodded to Sparkler. The pair arose. They went to the door and Duke opened it. A square-faced, beady-eyed man was standing there.

"What is it, Lassop?" demanded Duke. "Why aren't you covering the lookout?"

"The man I relieve is still there, Mr. Hydon. I thought I'd better speak to you before I went on duty."

"All right. Go ahead."

"But"—looking at Meldin—"I'd like to talk privately—"

"It's all right; this gentleman can hear what you say."

Lassop eyed Sparkler Meldin. The man from Havana met his gaze with shrewd eyes. Lassop twitched nervously; then spoke to Duke Hydon.

"It's just a crazy hunch, maybe," he said, "but I can't get rid of it. I'm worried—about The Shadow. He knocked off the Hilo Club last night."

"What if he did?"

"Well—it means that he may be coming here. I've heard a lot of talk about the way The Shadow pulled that job last night."

"You mean about Louie Zutz? The lookout? The fellow who sold out to The Shadow?"

"Zutz wasn't phony. They say he was a good guy. The Shadow knocked him off. At least, that's what a lot of birds think."

Duke Hydon was stroking his bearded chin; his eyes glared toward Jake Lassop.

"So you're turning yellow, eh?" jeered the proprietor. "Afraid that maybe you'll be next? Well, that's settled, Jake. You won't be. You're fired! I'll put one of the table men on lookout, down at the side door tonight."

"You've got the wrong slant, boss," pleaded Lassop. "You'll only be putting another guy in the same jam that I'd be in. I don't want to crawl out of duty. What I want is somebody with me. Then if The Shadow does show up, there'll be two of us to handle him.

"What's more"—Lassop's beady eyes were shrewd—"it ain't fair to throw too much on one guy. Suppose The Shadow does get past him? What then? I'll tell you. They'll be saying the same things that some wise mugs have said about Louie Zutz—that stuff about going over to The Shadow."

Duke Hydon's expression changed.

"So that's the trouble, eh?" he demanded. "Why didn't you say it in the first place? Sure—you can have another fellow with you. Both of you will be inside the door. Besides that, there's the street man—"

"He doesn't stay too close. He's usually half a block away, keeping an eye out for dicks."

"He'll be near enough if you need him in a pinch. All right, Jake—you're hired again. Stick here, and I'll send one of the table men to join you."

DUKE HYDON walked away, with Sparkler Meldin following. Jake Lassop watched them turn a corner and approach the gambling tables. Apparently Duke intended to show his visitor some of the features of the gaming place. Tensely, Jake entered the office and closed the door behind him.

"Calakor."

Jake whispered this odd word, as he approached the desk. Taking paper and pencil, he printed the letters in sprawling fashion. Picking up the telephone, he began to dial. But instead of using numbers, he referred to the letters that he had written.

"C-A-L-" Jake mumbled in an undertone "-A-K-O-R—"

A turn of the dial with each letter. Jake listened; a bell was ringing over the wire. But no one answered. Jake darted a glance toward the door; then concentrated on the telephone. As he did this, his elbow brushed the sheet of paper. Lazily, it floated from the desk, fluttered over and over and finally landed near the door, the printed letters upward.

Jake did not notice the paper's fall, nor did he see the door as it opened inward. A sharpish face peered into the room. The light caught the glitter of a diamond stickpin. Sparkler Meldin had returned to Duke Hydon's office.

Shrewdly, the man from Havana had guessed that Jake Lassop was up to something.

Sparkler was just in time to note the falling paper. Looking downward, he read the odd word "Calakor." He watched Jake; he saw the beady-eyed lookout hang up the receiver.

Jake was impatient while he waited to make the call again. Sparkler saw him peer about for the paper. Wisely, the Havana big shot edged back from the door.

When he looked again, Sparkler saw that Jake had found the paper. Jake was referring to it as he dialed. Sparkler guessed the game. Jake was calling someone who had not entrusted him with an actual telephone number. Instead, that person had transcribed the number into letters, by reference to a telephone dial, and had thus produced the word "Calakor."

This time, Jake received an answer. Sparkler listened intently to the lookout's conversation. Though he was hearing only one end of the talk, the man from Havana learned much.

"Listen, pal"—Jake was talking tensely. "It's going to be a giveaway if I let you through, like Zutz did at the Hilo... Sure, I could take it on the lam, but that would queer your racket. No, no! I ain't pulling out. I told Gonley I'd go through with it... Only they'd have me ticketed, and it would be tough for both me and Zutz, wherever he is...

"Listen, here's our out... Yeah, a way to work it better... The old elevator, up from the basement... Yeah, the service car—it's supposed to be on the fritz, but it ain't... I found it out this afternoon... It's your bet...

"I'll be at the side wicket, another lookout with me. Get it? An alibi for me, to fool Duke... Sure! That's it... If you have to make a break for it, I'll stick by when you scram through the side door. But lay off unless there's no other out...

"It ought to be a pip... Sure! All the tough mugs will think that you're The Shadow. There won't be many of them around, anyway... The front door? Don't worry about it... Yeah, the guy that covers it is downstairs with the headwaiters, working outside... Sure... Anytime..."

SPARKLER guessed that the telephone call was ending. He drew back from the door, closing it softly. He stepped out toward the gaming room and arrived there just as one of the roulette operators left his place and started for the office. This was the table man whom Duke had promised to Jake.

With sidelong glance, Sparkler saw Jake Lassop come from the office, just in time to meet the roulette operator. The two went toward a stairway at the side of the gaming room. Sparkler watched them descend.

He strolled to the office. Opening the door, he noted a curl of smoke coming from the interior of a tall ashtray. Jake had burned the paper on which had been written the word "Calakor."

For a moment, Sparkler Meldin looked toward the telephone, as if wondering what might happen should he call the cryptic number represented by the word "Calakor." Then a shrewd smile came over the big shot's darkened features. Turning about, the man from Havana went out to the gaming room.

Always an opportunist, Sparkler Meldin saw a chance that might work to his advantage. He knew that he had nothing to lose; perhaps he would find gain through coming developments. Sparkler had offered to buy Duke's gambling joint, here above the Club Torreo; but it was not the only spot that he had considered as a possible purchase.

Trouble tonight might kill the Club Torreo. On the contrary, it might lead to a lower purchase price. Those were possibilities that Sparkler Meldin studied. But there was another factor that impressed him even more. Sparkler had heard of last night's raid at the Hilo Club, even before Jake Lassop had mentioned it. Like others, Sparkler had believed that The Shadow had done the job.

He had learned that such was not the case. Chance had put Sparkler Meldin "in the know." He had uncovered a fact that would have startled all gangdom; the very one that Commissioner Weston and Joe Cardona were keeping to themselves. A fake Shadow was at large; a second worker garbed in black; a rogue who was trading on a master's reputation and damaging it.

Here was a chance to see the game in progress. Sparkler Meldin had heard of the awe that The Shadow could create. He had attributed it to The Shadow's own power; not to mere nerve, coupled with a guise of black. Though most of the customers in the Club Torreo were persons not engaged in crime, Sparkler could see a few toughs among them.

Would those ruffians wilt at the sight of an imitation Shadow? It would be worthwhile knowing. So Sparkler Meldin reasoned, as he looked about and located an obscure door in a front corner of the compact gambling room.

The door was a sliding one; obviously the entrance to the little-used elevator shaft. Shrewdly, Sparkler posted himself where he could watch it; and at the same time, he chose a spot that was near a little alcove. A good place to duck if heavy trouble started.

No word to Duke Hydon or any other. Sparkler Meldin intended to play as dumfounded as all the rest. To himself, he kept repeating a word that might be useful later. "Calakor"—the cryptic key that Jake Lassop had written, then destroyed.

Jake Lassop, through his failing nerve, had been the instrument through which a new factor had entered the game. Unwittingly, he had put Sparkler Meldin wise. Coolly, the man from Havana was awaiting the arrival of the second Shadow.

## CHAPTER X
## SHADOWS OF NIGHT

DOWN at the side entrance to the Club Torreo, two men were standing by a half-open door. One was Jake Lassop; the other was the roulette operator whom Duke Hydon had posted with the lookout. Jake was explaining matters.

"The street man's around here somewhere." Jake spoke nervously. "His job is to watch for dicks. He'll stop by, every now and then, to let us know he's on the job."

"How does he do that?"

"Four short raps, like this." Jake tapped his knuckles against the woodwork. "That means O.K.; if he repeats, it means he wants to say something. Then we open the door for him."

"What if he spots the bulls?"

"Two raps. Quick ones. Then we pass the word upstairs to duck the outfits. Duke can stow the wheels before the coppers bust into the joint."

"What about the front way?"

"That's safe. They'd have to go through the nightclub. The headwaiters would shoot the word through fast. Not a chance for anyone to barge through there."

"Anyone? You mean the bulls?"

Jake considered the question; then spoke in a hoarse whisper.

"The bulls?" he repeated. "Well, ordinarily, I'd say they might be the only guys who'd want to crash this joint. But tonight, it's different. You heard about the Hilo Club, didn't you?"

"Sure! Who hasn't? They say The Shadow knocked off that joint."

"He did. And there's a chance The Shadow may breeze in here. That's why there's two of us on the job. We'll be careful about who we let come in."

"How do you know when a customer shows up?"

"One rap—then two. If he repeats, we open the peekhole. There's enough light to spot a guy's mug. If he's all right, we let him through."

Jake was right in his reference to the light. Though the doorway where the pair stood was dark, a street lamp threw a mellow glow to the inner edge of the sidewalk. Beyond that were dusky spots; it was from one of these that a strolling man emerged. He darted a glance at the doorway as he passed. He gave a nod when he saw Jake.

"The street man," said the lookout to the roulette operator. "Everything's all right. Come on; we'll move in and close the door."

WHILE Jake was speaking, the muffled sound of voices was audible from above. It was the noise of chatter in the gaming room, that came continually to the lookout post. The sound hushed when the barrier closed.

A figure stirred from blackness. Close against the wall, it emerged into the edge of light. A black arm raised in signal to watchers across the street. Then, as silently as it had appeared, the phantom figure faded back against the wall. Its brief appearance had been ghostlike; so was its evanishment.

This shape had been no impostor. Only The

Shadow could have lurked in such narrow space of darkness. Only he could have approached so close to the conversing men; and The Shadow alone could have avoided the gaze of the stealthy street man.

The Shadow's purpose here was plain. He knew the arrangement of the Club Torreo.

The Shadow had expected to find Jake Lassop on side door duty. He knew that this would be the logical spot through which George Corbal would enter. Close at hand, The Shadow was ready to intercept his imitator. He had also provided for others to be present to take away Corbal if The Shadow found it necessary to deal with Jake or the street man.

Cliff and Hawkeye were across the street, hiding in an alleyway beside a darkened building. It was to them that The Shadow had signaled. His motion meant that the stage was set. The aides were to be in readiness. For The Shadow could already see possible complications. Jake Lassop usually performed lone lookout duty. Tonight, he had a companion.

Though familiar with the interior of the gambling hall above the Club Torreo, The Shadow did not know full details. He had not learned that the old elevator was still in operation; hence he considered the side door to be Corbal's lone way of entry and departure. Concentrated upon that assumption, The Shadow was considering Jake Lassop's position.

Alone, the lookout could easily pass Corbal through. With a companion, Jake would have to stage a bluff; and a good one. True, he could let Corbal—as the false Shadow—cow himself and the extra lookout; but once Corbal continued up to the gambling room, Jake would have difficulties.

The only out that The Shadow could see would be for Jake openly to turn traitor and cover his companion. That would do while Corbal was rifling the joint. Then, making a getaway, Corbal could shoot down Jake's companion, thus eliminating the only witness to Lassop's treachery.

Did Corbal have the nerve for such a game? The Shadow decided that he had. Last night, Corbal had used a gun to drop a patrolman. He had branded himself a man of murderous intent.

From now on, he would shoot to kill, whenever occasion called. The Shadow had dealt with others of Corbal's ilk. He knew their ways when they had tasted blood. Hence The Shadow waited in darkness, confident that Corbal would stage his raid, despite the fact that Jake might have warned him that a second lookout would be posted. In their conversation, neither Jake nor the other man had mentioned that Jake himself had called for a companion. That vital fact would have been a tipoff to The Shadow. Unfortunately, it had not reached him.

UPSTAIRS, business was brisk. Duke Hydon's place, though small, was large enough for two roulette tables. Both were working at full capacity. Men and women, all in evening attire, were flooding the boards with stacks of currency. Duke Hydon's stakes were high. He called for cash, not chips.

Standing near one table was a keen-faced young man who watched the players as well as the play. This was Harry Vincent, agent of The Shadow. Harry was sizing up the crowd.

As yet, he had seen no one who resembled George Corbal. Though he knew the man by description only, Harry was sure that he could spot him. Corbal's absence was proof that the crook intended to crash through from the outside. Hence there was no reason for Harry to seek contact with The Shadow.

Harry was interested also in watching any thuggish customers. There were a few about the tables; these were fellows who might figure, if gunplay broke loose. There was one man, however, whom Harry scarcely noticed. That was Sparkler Meldin, standing in his corner.

The big shot from Havana had arrived quietly in New York. No one here had recognized him. Duke Hydon, busy with the customers, had not had time to chat again with Sparkler. Though Harry did observe Sparkler's flashing jewelry, he did not grasp its significance. He took the tuxedoed big-shot for a customer who was awaiting a chance to play roulette.

Only Sparkler was watching the elevator door. He was the sole person who saw its slight tremble. Calmly, the big shot waited. He spotted eyes that were peeking through to study the roulette tables. Then the door slashed open with a clatter.

A man in black bounded out. From the folds of a high-tucked coat collar, the intruder delivered a harsh, almost snarling laugh.

To Sparkler, the imposture was plain. That hurried spring was a giveaway that this could not be The Shadow. The laugh, too, sounded false. The high-raised collar, the low-jammed slouch hat, seemed part of a masquerade.

Others, however, had not turned in time to see Corbal's anxious leap. The discrepancies of attire were overlooked by them, and so was the oddity of the laugh. For this false Shadow had actually brought startlement by the suddenness of his entry. More than that, he was ready with two automatics by the time the players turned.

"HANDS up!" snarled the intruder. "Hands

up—and keep them up! Back away from the tables!" Sparkler Meldin acted with the others. When he raised his hands, he spread them palms forward. Only the plain gold of his jeweled rings was visible.

The cloaked impostor could not see the gems behind Sparkler's fingers. Nor could he spy the glitter of the huge stickpin. Sparkler covered it by hunching his shoulders upward and lowering his long chin to the bottom of his neck.

The pretender who wore the guise of The Shadow was quick to size up troublemakers in the room. He had eyed them from the elevator shaft; with both guns, he was motioning certain men into a huddled group. The few thuggish customers lined up beside Duke Hydon.

Awkwardly, the false Shadow poked one automatic beneath his cloak. Sparkler Meldin observed the clumsiness of the move; but others were still too bewildered to catch it. All except Harry Vincent. He knew who the impostor must be.

Silence held the room in its grip as Corbal stalked forward to the tables and began to gather up cash with his gloved left hand. He was hasty, almost fumbling; yet nervy enough to make his bold game pass.

Harry Vincent strained, a dozen feet away. He wanted to spring upon Corbal; but he withheld himself.

He knew that the fellow might go wild with his one gun. A barrage of frantically pumped shots could injure helpless patrons of the gambling room. It was best to wait for a better moment of action.

Particularly because Harry had a confident feeling that The Shadow, even though tricked, would arrive before Corbal made his getaway. Hence Harry waited, watching the black-clad rogue unscramble thousands of dollars from the green squares of the roulette layout.

DOWN at the side door of the Club Torreo, two men had noted the sudden hush that had begun above. Jake Lassop had been the first to sense it. Wisely, he had said nothing. But his companion, ordinarily a croupier at one of the roulette tables, had been thinking in terms of cash upstairs. The lack of buzz impressed him.

"What's gone haywire?" he questioned. "They've quit playing. Maybe we'd better go up and find out what's happened!"

"Not a chance," snapped Jake, quickly. "We're lookouts. We belong down here."

"One of us can go up. You stick here while I—"

"No, no! We *both* belong here."

"But maybe the joint's been raided from the front. I'm going up!"

The croupier pulled a revolver from his pocket. Jake sensed instant complications. He knew that the false Shadow was at work. Moreover, he believed that the man would make a getaway through the elevator. Jake decided to work hard to keep his alibi.

"Hold it," he said, gripping his companion's arm. Jake drew a revolver of his own. "We'd better tip off the street man. Wait until I see if he's around."

Jake opened the door and peered out. He came back, shaking his head. He closed the door and locked it.

"No sign of him," he stated. "That means that everything's all right. The street man would have come here to tip us, if there'd been a front raid."

OUTSIDE, a figure was gliding from the darkness of the wall, close beside the door. The Shadow had seen Jake Lassop bob into view. That, however, was not all that The Shadow had noted. Though the door had been opened for brief seconds only, The Shadow had detected the lack of distant buzz. He knew that a hush had fallen in the upstairs gambling room.

Approaching the door, The Shadow gave four short raps. He waited a moment; then repeated the signal. With his other hand, he was flashing a sign to his aides across the street. Against the door, The Shadow formed a blotted outline, his shape revealed by the street lamp.

The door swung inward. Jake had heard the signal. He thought it was the street man wanting to say something. He welcomed this opportunity to stall and help his alibi. Close beside Jake was the croupier; both men were holding their revolvers.

The Shadow stepped back instantly; from his cloak, he whisked a brace of automatics.

"The Shadow!"

Jake gasped the recognition. Startled to helplessness, he knew that this was the genuine cloaked master. His game was up; so was that of the impostor whom he served. At that moment, Jake—like the goggle-eyed croupier—was incapable of action.

Then came a break. The Shadow wheeled; his guns uncovered the two men before him.

The answer came lunging from the dark. It was the soft-footed street man, springing forward with leveled revolver. Coming back from the corner, the fellow had spied The Shadow. But he had not been stealthy enough to complete a surprise attack. The Shadow dropped as the street man aimed the revolver. While the fellow faltered with the trigger, The Shadow lunged forward, upward. Locking with the attacker, he sent the outside man sprawling sidewise. The fellow rolled to the wall, his revolver clattering from his grasp. The Shadow wheeled and dived straight into the doorway. The croupier, jabbing forward, was the first to meet him. The Shadow jammed the man's gun arm upward; despite the thrust, the fellow offered resistance.

Jake Lassop scrambled for the stairway. He clattered upward, wildly hoping to give the alarm. He glanced madly downward, to see the croupier's body spinning about like a dummy figure. He saw The Shadow loom forward, heading for the steps. Jake made a last, terrified dive for upstairs safety.

Cliff and Hawkeye had come from across the street. Cliff had overpowered the street man while the fellow was snatching up his lost gun. Hawkeye piled upon the dazed croupier, who was sprawled across the doorway. Neither prisoner realized fully who their conqueror had been. Both helpless men were staring at new faces; those of Cliff and Hawkeye.

JAKE LASSOP had reached the head of the stairway just in time to witness the beginning of a departure. Corbal had gathered up the swag. He had backed almost to the door of the elevator. A lone gun loomed from his right hand; his left was filled with crumpled, pilfered currency. He still held those before him at bay.

But Jake's arrival forced a change.

Instinctively, many persons turned toward the sound of the clatter. Like Corbal, they saw the wide-eyed lookout waving his revolver, ready to shout out news.

"The Shadow!" screamed Jake. "The Shadow! He's—"

As Jake shouted, Harry Vincent saw George Corbal aim. With a quick lunge, Harry dived straight for the elevator, to snatch down the impostor's gun arm.

Harry was too late. Corbal pumped two shots as he arrived.

Jake Lassop sprawled; his writhing ceased as Harry grappled hard with Corbal. The crook managed a swing with his gun. His heavy gun fist clipped the side of Harry's head and sent The Shadow's agent to the floor just outside the elevator.

But Corbal took no advantage of his chance to riddle Harry. Instead he threw the money to the floor of the elevator and tugged at the door with his left hand, while his right aimed and pumped new shots rapidly toward the stairs.

Corbal had guessed who would be close behind Jake Lassop. Those shots were meant for The Shadow; and the sizzling bullets nearly gained their mark. For, as Corbal opened angled fire, he alone saw a cloaked shape weave into view.

The Shadow dropped. Head and shoulders alone revealed, he was just below the line of Corbal's hasty fire. In slipping downward, The Shadow lost his own chance for immediate gun-work. It was not until he had gained entrenchment that he had opportunity to use an automatic. Then his .45 boomed its answering message.

The Shadow's opening came just as the elevator door clanged shut. A stream of rapid bullets mashed the steel barrier. The delayed slugs were too late. Corbal was on his way to safety. He had left one victim behind him: Jake Lassop, the man who could have blabbed.

THOSE in the gaming room heard The Shadow's shots. They thought that another lookout had fired them; for they could not see The Shadow, because of the stairway's angle. Harry Vincent's bold attempt to grab the false Shadow had also shown the intruder to be vulnerable.

With mad accord, the huddled men beside Duke Hydon began to come to action. Yanking revolvers, they fired useless shots against the closed door of the elevator shaft.

"Try to head him off!" roared Duke. "Down through the side door—down through the front—around the block! Anywhere—" The Shadow had headed down the stairway while Duke was beginning his order. Sweeping out into darkness, he hissed an order to his aides.

Cliff and Hawkeye had shoved their prisoners into a doorway; hearing The Shadow's command, the two agents followed him. The Shadow led the way through a darkened alley that extended to the next street.

The roar of a departing car echoed from beyond. The Shadow and his agents reached their goal too late. A sparkling taillight twinkled around a corner, almost a block away. George Corbal, the second Shadow, had made his getaway; once again, he had left murder in his wake.

When pursuers arrived from the Club Torreo, they found no trace of the pretender who had raided the gambling lair. Duke Hydon's strong-armed men ducked their revolvers when patrol cars appeared upon the scene. Stating that they were patrons of the downstairs nightclub, they urged the officers to join in the search.

The quest was futile. No clue remained to tell of the invader's getaway, though officers scoured the entire area. And in their search for the false Shadow, they found no sign of the real. The neighborhood was vacant.

First to be balked, The Shadow and his agents had departed from the terrain. Their score with George Corbal was one that would require later settlement.

## CHAPTER XI
## A BIG SHOT PLANS

TWENTY-FOUR hours had elapsed since the affray at the Club Torreo. New headlines had gripped the front pages of the New York dailies. Again, the supposed activities of The Shadow had created a sensation. Yet a strange note of doubt had been forced upon the press.

Commissioner Ralph Weston had refused to admit that The Shadow existed. Wisely, Weston had refrained from giving the real reason for his statement; namely, his belief that The Shadow was not involved in crime. Instead, he had pretended the opinion that he had once held, long ago: that The Shadow—in name and in appearance—was merely an alias for some unknown person.

Until an actual identity could be given to the black-cloaked marauder, Weston was unwilling to declare a policy. At first, the press had stormed; then one newspaper had swung to the commissioner. That sheet was the *Classic,* on which Clyde Burke served as a reporter. Secretly an agent of The Shadow, Clyde had urged such procedure; and he had won his point.

Usually, other journals did not follow the example of the *Classic;* for it was a tabloid of yellow dye. In this instance, however, the other newspapers showed a trend toward the lead that the *Classic* had instituted. When a sensational daily turned conservative, editors suspected that something lay behind the actual news. Thus the soft pedal was applied to mention of The Shadow.

THIS day had been a difficult one for The Shadow. Counting heavily upon Clyde Burke, he had ordered the reporter to keep in constant touch through Burbank. Late in the afternoon, Clyde had shot through an unexpected report—one that caused The Shadow to form an immediate cause of action, for it concerned a man who had been present at the Club Torreo. Because of the tip that Clyde had gained, The Shadow appeared at the Cobalt Club, in the guise of Lamont Cranston. The time of his arrival was exactly eight o'clock.

The Shadow did not have long to wait. At ten minutes past the hour, a sharp-faced man entered the lobby of the club. Well-attired, brisk in manner, the visitor gave his name to the doorman. The attendant shook his head.

"Sorry, sir. We have orders that no one is to see Commissioner Weston even—"

Feigning the leisurely manner of Cranston, The Shadow sauntered forward. He eyed the sharp-faced man, then delivered a half-drawled exclamation.

"Sparkler Meldin!" ejaculated The Shadow. "Am I right?"

The arrival turned about. He nodded; his smile showed a gold-toothed gleam. He was puzzled by the face before him; yet he was pleased to know that he had found an acquaintance here. The Shadow extended his hand.

"Lamont Cranston is my name," he stated. "I met you in Havana, Meldin. Quite a fine place you had there. What are you doing in New York? Why, of all places, have you picked the Cobalt Club for a visit?"

"I want to see Commissioner Weston," returned Meldin. "I dogged his office all day. He wouldn't let me talk to him. So I came here, because some reporter told me that I might find the commissioner at the Cobalt Club."

"So you will." The Shadow nodded approval to the doorman. "Come along with me, Meldin. We shall find the commissioner in the grillroom. He is a friend of mine. Let me make the introduction."

THE friendship between Weston and Cranston was due for a severe strain. It came when The Shadow arrived in the grillroom accompanied by Meldin. One look at gleaming teeth and diamond stickpin told Weston who the arrival was. The commissioner began to storm.

"I don't want to talk to you, Meldin—"

The Shadow interposed.

"One moment, Commissioner," he remarked, in the calm tone of Cranston. "I promised to introduce Mr. Meldin to you. Really, he is a man of keen perception. I understand that he was present at the Club Torreo, last night."

"I know all about that," blustered Weston. "I have full reports on what happened at the place. If Sparkler Meldin thinks that he can tell me facts about this raider who calls himself 'The Shadow,' he will be wasting time—"

"That is not Meldin's purpose," interposed The Shadow. He gave a steady, knowing gaze to the Havana gambler. "I think, Commissioner, that you will be surprised when you hear this gentleman's actual business."

Weston subsided suddenly. Meldin grinned and nodded his thanks to The Shadow. He drew up a chair and sat down across from Weston. The Shadow's cue proved to be more than mere conjecture. Sparkler *did* have something else to talk about.

"Commissioner," he stated, "I want to open a nightclub, here in New York. A place to be known as the Casino Havanola. I needed to see you, in order to gain your approval."

"What an absurdity!" exclaimed Weston. For the moment, he was totally astonished. "A gambling establishment? Here in New York? It would be in defiance of the law!"

"You heard me wrong, Commissioner. I said a nightclub."

"Run by an outlaw, like yourself?"

"An outlaw?" Meldin's tone was suave. "Pardon me, Commissioner—the term is unwarranted. I have never defied the law."

"You ran a gambling place in Havana—"

"Where gambling was legal. You forget, perhaps, that I also had a nightclub in Miami—one, by the way, that was given a perfect rating as a place free from gambling. Moreover, it was an establishment where racketeers were never welcome."

Weston pondered. These facts impressed him. He looked at The Shadow. He asked: "Is this true, Cranston?"

The Shadow nodded.

"Perhaps I have been too hasty," decided the commissioner. "Yes, Meldin, I suppose that you can have a permit. After all, there is no record against you."

"None whatever," returned Sparkler. "The fact is simply this, Commissioner. At present, business is hopeless in Havana. The city is too disturbed by political troubles."

"Very well. Come to my office in the morning."

"One other point, Commissioner. About Duke Hydon, who ran the Club Torreo—"

"His place cannot stay open. We have sufficient evidence to close it. The Club Torreo is finished!"

"A good decision. I did not intend to ask you to permit its future operation. I merely wanted to know if I could hire Duke to work for me. I shall need a manager for the Casino Havanola—to open the place while I am absent. I must go to Cuba, to complete some business."

Once again, Sparkler Meldin had scored a surprise hit. Again, Weston gave agreement.

"Very well," decided the commissioner. "If you can show Duke Hydon the path to an honest living, I shall have no objection. My proviso, though, is that he shall have no financial interest in the business."

"None whatever. Thank you, Commissioner. And you, Mr. Cranston."

Wholeheartedly, Sparkler extended his hand. With a bow, he turned and walked from the grillroom.

WESTON twisted the points of his mustache: then glared at The Shadow.

"This was your doing, Cranston," he chided. "What did you bring the fellow in here for?"

"You had a right to refuse him," returned The Shadow, calmly.

"Perhaps," said Weston, sourly. "But he, too, has some rights; and Meldin is smart enough to know them. After all, the man has no court record against him. He could obtain an injunction—or try to get one—preventing the police from refusing him a license."

"He did not state so."

"Because he preferred to be friendly. He wanted a favor: that matter about Duke Hydon. So I granted it on policy. But we shall keep an eye on this new nightclub. You're leaving, Cranston? Well, we shall see each other later. When you have no new friend to introduce."

Weston was chuckling over his little jest when The Shadow strolled away. The commissioner did not observe the smile that appeared upon the thin lips of the supposed Lamont Cranston. This interview had developed certain possibilities that had been to The Shadow's liking. There was reason for his prompt departure. He intended to learn the sequel of Sparkler Meldin's interview with Weston.

THIRTY minutes later, The Shadow arrived at the Club Torreo. The gay night palace was glittering no longer. It had been closed by police order. Tables and furnishings had been removed. Two watchmen were on duty. They failed, however, to see the blackened shape that entered through the unlocked door. The Shadow had donned garb of black.

The front way to the second floor was open. Silently, The Shadow ascended. He reached the darkened gambling room. He saw a glimmer of a light beyond. Advancing, The Shadow reached the door of the office. It was ajar; the sound of voices reached The Shadow's ears.

"I'll fix it all tomorrow, Duke." The tone was Sparkler Meldin's. "The place—the time of opening—the personnel. You had a tough break here last night. As manager of the Casino, you'll receive a percent on the take. A chance to make a comeback."

"But it will go against us, Sparkler." The speaker was Hydon. "What chance have we got to make a cleanup, unless we have a roulette layout behind the front?"

"That's just what we will have," assured Sparkler. "But it won't come right away, Duke. We'll bluff Weston for a while; then we'll open wide. I know plenty of tricks that will foul the wise commissioner."

A chuckle from Duke.

"You ought to know them, Sparkler—All right. I'm in on it. When do you leave for Havana?"

"Three days from now. I'll leave the train at Miami, spend a day there, and fly to Cuba.

Meanwhile, Duke, I'll make a complete list of the things I want done. The rest of the job is yours."

THE two men were coming to the door. The Shadow drew back in darkness. Sparkler and Duke went by. Their footsteps faded upon the front stairway.

A soft laugh whispered through the gloom. The Shadow had checked upon what he had already surmised. Sparkler Meldin was planning a New York gambling house, with the proposed Casino Havanola as the blind.

Moving to the side stairs, The Shadow descended. He found the lookout door boarded shut. He pried away the inner fastening and stepped out into the night. The sequel had ended. The Shadow had placed the part that Sparkler Meldin had planned to play. The man from Havana could be forgotten for the present. The task of locating George Corbal was paramount.

In this assumption, The Shadow was not wrong. Yet he was only partially correct. Sparkler Meldin did intend to open the Casino Havanola; to turn it into a gambling den deluxe, ready for profits that would put the Club Torreo in the shade. His new place would be a blind, with Duke Hydon as its capable manager.

But there was another purpose behind Sparkler's game; one so well veiled that it had slipped past The Shadow. That other purpose concerned the second Shadow. Sparkler had not forgotten the facts that he had learned by listening in on Jake Lassop. Nor had he failed to remember the amateurish deeds of the cloaked pretender who had raided the Club Torreo.

Another sequel came when Sparkler sat alone, in the bedroom of an elaborate hotel suite. By a window that opened high above Manhattan, the Havana big shot reviewed a list of telephone numbers. Sparkler was working out the meaning of the word "Calakor." He had marked out a circled diagram that represented the dial of a telephone.

The first hole of the dial contained the number: one, but no letters.

ABC were the letters in the second hole of the dial. From these, Sparkler had decided that the exchange name must begin with two such letters. A telephone book listed an exchange as Abbott-5. A and B fitted. In hole No. 5 appeared the letters JKL. Thus "l" became 5.

The letter "a"—after "l"—stood for the figure: two. The letter "k," like "l," appeared with the number five. The "o," Sparkler had decided, must mean six. Since PRS appeared on the dial with seven, the final figure was established. The complete number became Abbott 5-2567.

SPARKLER had already called that number, with no success. He picked up the telephone and called the hotel operator. He asked for Abbott 5-2567. A bell began to ring; Sparkler listened for half a minute. Suddenly, a *click* reached his ear. A voice followed, growling the word, "Hello!"

Sparkler responded. Suavely, he asked if this was the Acme Hotel. A laugh came across the wire.

"Got the wrong number, friend," said the man at the other end. "This here is a pay station."

"A pay station?" inquired Sparkler. "Are you positive?"

"Sure! I was just coming in to make a call, when I heard you ringing. Better take another look in the telephone book."

"Whereabouts is the pay station?" asked Sparkler, casually. "I'd like to kid the sap who told me it was the right number."

"Downstairs in the Tyrone Drugstore," returned the speaker. "The one on Eighth Street, near Seventh Avenue. That's where they have the phone booths: downstairs."

Sparkler hung up. His gleaming teeth showed satisfaction. He had learned the location that Jake had called. The place where the second Shadow received telephone calls from bribed helpers who knew the key word "Calakor." Perhaps that device—a word instead of a number—could fool such men as Zutz and Lassop; but it had not passed by Sparkler Meldin.

Moreover, the man from Havana had another guess. A hideout could be located in that neighborhood. A crook pretending to be The Shadow would want to be quick when he ducked into cover and out. It might take a while to find the fellow; but it would be worth the trouble.

For Sparkler Meldin wished an interview with the second Shadow, one that would be brief and pointed. Sparkler had bluffed Duke when he had said that he was going to Havana. Instead, he intended to remain in New York. His evening strolls, moreover, would be in the neighborhood of Eighth Street, on the fringe of Greenwich Village.

Sparkler had bluffed more perfectly than he had guessed. Unwittingly, he had gained a march on The Shadow. Though Sparkler did not know the identity of George Corbal, he was close to the second Shadow's trail. With Sparkler lay present opportunity for a meeting with the man The Shadow sought.

The man from Havana had thrust himself deep into the game. He would be in deeper still, before either The Shadow or George Corbal would know of his clever entry.

## CHAPTER XII
## THE LINK TO CRIME

FIVE nights later. The Casino Havanola was holding its gala opening. Thanks to Duke Hydon, Sparkler Meldin had gained a New York nightclub much sooner than he had expected. The Club Galaxy, an old Manhattan bright spot, had been losing business. Duke had arranged for its purchase.

Since the Club Galaxy was already licensed, Sparkler Meldin encountered no red tape in the transfer. Almost overnight, the place was transformed into a new establishment. Its glittering sign proclaimed it as the "Casino Havanola." Spanish entertainers, already in New York, had been engaged for the opening performances.

Sparkler Meldin had presumably left for Cuba, via Miami. Duke Hydon believed that the big shot had gone; so did The Shadow. For both had every reason to suppose that Sparkler had found the opportunity he wanted. The Shadow, moreover, had received a report from Clyde Burke. The *Classic* reporter, on a special assignment in Washington, had interviewed Sparkler when his train stopped at the capital.

That had been two nights ago. The next day, Sparkler had been interviewed in Miami. A brief item to such effect had been wired to New York. Presumably, Sparkler had taken a plane to Havana. But therein lay the flaw. Though Sparkler had actually left Miami by air, his plane had secretly turned northward, instead of making for Cuba. As it was a private plane, its course was not noted.

Tonight, the big shot was back in New York. Though he had spent the last few years in Cuba, Sparkler was an old resident of Manhattan. Familiar with every quarter of the city, he had chosen several places where he knew he could dwell unnoticed. The first of these was an apartment in Greenwich Village, catty-cornered across from the Tyrone Drugstore.

MEANWHILE, The Shadow had continued with his quest. A lull had followed George Corbal's raid at the Club Torreo. Evidently, the pretender had decided that his next move could wait. He had learned that he needed craft as well as nerve.

The underworld had been perplexed by this sudden change of policy. Men of crime wondered what The Shadow's next move would be.

They still thought that Corbal had been The Shadow. Moreover, the killing of Jake Lassop had left a tinge of mystery. Presumably, aides of The Shadow had attacked the side door of the Club Torreo while The Shadow, himself, was gathering the swag. Jake Lassop's intervention had given the bribed lookout a clean bill. No one suspected that Jake had been serving the man who had killed him. Corbal had worked a smart trick when he had shot down his excited hireling.

In consequence of the Torreo affray, crooks had ceased their criticism of Louie Zutz, the lookout at the old Hilo Club. Zutz had been under suspicion; for it was conceded that he had ducked for cover after the raid by the pretended Shadow. Gradually, the opinion had grown that Zutz was hiding out because he feared The Shadow—not because he had served that foe of gangdom.

The waning of suspicion had proven advantageous to The Shadow. He knew that there had been three links to crime. One was Spike Gonley; the second, Louie Zutz; the third, Jake Lassop. Each of these had dealt with Corbal. Gonley had traveled to Mexico, after parting with Jerry Renwood in San Francisco. Lassop had been shot down by Corbal. Only one of the three links remained: Louis Zutz.

The Shadow had sensed that the Hilo lookout was still in New York. Hence he and his agents had engaged in an intensive search for the missing man. So far, they had achieved no luck, although The Shadow himself had visited notorious dives, garbed as a sweatered hoodlum.

Tonight, the search had spread. Cliff Marsland was scouring Brooklyn; Harry Vincent was in New Jersey. Hawkeye was making the rounds of hangouts in the Bronx.

AS for The Shadow, he had declared a temporary holiday. Tonight, he had chosen to view the opening of the Casino Havanola. Attired in evening clothes, he had appeared in the guise of Lamont Cranston. Recognized by a courteous headwaiter—a former employee of an exclusive hotel—the millionaire visitor had been assigned to a choice table near the entertainment floor.

Mexicans in native attire were strumming guitars, while a senorita crooned a Spanish melody. Surrounding tables formed terraced layers; the nightclub was two-thirds filled, although the evening was young. Apparently, the Casino Havanola was heading for a profitable business, even on a legitimate basis.

The headwaiter approached The Shadow's table. Courteously, he requested that Mr. Cranston visit the office.

The Shadow arose and strolled through a curtained archway. He passed between paneled walls, and was ushered through an open doorway. His disguised lips formed a smile as his eyes perceived the persons present.

Police Commissioner Ralph Weston was seated

in the office with Duke Hydon. The nightclub manager came to his feet. Beaming, he thrust his hand to grasp The Shadow's.

"My thanks, Mr. Cranston," he declared. "Commissioner Weston has told me that it was you who introduced Meldin to him. I appreciate the favor, sir."

Duke Hydon formed a bowing figure. His trimmed beard lent him a polish that befitted his nickname; for with it, Duke affected the air of a foreign nobleman. Evidently Sparkler had ordered him to add class to the Casino Havanola.

"Let me show you about," suggested Duke. "I should like you both to see the new appointments of the nightclub. We have intended to use all the space in the two floors that are at our disposal."

The Shadow was studying the paneled walls of the downstairs office. His survey was casual; he turned when Duke bowed and indicated the door. With Weston, The Shadow left the office. Duke conducted them to a broad stairway at the front of the nightclub.

This led to the second floor. There they entered a passage with wide, open doorways on either side. At each stop, Duke pressed a light switch, to show an elaborately furnished room. There were four such apartments, each still undergoing decoration.

"Rooms for special parties," explained Duke. "Each to be decorated after a different pattern. All will be ready for use within the coming week. When they are not needed for private parties, we can use them for overflow customers."

"Gamblers, perhaps?" quizzed Weston, significantly.

"No, no, Commissioner," laughed Duke. "See for yourself. The entire floor is open. Above it, there is nothing but the roof. Meldin's promise remains good, Commissioner. The Casino Havanola will be a nightclub only. Not a gambling establishment."

THEY had reached the end of the corridor. The wall ended with a dome-topped niche, wherein a fountain and its basin had been set. Duke switched on some hidden lights, to throw a glow upon the imitation marble.

"When the fountain plays, the effect will be excellent," he stated. "Colored lights upon spraying water; changing hues to add more beauty. Meldin brought the plans for this fountain. There is one like it in Havana."

On either side of the hallway were open-centered doors that served as entrances to cloakrooms. Noting the interiors of these long, narrow rooms, The Shadow saw that the walls were paneled, like those of Duke's downstairs office. More

than that, he had observed a deceptive fact about this upper story.

The second floor of the Casino Havanola did not occupy as much space as the first. The grand staircase was a winding one; that accounted, in part, for the illusion.

The Shadow had counted paces as they walked along. He had made an estimate which he knew must be correct. This upper floor had a depth that was no more than two-thirds of the lower nightclub. In addition, there must be a space above Duke Hydon's lower office.

The supposed cloakrooms were secret entrances to the space beyond the final wall; just as Duke's office served as the hiding place of a secret stairway. Customers, once on the second floor, could be admitted to a gambling palace through an unused cloakroom. Similarly, Duke Hydon could go up and down from his lower office, unnoticed.

Everything was fixed to open wide, once the Casino Havanola had established itself as a legitimate nightclub. Commissioner Weston had been completely deceived by the arrangement. The Shadow could see a pleased expression upon Duke Hydon's bearded visage. It was Sparkler Meldin who had arranged the layout; Duke was overjoyed to know that his chief's craftiness had scored.

THE trio returned to the nightclub. The headwaiter spied them and approached. He gestured toward the archway that led to Hydon's office.

"A telephone call," he explained. "For Mr. Cranston. I had it transferred to your private wire, Mr. Hydon."

"That was right," nodded Duke. "Go right ahead, Mr. Cranston. The office is yours."

The Shadow went to the office. He picked up the loose receiver and announced himself in a quiet tone. It was Burbank on the wire. The contact man had news. Briefly, he gave it: a report from Cliff Marsland. The roving agent had located Louie Zutz in Brooklyn.

The report received, The Shadow strolled from the office. Outside the door, he met Weston and Hydon. The commissioner was satisfied with his inspection of the Casino Havanola, and was about to leave.

The Shadow remarked that he had received an urgent call from New Jersey, and was therefore returning to his home. In the leisurely manner of Lamont Cranston, he went from the nightclub.

The limousine was not awaiting him. Instead, The Shadow took a taxi; but he was careful in his selection. He entered a cab that was parked fully half a block from the Casino Havanola. The driver did not hear him enter. In fact, his first knowledge of The Shadow's presence came when he caught the order of a whispered voice.

The driver knew the command. For this was Moe Shrevnitz, an independent cab driver who was in The Shadow's service. It was Moe who had trailed Jerry Renwood, that day on Broadway. Tonight, Moe had been in constant readiness for The Shadow's order.

There was significance in the order that The Shadow uttered. Moe interpreted its importance. He nodded to himself as he pulled away from the curb, swinging about to head in the direction of Brooklyn Bridge. Moe, like other agents of The Shadow, knew the present urgency. He could guess that The Shadow's present mission concerned the search for Louie Zutz.

The link to crime had been uncovered. The Shadow had gained his chance to resume a lost trail. Through Zutz, he might find a clue to the whereabouts of George Corbal, the skulking pretender to The Shadow's power.

Yet the mere finding of the link did not insure success. Long experience had told The Shadow that sometimes the simplest of tasks produced great complications. Small fry though Louie Zutz might be, The Shadow did not intend to seek him out too openly.

As the cab rolled onward, long hands opened a bag that lay upon the floor. Garments of black came forth; folds of cloth rolled over stooping shoulders.

Slouch hat, gloves, automatics—all these items of equipment became The Shadow's. His figure blackened within Moe's cab. A chance observer would have thought the taxi to be unoccupied. The only token of the unseen passenger was the slight whisper of a laugh that issued from invisible lips.

Louie Zutz, server of the second Shadow, would be due for a surprise tonight. Before an hour had passed, he would stand face to face with the superfoe who fought all evildoers; Louie Zutz was destined to meet The Shadow!

## CHAPTER XIII
## CLOAKED RIVALS MEET

MOE SHREVNITZ stopped his cab beside the blank wall of a Brooklyn warehouse, near the side door of a garage. As he extinguished the cab lights, the taxi driver heard the rear door close. The Shadow had stepped from the cab.

A voice whispered from the darkness. Cliff Marsland was here, reporting to The Shadow.

"Zutz lives across the street," informed Cliff. "I tracked him through a pal who works in the garage. Zutz just did a sneak into the garage—to make a telephone call, maybe. I think he made one a short while ago; because he was in the garage before."

The Shadow headed to the garage door. He found a small, hinged entrance in the center of the sliding panel. Entering, The Shadow found a dimly lighted interior. Past a cluster of stored cars was the door of an office. The Shadow approached; he heard a man talking breathlessly across a telephone. It was Louie Zutz, a pasty, rat-faced rowdy.

"Honest, I'm scared!" Louie's voice was a half whine. "I can't get no job at no other joint. There's mugs that are leery about the gag I pulled at the Hilo... Sure, I told Spike Gonley I'd work with you... Yeah, before he took it on the lam for Frisco... Well, I worked for you for a while, didn't I, at the Hilo Club?

"I've doped it that Jake Lassop was working for you at the Club Torreo. What's that? You plugged Jake because he tried a double cross? That don't change matters. One job's all a guy can pull... If those other guys won't go through with it like they promised Spike Gonley, why should I? I ain't no fall guy... What's more, this Shadow racket ain't so hot...

"I wouldn't worry if I ran into The Shadow himself, after seeing the way you pranced around in that black nightshirt... What's that? You want me to think it over and call again in fifteen minutes? All right..."

ZUTZ banged the receiver. Muttering to himself, he turned about. His eyes became goggly. Zutz was staring at The Shadow.

Though he displayed no weapon, The Shadow's hands were ready at the borders of his black cloak. Zutz forgot his recent boast. His impressions of Corbal, the false Shadow, were dimmed when he saw the real Shadow in person.

"I don't know nothing," whined Zutz, guessing that The Shadow had overheard his telephone call. "Honest! I was only helping a pal! Spike Gonley said I'd hear from a guy who wanted to knock off the Hilo Club. I did, and the mug told me where to call him. He came rigged up like you; but it was him, not me, that bumped the copper. I don't even know the number I just called. All I've got is a word the guy gave me. I spell it on the dial when I call him."

Zutz displayed a piece of paper. The Shadow plucked it from his fingers. On the paper, The Shadow read the word: "Calakor." Stepping past Zutz, he picked up a telephone book. His gloved finger found the page with the exchange list and marked the first exchange. The Shadow's eyes had noted the dial on the telephone. That was sufficient.

Disregarding Zutz, The Shadow called Burbank.

"Consult reverse number book," he ordered. "Report on Abbott 5-2567."

A pause; then Burbank's response:

"Abbott 5-2567. A pay station in the Tyrone Drugstore near Eighth Street and Seventh Avenue."

**Stopping short, fading backward, The Shadow thundered bullets from his automatics. Wild-stabbing revolvers were his targets.**

"H to cover," instructed The Shadow. "C may be there."

"H" meant Hawkeye; "C" meant Corbal. The Shadow's trail was settled. Hawkeye could take it

temporarily. Turning, The Shadow faced Zutz, who had stood puzzled during period of the telephone call to Burbank.

"I was to lay low," blabbed Zutz. "I called

tonight to ask about my cut; but the guy wants me to take on another lookout job—"

"Remain at your hideout," ordered The Shadow, his whisper sinister. "Later you will receive my order. Obey when it arrives!"

THE SHADOW was giving Zutz a break. Though a rat, the fellow had wanted no part in murder. The Shadow was willing to let him travel from New York.

Zutz appreciated the favor. He proved it, suddenly, when he emitted a hoarse cry of warning. Zutz was looking toward the door; The Shadow wheeled, knowing that the man had spotted some danger.

On the threshold stood a scar-faced bruiser, gripping a .38. The rogue was some unexpected killer, whose snarl told that he recognized The Shadow.

But before he could aim his revolver, The Shadow was upon him, pulling an automatic as he came. Sledging a backhand stroke, The Shadow used his left to clip the ruffian's jaw.

The fellow sprawled clear through the doorway. The Shadow hissed an order to Zutz:

"Stay where you are!"

Springing out into the garage proper, The Shadow encountered new foemen. A squad of hoodlums had arrived at the front door; they were jabbing bullets at The Shadow. A hoarse voice roared from a touring car that stood with motor running.

"Get The Shadow! Two grand to the guy who croaks him!"

The Shadow knew the shouter. He was "Skate" Dover, the "wanted" leader of a murderous crew who had been running bootleg gas to Long Island. This garage chanced to be their headquarters; returning from a run, the thugs had found The Shadow.

Stopping short, fading backward, The Shadow thundered bullets from his automatics. Wild-stabbing revolvers were his targets. He dropped the men behind him.

Skate shouted for crooks to dive behind parked cars. As they obeyed, The Shadow leaped beyond a big sedan. He had clipped three foemen; he dropped another who came over the top of a coupé.

Skate shouted for a charge. His remaining followers closed in toward The Shadow, who bobbed suddenly into view to meet them at close range. As he fired withering shots, a new gun blasted from the side door of the garage. Cliff had heard the shots. He had arrived to deliver a flank fire.

Into the barrage came a wild-eyed man fleeing for safety, he ran straight into doom. It was Louie

Zutz, forgetful of The Shadow's orders. Bullets riddled the scared rat. Louie rolled over dead, just as The Shadow and Cliff broke the charge of the foe.

As The Shadow spilled a last attacker, Cliff aimed for the touring car at the front of the garage. A door of the car wrenched open; Skate Dover came diving, aiming for The Shadow.

Cliff fired; his shot went wide. Fading, The Shadow rolled on the oily surface of the garage floor. As Skate missed a shot, The Shadow tongued a bullet upward. Skate sprawled, rolled over and lay still.

With Cliff behind him, The Shadow headed for Moe's cab. Hastily, they rode away, for sirens told that gunfire had been heard and police were heading to the spot. Moreover, The Shadow had other work ahead. He must take up the trail that he had left temporarily to Hawkeye—the trail of the second Shadow, George Corbal.

ALREADY Hawkeye, at the Tyrone Drugstore, had spotted a man who was pacing impatiently by the telephone booths. Hawkeye was sure that this man was George Corbal. He watched the fellow glance angrily at his watch and suddenly stalk from the store.

Hawkeye trailed.

After a few short, twisted blocks through Greenwich Village, Corbal descended stairs that led to a basement apartment. Behind an old-fashioned picket fence, two doors away, Hawkeye heard Corbal click a key in a lock. After the sound ended, Hawkeye came out from cover. Shambling past Corbal's door, he noted the number.

Hawkeye kept on around the block and picked what he thought must be the rear door to Corbal's hideout.

Hurrying back to the drugstore, Hawkeye made a call to Burbank. The contact man told the spotter to stand by. Soon, a bell rang in a booth. It was Burbank; when Hawkeye answered, the contact man ordered him off duty.

The Shadow had stopped off and called while riding in from Brooklyn. He had gained Hawkeye's report. From now on, Corbal belonged to The Shadow.

WITHIN his basement apartment, George Corbal had chosen darkness; a matter of usual policy. Finally, when he reached an inner room, he risked a light. The glow showed that the room had only one small window. It was high up; Corbal had covered it with composition board so that no light could trickle through.

The sallow-faced crook opened a table drawer and produced two lists. One covered gambling houses. Corbal had already crossed off the Hilo Club and the Club Torreo. Muttering, he ran lines through the other places on the list. He was through with the risky racket of raiding such clubs.

The other list had names of individuals, half of them crossed off. This was the list that Corbal had worked with Renwood, before Renwood went West. Corbal studied the remaining names carefully. He found one that suited him. He made a check mark beside it. Corbal still saw a chance for crime.

Opening a closet door, Corbal drew out garments of black. Donning cloak and slouch hat, he picked up gloves and automatics. He took them to the table, laid them upon the lists. The apartment had no telephone; but Corbal had previously supplied himself with a directory. Opening the telephone book, he found the name that he had checked on the list. Corbal copied it as it appeared in the book, using a small piece of paper.

The pencil point snapped. Corbal threw the pencil aside. Some pages of the telephone book flipped shut upon the paper that bore the written name. Finding another pencil, Corbal was about to slide back the flipped pages when he heard a whispered tone behind him. Chilled, Corbal turned about. His fresh pencil dropped from his nerveless fingers.

Standing within the door was a figure whose attire resembled Corbal's own. Slouch hat, cloak of black—there the similarity ended. The arrival had provided himself with accouterments that Corbal had as yet neglected. He was wearing black gloves; each fist clutched an automatic.

"The Shadow!"

CORBAL gasped the name. His cry was an admission of his own imposture. The cloaked intruder gave another laugh. Corbal trembled. Here was The Shadow, almost as Corbal remembered him from that hazy night when the cloaked avenger had entered to bind and gag him and keep him from Garraway, the banker.

"Don't—don't kill me!" pleaded Corbal. "I'll—I'll talk—"

"Proceed!" ordered the intruder, a sharp hiss to his voice. "Your life shall be spared!"

Corbal backed away from the table on which rested his own guns.

"I shot Patrolman Jennings outside the Hilo Club," he admitted, "but I wasn't out to kill him. I had to plug Lassop, because he was a double-crosser. I was through with the racket. You can see the list, with all the names crossed off."

Corbal made a pitiful sight; his black garb was flappy as he cowered.

Compared to Corbal, the new entrant was an imposing figure. With a swish, the intruder reached the table. Putting away one automatic, he lifted the list. Laying it aside, he picked up the other sheet.

"You have dropped one racket," he sneered, "but you have chosen another!"

"No, no!" protested Corbal. "The list is an old one!"

"One name is checked."

"I—I—yes. I intended to visit that man tonight, to learn if he had funds available. I never had enough on him for blackmail. He is a philanthropist; sometimes he keeps as much as fifty thousand dollars in his home. He has jewels, too."

A laugh followed Corbal's statement.

"You speak of funds," came the significant tone. "Where are those that you stole in the past?"

"In the large box." Corbal gestured toward the closet. "On the floor, to the left of the door—"

Words failed Corbal. He uttered a piteous cry. A gloved finger was ready on the trigger of its .45, beginning a squeeze.

"I confessed!" bawled Corbal. "You promised mercy—"

The automatic muzzle delivered flame. Hard on the first blast came another; then a third, a fourth. Bullets at close range, delivered for the heart of a cringing victim. Corbal sprawled crazily on the floor.

A HOLLOW laugh sounded, as a gloved hand put away the automatic.

Corbal's slayer stepped to the closet; found the box and opened it to view the swag. He picked up the lists, noted the one with the checked name and chuckled harshly as he folded the lists and added them to the contents of the box.

Stooping, he wrenched the black cloak that covered Corbal's shoulders. He raised the slouch hat, laughed as he studied Corbal's sallow face. He put Corbal's hat, guns and gloves upon the cashbox; then wrapped all within the dead man's cloak. Bundling the burden, he strode through darkness and reached the front street.

There, the departer heard shouts; also the sounds of approaching sirens. His shots had been heard. Police were closing in.

Quickly, the cloaked departer dashed for a space between two buildings. An approaching officer saw him and hurried in pursuit. The cloaked fugitive turned and fired three shots. One bullet found the patrolman's shoulder.

The fugitive dashed onward. A police car arrived on the street behind Corbal's hideout. The wounded patrolman was clattering the cement with his club, using his good arm. Two officers came to his rescue.

"The fellow beat it!" gulped the crippled cop. "He headed off! Maybe you can nab him; but he's got a start—"

"What did he look like? Where did he come from?"

"He was all in black! He came out of a basement on the front street, where the shooting was!"

"All in black? You don't think he was—"

The wounded patrolman grimaced as his shoulder twinged with a knifelike pain. He set his lips and nodded, as he gave answer:

"That's who he was: The Shadow!"

## CHAPTER XIV
## THE NAME IN THE BOOK

THE law had acted swiftly this night. Within fifteen minutes after the death of George Corbal, patrol cars were scouring the terrain for blocks about. A complete cordon had been established, in case a desperate killer should still be in the vicinity.

Within thirty minutes after Corbal's death, Joe Cardona had arrived upon the scene. The acting inspector had gained word of the killing. He had come to take charge of this case which appeared to involve The Shadow.

"It was The Shadow all right. Look at this, Inspector."

A detective made the statement, pointing to Corbal's body as he spoke.

Stooping, Cardona examined a trophy. It was a short strip of black cloth, twisted half about the dead man's neck, like a portion of a hangman's noose.

"This guy must have grabbed the killer's cloak," stated the dick. "Got away with a chunk of it. Funny, though, that he isn't clutching it."

Cardona started to make a comment. He stopped suddenly. He was wondering about this clue. That piece of cloth looked like a portion of a garment that the dead man had been wearing. Could someone have killed this victim; then snatched a cloak from his body?

Plausibly, yes. Yet the dead man could not be The Shadow. Cardona could not picture that sallow face as The Shadow's own; nor could he visualize The Shadow, trapped and slain, in so poor a hideout as this one.

"He took it on the lam, The Shadow did," the detective was reporting. "Patrolman Ruskin saw him. He was carrying what looked like a box of swag. Fired three shots at Ruskin. Got him with one of them. Not wounded bad, though."

CARDONA was nodding to himself. He was forming a reconstruction of this crime. One that did not hit the bull's-eye, yet which scored a marker. The dead man, here on the floor, had been wearing a black cloak. Therefore, Cardona knew who the dead man was. He was the one who had raided the Hilo Club; and afterward, the Club Torreo. This victim was the second Shadow.

Who had bagged him?

Not The Shadow. On that point, Cardona was positive. This episode had convinced him more than ever that a duplicate Shadow was in the game. The Shadow would not have shot down a helpless wretch, like this fellow on the floor. Nor would he have made a half maddened run for safety, pausing only to fire back and cripple a beat-pounding patrolman like Ruskin.

More than that, Cardona had just come from another case. Skate Dover, murderer, had been found dead in his Brooklyn headquarters. With him had perished members of his crew. Others—survivors—had blabbed of a lone fighter in black; then they had turned mum. Public enemies had been eliminated; and the one fighter capable of that deed was The Shadow.

Figuring the time element, Cardona calculated that The Shadow could not have come from Brooklyn to Manhattan within the period that had passed between the two events. Someone other than The Shadow had dealt death in Greenwich Village. One crook had guessed another's game; had slain him; had deprived him of spoils, as well as his false garments.

Cardona had scored close to a perfect hit. His one error came when he tried to visualize the killing of George Corbal. Cardona's guess was that another man had dropped the imitation Shadow; then had taken cloak and hat to mask himself in the getaway.

The actual truth did not occur to the ace sleuth. He never suspected that the slayer of Corbal had been guised in black at the beginning; that the dead man had believed himself faced by The Shadow.

Hence Cardona had no inkling of the cunning possessed by the man with whom he would have to deal. He thought that The Shadow duplication had ended.

Because of that, Cardona took it for granted that detectives had searched the place sufficiently. He finished his report then prepared to leave. He would have gone without a further clue, but for the comment of a detective present.

"FUNNY thing," remarked the headquarters man. "This guy having a phone book, but no telephone. What do you think of it, Inspector?"

Cardona shrugged his shoulders.

"What of it?" he inquired. He noted the directory on the table and began to thumb its pages.

"Probably he just carried it in here, along with a lot of useless truck—"

Cardona stopped suddenly. His moving thumb had struck the edge of a paper, wedged between two pages. Cardona opened the book. He found the sheet upon which Corbal had copied a name.

"Jothan Swedley," read Cardona. "That's an odd name. Wonder why this bird wrote that one, and left it here in the book. Hm-m-m. Swedley. Wait until I see if the name's listed."

He turned the pages, going toward the back of the book. He found the name Swedley listed half a dozen times. Among the group was a J. M. Swedley.

"That's the one," decided Cardona. "The only Swedley whose first name could be Jothan. I'll tell you what this means. This dead man must have known something about J. M. Swedley, in order to write down his first name, Jothan. Where's the nearest telephone?"

"Across the street," informed a detective. "That's where we called you from, Inspector."

"Show me the place. I want to make a call."

Cardona pocketed the sheet of paper. He wrote Swedley's telephone number in a notebook. He went across the street and used a private telephone.

There was no answer at the J. M. Swedley number. Coming out of the house, Cardona bumped into Markham, who had just arrived. He drew the detective sergeant to one side.

"I've got a theory, Markham," informed Cardona. "One crook bumped another. The killer took the swag—all the haul that the first guy made from the Hilo and the Torreo."

"You mean the dead man's The Shadow?" gasped Markham.

"Not at all," rejoined Joe. "You know the commissioner's decision. We're not looking for The Shadow. We're after a guy who has pulled some phony jobs, wearing a black cloak and hat.

"The dead guy across the street is the one we wanted. The killer took the cash he found there; and maybe he learned a few things besides. Like what the dead guy was going to do next, for instance. Well, in the telephone book, I found this paper. Look at the name on it: Jothan Swedley.

"There's a J. M. Swedley, and I've just called him. No answer. The man lives on East Eighty-fifth Street. That's where we're going, with a squad. Maybe the murderer will have some reason to get Swedley; and maybe he don't know about this paper that I found. Here's our chance to do two good bits of business. Protect Swedley and lay for the murderer at the same time."

TOGETHER, Cardona and Markham boarded a police car. They traveled along a narrow street, the headlamps cutting a wide swath. As they neared a corner, the glare of the lights fringed a doorway. Oddly, blackness refused to vanish in the momentary glow. That fact escaped the men in the car.

Blackness moved when it had again blended with deep darkness. A gliding figure began a silent course along the street. It drew aside when a searching patrolman went by, flicking his flashlight here and there. The officer's search was scarcely more than a routine. He did not believe that any fugitive would have doubled back so close to the scene of crime.

However, that stranger of the darkness was no fugitive. He was a different personage in black than the one who had made a wild flight from this district. The Shadow had arrived in person. He had been delayed in his approach, through the presence of a police cordon. From one spot of blackness to another, The Shadow had worked an irregular course inward to his objective.

He reached the basement doorway. He edged into darkness. There The Shadow saw the glow from the room where Corbal's body lay. Two detectives were coming out through the darkness; a uniformed policeman was following them to the door.

"So that's where the inspector has gone," remarked the policeman. "Up to see about this fellow Swedley. What do you think his idea is?"

"Swedley's name was on that sheet of paper, wasn't it?" retorted a dick. "That means the dead guy knew something about him. Maybe the murderer found it out, too."

"Yeah. But how many guys are there named Swedley? A lot, maybe."

"With a first name like Jothan? Say—there only could be one. I saw the inspector looking through the phone book. He found a J. M. Swedley. The only one it could be."

JOTHAN SWEDLEY. The Shadow remembered the name, as he made a circling course in darkness. When he neared the lighted room, he peered over his shoulder and saw the policeman at the outer doorway, still chatting with the detective. Gliding into the room, The Shadow formed a spectral figure in the light. He spied the opened telephone book. It lay beneath the glare of the table lamp. He noted the name of J. M. Swedley. The Shadow also made careful notation of the address. Not a wealthy neighborhood, where J. M. Swedley lived. The Shadow calculated it as being close to Third Avenue.

A black glove peeled from The Shadow's left hand, as his right drew it away. A gem, The Shadow's girasol, shone iridescent beneath the light. The Shadow's fingers rubbed the book page with their tips. That touch ended, they quickly turned the pages, to a section of the directory that was closer to the front.

The Shadow stopped among the names that began with the letter J. His fingers moved along the right-hand page, while his eyes scanned the left sheet. The Shadow made a double discovery. His fingers encountered indentations. Someone had written a name, while resting a paper upon the opened telephone book. Also, The Shadow saw the name he wanted.

George Corbal copied it directly from the book. Because of that, he had written the last name first, according to the usual listing. "Jothan Swedley" meant Swedley Jothan. There, in plain view was the name that The Shadow sought. "Swedley Jothan"—with an address on Madison Avenue.

VOICES from the front room. Turning swiftly, The Shadow swung back against a rear door in the farther corner. His shape was almost invisible, away from the light.

As he stood there, waiting, The Shadow stared toward the figure on the floor. He could see the sallow features of George Corbal. He recognized the man who had played the role of the second Shadow.

Two men entered. One was the bluecoat: the other, a new detective who had come with Markham. This chap was trying to explain things to the officer.

"The inspector don't know who we're after," stated the detective. "Didn't I hear him telling that to Sergeant Markham? So here's the stiff, eh?" He viewed Corbal's body. "Well, from what Cardona says, he may have been the guy in black."

"Yeah?" quizzed the bluecoat. "Then what was he doing on the next street, running away except when he stopped to plug Ruskin? Shot off some fireworks in here to begin with, then beat it, then ducked back and committed suicide without firing a shot? Is that the way you figure it? Say—if that's the way you hear things, you'll be pounding a beat before you know it."

"Get wise to yourself!" snorted the detective. "It could have been another guy outside. Some mug who snatched the black kimono off of this one. My hearing's good enough. How's your eyesight?"

"What do you mean, my eyesight?"

"Well, you'll have to do a lot of looking, won't you? Squinting around to see if you can spot a guy in black? Now you see him—now you don't—"

THE detective stopped short. All this while, The Shadow had been softly turning the knob of the door that led into the back room of the basement. He had opened the barrier; he was fading backward into darkness. By chance alone, the talking detective had looked up to catch a glimpse of his fading shape. The light showed one momentary outline of a hawkish silhouette.

"Say!" The detective stared. "Look at that door! I'd have swore I saw movement—"

The door was closing. The shine of its dark-stained panel replaced the deeper darkness of the room beyond. The detective grabbed the bluecoat by the arm.

"Some guy just ducked out of sight!" he cried, excitedly. "Come on! We'll get him!"

Yanking guns and flashlights, the pair sprang for the door and opened it. The glimmer of the torches flicked through the rear room, just in time to show a back door closing.

"He's gone that way! The key's still in the lock! Get him—quick!"

As the pair dashed for the back door, the inward-projecting key performed a singular action. Clipped by pincers thrust through the outside keyhole, the key itself was turning.

The detective reached the door and grabbed the knob. He tried to open the barrier. He failed.

"I can't get it opened—"

"Maybe it's still locked," put in the policeman. "That's the way it was when we looked the place over."

The detective turned the key. The lock clicked open. He turned the knob; the door swung inward.

"Well, I'll—"

The detective looked at the policeman, then shook his head.

"No guy could have locked it that quick," decided the dick. "Not with the key here in the door. Yet I saw the door closing—"

"Maybe you thought you did," interposed the bluecoat. "It sort of looked that way to me, too. But these flashlights do funny things when you swing them. Sometimes they make it look like something's moving when it isn't."

BOTH men swung beams about the rear steps. Discovering nothing, they went back into the basement, locking the door behind them. A silent, motionless figure detached itself from the wall. Gliding invisibly, The Shadow moved away.

Joe Cardona had been right; The Shadow, when he made a departure, did not take to maddened flight. The man who had slain George Corbal had been a masquerader, like the victim. The Shadow, too, had divined that fact from the talk that he had overheard between the remaining detective and the bluecoat.

Clearly, The Shadow pieced the circumstances, adding the finishing touch that Cardona had failed to get. Another crook had guessed Corbal's game. That new worker of evil had come here to murder the man who had passed himself as The Shadow. But such a crook, clever as a ferret, would surely have come prepared. More dangerous than Corbal, he had adopted the same ruse as the second Shadow, to try its working for himself.

A third Shadow had entered the game. One who had taken Corbal's swag. One who had probably learned of plans which Corbal, now dead, could not continue. One who would amplify the slain impostor's purposes with methods of his own. One who already might be threatening a man named Swedley Jothan.

Joe Cardona had guessed in reverse. He had gone to protect a man named Swedley, whose life stood in no danger. The Shadow, also, was starting on a mission of protection, following an urge that was the same as Cardona's. Chances were that The Shadow would encounter a superfoe of crime—one whose name he had not yet learned.

But on one point, The Shadow was sure. The enemy was a supercrook who had taken up the game where Corbal had left off; a new masquerader who had profited by his elimination of the old.

The Shadow was on the trail of the third Shadow!

### CHAPTER XV
### SHADOW VERSUS SHADOW

SWEDLEY JOTHAN'S home was a gloomy residence that had the appearance of a mausoleum. Though it stood close to modern buildings, it was not conspicuous; for a high wall surrounded the antiquated edifice. Passers on the street did not realize that a house stood beyond that plain brick wall.

Nor was Swedley Jothan widely known. He was not a man of tremendous wealth. His own fortune was less than a million dollars; and he had acquired it purely through his connection with large enterprises in which his name had not appeared. But Swedley Jothan was a philanthropist of unusual quality.

Unassuming by nature, he had retired from business to seek seclusion in this old Manhattan house. He had contacts with old friends who were men of greater wealth. He had impressed those former associates with his own belief in charity. Hence Jothan had become the handler of many anonymous gifts to worthy causes.

Tonight, Jothan was in his second-floor study. Usually, the philanthropist retired early; he had broken his regular rule because he had work to do. Seated at a cumbersome mahogany table, Jothan was marking notes upon the margins of typewritten sheets.

**SWEDLEY JOTHAN—**
**whose money and life**
**The Shadow saves.**

Stoop-shouldered, withered of frame, he made an almost pitiful figure. Yet when he looked up in response to a rap at the opened door, his face was a revelation.

Thin gray hair topped a smiling countenance. A friendly light sparkled from keen, understanding eyes. Jothan nodded, as he saw a sober-faced servant standing at the door.

"I know it, Rodney," chortled Jothan. "The hour is long past my usual bedtime. However, I shall still be busy for a while."

"Remember, sir, the doctor said you should retire early."

"This is an exception. I have important work, Rodney. I am revising the final lists that cover a half million in donations. Many worthy causes will derive benefit through these gifts. Best of all, Rodney, there can be no doubt about the money. All the funds have been delivered. The entire amount is in my safe."

"That is excellent, sir! But can you not leave the work to Mr. Dalley? He is your secretary."

"Of course. But Dalley needed a night off. He will be surprised when he learns that I have attended to the details of this work. Send him up here when he comes in, Rodney. Then you and Throckmorton can lock up. Where is Throckmorton, by the way?"

"On the third floor, sir. He has retired. You said that you would not need him."

"So I did. I had forgotten. Very well, Rodney. You can go downstairs and wait for Dalley. He stated that he would be back by midnight. That allows him about fifteen minutes longer."

RODNEY went away. His footsteps echoed from a flight of stairs. Jothan resumed his work. A hush filled the large, old-fashioned room. Wall brackets formed a mellow glow; a table lamp concentrated a brighter gleam upon Swedley Jothan.

The open door where Rodney had knocked was located mid-center in a long wall. It was directly opposite Jothan's table, and the door gave access to the hall. In addition, there were two other doors, each in a separate wall. One opened into a front room; the other into a room at the back.

This second door was close to the wall that separated the study from the hall. The door was to Jothan's right; beside it stood the safe of which the philanthropist had spoken. Large, modern in design, that strongbox formed a formidable device, one which would have taxed the supreme efforts of any safecracker.

The door in the right wall moved slightly open, immediately after Rodney's departure. The servant could not have spied it; for the door was not quite visible from the hallway entrance.

Nor did Jothan observe the motion of the barrier. He was too deeply engrossed with his papers. Nevertheless, the philanthropist must have remembered Rodney's reminder of the lateness of the hour. A few minutes after the secretary had gone, Jothan arose and went to the safe.

He fingered the combination. He opened the big door, swinging it toward the side entrance of the room. Jothan started to put his documents away. As he did, he heard a harsh chuckle from his left. Looking up, the philanthropist saw a strange figure looming beside the edge of the safe door.

The intruder was in black. The collar of his cloak fringed his lower features. His slouch hat, slanted downward, served as a mask for his eyes. The arrival was wearing gloves. In one hand he held a businesslike automatic. He was leveling the gun toward Jothan.

"PASS over the swag," hissed the intruder, his tone an evil jeer. "I know it's here. Pass it to me!"

Jothan hesitated, trembling. His eyes glanced inadvertently toward the safe. The intruder spied the action and glimpsed a square-shaped box. Stepping forward, he thrust Jothan back with a jab of the automatic. With his free hand, the threatening intruder grasped the box.

Moving away, he laid his prize upon a chair. He yanked open the top of the box; then laughed insidiously when he saw the contents. The box held currency of large denominations: five-hundred-dollar bills, and thousands. It also contained securities.

"What about these?" demanded the man in black. "Are they all negotiable?"

Pitifully, Jothan nodded.

"And the records of them? Are they listed on your documents?"

Jothan started to nod; then restrained himself. But the invader had caught the tip.

"Pass them across!"

Jothan obeyed the command. He drew the papers from the safe and gave them to the man who held him covered. The invader added the documents to the swag. He closed the lid of the box. Lifting the burden from the chair, he made a gesture with his gun.

"Back away from the safe!" he ordered. "Toward the center of the room!"

Jothan complied. The cloaked crook swung toward the doorway through which he had appeared. Jothan could see him past the opened door of the safe, which formed a partial barricade.

"Stand where you are," instructed the man in black. "Don't make a move!"

Instinctively, Jothan knew what was coming. Death was to be his. Murder was to follow robbery. The philanthropist was too terrified to move. He was in the open, a sure target for the killer's gun. The only point that delayed the delivery of bullets was the range. The intended murderer wanted to be sure of an immediate kill.

During those tense moments, a new motion occurred. One that neither Jothan nor the black intruder sensed. Another door was opening. It was the barrier at the front of the study. Slowly edging into the fringe of light came a figure that matched the one that Jothan faced. Another arrival cloaked in black.

This visitor differed from the first in one respect. His masking cloak collar and his down-turned hat brim did not totally obscure his countenance. They allowed a view of burning eyes— orbs that blazed from a shaded visage and sparkled with righteous fury.

Below the eyes loomed an automatic. Held in a firm, gloved fist, the .45 was leveled straight across the room. A ready finger was upon the trigger. The Shadow was present to deal with the impostor who sought murder.

Yet, for the moment, his hand was stayed; and with good reason. Swedley Jothan was almost directly in the path of The Shadow's aim.

"Move forward! Toward me!"

The snarl came from the cloaked faker beyond the safe. His command was directed to Jothan.

Faltering, the philanthropist obeyed. He knew that the move was intended as his death warrant, for it brought him to the closer range that the killer wanted.

A fierce burst of mockery filled the room. A rising, whispered taunt that commanded all attention. Jothan heard it as he was stumbling forward; it compelled the gray-haired man to turn. With the direction that he was taking, Jothan's new move threw him farther from danger. The sudden mirth gave startlement to the killer, also. The cloaked impostor saw The Shadow.

One more instant would have spelled the killer's doom, for The Shadow held him covered. The master-fighter was pausing only to draw the murderer's aim in his own direction, that no chance shot might find Jothan.

But at that vital moment, another factor intervened. A gun shot crackled; it came neither from The Shadow nor his imitator. The weapon that spoke was a small revolver. It was fired from the main door of the room.

By Rodney. The servant had come upstairs. He had heard the sound of voices. He had arrived at the hallway door. He had heard The Shadow's laugh; he had seen the cloaked avenger aiming with an automatic. Not knowing that The Shadow was a rescuer, Rodney had chosen him as a target.

THE servant's hurried shots were wide; yet they whistled close to the folds of The Shadow's cloak. Instantly, The Shadow dropped back into the front room; but he boomed quick shots as he fell away. His bullets sizzled toward the black impostor, far across the room. They missed their mark, for The Shadow's aim was spoiled, but they served their purpose.

The threatening killer dived for security beyond the open door of the safe. Jothan, seeking safety, staggered to the front of the open strongbox. The steel door lay between him and his foe. Only by leaning around it could the desperate killer hope to drill the philanthropist.

He took a chance on such action, for he saw Rodney hurtling through the room, on his way to block The Shadow's aim.

Again The Shadow's automatic stabbed from darkness. Picking a path past Rodney, the avenger sent a warning bullet that bashed against the projecting safe door. The would-be murderer dropped away.

Plunging forward, The Shadow met Rodney head-on. The servant was aiming madly with his revolver. With free hand, The Shadow drove Rodney's gun arm upward and sent the fellow over his shoulder with a quick jujitsu grapple. Again The Shadow clanged the safe door with a bullet. Then a new antagonist was upon him.

It was Dalley. The secretary had arrived home. A thin, bespectacled man, he was coming in from the same door that Rodney had chosen. Dalley clutched at The Shadow. With a quick jolt, the cloaked battler sent the unarmed secretary rolling across the floor.

One flash of a black-clad rogue in flight. The impostor had leaped away from the space beyond the safe. The box of wealth beneath his arm, the crook fled just in time to avoid another bullet from The Shadow's ready gun.

A shot thundered, just too late. Then The Shadow took up the pursuit through the far door.

Hardly had he passed from view before Rodney and Dalley came to their feet and started a chase. They had seen only The Shadow. They pursued madly, in spite of Jothan's blurted protests.

THROUGH the rear room, The Shadow burst into a dim hallway. Here he plunged squarely upon two grappling figures at the foot of the stairway leading to the third floor. Throckmorton, the other servant, had come down from above, just in time to meet the invader who wore the imitation cloak.

With one fierce clutch, The Shadow seized the black-clad impostor. He sent the killer sprawling to the floor, headlong toward a flight of stairs that led down to the back kitchen. The box of wealth went bounding to the wall. Stepping above it, The Shadow aimed his .45 to cover the crook whom he had spilled.

Throckmorton saw The Shadow. Dazed by a blow upon the head, this second servant thought that he had spied his former antagonist. He leaped upon The Shadow and tried to grab the avenger's automatic. As they wrestled, the crook by the stairway came to his feet.

The Shadow's .45 stabbed the dim light of the hall. The bullet went wide, for Throckmorton had grabbed The Shadow's wrist. But the shot was too close to suit the rising crook. With maddened plunge, the thwarted murderer scudded down the backstairs.

He was none too soon. Upon that instant, The Shadow broke Throckmorton's clutch and sent the servant tumbling to the floor.

The fray had required a scant four seconds; but it had carried the grapplers past the stairway. Throckmorton, groggy, sprawled wearily upon the money box. The Shadow, half off his footing, thrust out a hand to stop his fall. His fist encountered a loose door. The barrier swung inward. Slipping, The Shadow tumbled sidewise into a long, narrow linen closet.

The chance misstep halted his opportunity to pursue the fleeing murderer; and it produced another twist of circumstance. Just as The

Shadow slipped from view, Rodney and Dalley came dashing into the rear hall. They saw Throckmorton rising, his hands to his head. They heard the final clatter at the bottom of the stairway to the kitchen.

Brandishing his revolver, Rodney dashed down the back stairway. Dalley followed at his heels. Neither had seen the reclaimed box. It lay beyond Throckmorton's half-huddled figure.

The Shadow, coming to his feet, stepped out into the hall. He heard the descent of the pursuers. He saw the box upon the floor.

Head bowed in hands, Throckmorton had stumbled to the steps leading to the third floor. He was slumping to a seated position. He did not see the spectral, black-clad figure that stooped and plucked the box from the floor. The spoils regained, The Shadow strode back through the rear room. The first man to view him was Swedley Jothan.

The philanthropist had faltered to his table. He was seated there when The Shadow entered. A cry of alarm stopped short on Jothan's lips. For an instant, the philanthropist had thought this to be the murderer returning, for The Shadow held the precious box. Then the gleam of The Shadow's eyes told Jothan that this being was his rescuer.

The Shadow knew that Jothan, alone, had seen two figures in black. He placed the box in front of the philanthropist. He opened the cover to display the reclaimed contents. In a quiet whisper, The Shadow spoke:

"Your servants will speak of one intruder." The Shadow's words were like a prophecy. "Do not dispute their statements. Let them believe that they drove off the murderer. That you found the box yourself, in the back hall."

Jothan nodded his understanding. The Shadow resumed:

"Soon you will meet a man named Cardona," whispered the cloaked rescuer. "He will be the police inspector in charge of this investigation. Request an interview with Commissioner Weston. Tell your complete story, with Cardona present."

"What shall I say?" asked Jothan. "Shall I tell them—"

"State that The Shadow gave you rescue," ordered The Shadow. "Tell them that the man who robbed you was obviously an impostor. Affirm your belief that the thief will have a short career. State that he has supplanted an impostor who preceded him."

"But if I express such opinions—"

"They will believe you. They will express their thanks, for they will know the course to follow."

Footsteps were sounding from the rear stairway. The buzz of voices came from the rear room.

Swedley Jothan saw The Shadow wheel about, then stride toward the doorway into the front room. His figure faded into blackness. A whispered laugh—no more than an echo—reached Jothan's ears as a final reminder. The Shadow was gone.

Dalley and Rodney entered the room, bringing Throckmorton with them. They uttered happy exclamations when they saw their master seated at his table. They gave new expressions of satisfaction when they spied the open box, with all its wealth secure.

Swedley Jothan smiled serenely when he heard his servants tell their versions of the fray. The Shadow was right; not one of them knew that there had been two black-clad visitors to this study. Jothan alone had seen Shadow versus Shadow. He had seen the real deliver bullets at the false. Shots which the servants thought had been intended for their master.

True facts would be kept until the proper moment. That time would be when Swedley Jothan held conference with Commissioner Ralph Weston. So had The Shadow ordered; and Jothan, knowing that he owed a debt of rescue, intended to obey.

## CHAPTER XVI
## THE SHADOW KNOWS

TWELVE days had passed since the attack at Jothan's. Startling events had gained new repetition. Again, a roaming, black-clad raider was at large. In swift, successive strokes, a new crook was spreading consternation. Like the Hilo Club and the Club Torreo, four gambling places had been pillaged by a cloaked intruder whom the underworld declared must be The Shadow.

New evening had settled upon Manhattan. Commissioner Weston was still in his office, tarrying late because of overwork. Joe Cardona was announced and admitted. Weston eyed the acting inspector with impatience.

"Well, where are the results?"

"I don't know, Commissioner," admitted the ace. "We're up against something tough. But for that matter, so is The Shadow."

"Bah!" ejaculated Weston. "He has taken on too much—that is the whole trouble, Cardona. It's time that we stepped in."

"I don't think so, Commissioner. I believe that The Shadow is due. Everything has worked against him since that night he rescued Swedley Jothan. It's time that a break was coming in his favor."

"Be more specific, Cardona."

"All right, Commissioner. Suppose we take it from the beginning. We guessed that faker was pretending to be The Shadow. We decided that the best way to handle that crook was to let The Shadow cover him."

"By the faker, you mean Corbal. The second Shadow, we might term him."

"That's right. The Shadow was out to get Corbal. To turn him over to us—"

"But The Shadow failed."

"Because he was busy elsewhere, doing the law a more important turn. Another criminal found Corbal ahead of The Shadow. This new factor bumped Corbal and took up his game."

"To become the third Shadow."

Weston banged his fist as he spoke. Pounding the desk repeatedly, he stormed at Cardona.

"Jothan told us all we needed," flared the commissioner. "He practically delivered a message from The Shadow. We were ready to put the clamps on the gambling places. We waited, to give The Shadow opportunity, in case this new impostor chose to raid.

"What has happened? Four raids by the criminal! The Shadow has not stopped him. What has been gained? Nothing! Nothing, I tell you! We should have clamped the lid on every gambling room in town. At least you agree with me on that, Cardona?"

Joe shook his head. "I don't agree, Commissioner," returned the ace. "I'll tell you why. If we had closed the joints, new ones would have opened. You know how they work it. Always a jump ahead of us. But by sitting tight; we've accomplished something. Do you know what the joints are doing? They're closing of their own accord.

"Yes. They're scared, Commissioner. Scared because they think it's actually The Shadow who's raiding them. I've got some straight reports here. The gambling racket is nearly finished, of its own accord. The places have wilted—folded up—within the past week."

WESTON began to look somewhat mollified. Suddenly he stormed again.

"But all this while," he roared, "a murderer has been at large! He has not dealt in slaughter since he killed Corbal; but that is only because he has not found it necessary. Surely, The Shadow must recognize the menace that is abroad."

"Probably he does," assured Cardona. "That's why he has chosen the only way to get this crook he's after. Don't you get it, Commissioner? Like us, the Shadow is dealing with a lone crook—a smart one—who uses no pals. The dragnet won't land him. We wouldn't know him even if he walked into this office.

"We've got to let him show himself. So does The Shadow. And if we clamp down on all the joints, where will that crook pop up? At some place like Jothan's, to murder when he robs. But as long as the joints stay open, that thief has got a racket to his liking."

"But you just stated that the gambling places are closing."

"They are. The list is narrowing. There are less places for this crook to raid. He's cornering himself, Commissioner, and he doesn't know it. But The Shadow does. That's why I say he's due to get the crook. Look at this list, Commissioner."

Cardona reached for a report sheet. He pointed out a name.

"Slook's Cafe," said Joe. "Sounds like a hash house; and that's all it looks like. One of those places with armchairs. But upstairs, they tell me, it's got one of the fanciest layouts in New York. Roulette and faro. Plenty of people with dough sneak into Slook's. Ones who are socially prominent, too.

"It's miles ahead of any other joint in town. Any of those that are left, I mean. That's where this stickup guy is due tonight; and if he's due, so is The Shadow. Don't think The Shadow is letting us down, Commissioner. The Shadow will be there."

"I'm not taking chances!" banged Weston. "At last, Cardona, you have shown some brains. Get ready. Pick your squad and join me."

"You mean we're raiding Slook's?"

"Exactly! We shall go in there and take charge. When the raider arrives, he will have to deal with us."

"But he may get wise and stay away."

"We shall take a chance on that, Cardona. We must venture, if we hope to gain."

"But The Shadow—"

"Bother The Shadow! Why should we depend upon him when our course lies open?"

ON a side street west of Broadway stood Slook's Cafe, a place that fitted Cardona's brief description. The armchair lunchroom was a blind for the upstairs gaming house; but there were other entrances also. Street men and lookouts were many hereabouts.

One side of the gambling hall flanked a low-roofed space between this building and the next. Shuttered windows were all along the wall. One of these, at the very end, opened into a hallway that adjoined the gambling room. That passage was unwatched. Some outsider must have guessed it.

For on this important evening, an intruder was prying at the shutters. Black against the side of the wall, he was clumsily trying to jimmy the barrier. He might have failed with other windows; but this one chanced to be comparatively weak. The shutters opened with a sudden jolt. The interloper entered.

A large crowd was at play within the bare-walled gambling room. The place lacked class; but the customers were not particular. All of the fancier gambling halls had closed. This one had gained the more exclusive patronage. Tuxedoed patrons rubbed shoulders with less genteel habitués. At one roulette table, a bejeweled dowager was staking heavily on the play.

"That's Mrs. Randolan," someone was saying. "She must have stopped here on her way to some swanky party. Look at that lot of gems. The pearl necklace—"

Someone uttered a shrill cry. All eyes turned toward the side passage. A black-clad raider was advancing: an automatic in each hand. Babbling voices ceased as the intruder uttered a fierce laugh. The automatics moved from side to side, edging players to the walls.

Croupiers heard a snarl. Nodding their willingness, they began to push money toward the center of the board. Others added house cash to the stakes that players had wagered. Quivering lips were muttering the identity that they thought belonged to the raider: "The Shadow!"

SHOVING one gun beneath his cloak, the raider pulled out a cloth bag and tossed it on the table. The cowed attendant hurriedly gathered the money into the bag. With a contemptuous laugh, the cloaked man stared along the wall. His eyes caught the glitter of jeweled finger rings. He beckoned to the croupier who held the bag. The man came toward him.

"Hold it out," ordered the raider. Then, to Mrs. Randolan, he added: "Shed those rings! Into the bag! And add the necklace for good measure!"

There was a snarl to the tone. Trembling, the dowager delivered the jewels and the necklace. The raider whisked the bag from the croupier. Retreating, he made his way to the passage. He tossed the closed bag through the window, then turned to make his departure.

At that instant, a door sprang open. The barrier was down the passage, at the farther end, where only the departing raider could observe it. Swinging, the impostor saw a swirling shape in black. He caught the gleam of eyes that blazed. An automatic muzzle leveled in his direction. Again, the impostor was faced by The Shadow.

Wildly, hopelessly, the crook scrambled for the window.

As The Shadow pressed the trigger of his automatic, a man sprang upon him from in back. The Shadow's aim was wide. His bullets found the open shutter; not the diving man who was going through the window. Coming in, The Shadow had overpowered one lookout; he had bound and gagged the fellow. This unexpected attacker was a second lookout who had chanced to find the first one.

Twisting, The Shadow fought to fling the man aside. Together, they staggered through the passage. There, The Shadow gave an upward heave and sent the man spinning headlong. The very power of his fling kept The Shadow moving forward. Half staggering, he stopped against the wall, just within the gaming room.

Sounds of pistol shots and scuffle had aroused the bolder persons present. Revolvers were flashing as thuggish gamesters leaped forward to begin a fight.

The Shadow wheeled. His laugh rose strident as his .45 broke loose with flame. He was firing high, above the heads of people; but his action was effective. Armed men broke; they dived for the cover of the tables.

Then came the shrill blasts of police whistles. One door splintered beneath the driving power of an ax. The Shadow turned, to choose the window through which his imitator had fled. He wanted to make pursuit before the law arrived.

The Shadow was too late. Officers were on the roof.

SPEEDING through the passage, The Shadow gained the stairway by which he had reached the gambling joint. At the bottom, he flung open the street door and sprang to the sidewalk. A policeman pounded upon him, driving down with a revolver.

The Shadow's fist caught the bluecoat's wrist. With a powerful twist, he wrenched away the officer's gun and sent it skidding along the sidewalk. Another twist and he was free.

Two dozen forward paces, as if in hasty flight. The Shadow stopped short and flattened against a wall beside a pair of steps. He did this in a space of darkness, just as the policeman fired with his regained gun.

As the revolver spurted, The Shadow delivered a strange, wild cry. More shots jabbed from the revolver. Again The Shadow gave a cry; this time, a trailing one that ended with an anguished choke.

The bluecoat pounded by, shouting as he ran. He thought that he had bagged his quarry. The Shadow's deceiving call had made the officer believe that a wounded man had kept on staggering. A patrol car skidded past The Shadow, to aid the bluecoat in his imaginary chase.

For a moment, the way was clear. The Shadow glided swiftly across the street and edged beneath a flight of high steps. He found an unlocked basement window; he opened it and entered a darkened house. With tiny flashlight glimmering, he picked his way through deserted rooms, opened a rear window and stepped out to a passage that led to the street beyond.

THE law's invasion of the gambling den had come too late to trap the raider whom both police and The Shadow sought. Worse than that, it had brought disaster to The Shadow's chase. His chance to overtake the impostor had ended, at least for this night. Commissioner Ralph Weston had staged a bad blunder.

Joe Cardona guessed that fact when he heard the reports of an unsuccessful search for a supposedly wounded raider. The jimmied window looked like a spot of entry. Yet lookouts testified that The Shadow had come by the stairs at the rear. Moreover, the sparing of the officers; the weird evanishment of a pursued departer—these were proof to Joe that The Shadow had been on the raider's trail.

Cardona, however, was wise enough to keep his theory from Commissioner Weston. That worthy was in no mood for criticism.

LATER, The Shadow stood within his sanctum. Burbank was speaking quietly across the wire. The contact man was relaying a report from Clyde Burke, who had just talked with Joe Cardona. The *Classic* reporter had learned the details of the raid at Slook's Cafe.

The Shadow made notations. When the call had ended, he brought typewritten report sheets into view. There were permanent records—statements gained through agents. Reports that The Shadow intended to keep for his archives. One was an old one. It referred to Corbal's raid on the Club Torreo.

Harry Vincent had been present on that occasion. Yet Harry had scarcely noticed Sparkler Meldin, who had also been on hand. Moreover, the jewel-sporting big shot from Havana had escaped Corbal's notice as well. The Shadow already knew that Corbal had missed an opportunity when he had failed to lift Sparkler's diamonds.

Corbal was dead. Another raider had taken up his game. A daring, cool-headed crook who did not overlook opportunities. Tonight, according to Clyde Burke, this new impostor had grabbed more than the money on the gaming tables. He had also bagged a dowager's jewels. A direct contrast between this rogue and Corbal.

A whispered laugh pervaded the sanctum. The Shadow's hand produced a sheet of paper. It was a cablegram from Havana. Addressed to Rutledge Mann, the investment broker, and signed Marsland. One week ago, Cliff had gone to Cuba at The Shadow's order.

**"SPARKLER" MELDIN— gambler from Havana.**

Though the cable referred to stocks and bonds, its actual message was a hidden one. Its wording was simply an answer to a question that The Shadow had ordered Cliff to discover. The cable told that Sparkler Meldin was not in Havana; nor had he been there since his first trip to New York.

Jewels overlooked; jewels seized. These showed a contrast between the second Shadow and the third. Only a person who had noticed Corbal's lapse would have remembered not to make one of his own, where gems were concerned. Particularly a person who could recognize rare stones when he saw them.

The Shadow had done more than guess the identity of the third Shadow. He knew the impostor for what he was; and who. The man with whom The Shadow still must deal was Sparkler Meldin, the big shot from Havana.

But in police headquarters, discussion still ranged over the mysteries of the gambling dens thefts.

### CHAPTER XVII
### WESTON TAKES ADVICE

"WELL, Commissioner, our chances ended with last night. That raid at Slook's has clamped the lid. There's not a first-class gambling joint in operation."

"Good riddance, Cardona. We shall try my policy a while. I told the reporters this morning that these raids by an unknown crook will end. For the simple reason that he will have nowhere to strike."

"Which makes it tough for The Shadow, Commissioner. And forces a mighty dangerous crook into new channels. Ones that we can't guess at present."

Weston made no comment. He merely passed a newspaper across the desk. It was a late edition; one that Cardona had not seen. A five o'clock final.

"There is my statement, Cardona," announced the commissioner. "The morning newspapers will pick it up and elaborate it. The public will know exactly how I stand."

"So will The Shadow," observed Cardona, ruefully. "Unless he already knows. That's not all I'm thinking about, either. The crook is going to read this stuff, Commissioner."

"Let him," decided Weston. "Perhaps he will recognize the futility of his misdeeds. We must find that man, Cardona. But not by allowing him open opportunity for crime."

The telephone bell rang. Weston picked up the instrument from his desk. Cardona heard his chief's tone change from brusqueness to affability; then to surprise.

"Hello, hello," said Weston. "Ah! Judge Trostler. Glad to hear from you... Certainly. I should be glad to learn such information... What's that? The Casino Havanola?... This positively amazes me."

Hanging up, Weston turned to Cardona.

"Rumor is rife, Cardona," declared the commissioner. "Someone has informed Judge Trostler that the Casino Havanola has gone in for heavy gambling! With the highest stakes ever played in New York!"

"Where did he get that dope?" demanded Cardona. "I was down there night before last. The place looked quiet enough. Duke Hydon showed me through there."

"I have seen the place also," stated Weston. "I cannot understand how gambling could go on there. Those rooms upstairs are open. Accessible to anyone."

Again, the telephone was jangling. Weston held another brief conversation. "Hello, Parrow... Yes, I have heard... No details, however... Yes, it may only be a rumor; still, it is a likely one..."

Hanging up, Weston stated more to Cardona.

"That was Parrow. Assistant to the district attorney. He has heard it also. There must be something to this rumor, Cardona. I wonder who else could tell us facts about the matter?"

"What about your friend Cranston?"

"Cranston?" Weston laughed. "He knows nothing, Cardona. A keen enough chap when it comes to big-game hunting. Bagging elephants and tigers. Or fishing for barracuda. But gambling is not within his range."

"He knew Sparkler Meldin," observed Cardona. "It was Cranston who introduced Meldin to you."

"That is true. I had almost forgotten. By the way, Cranston was with me when Hydon showed us about the Casino Havanola. Hydon was pleased to see him at the place. I wonder if Cranston has been going there regularly?"

"Why not ask him?"

"I shall." Weston glanced at his watch. "It is after six o'clock. We may find Cranston at the Cobalt Club. Come along with me, Cardona."

ARRIVED at the Cobalt Club, Weston and Cardona found the person whom they sought. Neither saw the semblance of a smile that appeared upon the fixed lips of Lamont Cranston. The Shadow had expected this visit; and with good reason. It was he who had made both telephone calls to Weston's office.

"Cranston," questioned Weston, "have you been at the Casino Havanola recently?"

"Yes," replied The Shadow. "Only a few nights ago. In fact, I am going there this evening."

"Tell me something about the place. Could it be a blind for a gambling room?"

"A perfect one! Except for one detail."

"And just what is that?"

"There would be no place to put the roulette tables, except on the roof."

Weston looked piqued. Cardona grinned.

"Nevertheless," added The Shadow, "I have heard that Sparkler Meldin is a clever chap. Gambling appears to be part of his existence. It is difficult to picture Meldin without also visualizing the background of a gaming room."

"You saw his gambling place in Havana?" inquired Weston. "How long ago, Cranston?"

"A year ago. Perhaps longer. I understand that Meldin is in Havana at present."

"He is. He will be back in New York later. Meanwhile, we would like to learn the real inside of this rumor."

"Is there a rumor?"

"Of course. That is why I asked you about the Casino Havanola."

"I see. Perhaps, Weston, the rumor is a trifle previous."

"Previous? You mean that gambling may not start until Meldin returns? Is that it?"

"Yes. Your trouble will begin then. You can

anticipate it, Commissioner. Do you know, I have felt quite guilty because I introduced Meldin to you. The man was merely an acquaintance of mine; not a friend. That is why I suggest that you end the nuisance before it begins."

"How can I do that?"

"By suspending the Casino Havanola's license."

"Absurd, Cranston! That would mean an injunction against the police department, to make us show cause why the club should be closed."

"Instigated by whom?"

"By Meldin, of course."

"From Havana?"

Weston beamed with sudden enthusiasm. "You have hit it, Cranston!" he exclaimed. "I shall do exactly as you have suggested! For a fortnight, the Casino Havanola had been under the sole management of Duke Hydon. I was given to understand that Hydon would be merely a subordinate.

"Since Meldin has not performed the duties of an actual proprietor, I am quite within my rights in giving this decision. It is for the public welfare. To protest, Meldin will have to come from Havana. When he does arrive, he will be at a disadvantage—thanks to his own negligence."

JOE CARDONA indulged in a grin.

"How soon are you going to shut down the place?" he asked. "Will you give them to the end of the week, Commissioner?"

"Yes," replied Weston. "That allows three more nights, including this evening. I shall call Hydon from here. In a way, I feel sorry for the fellow; he has a pleasant personality. At the same time, he knows that I cannot grant him a nightclub license after our experience with the Club Torreo. Therefore, I shall tell him that I cannot tolerate the Casino Havanola, since he—rather than Meldin—appears to be the proprietor."

"Better not mention Mr. Cranston's name," put in Cardona. "He's going down there tonight. Better let him appear to be surprised, if Hydon weeps on his shoulder and begs him to put in a good word with you."

"An excellent suggestion," interposed The Shadow, "and I have another, Commissioner. This was an interesting statement that you made today." In leisurely fashion, The Shadow picked up an afternoon newspaper. "People are probably pleased to learn that you have clamped down on the gambling racket. Why not announce that you are closing the Casino Havanola because of Duke Hydon's former connection with the Club Torreo?"

"I shall," agreed Weston. "That will make a story for the morning newspapers."

ONE hour later, The Shadow arrived at the Casino Havanola. Scarcely had he taken a table before the headwaiter arrived with a request. Addressing The Shadow as Mr. Cranston, he asked if the guest would be kind enough to come to Mr. Hydon's office.

The Shadow went to the office. He found Duke Hydon pacing the floor, muttering epithets into his beard. Seeing the arrival, Duke's manner changed. He became wheedling.

"A favor, Mr. Cranston," he pleaded. "One that only you can supply. I have received bad news—very bad news—"

"From Havana?"

"No, no! I have had no communication from Meldin. This word came from the police commissioner. He has ordered me to close this nightclub."

"On what ground?"

"He has not stated his true reason." Duke wagged a knowing finger. "I know what the commissioner believes. He thinks that I am running a hidden gambling establishment. That is why I should like you to speak with him, Mr. Cranston. You have been here often enough to know that the charge is false."

"My testimony would be rather negative," expressed The Shadow, in a dry tone. "The fact that I have seen no gambling room is not proof that such a place is absent."

Duke beckoned. They went from the office. As on the opening night, they ascended to the second floor. Like the space downstairs, the upper rooms were filled with diners.

"The cover charge is less up here," explained Duke. "Look, Mr. Cranston. Is there any place for gambling? See for yourself."

The Shadow nodded; then he eyed the fountain at the end of the hall. The water-spray was in operation, flooded by changing lights. The Shadow approached it.

"Quite a splendid sight," he observed. "I suppose that Meldin will enjoy seeing it?"

"Not if the place is closed when he gets back," grumbled Duke. "I don't know what is delaying Meldin. He should have been back in town this week. Well, Mr. Cranston, you have seen everything. I hope you will see fit to speak to the commissioner."

As they turned about, The Shadow noted the two cloakrooms; both were filled with garments. Two wiry Cubans were in charge, one behind each counter.

"Good workers, those Cubans," remarked Duke, as he and The Shadow walked away. "Sparkler Meldin brought them with him from Havana. He left them here. Competent, both of them, and courteous."

As they reached the top of the staircase, The Shadow paused to light a cigarette. Duke stopped several steps ahead. A young man was coming up the stairs. It was Harry Vincent. He strolled straight past The Shadow and continued along the hall.

"Coming downstairs, Mr. Cranston?" queried Duke, anxiously. "The floor show is just beginning. You should not miss it."

The Shadow followed the bearded man. He saw Duke show an expression of relief. The Shadow knew the reason. It was because of Harry Vincent. A former patron of the Club Torreo, Harry had gained special privileges at the Casino Havanola.

Going along the upstairs hallway, Harry stopped at the cloakroom on the right. He spoke to the white-jacketed Cuban, who nodded his approval. Harry waited while the fellow drew back the cloakroom door. Then The Shadow's agent entered.

Going deep into the cloakroom, he knocked upon the paneled end wall. A door swung inward at his signal.

Harry had gained admittance to the gambling room of the Casino Havanola. Harry had been there nearly every night since the opening of the place. He had forwarded regular reports to The Shadow. Those reports explained the telephoned tips that Weston had received. Yet The Shadow, though he knew the full secret of the Casino Havanola, had not revealed the complete facts to the law.

He had delivered enough to insure the closing of the nightclub. Beyond that, he had furnished nothing. Weston had failed to give complete cooperation; The Shadow's only course had been to use the commissioner as an unwitting aide in a new plan of action.

IT was after nine o'clock when The Shadow strolled from the Casino Havanola. On the avenue, enterprising newsboys were already shouting out the death knell of the glittering nightclub. Patrons were eagerly buying newspapers.

"Commissioner orders nightclub to close—"

The Shadow bought a copy of the morning *Classic*. This was the bulldog edition, on the street before nine p.m. He smiled as he noticed Clyde Burke's name as having written the nightclub story. The Shadow's own agent had been the reporter who had gained an interview with Weston.

The police commissioner had taken advice from The Shadow. Tonight; then two nights more. Those alone remained for the Casino Havanola. A fact that was doubly to The Shadow's liking. First,

because the law would investigate no further. No need to molest the Club Havanola on the flimsy strength of rumor; for the place would soon be ended.

The second reason was quite as important as the first. The Casino Havanola hid the only remaining gambling joint that catered to wealthy, carefully chosen customers. Sparkler Meldin had not raided it, for the place was his own. But since the Casino's career was doomed, Sparkler might form other plans.

Wealthy customers, with rolls of cash that would not cross the gambling tables; patrons loaded with jewels—bait for Sparkler Meldin. One more chance for the crook to play the role of the third Shadow. To give himself an alibi, when he did.

Tomorrow night. Then would come the best time for opportunity. Sparkler would be too wise to wait until the final evening. Thus did The Shadow reason, as he entered his limousine and ordered Stanley to drive eastward. The car was headed for the vicinity of the sanctum. The Shadow was donning cloak and hat.

Well had The Shadow begun to gauge his plans. Yet always, there was the chance of unexpected circumstance. Though The Shadow had not learned it, trouble had already begun to break.

## CHAPTER XVIII
## CROOKS SURPRISED

COMMISSIONER WESTON had been a bit too eager in his contact with the press. Therein lay the source of the trouble that was to show a marked effect upon The Shadow's plans. Had Weston been slower in making his statement, it would not have appeared in the early edition. Hence patrons of the Casino Havanola would not have learned the nightclub's fate until the next morning.

As it chanced, however, a buzz began to hover about the Casino Havanola, shortly after The Shadow had departed. The stir spread through the lower floor. It reached the dining rooms above. At last it filtered through to the hidden space beyond the end wall of the second floor.

There, the news spread again. Half a hundred wealthy customers suspended play. The Casino Havanola was through, according to report. Until the rumor was settled, no one cared about the spinning roulette wheels. They must have the answer, these patrons of the Club Havanola.

Duke Hydon appeared. The bearded manager came from a tiny office beyond the gaming tables. He waved his arms and called for silence. Commotion ceased. Duke waved to an attendant; the man brought a stack of newspapers.

"Ladies and gentlemen," announced Duke, "I regret to announce that the Casino Havanola will soon be closed. At the same time, I take pleasure in announcing that it will continue business for two nights more. Therefore, I suggest that all patrons take advantage of the remaining opportunity.

"I can assure you that the police will not interfere tonight; nor on the coming nights. The commissioner has said that we must close. We have agreed. The commissioner is satisfied, and pleased because of our good behavior."

A round of laughter came as Duke made pause. The bearded man chuckled.

"I have just talked to the commissioner on the telephone," he stated. "He said that he was pleased because I accepted his decision. Of course"—Duke paused to chortle dryly—"our friend, the commissioner, has not visited every part of the Casino Havanola."

More laughter. Duke finished his announcement. His final words were significant.

"As for other interference," he declared, "such as other establishments have experienced, you need fear nothing. We are quite prepared to handle all intruders. Your valuables are safe when you come here."

Duke ordered the attendant to distribute the newspapers among the customers. Players scanned the headlines, then threw the journals aside. Wheels resumed their spinning. Currency flooded the tables. Women who wore jewels laughed with their companions. A carefree atmosphere had been regained.

FEW persons noted the two men who strolled into Duke Hydon's tiny upstairs office. The customers took them for other players, since they were attired in well-fitting evening clothes. But the conference that developed proved these men to be of different ilk.

"Hello, Kidder; hello, Brad." Duke nodded to each man in turn. "Sit down. I want to talk to you. You know, there's something fishy about this racket going sour."

"Do you think The Shadow's in it?" growled the man called "Kidder."

"He may be," replied Duke. "Perhaps he was afraid to crack this place. He may have passed word to the commissioner."

"Not likely," put in Brad. "You can't tell me that The Shadow would be showing any favors to the commish. Not with the way The Shadow's been acting lately."

"You never can tell about The Shadow," observed Duke. "It was on his account that I brought you fellows in from Chicago. Kidder Dagland and Brad Stuggart. You two always did

work together. Keeping up a swell front. Kidder and Brad—the alibi dudes."

"A good racket, in the old days," remarked Kidder. "A guy needed an alibi out in Chi. It didn't count for much, either, unless two people backed him on it. That was our specialty, all right."

Duke raised his hand impatiently. He spread out some sheets of paper.

"Look at these," he said. "List of people here tonight. All about them—how they became acquainted with the place. That's one reason I brought you fellows in here—you and those other torpedoes who are working as attendants. I wanted you to keep an eye on the customers."

"We've been doing it," stated Kidder.

"All right," returned Duke. "Tell me who's phony. I think that some stoolie has muscled his way into the place."

"Not much chance of that," observed Brad. "I'd have spotted a phony the first time he showed up."

"No suggestions, then?" questioned Duke.

Both men shook their heads.

"Very well. Go out and watch—"

Duke stopped. Someone was at the door. It proved to be the gaming tables banker.

"One fellow going out, Duke," he informed. "The house owes him two hundred bucks. Says to keep it until he gets back. He's going to get dinner."

"Who is he?"

"His name is Vincent."

Duke turned to Kidder and Brad. "It's just a hunch," he admitted, "but maybe it's a good one. You two cut down the secret stairway to the lower office. Then come upstairs again by the outer stairway and spot this bird. Watch him."

Kidder and Brad nodded. The former pressed a side-wall light switch, with quick up and down *clicks*. A panel slid open, to show a spiral staircase. The pair descended, closing the panel behind them. Duke turned to the cashier.

"Stall him for a few minutes," he stated. "Maybe he wants an IOU, so he can have evidence against us. Tell him we don't give them. Put his name in the book and have him wait while you bring it to me for an O.K."

IN the gaming room, Harry was awaiting the banker's return. Chips were used, within certain limits, at the Casino Havanola. Harry had turned in his supply; he had asked that they be credited to his name. He had done this with a purpose; namely, to find an excuse for visiting Duke Hydon in the office.

When the banker arrived to state the arrangements, Harry caught a glimpse of Duke. The man-

**Two men landed suddenly on Harry's shoulders.**

ager was standing in the open doorway of the little office. Harry could see an empty room beyond. He decided to drop the matter as soon as possible.

"Very well," he said, when the banker had explained. "Put my name in the book. Your word will be all right." This time, it was the banker who played for time.

"Mr. Hydon will mark it with his O.K.—"

"That will not be necessary," interposed Harry. "I'll only be gone half an hour."

"But if you can wait for only a few minutes—"

Harry shook his head. He strolled toward the exit. A watcher opened the sliding door. Harry stepped through to the cloakroom. The Cuban signaled him through. Harry reached the hallway. He continued along the passage and down the circular stairway. There he stepped into a telephone booth and dialed a number.

Two men spied Harry in the telephone booth. They were Kidder and Brad, coming through from the lower office. Kidder waved Brad back; then slipped into a vacant booth next to Harry's. He caught the finish of a conversation.

"Business resumed..." Harry was evidently describing to Burbank, The Shadow's contact man, the scene in the gaming room. "Yes, everything will be the same tomorrow... I'm going up again, to collect some money. Shall I fake an excuse to get into the office?...

"Yes, I can call again in fifteen minutes... Wait." Harry glanced from the telephone booth. "There's a vacant table right here. If you call me, I can answer promptly... Yes, anytime within the next half hour..."

Kidder slid from the booth. He joined Brad and motioned him toward the stairway. They watched Harry come out and take the table nearest to the telephone booth. Kidder whispered to Brad, who nodded and went up the stairs. Then Kidder went over to Harry's table.

"Mr. Vincent?" he inquired, in an undertone.

Harry nodded.

"Duke sent me down," confided Kidder. "He wants to see you about that credit. Could you come up with me before you begin dinner?"

"Certainly!"

HARRY had noted Kidder in the gaming room, but had supposed the man to be an ordinary patron. Apparently, Kidder had some connection with the house. Harry was interested in this finding. He followed the man to the second floor. They went through the cloakroom at the right.

Always the one at the right, Harry had learned. There was a door from the left cloakroom also; but Harry had never seen it used. Probably it had been provided only in case large groups of players crowded the gambling hall.

Harry followed Kidder through to the upstairs office. The man opened the door and stood aside to let Harry enter. The Shadow's agent found Duke at his desk. The manager arose and nodded affably. He spoke in a rather loud tone.

"There has been a slight error in calculation, Mr. Vincent. Only a matter of a few dollars; but I thought it best to inform you—"

Two men landed suddenly on Harry's shoulders. The Shadow's agent twisted; punching hard, but uselessly, he sprawled beneath the combined attack of Kidder and Brad. The second rogue had been waiting outside the office. He had followed Kidder and they had quietly closed the door. Swift and efficient in their attack, they were choking Harry into submission.

Duke bounded forward and plastered a piece of wide adhesive tape across Harry's mouth. Kidder was holding Harry's legs, while Brad was twisting a strap around the victim's wrists. Three against one, with a surprise at the beginning, they had The Shadow's agent helpless.

"I'll get the call downstairs," declared Kidder. "I'll tell you more when I come back."

He went out through the gaming room. Going down the stairs, Kidder heard the ringing of the bell in the telephone booth. He hurried his descent and answered the call. Though out of breath, Kidder managed to fake Harry's voice:

"Hello, hello! This is Vincent on the wire."

Kidder waited. A quiet voice responded: Burbank's.

"Off duty."

"What about the office?" queried Kidder. "I may get a chance to talk to Duke Hydon—"

"Off duty."

"Until when?"

A pause; then the quiet voice replied:

"Until tomorrow night."

Kidder made no response. He waited, hoping that a new statement would come over the wire. A dozen seconds passed; then Kidder heard the click of the receiver. The rogue hung up his own receiver. He had learned nothing of much consequence; but he had staged a bluff.

KIDDER took his time about returning through the front way to the gaming room. He supposed that Duke expected him back by that route; but he did not want to go in and out at too frequent intervals. It was ten minutes before he arrived at the tiny office—to find Harry Vincent propped in a chair, staring helplessly at Duke and Brad.

"Will he talk?" demanded Kidder.

"We haven't tried him yet," replied Duke. "We wanted to hear from you, Kidder."

"I talked to the mug at the other end. Learned nothing, except that this guy is off duty until tomorrow night. When I talked, I said that I was Vincent."

"Off duty? What do you think that means?"

"It's easy enough to find out."

Kidder turned to Harry. He snarled as he faced the bound man. There was venom in Kidder's tone.

"You're telling us who you're working for!" he announced. "Who the guy was that you called! Everything else we want to know! Do you get me?"

Kidder expected a nod. Harry did not give one. Kidder spat a threat.

"I'll *make* you talk! I've handled tougher eggs than you. I'm putting you wise; you'll save yourself a lot of misery if you don't hold out."

Harry remained motionless. Kidder moved over to talk with Brad. They buzzed a low conversation, one that required a full five minutes. With nods and glowers, the two were building up some scheme of torture. A crafty preliminary, capable of jangling a strong man's nerve. Harry could feel the strain, for he knew himself to be the topic of conversation.

"All right," decided Kidder, finally. "Get ready, Brad. We'll hand him the heat treatment, for a starter."

"Not here!" protested Duke. "We've kept him here too long already! It's been twenty minutes since you went down to get that telephone call, Kidder. We'll have to take him to the lower office."

AS he spoke, Duke arose and went to the wall. He gave the switch its rapid clicks. The panel opened. Duke motioned to Kidder and Brad. The pair hoisted Harry and lugged him down the spiral staircase.

It was a precipitous trip into lower darkness; and a rough one, for the stairs were narrow. Nor were Harry's captors gentle. Harry was aching from a dozen jolts when they reached the bottom.

There they waited for Duke. Evidently the manager had made a brief trip into the gaming room, for it took him a few minutes to arrive. Coming down in the darkness, Duke pressed by the two men and their burden. He opened the panel into the lower office. He stepped into deeper darkness.

"Bring him through," whispered Duke. "Say— why did you fellows turn out the light? Wasn't it on when you came down here before?"

"Sure," growled Kidder. "What's more, we didn't turn it off. It must have been one of the headwaiters."

"I've ordered them to stay out of here," snarled Duke. "I'll find out who went against my order! I'll—"

Duke's speech ended. He had found the light switch and had pressed it. His words were frozen by the sound of a harsh, gibing laugh. Duke saw his companions staring toward the far wall of the room, with Harry Vincent slumped between them. Duke turned. He saw the object of their gaze.

A shape in black. A fisted form with leveled automatics. A figure that Harry's captors recognized. A sight that brought quavered gasps from their lips.

"The Shadow!"

Harry Vincent's eyes had filled with hope. Though the laugh, when repeated, was echoless, Harry had no fear. Rogues were trapped. He was rescued. Such was Harry's swelling thought; then, in an instant, his bubble burst.

The folds of the cloak dropped as the head tossed backward. The sneering laugh changed to a

raucous snort. Duke and his companions stared at a sharp-featured face. The long chin, the beady eyes—those were features that Duke Hydon recognized when he uttered an elated cry: "Sparkler Meldin!"

## CHAPTER XIX
### SPARKLER'S STORY

A GLEAMING smile flashed from the features of Sparkler Meldin. Gold teeth were glittering in the light. Then came the sparkle of large gems, as the arrival drew away his black gloves. Last, the huge flash of a diamond stickpin when the cloak was tossed aside.

Kidder and Brad gaped. They had heard Duke describe Sparkler; this was the first time they had seen the man from Havana. Sparkler had few friends, even in New York; and he had none in Chicago. Yet any crook would have guessed his identity, once having heard of him.

"What—what's the racket, Sparkler?" queried Duke, his voice a stammer. "We thought you were The Shadow!"

"You're not the first who fell for it," snapped back the jewel flasher. "The only trouble is that the racket's through. Well—it was good while it lasted."

"You saw the early newspapers! You know about the commissioner closing the joint?"

"Sure! But that's not the racket that I mean. I'm talking about this Shadow business. That's what brought me here—after I saw a newspaper."

Duke looked puzzled. Sparkler's laugh was harsh. Narrowed eyes studied Kidder and Brad, also the prisoner between them.

"Who are these fellows?"

"Kidder Dagland and Brad Stuggart," explained Duke. "A couple of regulars from Chicago. They brought a bunch of torpedoes with them. I've got the trigger crew working as attendants in the joint. Your Cubans are on the front."

"All on account of The Shadow?"

"That's why. I wanted to be ready in case he tried to knock off the joint."

Sparkler's lips phrased a chuckle.

"Even *you* didn't get it, Duke," laughed the sharp-faced visitor. Gem-laden hands were placing automatics on the table. *"I was The Shadow! I'm* the bird who staged the knock-offs!"

"Don't kid me, Sparkler! You were in the Club Torreo the night The Shadow raided it."

"Sure! That was before I muscled in on the racket. The guy that raided the Club Torreo was a phony. I guessed it. I bumped him and went after the gravy for myself."

"Who was the guy?"

"The stiff they found in Greenwich Village. The one they identified as George Corbal. I croaked him in his hideout. Took his swag; his cloak and hat, too."

"You've been wearing them?"

"No; I had an outfit of my own. Listen, Duke; I figured the fellow was a phony—that he was getting by on The Shadow's rep. I saw a swell opportunity. I started for Havana, but doubled back. Rigged up my own black outfit; then breezed in on Corbal to see how he'd like it. He thought I was The Shadow."

LIGHT was dawning on Duke. He started to ask a question. Sparkler's rasp intervened. Duke listened.

"I figured that the lid would be coming soon." Gold teeth gleamed in a wise grin. "That it wouldn't be long before the commissioner clamped down. This place being my joint, the thing to do was make business better for it. So I knocked off the others."

"Like you were The Shadow!"

"That's it! I threw the gravy to you, Duke. Naturally, I laid off this joint."

"Smart business, Sparkler. I never guessed it."

"I've used my hideouts; I've grabbed my swag and stowed it. But the racket was to work entirely on my own. You didn't even need to be wise, Duke."

"Why not, Sparkler?"

"Because I figured I might have to stage a knock-off here. That's why I blew in tonight: thinking that it might be a good stunt."

Duke was staring; his bearded face showed anger. It was Kidder who chuckled; his tone showed admiration.

"I get it," he volunteered. "The clamp has been put on, Duke. The Casino Havanola is through. The best bet was to pin another job on The Shadow."

"And an alibi for myself," came Sparkler's addition. "Nobody—not even you, Duke—would have doped it out that I was passing myself as The Shadow. I came in here through the side door. It's easy to pull a sneak, when you're tricked out in a black cloak. I intended to go up through the upstairs office. As luck had it, you fellows came down. So I figured the best bet was to let you in on the know."

"You fooled us, Sparkler," Duke said. "If you want to go up and stage the raid, I'll fix it. Kidder can pass the word to the torpedoes to act like dummies. Only—"

"I know what you're going to say, Duke. That it might hurt you. Particularly since the police commissioner is closing the joint only on suspicion.

I thought of that, Duke. It was the one reason I wanted to lay off."

"I'd have to take it on the lam because it would expose the gaming tables to the police—"

"I know. Two blacklist markers would ruin you. But I knew where you would hop. To Havana. I intended to give you the whole low-down when you got into the clear. Well, I can stage a raid if you want it. We'll talk that over. Meanwhile, who is this mug?"

A glittering hand flashed toward Harry Vincent.

"His name's Vincent," stated Duke. "We think he's working for The Shadow."

"What makes you think that?"

"Kidder spotted him putting in a phone call—making some kind of a report. There was a return call. Kidder answered it and pulled a bluff. They don't expect to hear from Vincent until tomorrow night."

"Yank that adhesive off his face. I want to look at him."

BRAD wrenched away the tape. Sparkler's face was glaring down at Harry's. A nod followed.

"I thought I recognized him. I saw this guy at the Club Torreo."

"Sure he was, Sparkler," agreed Duke. "That's why I let him come in here. I thought he was all right."

"He was the bimbo who made a grab for the phony Shadow."

"Say—that's right! What do you make of that, Sparkler?"

"It's simple enough. This fellow Vincent knew that it was Corbal. How about it, Vincent? The Shadow planted you at the Club Torreo to grab the phony. Is that it?"

No comment from Harry.

"I'll make him talk," growled Kidder. "That's what we brought him down here for. Come on, Brad—"

"Wait!" Gems flashed from a restraining hand. Sparkler's voice was hard. "If Vincent was there to grab Corbal, he was here to grab me. Don't worry about putting the heat on him. We won't need to."

"Why not?"

The query came from Duke. Sparkler's answering rasp was prompt.

"Because," came the comment, "if Vincent makes no report tomorrow night, The Shadow will come here himself. He is liable to come anyway. He's been trailing me all along the line. I was lucky to get away from him at Slook's Cafe.

"The Shadow knows about this joint of ours, Duke. If he didn't, this stooge of his wouldn't be here. The Shadow knows a lot; but there's one thing he doesn't know. He hasn't guessed that I'm the fellow who's trading on his rep. He knows there's a phony—that's all.

"On that account, he'll figure that I'm due here. Since the joint is closing, there are only two chances left. Tomorrow and the night after. The Shadow will show up tomorrow, figuring that it's the best bet. He may come here ahead of me; that would be his best bet. Yes, The Shadow will be here and waiting.

"That's when we'll get him. He won't have a chance! We'll put the finger on The Shadow. We'll rub him out! Everything will be planted on him. We'll get a handshake from the police commissioner, as well as from every big shot in New York. It's a perfect setup! I'll be in the upstairs office, covering, while you fellows stick to the gaming room."

HARRY VINCENT repressed a groan, as he heard the rasped arrangement. He had failed The Shadow. On his account—if for nothing else—his chief would be sure to enter the trap. Harry's groan was audible; The Shadow's agent heard a harsh chuckle.

"We've found our ticket." The rasp was Sparkler's. "We'll hold this prisoner, and let him talk afterward—when we have bagged The Shadow. Maybe we won't need to hear him then. He's nothing but bait, anyway. Where can you stow him, Duke?"

"In here." The bearded man opened a farther panel, to show a small, windowless room that adjoined the spiral stairway. There was a cot in the closet-like compartment. "It's got a ventilator, so he won't suffocate."

"Cut him loose and stick him in there on the cot. We'll lock the panel from this side."

"But what if he starts to raise a row?"

"He won't. Because I'm parking here for the night. So are you fellows. We'll take turns sleeping on the couch. Tonight and all day tomorrow. There'll be three of us always on watch."

"Just on account of Vincent?"

"No. I tell you he means nothing. Our job is to be ready all the time, in case The Shadow shows up before we expect him. We take no chances where The Shadow is concerned."

Bonds were cut. Harry was shoved into the little room. Kidder sprawled the prisoner on the cot. The panel clicked shut. Harry heard it being locked. Again, The Shadow's agent groaned.

His case was hopeless, with three men on constant watch outside. The Shadow's plight would be hopeless also, when tomorrow night arrived. So thought Harry Vincent.

## CHAPTER XX
## DEATH IS DEALT

EARLY the next evening. Business as usual at the Casino Havanola. Except for one point: Duke Hydon was allowing no visitors in his downstairs office. Whenever a knock sounded on the door, Duke answered by stepping out and conducting conversation in the passage. In this manner, he blocked the only direct entrance to the downstairs office.

Duke had just held a five-minute conversation with one of the headwaiters. The fellow went away; Duke stepped back into the office and locked the door behind him. He turned to the desk, to see Sparkler Meldin playing solitaire. Diamonds glittered as fingers turned up cards. Gold teeth gleamed as the sharp features grinned.

"Kidder and Brad just went upstairs." Sparkler's thumb nudged toward the panel that hid the spiral stairway. "They lugged Vincent with them. Going to park him in a corner of the upper office. Bound and gagged."

"They could have left him down here—"

"It was Kidder's idea, and it sounded like a good one. He said we ought to have Vincent where we could watch him. What's more, we might need to use him."

Duke nodded.

"Let's go up, Sparkler," he suggested. "We'll use that upper office as headquarters."

They arrived in the upper office, to find Harry Vincent tied up in the corner. Duke motioned Sparkler to the chair at the desk. Nervously, the bearded manager kept pacing about.

"Worried, Duke?"

Duke nodded at Sparkler's question.

"Yes," he admitted. "My part is a rather tough one. The others are outside; you are stationed here. Which means that I have to keep moving in between. I wonder just where I'll be when The Shadow shows up."

"It won't matter, Duke. Everything is arranged—"

A knock at the door. Kidder's voice. Duke called the man into the room. The buzz of conversing players, the clatter of the gaming room— both were audible during the short interval when the door was open.

"A hot tip, Duke!" informed Kidder. "Joe Cardona just dropped in! He's having a dinner in one of the second-floor rooms."

"Joe Cardona? Is anyone with him?"

"A couple of guys that look like dicks. Brad was outside; he spotted them."

"Humph! Just snooping around, so they can rub it in. Well, they don't matter. We expect the police in anyway, after the fireworks are over. All I'm wondering is, who tipped them off to come here."

JOE CARDONA was wondering on that very point himself. Dining in one of the second-story rooms, the acting inspector was thinking over a telephone call that he had received at headquarters. The voice had been that of Swedley Jothan.

Cardona happened to know that the philanthropist was out of town. Yet Cardona had not forgotten the night when he had dashed off to save a man named Swedley, when he should have been looking out for Jothan. J. M. Swedley's first name had proven to be James, a fact which had irked Cardona somewhat.

Swedley Jothan, however, had been rescued by The Shadow; and he had delivered a message that he had received directly from the sleuth in black. Jothan's story had clicked with both Cardona and Weston. It had restored the commissioner's confidence for a while. Only Cardona and Weston had heard the true description of Shadow versus Shadow.

So tonight, though Cardona was puzzled by the telephone call from Jothan, he had no question regarding the authority behind it. He was confident that he had received a message from The Shadow. His speculation concerned the actual speaker, only.

No word to Weston. Cardona had promised that to the man who talked like Swedley Jothan. Instructions to be followed to the letter. Cardona had accepted them. He could remember the terse statements:

"Casino Havanola—upstairs dining room—cloakrooms at the end of hallway—investigate as soon as both Cubans have left—"

Cardona had seen the Cubans when he had strolled down the hall to look at the shimmering fountain. From where he was at present seated, Joe could see almost to the end of the hall. He had noted several persons going to the cloakrooms. A few of them had not returned.

Joe signaled to a plainclothes man at another table. The fellow nodded. He sauntered into the hallway and strolled toward the fountain. Soon he returned. A shake of his head was indication that neither Cuban had left his post.

Five minutes followed. A stooped man with gray beard passed along the hallway, leaning on a bamboo walking stick. The man was wearing hat and overcoat, and he was carrying a satchel. Cardona wondered if he would return from the cloakroom. Joe watched; then saw a white-jacketed Cuban come along the hall.

This was not astonishing. Obviously, two were on duty at the cloakrooms, so that one could go on errands whenever necessary. Nevertheless, Cardona was particularly interested in the activities of the Cubans. Seeing one of them depart, Joe wondered about the other.

FINISHING a plate of spaghetti, the acting inspector arose and strolled along the hall. He stopped at the fountain. He looked to the right. There was no Cuban behind the window of the cloakroom. A quick glance to the left. The second Cuban was also gone.

Quickly, Cardona thrust his head through the open window on the right. No sign of a hiding Cuban. Going to the other window, Cardona craned his neck. He spied something white upon the floor. He yanked open the door and entered. Brushing overcoats aside, he reached the rear of the room.

He found the Cuban, bound and gagged in a corner. The man's eyes were closed. The white that Cardona had spotted was part of the fellow's jacket. Cardona saw a satchel in the corner. He yanked it open; within he saw the gray mass of a false beard; with it the bamboo cane, crushed in telescopic fashion to a mere six-inch length.

Beside Cardona was an end wall panel, cleared of coats and hats. Joe pressed his hand against the woodwork. The panel yielded; it slid sidewise into the wall. Fingers sliding to his pocket, Cardona gripped the butt of his revolver. He drew the weapon while he stared at the sight before him.

Cardona was looking into a lighted room, a gambling hall half-filled with well-dressed patrons. Standing at a central spot was a figure cloaked in black—a menacing intruder who slowly gestured with a brace of automatics. Silenced customers were backing to the walls; attendants likewise. Tables lay clear to view, displaying a harvest of cash for this unexpected reaper.

With sidelong glance, Cardona noted another door in this same wall. Its guard was standing with upraised arms. Apparently the cloakroom on the right had served as the only regular entrance. That was why this intruder had chosen the cloakroom on the left. He had been the stooping, bearded man. His satchel had contained the raiment of black.

One Cuban gone, the bold visitor must have overpowered the other, single-handed.

Cardona's gun stopped halfway to levelness. For an instant, Joe had been ready to cover the cloaked intruder; to shoot him down before he had a chance. He thought that he had trapped the third Shadow. Then realization froze Joe to inaction.

This was no impostor! This was *The Shadow!* It fitted with that telephone call that had come in

Jothan's voice: "—cloakrooms at the end of hallway—investigate as soon as both Cubans have left—" Remembered words thrummed through Cardona's brain.

The Shadow had predicted what had happened; he had relied upon Cardona's keenness to spot the game, once the lead had been given. This must be The Shadow, revealing a hidden gambling den. Holding everyone at bay, waiting for the law to raid!

Cardona dared not leave. He foresaw hazards for The Shadow. It was better to wait for the squad to come here. Cardona knew that his men might arrive any moment, since he had not returned to the dining room.

Hence Cardona waited, drawing back into the cloakroom, ready to warn his followers for silence, until they could spring a sudden entry. By that plan, he could shift others through the opposite cloakroom.

ACROSS the gambling hall stood Duke Hydon. He was just outside the tiny office. Duke could not see Cardona, for the cloaked invader stood directly between him and the exit to the cloakroom. Duke's hands were raised; his eyes were staring. His lips, however, were mumbling words.

"It's The Shadow—he's got the lead—too quick for Kidder and Brad—but they'll jump to it if they get the break—so will the torpedoes—"

"Edge over, Duke!" came a whispered rasp through the crack of the office door. The barrier was slightly ajar; Duke could catch Sparkler Meldin's harsh tone. "I've got him covered! That's it—stick right where you are. Your shoulder is clear of my gat. The old smoke wagon is ready."

"Let him have it!" mouthed Duke. "Drop him, Sparkler! You've got the range. Drill him, quick—"

"Not yet. Wait until he moves forward. Closer to the tables. We're framing him, Duke. We want it to look like he's come to grab the cash. So all the people will swear he's crooked."

Sparkler's whisper ended. The cloaked invader was advancing toward the very center of the room, straight to a table where stacks of money lay. A gibe came from lips that were masked by upturned folds of cloth. The sneer caused frightened players to back closer toward the walls.

Duke noted, however, that some were reluctant to yield their ground. Kidder—Brad—torpedoes—

"Now!" whispered Duke. "Start it, Sparkler! He's almost at the gaming table—"

DUKE broke off. An attendant, close beside another, had edged over to hide his right arm behind his pal's left shoulder. The moving man was one of the torpedoes. His raised arm was dipping down. It snapped upward as the fellow sprang suddenly to the left. A revolver flashed. The torpedo fired.

The cloaked invader wheeled. Furiously, he aimed and pressed the trigger of a .45. The torpedo's shot had sizzled wide. The first bullet from the automatic clipped the fellow's shoulder.

"The Shadow's dropped him!"

People along the walls were rolling to the safety of the floor when Duke gasped the words. Others, however, still retained their feet: men who were spread about in a semicircle. Kidder and Brad had posted their marksmen for just such a job as this. Half a dozen revolvers were flashing; muzzles jabbed simultaneous spurts toward that wheeling, black-clad fighter in the middle of the room.

A big gun roared from beside Duke Hydon's ear. Its aim was perfect. Duke had expected such a shot from Sparkler. Yet the blast was unnecessary. Already other sharpshooters had done their work. Springing from every side, they had riddled their lone foe. A cloaked form was sprawling forward. Killers had loosed the venom that they had reserved for The Shadow.

Automatics clattered from loosening fists. The black-clad fighter rolled grotesquely, then lay motionless, almost at Duke Hydon's feet. His slouch hat wavered, then fell from his head.

Duke, leaping forward, spied the upturned face. The cry that Duke emitted was one that came convulsively to his lips.

"Sparkler! Sparkler Meldin!"

ONCE again, Duke had recognized a face that had been hidden by a hat brim. The same face that he had seen last night: Sparkler Meldin's. Only a moment ago, Sparkler had been in the office, whispering harshly to Duke. Yet here was Sparkler, riddled with slugs, dead upon the floor of the gaming room! It was incredible!—impossible!—yet Duke could not stop to reason. Nor could Kidder and Brad. They, too, were staring at that upturned, blood-streaked countenance. They saw the widespread lips, the gleaming gold teeth that glittered with a frozen leer. The cloak had fallen away; a diamond stickpin flashed from Sparkler's collar. Gloved fingers bulged with rings beneath the cloth.

Sparkler Meldin!

The name crowded three startled brains. Then came an answer to the riddle. A taunt that left no doubt concerning the identity of the dead man on the floor. The laugh that swept to startled ears was

Boldly, The Shadow had stepped forth to deal with danger. He was faced by men who had a zest for blood.

proof that Sparkler Meldin had been slain; for it was proof that The Shadow lived.

The office door had swung wide open. From the space within had stepped a cloaked and shrouded figure. A being in black, whose mirth rang out defiant challenge, whose vivid laughter swept to high crescendo; then staggered the room with shivering echoes.

The Shadow—not Sparkler Meldin—had come to the Casino Havanola last night. Made up to look like Sparkler, The Shadow himself had planned a successful trap. His mesh had snared a murderer. The Shadow had resumed his garb of black.

Ready with huge automatics, The Shadow was prepared to deal with foemen. Gun-bearing crooks were faced by the real avenger whom they had failed to conquer!

## CHAPTER XXI
## CRIME'S AFTERMATH

BOLDLY, The Shadow had stepped forth to deal with danger. He was faced by men who had a zest for blood. The same guns that had downed the interloper were still in ready fists. Kidder, Brad, and their squad were ready to battle The Shadow as they had fought with Sparkler Meldin.

The odds were better in their favor. They had started from scratch with the false Shadow; but their weapons were already drawn when they faced the real. Revolvers sprang to action; fingers were quick on hair-triggers. But bullets came too late.

The Shadow had swung forward, whirling as he came. He feinted to the left. His trigger squeezes answered the finger pulls of crooks. The Shadow's shots were swift and crippling.

Kidder Dagland, as he fired one faulty shot, received a bullet in the wrist. His gun slipped from his fingers. Brad Stuggart, leaping forward as he thrust his gun, was stopped by a second winging shot. Brad spun about and sprawled. The bullet had clipped him in the shoulder.

Crooks were backing as they fired. Though desperate, the torpedoes wanted to avoid The Shadow's aim. Their one chance to find the whirling target depended upon Duke Hydon. The bearded man was in The Shadow's course. Bare-handed, Duke was springing in to stop the cloaked fighter's elusive drive.

A black-gloved fist swung sidewise to gain aim at a distant foe. Well calculated, that maneuver. The hand stopped short as it encountered Duke's jaw. The bearded man went floundering backward.

The Shadow boomed an instantaneous shot toward a diving gunner. The bullet missed its mark by a scant fraction. But its effect was as good as a hit.

Henchmen had lost their nerve. They were ready to drop their guns and cry for mercy. Kidder and Brad were downed; the remaining crooks had no leadership. Guns were about to drop from yielding hands when The Shadow's swift work ceased. Staring crooks saw gloved hands thrust smoking automatics out of sight.

Then came the reason. Hurtling men were bounding in from the cloakroom entrances. Savagely, they fell upon the thugs and bore them to the floor, wrenching their guns away. Struggling crooks tried to break free. They were bowled against roulette tables. Boards were overturned; wheels went clattering, rolling; cash and chips spread everywhere.

Cardona and his squad had broken in upon the scene. The Shadow had deliberately spared the defeated rowdies that the law might have its opportunity. Duke made a wild grab for a lost revolver, while Kidder and Brad staggered about, looking for an avenue that would offer a getaway. All acted hopelessly; detectives pounced upon them.

Startled players were rising from along the walls, freed from the menace of conflict. They had witnessed two swift frays; they were watching a third, its finish a foregone conclusion. Beaten crooks were in the hands of the law.

JOE CARDONA saw The Shadow above the body of Sparkler Meldin. The ace watched The Shadow rip away the bloodstained cloak that covered the impostor's form. The Shadow's hand plucked up the hat that lay upon the floor; then tugged away the gloves that covered Sparkler's hands.

A solemn laugh was audible, as The Shadow held these trophies high. It was his denouncement of the murderer who had played the imitation game. A final reminder that the third Shadow, like the second, had received just doom.

Two murderers had died in false attire. There would be no more. With a last laugh, The Shadow swung about and strode into the little office. His chilling mirth gained a sudden muffle, as the door swung shut behind him. The key clicked in the lock.

Harry Vincent was standing by the desk, holding an automatic. Harry had been released by The Shadow; the agent had backed his chief. All the while that The Shadow had battled, Harry had been just within the doorway, ready to join in the fray. His shots had not been needed.

Seconds only had marked The Shadow's fight. Kidder—Brad—Duke—all had staggered in swift procession. Harry, aiming for thugs, had stopped when The Shadow had ceased fire. Harry, too, had seen the invading representatives of the law.

The Shadow tossed a black bundle to Harry. It was Sparkler Meldin's cloak, slouch hat and gloves rolled tightly within it. Followed by his agent, The Shadow led the way down the spiral staircase. They reached the lower office. The Shadow unlocked the door.

Crowds were making for the front exit of the nightclub. Confusion had swept the Casino Havanola. The Shadow took a pathway to the left. Close behind him, Harry followed, through a doorway to the street.

Moe's cab was parked there, waiting. Harry boarded it in response to a hissed order. He looked about for The Shadow. His chief was gone.

Swallowed in the darkness of the thoroughfare, The Shadow had chosen his own course. The lingering echoes of a whispered laugh: those were the only reminders of the victor's presence. The cab rolled away, with Harry its lone passenger. Through Harry's brain was running the solution of strange events.

That call from Burbank; the one that Kidder had answered last night, posing as Harry. Well had The Shadow chosen Burbank, to serve as contact. Burbank had spotted the false notes in Kidder's voice. The contact man had called The Shadow, to state that Harry was in trouble.

The Shadow had come at once, prepared for a double part. Himself upon the surface, he was masked as another beneath. The Shadow knew that Sparkler Meldin was passing himself as The Shadow. To beat the crook at his own game, The Shadow had passed himself as Sparkler Meldin.

Other points were still bewildering; but Harry knew that he would learn the answers later. Vaguely, he grasped the clever features of The Shadow's stern campaign to end the menace begun by one imposter and carried on by another.

IT was Joe Cardona who presented many of these details, one night later. Not to Harry Vincent, but to Commissioner Weston in the police official's private office. Cardona had learned facts; some through men who had talked, others through straight investigation. He had also followed another tip from The Shadow. One that concerned Miami.

"The Shadow guessed who Meldin was," assured Cardona. "That's why you got those telephone calls, Commissioner. They weren't from the judge and the district attorney's office—I've been checking. The Shadow paved the way to the closing of the Casino Havanola.

"So Sparkler would come there, as the third Shadow. With the clamps put on, his best chance was a cleanup. To get jewels, cash—best of all, an alibi that would pin things heavy on The Shadow. Nobody would ever have figured Sparkler raiding his own joint.

"Yet the whole thing was a setup. Sparkler had his own man in the cloak rooms. He blew in wearing a phony beard. One Cuban helped him tie up the other; then the first one went away. This to make it look as though The Shadow had pulled the trick. What's more, Sparkler went through the entrance that nobody was using. There wasn't even a lookout to stop him."

Weston nodded; then inquired: "But what about The Shadow?"

"He must have figured Sparkler perfectly," returned Cardona. "He knew that Sparkler wasn't going to let Duke in on it. Sparkler was playing a lone game. What did he care if Duke got into a mess? Sparkler made a boner, though. He didn't know about Duke's strong-arm crew."

"Didn't the Cubans tell him?"

"They weren't in the know. They thought that Kidder and Brad were customers. They didn't guess that the attendants were yeggs from Chicago. The Cubans never went into the gaming room. They were part of the front."

"And The Shadow stole Sparkler's own game?"

"He did. He walked in on Duke one night early. All in black; but when he dropped his cloak, he was disguised as Sparkler. The Shadow wanted to be on the inside when Sparkler arrived. He picked the surest way. As Sparkler, he was welcome. What's more, he told Sparkler's own story, as near as I can figure it. Duke fell for it.

"So did the others. They were so sold that they were sure Sparkler was The Shadow, when he showed up. The Shadow let them get Sparkler. Handed over the lone wolf to the foxes. I saw it, Commissioner. I fell, too. I was paralyzed when I saw Sparkler drop. I thought he was The Shadow; that I was too slow to save him."

Pausing, Cardona drew a sheaf of papers from his pocket. He added final data.

"ON account of the funny beard," stated Joe, "we've traced the places where Sparkler stayed. Always in good hotels, sticking pretty close to his room. We'd never have landed him in the dragnet. The Shadow had practically no chance to locate him.

"I've wired Miami." Cardona paused. He had sent the telegram at The Shadow's telephoned suggestion. "Asked the police to look through Sparkler's nightclub there. They found that the manager had been getting registered packages by mail. They were in a safe. The police opened them. The packages were full of swag.

"The stuff that Corbal swiped; the money that Sparkler grabbed. And the jewels. Sparkler was probably afraid to ship them to Havana. Miami was a better bet. He would have collected the swag later."

"One point, Cardona," put in Weston, suddenly. "How did you happen to be at the Casino Havanola?"

"I meant to tell you that, Commissioner," returned Cardona, cautiously. "It was a telephone call, from Swedley Jothan. That is, it sounded like Jothan, but since he was out of town, I thought it might be a hoax. I hopped up to the Casino anyway, with a squad. I was going to call you from there. But the trouble started before I had a chance."

"Do you think the telephone call was from The Shadow?"

"I *know* it was. He had plenty of chances to make it, right from Duke's office. That's where he was staying, all along. Duke and the others were up and down, in and out. The Shadow must have called me when he was alone."

THE telephone bell jingled alongside Weston's desk. He picked up the instrument and spoke abruptly. Recognizing a voice, he smiled.

"Thanks, Cranston," remarked the commissioner. "I am glad to receive your congratulations... The details? You would like to hear them?... Very well... I shall meet you for dinner at the club..."

Weston started to hang up; he paused suddenly.

Cardona did not notice the commissioner's rigid gaze. Joe spoke, in a tone of recollection.

"I heard The Shadow's laugh," he remarked. "When the raid was on. It was uncanny! Different from the laugh Meldin gave. When The Shadow laughed, he—"

"What was that?" demanded Weston, suddenly.

"The Shadow's laugh," replied Cardona, puzzled. "I heard it—"

"Just now?"

"No. Last night."

"Odd." Weston was musing. He pointed to the telephone: "Just as I hung up, I heard a laugh. Strange, uncanny, distant. I am sure that it came after Cranston had clicked the receiver hook."

Pondering, Commissioner Weston sat solemn as he recalled that fading, chilly tone.

Cardona, eyeing the commissioner, knew that his chief had caught an echo from the past. The same sound that Joe had heard last night—the spectral mirth that he could never forget.

The triumph laugh of The Shadow!

THE END

## Coming in THE SHADOW Volume 8:

Two world-famous crimefighting agencies join forces: The Shadow—America's foremost crimebuster, feared all over the world by men of evil—and Scotland Yard—England's master law-enforcement organization, dreaded by all of London's hoodlums. The world's greatest investigators team up to bring an end to ...

# THE LONDON CRIMES

Then, within the walls of an ancient castle dwelt the tradition of a noble family— the history of men who fought for right; men who knew gallantry and honor. But an oppressive atmosphere shrouds the building—an air of dire foreboding which makes it a

# CASTLE OF DOOM

with death occupying its battlements, and crime lurking deep within its dungeons. This dark mystery can only be unraveled by the supersleuth known as...

**Only $12.95.  Ask your bookseller to reserve your copy now!**

# THE SHADOW'S SHADOWS by Anthony Tollin

Radio listeners experienced two very different Shadows over the airwaves. While the classic 1940s Mutual series featured Lamont Cranston as an invisible crimebuster who was "never seen, only heard" in his battles against the underworld, the earlier CBS broadcasts had first introduced The Shadow as a sinister storyteller.

Frank Readick's mocking laugh and venomous tones made The Shadow a national sensation on *Street & Smith's Detective Story Program.* In 1931 he became the first actor to portray the mystery man on the silver screen when he reprised his radio role in *Burglar to the Rescue,* the first of six "Shadow Detective" two-reel "filmettes."

The Shadow was a superhero who owned the charismatic darkness of the melodrama villain. The Dark Avenger inspired many successors, so it should come as no surprise that such a dynamic crimebuster would eventually be confronted by impersonators. After all, sinister dopplegangers, cloaking themselves in the hero's trappings, had been the bane of pulp heroes since the early adventures of Nick Carter, Tarzan and Zorro.

The Master of Darkness confronted not one but two evil impersonators in *The Third Shadow,* but those were far from the only deadly doubles he encountered during his long career.

In *The Shadow Challenged* (broadcast January 19, 1941), an archeologist discovers the secret of hypnotic invisibility from ancient Hindu manuscripts, and uses those powers to murder his rivals as The Shadow. Newspaper headlines blaming the Master Avenger for the murder of a museum professor force Cranston (Bill Johnstone) and Margo (Marjorie Anderson) to cut short their vacation and return to New York. Investigating the case, Cranston falls into the clutches of his shadowy impersonator who boasts:

> I've known for some time now you are The Shadow. I've followed the activities of The Shadow for many years. I was most curious to learn his real identity. I began keeping track of the people who were present before and after all of his appearances…. Having learned your secret of invisibility, I have hypnotized your mind before you were aware of me. This time, the real Shadow is visible—and I am the one unseen!

The usurper admits he committed his murders in The Shadow's name to lure Cranston into a trap:

> … I wanted to attract the attention of you, the real Shadow! And I succeeded. I led you on, Lamont Cranston, with my phone calls and anonymous notes…. My purpose was—and is— to put an end to your activities. After tonight, Mr. Cranston, I *alone* will be The Shadow, and I shall capitalize on this power. You were a fool …

always working for the powers of good. I shall take real advantage of the name…. With the trick of invisibility, the world will be mine!

Of course, Lamont Cranston has the last laugh, as he gives the usurper a private lesson, powerfully demonstrating who is the true master of invisibility:

> Unlike your other victims, my mind is not receptive to your hypnosis…. I mean that you have been perfectly visible to me ever since you entered this room ... and now, if you observe closely, I shall instruct you in the true art of hypnosis. Look at me …Look at me! I am disappearing before your very eyes… *I am no longer Cranston … I am—The Shadow!*

In an ingenious piece of casting, Frank Readick returned to voice The Shadow's evil impersonator. The radio veteran had departed the series at the conclusion of the 1934-35 CBS season, though his sibilant opening and closing signatures were rerun throughout Orson Welles' 1937-38 seasons.

Perhaps Readick was recruited for the role by Shadow regulars Bill Johnstone and Dwight Weist (Commissioner Weston) who rented an apartment with Frank near the broadcast studios where they pursued their separate hobbies (woodworking, photography and model railroads) between shows.

On occasion, even members of the fair sex donned The Shadow's cloak and slouch hat. In Walter Gibson's *Smugglers of Death,* after being rescued by Harry Vincent, ace swimmer Myrna Elvin discards her "handicap" of clothing for an

Frank Readick as The Shadow

Bill Johnstone and Frank Readick costarred as Lamont Cranston and his invisible impostor in *The Shadow Challenged.*

SMUGGLERS OF DEATH Complete Shadow Novel
AND OTHER STORIES

emergency night swim. Reaching her destination, she learns that criminals are occupying her cottage. Discovering The Shadow's unconscious form, Myrna arms herself with one of the avenger's automatics and wraps herself in his dark garb.

> The cloak, at present, was useless to The Shadow; but it was exactly what Myrna wanted. Eagerly, she slipped her arms into the cloak sleeves and wrapped the garment tightly around her body.... Her hands were lost in the sleeves; the hem of the cloak dragged the floor.... she was clothed in complete blackness, except for her hair. She could not risk a venture into the night with her blond locks in sight.
> Picking up the slouch hat, she combed her bobbed hair upward and clamped the headgear in place. The transformation was complete. She felt a surge of confidence. The Shadow used these garments to blend with the darkness of night. Myrna could do the same.... What if crooks were suddenly confronted by The Shadow at a moment when they still believed they held him helpless!

> Sight of a cloaked foeman, ready with a gun, might drive them to frantic flight. Frenchy Brenn, a double murderer, had fled when faced by The Shadow.... She could masquerade as The Shadow!

While Myrna's daring plan only briefly delayed the villains' machinations, it certainly resulted in one of *The Shadow Magazine*'s more provocative covers (above).

Not to be outdone, the lovely Margo Lane (played by Barbara Reed) donned The Shadow's ebony garb for a comedic sequence in *Behind the Mask,* the middle installment of Monogram's 1946 Shadow film trilogy. When Lamont and Margo's wedding plans are delayed after an impostor frames The Shadow for an unusual series of murders, Cranston's "friend and companion" dons a spare Shadow costume to investigate the crimes, in a brash attempt to get her wedding back on track. Margo briefly establishes herself as the film's third Shadow, until the true Master of Darkness rescues her from both the murderer and the police.

The Shadow (Kane Richmond) tangles with a masked double, unaware that it's Margo Lane (Barbara Reed) in disguise.

A Shadowy impersonator kills by lethal injection in *Behind the Mask.*